*In*
*her i...*

"This is Egypt, Princess," he whispered, and let the sand trickle over her arm and her breasts.

She looked down at the golden grains, then back up at his face as he drew her close. She could read the look in his eyes . . .

His lips tasted of salt, and his arms pulled her so close she thought she could not breathe. But then his hands began to move against her back, stroking and encouraging, as his tongue pressed against her lips. She parted them, allowing him entry, wondering at the sudden liquid throbbing that his touch had released inside her . . .

# Desert Nights

## Susan Stern

DIAMOND BOOKS, NEW YORK

DESERT NIGHTS

A Diamond Book / published by arrangement with
the author

PRINTING HISTORY
Diamond edition / February 1991

ISBN: 1-55773-457-7

Diamond Books are published by The Berkley Publishing
Group, 200 Madison Avenue, New York, New York 10016.
The name "DIAMOND" and its logo are trademarks
belonging to Charter Communications, Inc.

PRINTED IN THE UNITED STATES OF AMERICA

10 9 8 7 6 5 4 3 2 1

# One

SHANDA STARED NUMBLY at King Hattushil. She could see that he still spoke, but her ears were filled with the pounding sound of the blood in her veins and his words were lost to her. It was with a great effort that she remembered she called this man father, that the court looked upon her as his blood. She had never felt more foreign in her life.

She darted a quick glance at Nemshet, hoping he, at least, would speak up for her, that he would protest her being sent away. But his face remained impassive, and he seemed as disinterested as all the others in the huge audience room. He appeared to have no personal interest in the matter being discussed. His apparent indifference opened a dark place inside her that grew numb with hurt and larger as the seconds passed.

Bewildered, she turned her attention back to the king.

"I would have your word, Shanda, that you will accept the Egyptian as your lord and obey his word as you would my own."

There was, of course, no choice for her, no possibility of crying out that she would not do as he commanded, that the thought of this foreigner disgusted and repelled her, that she would not go willingly to his bed as the king's gift. Instead, she inclined her head with the minimum show of meekness she knew Hattushil would require of her.

"As you wish, my lord. I have no choice but to do as you have bidden me."

Hattushil looked down at her and his brow furrowed. He did not quite accept her submission, nor had she given him what he had demanded.

"Do I have your word, Shanda?" he demanded, his tone more vexed than usual when speaking with her.

She bowed her head a bit lower, knowing he was on the edge of anger. "Yes, my lord, I give you my word."

For the first time since he'd watched her enter and cross the length of the huge audience room, a smile touched the lips of the king. "It is done," he murmured softly and waved his hand, dismissing her, to seek his advisers.

Shanda saw Nemshet lean toward him and whisper something to him, a smile gracing his lips, too. She had never known the king to allow him such informality. She wondered if he had sold his love for her for that privilege.

She straightened, determined to leave the room before allowing the tears to come. She swore to herself she would not show such weakness before this lot of mewling courtiers. She would not give them even a taste of her misery upon which to feed.

She felt their eyes on her as she turned and strode the length of the seemingly endless hall, her chest tight with the pressure inside her, her eyes unseeing. Only when the doors swept open for her passage, when she saw the guards in the outer hall salute her and heard the huge doors swing shut behind her, did she falter. She reached for the support of a tall gilded pillar and stood grasping it, breathing hard and trying to summon her control.

"Princess? Is something wrong? Are you ill?"

She turned to the weathered face of the old guard, knowing he would offer her an arm and his escort if she asked it. Still she refused, aware that Hattushil would learn of her distress and unwilling to show that weakness to him.

She shook her head. "No, thank you, Ikira. But I thank you for your concern."

She felt his eyes on her as she straightened and continued along the corridor. She paused for a moment when she reached its end, considering. The corridor divided in two there, the left hand taking her toward the women's hall, the right to the palace garden. Even if she were to go directly to her own rooms, she knew the others would be watching her, silently laughing at her. She was not yet able to bear that.

She turned to the garden, aware that it might shelter some of the members of the court, but sure, at least, that she would not be subject to the eyes of any of the king's women there.

When she reached it, she paused at the garden gate. The plantings were coolly bright and inviting, the air scented with the perfume of a dozen different flowers and musical with the gurgling of water as it splashed from rock to rock before reaching the garden pool. She moved forward cautiously, knowing Hattushil did not like her to come here without proper escort, that he would send her to the women's garden with a rebuke and perhaps a taste of his anger. She edged her way to the pool, relishing the small sense of freedom it gave her to be there alone, and seated herself on a carved stone bench that stood half surrounded by small palms and flowering hibiscus.

Hoping to distract herself, to keep herself from any thought at all, she concentrated her attention on the falling water, watching each successive splashing descend from rock to lower rock, each repetitive and expected and yet none entirely like any other. There was beauty all around her. Surely she could lose herself in it, if only for a while.

"You ought not to be here alone, Shanda."

At any other time she would have known the voice without needing to turn to see who spoke. The mere sound of it would have given rise to an oddly pleasurable shift inside her. Just then, however, she had managed to expunge that voice from her memory, just as she had expunged the features it evoked. She turned and stared at Nemshet, looking at him as though he were a stranger to her, as though she had never seen him before.

He was decidedly handsome, she thought with an uncharacteristic objectivity, the heavy, dark curls that hung across his brow oddly boyish, especially when they fell near those dark, dark eyes, so dark it was nearly impossible to see where the iris stopped and the pupil began. It was his eyes, she thought, more than anything else about him, that held her in his power.

"There have been a number of times when you were more than happy to find me here alone, Nem," she answered quietly. "Have you so easily offered up your claim to me? I remember a time when you swore you would sooner die than face the prospect of living without me."

He moved to the side of the bench and brushed away a branch at its edge before he sat. When he began to move closer to her, she backed away from him, her eyes so condemning he kept his distance from her. She was resigned to sharing the bench with him, however, and when he came no closer to her, she returned to her contemplation of the waterfall. It could not, however, hold her glance as she would have it do. Slowly her gaze drifted first to the edge of the pool and then along the smooth colored stones that edged it until it stopped at his feet.

He wore boots, as he always did, not a gentleman's tooled leather sandals, but boots befitting a young general, although there was little possibility that he would find either horse or battle at the palace. It occurred to her that the boots were an affectation, a mark of his ambition as much as his position.

"Nothing has changed, Shanda," he told her quietly. "I still love you."

He leaned toward her and put his hand on her arm. She would have pushed it away had she not heard the words, had she not believed them.

"Is it true, then?" she asked breathlessly as relief swept through her. She was aware that he was moving closer to her once more, and she was now eager for his touch. "You do love me?"

"You know I do, Shanda. You are my life," he whispered before he kissed her with feverish ardor.

It was what she wanted from him, she knew, both the words and the reaffirmation the touch of his lips brought. The previous hour might never have happened. She let herself melt thankfully against him.

"Then you will go to him?" she asked him, her words breathily intense in the aftermath of his kiss. "You will beg him not to send me away, to allow us to marry?"

He pulled her close and put his cheek against her hair, inhaling its perfume before he replied.

"You know that would be useless, Shanda, just as I do," he told her mournfully. "Were my family more illustrious, my fortune greater, perhaps. But as things are, he would not consider it."

"You're a general," she protested, pressing her cheek against his chest. She could feel his heartbeat, a slow, steady throb that seemed to echo her own.

"With nothing more to my credit than a few border skirmishes. And one of a score of young generals at that. No, Shanda, you are far too precious for him to waste on the likes of me."

"Then we could leave, Nem. We could go to the far north, to my mother's people. I would like that." She would more than simply like that, she realized. It was a childhood dream that she'd never given up, the thought of escape, of no longer being an outsider, of feeling that she belonged somewhere. Her mother's people surely would accept her, as Hattushil's never had.

He shook his head. "Don't talk nonsense, Shanda. Running away like fugitives? We would be beggars. What kind of a life is that?"

"We would have each other," she whispered, more to herself than to him, because the paralyzing reality was once again beginning to return. "We would have our love."

"It would do us little good were we to die of starvation." He held her quietly for an instant. "No, Shanda, there is only one way, and that is to provide myself with a military victory so great that even the king would have to honor it. And so you must go to Egypt."

She pushed his arms away, noticing as she did so that the warmth she'd found in them had suddenly turned cold.

"And this is part of it? That you send me to another man's bed?" she cried softly, her voice taut with disbelief.

"Do you think it is easy for me, knowing that another will claim what ought to be mine?" he asked her. He put his hands on her shoulders, holding her firmly when she began to try to move away, his fingers biting into her flesh. "I swear to you, Shanda, it will not be for long. And when it is done, we will be together, with the king's blessing. It is the only way."

She stopped trying to pull away when she heard the words, and the pressure of his fingers eased. "I don't understand, Nem. What is it you plan? What will happen?"

"It is safest for you that you do not know, Shanda," he replied.

"Safest?" she cried. "You tell me you love me and then you send me away to another man and say it safest that I do not know why?"

"Can you not trust me, Shanda? Is that so very much to ask?" He looked down at her accusingly, and she found herself cringing at that look even though she knew he had no right to it. "Go to Pharaoh. Make him fall in love with you."

"Let the king send another woman," she replied petulantly. "He has a dozen daughters."

His hand stole from her shoulder to wrap itself in a handful of her hair. He raised it, watching the way the sunlight turned it into undulating ribbons of gold. "There is none like you, Shanda. No other woman can do what you do to a man."

She jerked her head, pulling her hair from his hand. "I hate it," she told him. "It has always made me different, strange to the others, something to hurt. I'll cut my hair off, make a wig of it, then give it to Hali. Or Lesha. You can send one of them to Pharaoh."

"Hali and Lesha," he replied softly, "are beautiful, Shanda, but not half so beautiful as you. And your beauty cannot be given to them, for it is more than your hair. You cannot give them your smooth, pale cheeks, your fine straight nose"—he placed his finger on its tip—"or eyes the color of the sky. The others do not have lips like yours that swell like warm new-opened roses, or cheeks so finely carved from silken stone." Again he brought his fingers to her face, touching her lips and her cheeks. "And finally I can tell you, for I have done it many times, that a man can recognize you when you are among the others, even with your hair covered and your face veiled, for none of the others stand so tall or move with such fluid grace. If you are made to feel different from them, it is because you are a thing apart, Shanda. And the hurt they've given you is only to allay their jealousy, because they know that they simply disappear when they stand at your side."

His words were sweet poetry to her ears, as they always were. He had a gift with words, an ability, when he chose to use it, to make whatever he said sound like a treasure, something to be held on to, to be cherished. But they were just words, she told herself sharply, refusing to let herself give in to the impulse to acquiesce, to accept what he said. If he truly loved her, he would prove it to her by his actions, not attempt to persuade her with mere words. She wondered if she had ever really known him, known any more of him than the paeans he so glibly offered her.

"Enough of this, Nem. It is all just words," she said angrily, her eyes flashing as they met his. "If you find me so beautiful, how can you let him send me away?"

He put his hand on her chin and forced her face up to his, until her gaze wavered as she saw the certainty in his eyes.

"We need not give it all to him, Shanda," he whispered. "We could steal the first pleasure before you leave." He began to lower his lips to hers once more.

Shanda realized that his eyes were almost hypnotic, that she was becoming weakly pliant as she always did when his arms were around her and he stared at her with those dark, potent fires. But then she realized what it was he had agreed to send her to do and she awoke abruptly, pushing him away before she could taste his lips on hers once more.

"You stood mute while I gave my word, Nem," she said evenly. "You could have spoken then, but you did not. I will not break my promise now, not even for you."

It frightened her to think how close she had come to breaking that word. If he'd asked her to run away with him, she would have turned her back on her honor and gone with him. But that moment of weakness was past.

She had made a vow to Hattushil and she would keep it, remembering the lessons of honor her mother had taught her, remembering that honor was all she could count as her own, honor and pride. It was that more than anything else that had set Althea apart, for the Hittite women considered honor a man's realm; they believed that their own value lay in their ability to please men and bear children. But Althea had lived by a different code, and it was the rule of her people she had taught Shanda. Hattushil had known that when he demanded of Shanda her word, for he had known Althea, and although he had never understood her, he'd always known what he could expect from her. She had made a pact with him herself and had kept it until death had freed her from it. He could expect nothing less from her daughter.

She put her hands on his and pushed him away from her as she stood. "Whatever pact you have made with Hattushil, whatever prize it is for which you have bartered me away, I hope it pleases you."

He stood and reached out to her. "It is for us, Shanda," he told her, his eyes still on hers, holding them as they always did. "When it is done, you will understand."

There was no wavering in his voice or his expression, no willingness to recognize her fears or her doubt. That realization, Shanda found, frightened her almost as much as the prospect of being sent to Pharaoh's bed. She felt a cold numbness begin to fill her, to steal away the feeling she had for him.

"Perhaps, Nem, whenever that will be, however that will be. But I do not understand it now."

She turned and left him without another word. As she walked away from him, she thought her heart would shatter inside her. She had loved him. She had thought he'd loved her. And now he was letting her leave him as though they were strangers. She could feel his eyes on her as she fled from the garden and returned to the dark, cool palace.

The hall along which she ran seemed to disappear for her, the ornately carved columns of precious cedar, which awed visiting lords and emissaries, were transformed by her unseeing eyes into dim, tall shadows, a deep, thick forest of them, stretching on almost endlessly. Her feet carried her without her direction, finding their way out of habit, for she had little thought to instruct them. It was with an almost dumb surprise that she found herself before the great carved doors that opened to the women's hall.

She nearly shuddered at the sight of them. She hated this place, hated the women who dwelt there, with their smug indifference to her, hated even more the way they had condemned her as the foreigner's whelp. While her mother still lived, Shanda had had no need to think of their envy, for together she and Althea had occupied a small house at the far end of the palace compound, just the two of them and the servants who would never have dared to show any disrespect. But now the small house had been given to one of her half brothers and his favorite as a mark of the king's favor. And Shanda was relegated to the women's hall as though she were nothing more than one of the thirty other women the king counted as his daughters rather than the child of the only woman to whom he had ever sworn his love. It was almost as if he was punishing her for her mother's death.

Shanda took a deep breath as the great doors were swung open for her passage, steeling herself to meet the curious and amused eyes, the whispered words, mean and spiteful, that were really intended for her to hear. These sisters with whom she had nothing in common, whose mothers had taught them to hate and envy the foreign woman who had stolen what they thought should rightly be theirs, would show delight at her distress and would cause her more hurt if they could.

Shanda told herself that she would not give them the pleasure of seeing her pain, that she would bear their taunts with indifference so as to deny them satisfaction. Suddenly the thought of leaving became less odious to her. At least she would be done with the petty jealousies and the resentment with which she could not deal.

It was not as though she had wanted things to go as they had. When she was a child, she had been shielded from the pettiness of Hattushil's concubines. Her mother had seen to it that Shanda was carefully kept apart from the other women, carefully sheltered from the jealousy to which she herself had been subjected. But for two long years now Shanda had lived in this uncomfortable world, two years since Althea's death, and nothing she could do, it seemed, could change the hatred she herself had done nothing to create. At first she had felt it as a constant hurt, this rejection despite her desperate, often meek attempts to win their friendship. But nothing had helped her, and their rebuffs seemed all the more vicious for her futile tries, until finally she had withdrawn from them completely.

Indifference, however, would be hard to maintain after the audience with Hattushil. Somehow they would already know what had occurred, word coming, as it always did, with what seemed to Shanda impossible speed. They would already know, and they would make no effort to hide their glee that she was to be sent away, especially if she let them see that the prospect appalled her.

She squared her shoulders, standing for a moment longer before the open doors, then strode forward, determined neither to look at them nor to show them her distress. As she had in the long hallway, she cleared her mind and moved forward through the open courtyard determined neither to see nor to hear.

But either her determination was not strong enough or their spite was too powerful to ignore. The laughter and stares, the words whispered sotto voce—"See how the mighty are blessed" and "See the king's favorite now"— followed her as she ran blindly to her rooms.

# Two

"THE HITTITE EMISSARY."

The words seemed to echo along the length of the great audience hall, bouncing off the huge stone columns and the polished stone floor. Shanda could almost feel them pushing against her skin, forcing her to pay attention. The numbness inside her had grown over the weeks since she had left Hattushil's court. She told herself nothing could harm her now, that she was dead to any hurt this barbarian king might wish to do to her. By letting her leave as he had, Nem had killed whatever part of her was able to feel. Still, she knew it was not true.

For a moment she wished the floor would simply open and swallow her or that one of Hattushil's vengeful gods would strike her dead. But she realized it was no use to whisper a prayer to a god in whom she had no belief. Even if such a deity did exist, there would be no reason for him to show her the mercy of granting her wish.

It took all her strength to stride across the long, cool length of the room. Numbly she perceived the eyes of the courtiers—men with darkly bronzed bodies, naked except

for sandals, linen loincloths, and forearm and breast jewels;
women with bare breasts and near-transparent robes that fell
from the waist or, more modestly, from one shoulder, beads
and gold baubles hanging from their necks and arms, their
hair plaited in endless rows of tiny braids. Barbarians, she
thought, near naked and shameless.

She could not understand their seeming fascination with
her, the sudden hushed intensity of their inspection. There
had been a constant drone of murmuring and movement
during the previous audiences. She had heard the noise
even from the waiting room outside. As she walked forward, however, they hushed to silence.

She forced her attention to the man who sat in the gold
and lapis throne on the dais at the far end of the room. She
had hoped he would be old; past the age when a strange
woman would hold any interest for him. Instead she saw
a man of perhaps thirty-five summers, no longer a youth,
certainly, but decidedly not the ancient for whom she had
prayed. His body, like those of his councillors, was mini-
mally robed, and strong muscles rippled through his arms
and shoulders as he turned and spoke to the vizier at his
side. At his feet lay a lion, the huge cat apparently napping
peacefully, like an overgrown household pet.

Again there was the call, "The Hittite emissary. Who
speaks for the Hittite king?"

Shanda quickened her pace slightly. In the sharp stillness
of the hall it took all her courage for her to answer aloud.

"I speak for King Hattushil."

Pharaoh turned his eyes to her, and she saw them, even
from the distance of a third of the length of the hall, dark
gray and glittering. They peered out at her, showing a bit
of surprise and a decided attitude of disdain.

"A woman? The Hittite king insults this throne by sending
a woman to offer his tribute?" His voice boomed, deep and

resonant in the long, quiet cavern of the hall.

Shanda felt it like a blow, stopping her progress and nearly taking her breath from her. She had come to within a few feet of his dais when his words halted her. She stood there uncertainly for a moment, trembling inside, daring to go no farther. She knelt and bowed her head to him.

The silence became nearly as potent as his words had been. Shanda searched her mind for words, but found none. Even if they had been there, her tongue had suddenly grown too thick to let her speak. This man terrified her in a way she had never been terrified before, and she could not think why.

"What is this? The Hittite sends not any woman, but a mute, to speak his words. This must be some strange form of diplomacy we do not know here."

There was humor in his voice now, and the room filled with quick laughter at his words. His derision and the tittering amusement of the courtiers gave Shanda the impetus to speak. She might fear this barbarian king, but her pride would not allow her to become the brunt of his jokes.

"I assure you no insult was meant, lord, in sending me to speak for King Hattushil. It is his earnest wish that my words will please you, lord, and convey his deepest respect."

"I have no interest in his deepest respect, only in his tribute," came the deep resonance again.

Although she dared not look up to his face, Shanda knew it was he who had spoken. There was a power in his voice that she had never heard before, an arrogant certainty that said clearly he knew the import of his words and expected all those around him to know it as well. This man would be a formidable enemy, one who would be difficult to outwit. Whatever Hattushil planned, she prayed she had the strength to do her part and to survive.

"I am his tribute, lord," she murmured, remembering the words she had been tutored to speak.

She saw the feet in front of her stir, saw the well-muscled thighs shift as he stood and descended the stairs to where she knelt. He put his hand beneath her chin and raised it. With a sudden burst of courage, Shanda let her eyes find his.

She saw him now as he was, uncolored by her expectations of him. He was taller than the courtiers who surrounded them and powerfully built, with dark, thick hair that fell straight across his forehead, and those oddly piercing gray eyes. He stared indifferently down at her, his look coolly aloof and considering, as if he were possessed of a unique masculinity, as though it was an asset of which only he had possession. Arrogant, she thought, but even as she made the judgment, she became aware of an odd disquiet filling her as his eyes returned her stare, a disquiet that had nothing to do with her fear.

"You?" he asked, his tone incredulous. "Who are you that I should accept you in place of two hundred talents of grain?"

"I am Princess Shanda, lord," she replied slowly, remembering the words, "and I am sent to tell you that there is a drought in King Hattushil's lands, that if the grain is sent to you, many of his people will starve. He begs your indulgence, great lord, and asks that you accept me in its place. He places the lives of his people in your hands, relying on your mercy." She fell silent then and lowered her gaze respectfully. She had spoken the words as she had been instructed. What further would be asked of her?

Pharaoh stared down at her, at the deep purple silk that so completely clothed her body and yet, somehow, managed to reveal more of her long, slender form than could the brief, transparent costumes the women of his own court wore. She was tall, he realized, almost his own height, and he was half a head taller than any other in his court.

Of its own, his hand reached out to the thick cloud of golden hair, seeking some assurance that it was real and not some artifice of which his women had not yet learned. It was, he found, indeed her own hair, and not some unlikely wig; it was fine and incredibly soft to the touch, and filled with an unbelievable luster. He lifted a handful of it, then let it slowly fall back to her shoulder, the sunlight playing on the fine strands and setting them ashimmer, a soft golden curtain that framed the incredible paleness of her face. This was something he had never seen before, and he wondered what trickery had been used to turn it to that impossible shade.

"And if your father's gift does not please me, then what, Princess?" he demanded. His voice had softened somewhat, despite his intention.

"Then I shall return, lord, and the grain will be sent to you, despite the hardship to the people."

"What if I decide to keep you and demand the grain as well, Princess?" he asked slowly, reaching once more for the soft, loose cloud of her hair.

She knew now that she had been right to wear her hair loose this way. She had seen the look now in his eyes many times before in the eyes of men in Hattushil's court. That fact returned to her a good deal of her composure.

She tossed her head back, pulling her hair from his hand. "That cannot be, lord," she replied sharply. "If you choose the grain, it will be sent to you, but I must be returned to my father's court first. Take me or the grain. You may choose only one."

She held his gaze, her eyes defiant. Her courage had come with her composure and the realization that he was simply a man like any other. But then she saw the muscles of his jaw grow hard, and she understood that, despite Nem's words to the contrary, it would take a good deal more than a smile and a glimpse of her golden hair to charm him. Her words had angered him, and a tremor passed through her. She fought to keep it under control and hidden from his gaze.

"You dare to dictate to me?"

This time his voice was closer to a roar than to the low rumble it had been at first. It seemed to shake the very stone on which she stood. The certainty she'd felt a moment before disappeared, leaving her with only her terror of this huge, fearsome man.

"I must, my lord," she murmured with all the strength she could gather. Still her voice trembled. "It is the message I have been instructed to deliver to you."

She could taste her own fear now, and she lowered her eyes, knowing he could see it in her face. She half expected him to step forward and strike her, so heavy was the wrath in his words.

Instead he stood silent. His angry tone had awakened not only her fears but also the sleeping cat that had lain so quietly at his feet. The beast looked up, eyeing Shanda as he would have eyed a bit of small game that had foolishly wandered into his lair. Then he stood and spoke, too, his roar mimicking his master's, angry and loud as he slowly made his way toward her.

Shanda looked from the cat to Pharaoh, confused for a moment. Then she read the expectation in his eyes: he thought she would tremble at the sight of the approaching beast and beg him for his protection. She turned her attention back to the cat, then stood, moving very slowly as he neared her, holding her hands palm outward to him, murmuring softly the words she had heard spoken so many times by the priests at Hattushil's court.

Whether it was her stance, the words, or simply her calm, low voice, she did not know. But, like the great cats at Hattushil's court, this one came and stood docilely beside her, brushing his great golden mane against her leg, the force of his greeting almost pushing her aside. She reached down into the heavy mass of hair and scratched his neck.

Again Shanda became aware of the unnatural silence in the hall, but dared not turn to the courtiers' surprised expressions. Instead, she brought her glance back to Pharaoh's face, telling herself she was no more afraid of him than she had been of his ferocious pet. To her surprise, she found he was smiling, his lips parted to show his straight white teeth.

"How did you bewitch him, Princess?" he demanded, his tone genuinely perplexed. "He suffers no touch but mine and his caretaker's, and yet he sits beside you like an ancient house cat, demanding to be petted."

Shanda smiled at him, pleased with herself and not unwilling to let him see. "The lion is sacred to the Hittite people, lord," she replied. "Many such beasts are kept as pets at King Hattushil's court. One quickly learns the words to calm them."

She spoke confidently, but Shanda knew she had been very lucky. If the pharaoh's pet had been less well trained, less used to the sight of strangers in the court, he might have reacted very differently to her advances.

Pharaoh, however, seemed pleased with her feat. He held out his hand to her and smiled as she placed her own in it. The small contact produced an unexpected shiver in her fingers and palm. She realized with a start how much she had dreaded the thought of his touch and how little the actuality matched those expectations.

"You interest me, Princess," he told her bluntly. "Come sit with me while I ponder the choice your father has offered."

· He mounted the steps to his throne, dropping a large pillow on the dais near his feet before he sat.

Shanda followed him and obediently settled herself at his feet. She felt a decided thrill of triumph. This beast she had so dreaded seemed little more frightening now than his pet—and decidedly more handsome. If she was to be sold as a part of Hattushil's plan, whatever it might be, she was relieved to find that he was not the monster she had anticipated.

Pharaoh motioned and the vizier consulted his list, calling out for the next audience. Shanda was aware that there were still some in the hall who stared at her, but the low murmuring had once more begun to fill the silence. Normality was slowly returning to the court.

A small graying man made his way through the hall to the dais, stopping a few feet away as Shanda had done and making a low obeisance, lowering his head to the floor in deference. Shanda thought the display distasteful, wondering how any man could so lower his pride as to bow that way to another. When he spoke, however, there was no hint of fear in his tone or his manner. Shanda watched as he smiled at Pharaoh, and spoke in an almost comradely fashion, discussing the progress made at the quarry he managed, relaying the number and size of the great stone blocks that had been cut and made ready for transport for the building of Pharaoh's monument.

There were several exchanges, as Pharaoh asked questions about the type of wood used for the fires needed to heat the rock to force it to crack, and the depth of the holes that had to be cut in the stones to accept the flames. His interest in such details surprised Shanda. Hattushil and his courtiers concerned themselves with only one matter, the techniques of war. She had expected nothing else from Pharaoh, and his greater interests impressed her.

The quarry chief finished his report and took his leave. More names were called, and two men approached, one richly clothed, with gold bands on his arms and fingers, the other dressed in the plain, worn garments of a commoner. Shanda thought them an odd pair to be brought together before Pharaoh.

She was paying only slight attention as they spoke, each telling approximately the same story. Twice the richly dressed lord interrupted the poorer man, and both times the commoner yielded silently and without protest, obviously used to behaving respectfully in the presence of his betters. When he dared look up at Pharaoh, his expression was filled with awe. She remembered what she had been told by her tutors, that Pharaoh was believed to be a god by his people.

Finally it seemed that Pharaoh had heard enough. He waved his hand to silence them both, then turned to the lord, his eyes stern. "Then the work has been completely stopped?" he asked. "The laborers refuse to continue?"

"That is so, lord, despite all efforts, the men steadfastly refuse to return to work." There was a look of sullen satisfaction on his face as he spoke, as though he already considered himself the winner in the dispute.

Pharaoh turned his glance to the second man then. "And you claim you and your men are not being given your allotment of grain?"

"It is true, lord. My men have too little food to feed their families. We had no choice but to cease work. Two men have already died in falls that would not have happened had they not been weakened by lack of food."

"Lies, Pharaoh," the lord shouted, his look of satisfaction replaced by one of affronted innocence. It was quite plain he felt the challenge the other presented him was an insult to his dignity and position. "All lies. The workers have received their allotment, but cause this trouble to get more so that they can sell it and profit from your generosity."

Pharaoh raised his hand. "Enough," he said, his voice loud enough to interrupt the flow of protest that was about to bubble from the second man's lips. Then he turned to Shanda. "What think you of this, Princess?" he demanded abruptly.

Shanda looked up at him, perplexed. "Me, lord?" she asked, surprised.

He nodded, as if his request for her opinion were entirely normal. "One of these men is lying. Either the governor is stealing the grain that ought to have gone to the workmen, selling it, and keeping the profits, or else the workers are trying to extort more money from my treasury than they have the right to collect. Which of them shall I believe?" He stared at her, a hint of amusement in his eyes.

Shanda pondered a moment, trying to quell her surprise at his request. "May I ask a question, lord?" she demanded finally.

He smiled and nodded.

"These workmen, what is it they do?"

"They are preparing my tomb, Princess, carving and painting its walls, making a fit place for a living god to lie before making his journey to the afterlife."

This, too, surprised her, the way he spoke so casually of his tomb, of his own death, but she went on. "Then they are artisans, not common laborers?" she asked.

"Yes, Princess, they are artisans, the finest that could be found to perform this delicate and holy duty."

She faced the two men. "Real artisans care more for their craft than for riches; they ask just enough to keep themselves and their families. If only one of these men speaks the truth, lord, and I must choose between them, I call the governor a liar."

"What?" the lord cried in outrage. He turned to Pharaoh. "Surely, my lord, you do not take the advice of a woman?"

But Pharaoh turned to the vizier. "An inquiry will be made into the governor's finances. Until it is completed, he will be our guest, in prison." To the workman he said, "You will oversee the work in the interim." The man nodded, agreeing. "And the work *will* continue." This last sounded almost like a warning.

"We will resume immediately, lord," the man replied, bowing low, as guards appeared and bore the governor, still protesting, away. Then the workman, too, turned and left, melting into the crowd of courtiers as he made his way out of the hall.

Shanda looked up at Pharaoh and found he was staring down at her. His face spoke of amusement, she thought, or perhaps it was simply surprised interest.

"What if I was wrong, lord?" she asked him softly.

He leaned toward her. "A ruler must have the courage to make decisions, Princess. One always has choices to make and often little on which to base them but a feeling. In this instance, I had already made my decision. And I made it as you did, for precisely the reasons you did. We are probably correct." He watched her thoughtfully for a moment, then broke the silence once more. "And I have come to another decision as well, Princess. I have decided to keep the gift your father has sent to me."

Shanda looked down, hoping to hide from his eyes the feeling of triumph she felt within her. Whatever else, she had at least done as she had promised she would do, what she had been sent to do. For this, she was sure, Hattushil would reward her. He was, after all, not without his own sense of honor.

Pharaoh spoke to his vizier, and soon an escort appeared.

"I will join you later, Princess," he told her as he waved Shanda toward them.

She rose quickly, bowed to him, then walked down the steps to join the guard. She waited as the four men grouped themselves around her, then allowed herself to be led from the hall.

Pharaoh watched her as she left, the ranks of courtiers parting for her like an unruly but obedient tide.

His vizier whispered in his ear. "It is said, lord, that the Hittites guard their women, especially those of noble birth. They remain virgins until they are wed."

Pharaoh's lips curled into a smile at his words. "You are a wealth of unexpected information, Nofret," he said.

"It is my place to serve, lord," the vizier replied piously.

Pharaoh's smile suddenly disappeared. "I have heard no word of drought or famine among the Hittites," he said abruptly. "Send word to our spies. I will know more of this. And see that the garrison at Shunem is quietly enlarged. It is not wise, I think, to leave a wolf hungering at an unguarded door."

# Three

SHANDA STOOD QUIETLY as the great gilded doors were opened for her and the guard divided, drawing back, making room for her to enter. The doors were opened by two enormous eunuchs, both well muscled and well armed. For a moment Shanda was perplexed. No such guards stood at the entry to the quarters that housed King Hattushil's favorites and children. Still, she warned herself, this was a strange place and she must expect nothing familiar here.

Once she had entered and the doors had closed behind her, however, her confusion turned to anger. She realized quickly that this part of the palace, with its wide tree-shaded garden separating two long rows of separate rooms, did not house Pharaoh's favorites and offspring. There were no children here, no cries of babies or shrieks of youngsters at play. The silence made by the absence of their cries was oddly disturbing to her and pressed on her like an unpleasant weight. All she could hear was the dull hum of women's talk, punctuated from time to time by shrill laughter, and even that ceased abruptly as the occupants of the hall became aware that a newcomer had arrived in their midst.

They turned to stare at their new rival as Shanda felt the dull realization settling into her that she had been sent, not to live with Pharaoh's chosen favorites, as she had expected, but to his harem. As if she were a common peasant woman he'd seen and wanted, she'd been consigned to live where he went for amusement.

She walked through the paths of the garden, following the old eunuch who chattered at her side, only dimly aware of his words and of the open, appraising stares of the women. She felt a trembling rage growing inside her, anger and outrage at the insult being done to her. She held herself tight, knowing she could not allow these strangers to see how she felt.

She had been alone in the room for several minutes before she realized where she was, before the rage left her enough so that she might feel even the smallest nudge of curiosity. She looked about, saw the room was fairly large and quite bright, the bed and chair and dressing table well wrought, even elaborate, with carved feet and inlaid surfaces.

There was a small polished silver disk on the dressing table. Curious, she lifted it. Its shiny surface reflected her features. She realized this had been left so that she could present herself at her best to Pharaoh. She slammed it back down on the table, churning with anger, and turned away as a wave of misery washed over her.

It was then the eunuch's words returned to her, the words she had been too numb to consider. He had said that she was highly honored, for he had been directed to allot to her one of the finest rooms in the harem. She heard the words once more in her mind, saw the old eunuch's superior, knowing expression. To be considered one of Pharaoh's favorite whores brought her no pleasure at all. Filled with a dull misery, she asked herself how Hattushil could have sent her to this, sent her to be demeaned and treated with neither honor nor respect.

She found her trunk in a corner and went to it, fell to her knees beside it, then opened it. She rifled through the garments until she found the small cedar box that held her combs and hair ornaments. Opening it, she drew from it the single shining golden object it contained, and held it to her breast without looking at the intricate carving on its surface, knowing its every feature more familiarly than she knew anything else. It was the golden cuff that had once been her mother's. And before that, she knew, it had belonged to the man her mother had told her of, the tall, golden-haired man who had given all, who had fled his own home so that he would not lose the woman he loved. Shanda thought of that man whom Althea had loved all those years before, and she wept for him, bitter, painful tears that did little to ease the hurt she felt within herself.

She did not, however, have long to savor her misery alone. A few moments later the door opened and a horde of chattering dark-haired women entered the room without so much as asking her leave. She absently put the golden cuff around her wrist as she watched them move through the room, staring at her openly, reaching out to touch her hair and the silk of her gown. She could see their lips move, and was dimly aware that they were smiling at her even as they inspected her, seeming to tell her that she might be their rival, but they would accept her if she made an effort to become one of them.

Shanda kept her mind from hearing their words, turning away from their smiles. She wanted nothing from these women, certainly not to be taken into their company, to be considered one of them. She was a royal princess, not some hetaera whose favors could be purchased with a trinket or a handful of coins. Hattushil had been wrong to send her, to think that with a few words she could bewitch Pharaoh as her own mother had bewitched him. All she wanted was to be left to herself to contemplate her misery.

She allowed the women their distraction, however, letting them look through the clothing in her trunk, to chatter curiously about the color of her hair. She thought of them only as one might think of a swarm of bothersome flies—harmless, but annoying. It was only when one of them reached out to the golden cuff at her wrist, wanting to examine the detailed carving on its face, that Shanda awoke from her distracted daze.

She pulled away, pushing the woman from her, aware suddenly of the thick, musky scent of her body and the cloyingly sweet odor of the oils she wore. If the women had seemed like harmless flies only moments before, now they transformed themselves into harpies, evil spirits, grasping at her, tearing at her with sharp-nailed greedy hands.

She was sickened, revolted by the intimate closeness these strange women had imposed upon her, terrified that proximity to them might bear a contagion, that if she let them stay close she might find herself one of them, her face heavily painted, her body reeking of the thick, sweet scents. She grew ill, picturing herself a common street whore, plying her trade in some evil alley, begging coin from foul and lecherous men.

"Get out of here," she screamed suddenly, hearing the note of hysteria in her voice but unmindful of it. "Leave me alone. Get out!"

They stared at her a moment in silence as though she'd suddenly taken leave of her senses, but she screamed at them again and her second cry brought the ancient eunuch. He herded the women out of the room, ignoring their assertions that they had done nothing wrong, had meant merely to welcome the newcomer. Shanda saw his glance as he left her, following the women, a look of disapproval to tell her she ought to have accepted the inspection with more grace. She didn't care; she had no more thought for his sanction than for that of the women.

When she was once more alone, she sat on the edge of the bed and examined the bracelet on her wrist, studying the tiny figure of the warrior driving a chariot, his lance in hand, and the huge man-beast that approached him and threatened the beautiful, long-maned horse that pulled him. She knew this warrior was Pelias, the man who'd loved her mother and died for her, but soon her thoughts strayed from the story Althea had so often told her, and roamed unbidden to Nem.

She'd told herself a hundred times that she would never think of him again, that he'd abandoned her, and that the thought of him was as odious to her as the thought of the Egyptian barbarian to whom he'd allowed her to be sent. But she could not push him from her mind. Unbidden, he appeared before her, his dark eyes holding hers, a lank, dark curl falling haphazardly across his brow, a slyly self-assured smile curling up the corners of his lips.

She felt the familiar lurch inside herself, as though Nem were actually close to her, and she longed for the feel of his arms around her. She loved him, she told herself, and wished herself back at Hattushil's court with him. She thought of the words he'd spoken before their angry parting. He had told her she must do this thing if they were ever to be together. Surely he would not have asked it of her unless he felt certain they would soon be free to love each other. She vowed to cling to that thought, hold it fast, so that she could survive this demeaning reality.

"Excuse me, lady."

She looked up abruptly as the image of Nem shattered and

vanished. Its place was usurped by a boy, staring wide-eyed at her, apparently a bit frightened. At her glance, he fell to his knees and bowed, lowering his head to the floor at her feet.

"Who are you?" Shanda demanded irritably. Then, disgusted by his demeaning position, she snapped, "Get up."

"My name is Medinet, lady. I have been sent to serve you."

Still the boy did not move, but stayed on his knees, his head touching the floor. Shanda hated this show of his servility; disgust rose within her as it occurred to her that he must be a eunuch, for no others would be allowed to serve in Pharaoh's harem.

"Get up," she ordered again, this time sharply, and the boy, apparently unable to do as she bade, responded by looking up at her, his eyes still wide and frightened. "On your feet, boy," she snapped at him when he made no move to get off his knees.

He seemed to shudder; then he stood, silent and watchful, his eyes on hers.

He was only twelve or thirteen, Shanda realized, and small, with skinny arms and legs that seemed unable to settle themselves comfortably.

"You may tell them I do not care to have a eunuch serve me, that I have no need for any servants at all," she told him, then turned away, dismissing him from her thoughts.

It was only when she heard a muffled sob that she turned to find him still there, his face screwed up with his misery and tears streaming down his cheeks. She thought him about to fall once more to his knees, but obviously he thought better of it when he saw her expression, because he straightened himself somewhat at her glance.

"Please, lady," he begged, his voice pitiable, "how have I offended you?"

"You have not offended me," she snapped, almost repulsed by his misery, caring at that moment only for her own. "I simply have no need for a servant. Go."

"But if I tell them you rejected me, they will think I have done something wrong, lady, and they will beat me. I pray you, do not send me away."

Shanda considered him for a moment. His fear seemed genuine enough, and she had no desire to be the cause of hurt to him. She would swallow her distaste for eunuchs, she decided, as long as he behaved properly.

"Very well, you may stay," she said slowly, abashed at the relieved smile that spread across his face at her words. He drew the back of his arm across his nose and cheeks in a vain effort to dry them. He bobbed his head, and Shanda thought he was about to kneel before her once more. "But you are never to take that disgustingly servile position in my presence again," she warned. "Do you understand?"

He nodded and once more his head bobbed eagerly. "Yes, lady," he replied. "As you like, lady."

"Where are you from?" she asked, almost as an afterthought, realizing that his presence could at least serve to distract her.

"From the south, lady, from Kalabsche."

"And how did you come to be here?" she demanded.

The boy thought for a moment, as if unwilling to speak. Then he looked directly at her eyes and seemed to decide she would accept his past, or at least would not blame him for it. He lowered his gaze before he spoke.

"My father was a lord, an ambitious lord. He tried to take the place of the pharaoh's governor by force, telling the local people that a foreigner from the north could not rule them fairly and honestly. He lost his battle, however, and the governor sent his soldiers to our home. They killed my father, raped and killed my mother and sisters." He clasped his hands so tightly his knuckles turned white with the pressure, and his voice became a hoarse whisper. "They made me what I am now and took me to the governor. He decided to let me live and sent me here as a gift to Pharaoh."

Shanda felt a well of pity rising in her. This boy had suffered, known more terrible misery than she could even contemplate, through no fault of his own.

"I am sorry," she told him softly.

He shrugged. "It is an honor to serve in the pharaoh's harem," he told her. "Many willingly give up what was taken from me so that they can live here."

Shanda listened to his words thoughtfully. He had somehow found the courage to live with his situation, something she knew was not a simple feat. She would not see him hurt again because of her; she would give him a fair chance. She wished she had the power to free him.

He seemed intent upon pleasing her. As soon as he'd determined that she was willing to keep him, he began to busy himself, carefully gathering up the clothing the women had taken from her trunk and strewn about the room, folding the dresses neatly and returning them to the box. Then he disappeared silently, returning a few moments later carrying a tray laden with fruit and bread and cheese and an earthenware pitcher of wine. He set the tray down on the table near the fretted window that looked out at the garden, and set the food out for her. When he'd accomplished this task, he looked up at her expectantly.

At that moment, Shanda felt comfortable with him and almost glad of his presence. She seated herself at the table on the chair he held for her. The sounds of the women sporting in the garden beyond her window came to her as a reminder of where she was. She turned away from it, wanting to forget the presence of the women, wanting to forget where she was. She looked up at the boy.

"Will you not sit, too, Medinet, and share my meal?"

He was clearly shocked by her offer, but regained his composure quickly enough. Apparently he knew what had happened between her and the other women and recognized, even before she did, that she was lonely. He nodded gravely, brought a chair, and placed it at the opposite side of the table. Then he sat, waiting until she broke off a piece of bread and held it out to him before daring to touch any of the food. At her offer, however, he took the bread and set to, eating with the sort of hunger of which only young boys seemed capable.

Shanda smiled and took some of the bread for herself, then began to eat it absently, her eyes still on him. After the first bite, however, she realized that her stomach was completely empty and grateful for the offering. She took some cheese and fruit.

"How long have you been here, Medinet?" she asked between a mouthful of cheese and a swallow of wine.

"Med, please, Princess?" he suggested.

Shanda noticed the change in address and wondered if it was a conceit based on the fact that he served a princess, raising his position over that of the eunuchs who served less lofty concubines. She was used to the form of address, however, and so said nothing of it.

"Very well, then, Med," she replied, agreeing to the informality.

"I have been here less than a year," he answered. "The river had just overflowed its banks when I came."

"I have heard of this rising of the river," she said. "Will you tell me about it?"

And so he talked, telling her how the great Amun Rah, god of the sun, and Isis, goddess of heaven and earth, made the Nile overflow and the land become fertile each year, so that the crops would grow and bear fruit. She smiled at his words, encouraging him, but secretly feeling a bit superior, thinking his gods, like those of the Hittites, strange and foolish, like the gods of which her mother had once told her, gods with names like Zeus and Athena and Apollo.

She had long before stopped believing in gods, feeling that no fair or just god would have treated her mother so cruelly. Her thoughts were similar with regard to young Med. He certainly owed no allegiance to any gods who had allowed such horror to come to his short life.

But she was pleased nonetheless with his company, and the remainder of the afternoon passed quickly for her. It had grown dark when Med finished his tale and turned to the task of clearing away the remains of their meal. She watched him fill the tray with the empty plates and pitcher, the crumbs of bread and peels and pits of oranges and plums, sweeping up the lot until the table was shiny and clean once again. Then he lifted the tray and started to the door.

Before he reached it, however, there was the sound of a gong, loud enough so that it could not be missed, but high and sweet, without any sharpness to it.

Med turned to her. "Pharaoh is here, Princess," he told her. "You must go to the garden to greet him." Then he slipped out the door, bearing away his tray and disappearing from her view.

Shanda felt deserted. Med's advice, that she go out to the garden to greet Pharaoh, only roused her ire. Even her fear of the Egyptian king was supplanted by her anger at the common way he had treated her by sending her to live as another of his many whores. If he thought no better of her than that, if he could not show her the honor due her status, then he could send her back to Hattushil. No matter that being returned to the Hittite court would mean disgrace. To stay would be worse.

She would not go to the garden. She was a royal princess not bound by such harem laws. Let him amuse himself with some other woman of his harem. She may have given Hattushil her word that she would obey Pharaoh as her lord, but she had sworn no oath to demean herself. Clearly, Pharaoh sought nothing more from her than he would from some peasant woman who had taken his fancy.

The old eunuch bowed in welcome to him, and Pharaoh acknowledged his presence with an absent nod. He stared at the gathering of expectant, smiling women, but the one smile for which he searched was not among them. He turned to the old eunuch.

"The Hittite, where is she?" he demanded.

The old man seemed flustered by his abruptness. He turned to scan the group of twenty or more women who milled in the small courtyard. Ordinarily Pharaoh had a kind word for him and time to exchange a joke, perhaps, or a drink of beer.

"I do not understand why she has not come, lord," he answered quickly when it became obvious to him that Shanda was not there. "She must be still in her apartment. I will have her sent for."

Pharaoh waved his offer aside. "No matter. I will go to her," he said. Then, lest the old eunuch fear that he would be blamed for not having properly instructed the newcomer, he added, "First days are often confusing. Perhaps the Hittite did not understand what was expected of her."

With that he started along the path, nodding to the greetings the women offered him, but ignoring their smiles of invitation. He had other plans for the evening, and these women seemed suddenly unappealing to him. All he could think of was a pair of incredibly blue eyes set in a fine, pale face framed by hair with an unbelievable golden hue.

As they had several times during the day, at times when he should have been occupied with other matters, his vizier's words returned to him, that Hittite women remained innocent until they were wed. Those words had led him to moments of distraction, moments when his thoughts were firmly entrenched in the anticipation of teaching the golden-haired princess those arts from which she had so far been shielded. Several times he had come to an abrupt awareness that he had been silently musing while the whole court watched him, no doubt wondering what had so distracted their king.

It was with a pleasant sense of expectation that he opened the door to Shanda's room and looked inside. A small lamp had been lit and placed on the table in the corner, its flickering light casting a moving warmth on the walls and furnishings. As he entered, Shanda, who had been sitting in a chair by the window, stood and faced him.

He smiled at her. "Well, Princess," he asked, "how do you find your surroundings?"

It was obvious from his tone and expression that he expected her thanks for his largess. Shanda marveled at his manner. Was it possible, she wondered, that he thought he was actually honoring her by placing her here, treating her this way? Had he no thought of who she was and what she was? Surely nothing compelled her meekly and graciously to accept his disdain—not the oath she had sworn to Hattushil, not even the hope that her compliance would lead eventually to a life with Nem.

The arrogance of the man overwhelmed her. Was it truly that he could not understand that she was a royal princess, that in her own land she was accorded the same honors he was given in his? Never would Althea let her forget that pride and honor were her most precious possessions. She had no intention of humbly thanking him for his generosity. Instead, she would wait until he understood that she demanded to be accorded what was due her.

"Why have you placed me here?" she demanded, her voice shaking. The anger she'd felt earlier had returned at the sight of him. "I am a princess of royal blood, not some peasant woman who has aroused your lust."

Her lack of pleasant greeting surprised him. But it was her expression even more than her words that roused him from his stupor of satisfied expectation. His smile vanished. "And just what did you think I would do?" he demanded sharply. "Build you a palace? Make you my queen?"

There was an answering anger in his tone, and his words were heavy with sarcasm. Shanda heard it, but she dismissed it, unwilling to accept the nagging words of caution that the voice inside her was silently screaming at her. Her cheeks colored, and her hands balled up into useless fists.

"I expected you to treat me with the respect to which my position entitles me," she told him, mustering a vestige of her dignity. "Either that or send me back to Hattushil and tell him you would have your tribute of grain in my place."

"Perhaps I should instead send you to my troops, Princess. It would have been to them the grain would have gone."

He stared at her evenly, obviously hoping to shatter her anger with his threat and leave her begging his pardon. Instead, Shanda was filled with disgust. This man was indeed a barbarian, just as she had first thought him. But despite his swagger and his arrogance, she would not be cowed by him. His people might consider him a god, but she knew he was only a man, a man whose blood was no loftier than her own. She had known great men, important men, in Hattushil's court. She had even come to love Nem, but still she knew he was as much a man as any other. It was

impossible for her to see Pharaoh as anything more than just
a man, a powerful one, perhaps, but still a mortal. And she
knew from the lesson her mother's life taught her that even
the most powerful of men could be ruled by a woman.

She returned his stare as she drew herself up sharply,
her shoulders thrown back and stiff. "One barbarian or a
thousand," she replied, her tone like ice, "where lies the
difference?"

For a moment they stared at each other. Shanda saw
the anger seep from his eyes and something else take its
place, something all too familiar to her, something she'd
seen before in many men's eyes when they looked at her.
That was the reason, after all, why Hattushil had sent her
to Pharaoh.

For a moment she thought she had won, that he would take
her away from this dreadful place with its foolish, scheming
women and do as Hattushil had done for her mother. Indeed,
he had built Althea her own small palace, and if he had not
made her his queen, she had still, in many ways, ruled him.
Shanda permitted herself a small smile. As her mother had
done with Hattushil, she would do with this king. In the
end, he would be able to deny her nothing.

But he soon proved far less easily manipulated than
Hattushil had been. He moved toward her with a stealthy
determination, the look in his eyes telling her he was not
about to beg her for what he considered his right.

"I have paid a great price for you, Princess—the grain
your father owed me. Your blood may be royal in Hattushil's
court, but here it is no better than any other's. And you are
mine now, by payment."

For a moment, Shanda faltered. She'd been wrong to
think she could conquer him so easily, to think his will
any less strong than her own. He strode toward her slowly,
his step determined, and as she watched him she knew she

would have to give him what he desired—her willing acceptance of him. For just an instant she thought perhaps that
sacrifice would not be so great after all, for he was strong
and handsome and not without wit and intelligence, as she
had seen that afternoon in his audience hall. She thought of
the way Althea had described Pelias to her, how her mother
had used those very words to tell her daughter about the man
she had once loved, the man who had continued to rule her
heart even years after his death: strong and handsome and
intelligent. Perhaps Hattushil had unknowingly sent her to
the man who could steal her heart.

But then the thought of Nem bit at her mind, and she drew
back from the possibility. It was Nem she loved, Nem she
would sacrifice herself for if the need for sacrifice arose.
And to willingly give herself to Pharaoh would only cheapen
her in his eyes. Of that she was certain. He had more than
enough women, she reminded herself, women who were
doubtless practiced and talented in arts of which she had
only a distant knowledge. Once Pharaoh had taken her, he
would lose all interest in her, and that would make her sacrifice useless to Nem and Hattushil, who had told her to
make Pharaoh love her.

She realized he was close to her now, only inches away,
his dark eyes steely as they gazed into hers. For a moment
she felt a quiver of fear. She had to force herself to stand
still, to resist the urge to back away from him.

He reached out and put his hand on her shoulder where a
silver brooch held the soft drapery of her robe. He grasped
it firmly, then yanked it forward with a sudden sharp movement. She looked down, at the torn silk and her exposed
breast, then up at him.

Let him know that what he takes he steals, a voice within
her counseled. As long as he knows he has not completely
triumphed, he will continue the pursuit.

"You need not have torn my robe," she told him evenly. "I would have removed it, had you bidden me."

There was no softening in him. "Remove it," he ordered her.

As she had told him she would, she obeyed, slipping the remaining fabric down to her hips and then letting it fall to the floor, all the while watching his expression.

She stood before him naked, her feet surrounded by the circle of shimmering silk. He put his hand on her back and drew her close to him, letting his fingers slide across the soft skin of her back and down to her waist as he pressed his lips to hers.

The sudden contact of his lips was a surprise to Shanda, as was the firm, knowing touch of his hands on her flesh. No one—not Nem, not anyone—had ever touched her this way before. It was strange to her, this seeking, forceful, yet somehow gentle contact. He seemed to be telling her with his lips and his hands that he meant her no real harm, despite the ferocity of his manner and his words, that he wanted only that they both find pleasure in each other. And that, she knew, was the way to win him, by refusing to feel what he wanted her to feel.

She stood perfectly still, her hands at her sides, not sure what he expected of her and determined to give him only what little he demanded. But as his lips roamed to her neck, she felt a warm, liquid tide rising within her, and for the first time the pledge she had sworn to Hattushil seemed far from odious to her.

He released her finally, dropping his hands away from her and slowly drawing back to stare at her naked body with rapt appreciation. His expression, however, spoke to Shanda only of possession and triumph, as though he already felt sure he'd conquered her. She pushed aside the pleasure she'd felt in his kiss, telling herself that he had not won, that she would not let him. She would permit him what he wanted, but she would take no pleasure from it, somehow sure the knowledge of that fact would pain him far more than the sacrifice she would be forced to make.

He saw her diffidence and silently cursed her pride.

"Lie down," he told her, pointing to the bed, his tone one of command. He was determined to show her that he was her master now, that he held no regard for her Hittite pride.

He knew that if she melted, if she cried out to him or begged him, he would not be able to touch her except to comfort her like a brother. But when he saw her looking at him with anger and disdain and a rigid determination not to fear him, he resolved to conquer her with his passion.

Shanda stepped out of the circle of silk that lay around her feet on the floor and moved warily to the bed, knowing that the moment had come and wondering that she felt no fear of it but simply a dull acceptance. She sat down on the edge of the bed, staring up at him, waiting for whatever was to come with a stoic determination and a certainty that she would prove stronger than he was.

He stood staring at her for a long moment, neither of them speaking, and then he removed his robe, revealing his hard-muscled chest and arms and, when Shanda dared to look downward, ample evidence of his arousal. He sensed her shock at that, and realized that she was indeed innocent, that she'd never been witness to a man's naked body before. The thought did not generate enough amusement in him to moderate his determination. He sat beside her, put his hands on her shoulders, and pushed her down onto the pillowed softness of the bed.

Shanda was sure that she would feel nothing if she refused to feel. She closed her mind to the awareness of his touch as he caressed her breasts and her thighs, as his lips pressed against the warm flesh of her neck. A shiver of heat passed through her, a pulsing, liquid rush inside her, and she felt that it was wrong, that she should not allow herself to feel. She tensed her body and lay perfectly still, silently vowing that she would be stronger than he, that despite his hands and his lips, he would not really be able to touch her if she refused to be touched.

He felt her tense beneath him, but he would not let her escape him so easily. He forced her legs apart with his, and pressed his lips to hers as he entered her, wanting some reaction from her, anything, even a cry of pain if she would not utter a low moan of passion. But she remained still, and when he stared into her eyes, he found them blank and distant.

He moved inside her, and Shanda felt the hot, liquid press inside her, but she fought against it, putting her hands on her thighs and digging her nails into the skin to concentrate her thoughts elsewhere. She had sworn to obey him, and she would keep her word, but she would not give him the satisfaction of revealing to him the strangely pleasurable response of her body.

And then suddenly he found his anger gone and himself akin to a rutting animal. The comparison disgusted him. The thought that he did not please her bewildered him, for no woman with whom he had lain before had ever offered him any response but absolute and complete enthusiasm, sometimes so theatrical that it made him wonder what they expected of him in return. There was none of that with her, and he suspected that the lack of reaction was intentional, meant to show him that he held no mastery over her.

A sudden spark of anger returned, and it was enough to push him over the edge. He released himself into her with a powerful thrust, so strong she cried out softly, and then he lay silent, spent and still filled with ire, wondering what had happened to him, why none of it had been as he had anticipated it would be with her, why there had been no mutual pleasure in the play of their bodies. He drew himself away from her, stood, and grabbed up his robe from the floor where he'd dropped it, pulling it on, thrusting his hands sharply through the sleeves.

She stared up at him, and her beauty at that moment quite took his breath away. The golden halo was in disarray now, the blue eyes filled with anger and disdain. He'd possessed her, she was his property, but he knew he had not even touched her, that somehow she'd kept herself distant and as proudly aloof from him as she'd been when he'd entered the room. The realization saddened him more than he could have thought possible. In the strange battle that had been waged between them, she had defeated him without even fighting.

Even more maddening was the thought that he knew of no other course to take with her, no offensive other than this forthright attack she'd so successfully defeated. And as he stared at her, he wanted the victory even more than he had before.

He started to go to her, to try to make things the way he had thought they would be. Her voice stopped him.

"Barbarian," she said.

Just the single word, uttered slowly and with a sharp venom.

It was enough to call up his own anger once more. He turned away from her and strode quickly from the room, not even bothering to look back to the bed where she lay.

When Med found her the next morning, Shanda sat curled up in one corner of the bed, awake but bleary-eyed, staring at him as he opened the door and entered her room as though she expected to see some monster rather than his unprepossessing figure. He stared at her a long moment, realizing from the dark circles beneath her eyes that she had not slept.

So the gossip that had spread throughout the women's quarters was true, he mused, the gossip that was spread with glee by dozens of anxious tongues, that Pharaoh had lain with her but found no pleasure in her company.

"Princess," he said softly as he approached her, "are you not well? Can I help you?"

He moved slowly to her, holding out his hands to her as if to calm a frightened child. But the glazed look left her eyes as he neared, and she straightened herself slowly on the bed, unbending her cramped legs and stretching them as she wrapped the linen sheet around her body.

It must be morning, Shanda thought. That meant she had cried miserably throughout the night. Despite what Pharaoh had thought when he left her, she felt no glow of triumph over him, no thought that she had achieved anything near to victory. Mostly, she felt shame, shame that he had made her body stir and tremble despite her determination to keep herself aloof from him.

"I am well enough, Med," she said to him with determination but little conviction in her voice. "I want to bathe."

"Certainly, Princess," he replied and hurriedly fetched her robe and a small box from a chest in the corner of the room.

She sat and watched him, taking a great deal of interest in his actions, as though such ordinary movements had special meaning for her. When he stood before her once more, patiently waiting for her to rise, she pointed instead to the box.

"What is that?" she demanded abruptly.

He smiled at her, glad of the distraction. "Scented oils, Princess. All the ladies use them."

She drew back suddenly, as if the prospect physically repelled her.

"I will not," she told him, shaking her head sharply. "I am not one of those"—she paused, as though thinking of a fitting description, but finding none and finally settling for the word he had used—"those ladies. I have no desire to emulate them."

With that she stood, dropped the sheet, and held herself very erect, keeping her shoulders back as though proving her control despite the weary fear Med had seen in her eyes when he entered the room. As he helped her into her robe, he felt a sudden pang of sympathy for her and wished he dared to offer her the comfort of his touch. Instead, he bowed, returned the box to its place, then went to the door.

"This way, Princess," he told her as held the door for her.

He thought to warn her of the talk of the women, but she walked ahead of him, not pausing for him to catch up to her, and he was forced to hurry to keep within a few paces of her. As they approached the bath, he was aware of a sudden hush of voices. The women who were lazing there, seeing her, stopped their usually ceaseless chatter.

Med held his breath, wondering if they would be cruel to her now that they no longer felt her a threat to them, now that Pharaoh seemed to have dismissed her as an unworthy recipient of his attentions. They did not greet her, not even summarily or without warmth, the least he had assumed they would offer her.

Instead, from the far side of the pool came a voice, loud and clear in the unusual silence.

"It seems the proud Hittite, for all that golden hair, lacks the most basic equipment to satisfy a man. Perhaps the gold is as much artifice as the rest of her."

The words were followed by a general titter of laughter.

The laughter stopped as Shanda's eyes traveled to the opposite side of the pool, seeking out the one who had accused her, then gave up the effort. She owed no sign of regret to these women. She could almost feel Med's relief from where he stood behind her as she squared her shoulders disdainfully, giving no indication that she had heard.

But when Med took the robe from her, she made no move toward the pool. Instead, she stood naked, inviting the full and curious gaze of the women.

"Does this satisfy your curiosity?" she asked them haughtily as she glanced once more at the silent women, letting them stare openly at her naked body, at the thick thatch of golden hair between her thighs.

She stood for a moment, then turned around slowly, daring the others to meet her eyes, let alone taunt her further. Without exception, they turned away, embarrassed, and finally she, too, turned away, dismissing them and moving to the edge of the pool.

She stepped in quickly, feeling the water cool and fresh against her skin. When she stood waist deep, she turned her attention from her audience completely and dove toward the deepest part of the pool, wishing for a permanent escape rather than a short reprieve.

She stayed beneath the surface as long as she could, until she felt the pressure in her chest like a pounding throb inside her. Then she drifted upward and drank in a breath of fresh air like a cleansing draft. She swam then, from one side of the pool to the other and back again, over and over, concentrating on the movement of her arms and legs, wanting to tire her muscles enough to numb herself to thought completely. Then finally she turned and climbed from the pool, ignoring the still silent stares of the women and, without a word, allowed Med to drape the robe around her.

She slicked the water out of her hair and her eyes, then walked away from the staring women.

As she moved along the flower-lined path, she heard the sudden hum of talk as the women found their tongues. They were all anxious, it seemed, to discuss this new encounter with the alien Hittite creature.

When she reached her own room, Shanda crumbled. She waved to Med to close the door quickly, then allowed her shoulders to fall and her head to bow with the weariness and hurt she would not allow herself to show in front of the others. As she dried herself, she watched the boy straighten out her bed, then hurriedly find a clean linen shift for her to wear. She donned it and allowed him to lead her to the bed, knowing herself to be at the point of exhaustion, thankful for the exertion of the swim for her now tired muscles.

She lay back as Med drew the sheet up over her. Then she pulled it up to her chin, wishing it could protect her from the miseries she was condemned to face alone.

# Four

IT WAS LATE afternoon when Shanda woke. The rest had done her a great deal of good, she realized. She was almost able to dismiss the feeling of despair she had borne so acutely that morning. She knew she was far from healed, but the wounds no longer seemed mortal.

She washed and dressed, eyeing the torn gown that now lay on the chair in the corner of the room where Med had been mending it when she awakened. The garment brought back memories of the previous evening, painful memories on which, she knew, it would do little good to dwell. She pushed them aside.

She would not think of the previous night, she told herself firmly. At least she was certain of one thing: The remarks with which the women had taunted her were true. Pharaoh would not come to her again. He had certainly found little enough in her company to amuse him.

Med left for a few moments and returned to her with a tray of food, as he had done the day before. He silently laid out the fruit and bread and cheese for her, then waited until she urged him to make a place for himself at the table with her, watching silently as she picked at the food and then pushed it away.

"You should eat something, Princess," he chided her softly, sounding more like an aging nurse than a young boy.

Dutifully she nibbled at a piece of fruit before dropping it to her plate. He hastily finished what lay on his own plate, hungry as he always seemed to be, but not wanting to eat before her when she so obviously had no appetite.

But she smiled at him, gently encouraging, and pushed the platter toward him, silently inviting him to eat his fill.

"Young boys, I'm told, are always hungry," she told him.

He smiled shyly as he put some melon on his plate. "I don't know about others, but my belly never seems to be full," he replied, neglecting to add that in all too many instances that emptiness was due simply to the fact that he was given far too little with which to fill it.

"Well, fill it now," she commanded him with a smile. "There may not be many more chances for me to share with you. Perhaps Pharaoh will decide it is not worthwhile to waste food on one so worthless as I seem to be."

She'd meant the words in jest, but once uttered, they rang true in her own ears. She'd failed in everything she had been expected to do, failed to live up to Pharaoh's expectations of her, and Hattushil's and Nem's as well. Death by starvation seemed only too fitting a fate for her.

But Med shook his head vehemently. "You must not think such things, Princess," he admonished. "And you must not listen to the talk of the others."

Shanda turned away from him, staring out into the cool green of the garden. "It really matters little what I think," she told him. "After all, thoughts are useless to a sack of grain."

Or to a woman, she thought. In Hattushil's court and, it seemed more than obvious, in Pharaoh's as well, women served but one purpose. In her whole life, only one woman had urged her to think and act with courage and pride. All her life, she realized, she'd tried to measure up to the memory of her mother, judging her own actions by what she thought Althea might have done in her place. And she had, she thought, behaved courageously with Pharaoh, silently defying him even in the face of his anger. She wondered if it had all been useless.

She fell silent, oblivious to Med's confused stare. She turned her attention to the golden hue that colored the late afternoon sunlight, the rosiness that preceded the dimness of twilight. She wondered if Pharaoh would come again to his harem that evening, if he would feel it necessary to flaunt his rejection of her before the others, to demean her pride before he dismissed her and chose another to entertain him for the night.

Med finished his meal quickly and in silence. When he stood to clear the table, Shanda woke suddenly to his presence.

"It grows late, Princess," he told her when she turned to him. Then he nodded to the dimming light in the garden. "You must dress, ready yourself for Pharaoh."

She almost smiled at his serious expression. "I think Pharaoh will have little interest in my company this evening," she replied with a lightness she did not feel.

Med shook his head. "But your presence is required, Princess," he told her.

She didn't move, but watched him in silence as he busied himself clearing the table, then fetching and lighting the oil lamp. But finally she realized that he was right, that she had little hope of simply hiding in her room for the remainder of her life. She stood, resigned to the fact that if she ignored the summons to greet him, Pharaoh would consider her actions a blatant defiance of his power. Even if she could justify her spontaneous anger, she knew that Pharaoh would not condone open defiance.

She hated herself for having given her word to Hattushil, but she had sworn to obey Pharaoh, and she would keep her oath, not for her father, but for her own self-respect. Althea had taught her that her word was her honor. Without her honor, she knew, she had nothing left.

Finally she roused herself and donned the purple silk dress, hardly noticing how neatly Med had mended it until she saw the look of disappointment in his eyes at her indifference, and then she made a bit too much fuss over his work. In the end, they both felt awkward, and she turned away to draw her comb absently her disheveled curls, making an effort not to think.

When Med approached her with a box containing brushes, kohl, and pink, blue, and purple paints, she waved him aside, ignoring his disappointment. She realized he secretly wished that she would make some effort to improve her appearance by painting her face as the other women did. It occurred to her that Med's position was directly tied to her status. If she became a favorite, he would have far greater standing among the other servants. He would be elevated from mutilated son of a provincial rebel to servant to Pharaoh's beloved. She almost regretted her inability to oblige him.

She wondered idly why he thought there might still be a chance for her to reach so lofty a position. She herself was sure that Pharaoh had little thought for her beyond the possible determination to bend her to his will. In any case, she had no intention of allowing Med to transform her with his paints and oils into another characterless face in Pharaoh's harem.

It was late when the gong was finally rung, the sound of it echoing through Shanda's brain with a fateful finality, a tolling of her destiny. She felt a rigidity come over her as she rose and slowly walked to the door.

Med held it open for her, and she ventured out into the garden with as much trepidation as if she were facing the dark wilds of an untamed wood. Torches had been lit, brightening the paths and reflecting from the pool as she passed it. They flickered with a dancing gaiety on the soft night breeze, and she slowed her steps, letting herself admire the shimmering shadows the flames cast on the night green of the garden.

It was several moments before she heard the murmured sounds from the central pavilion. She knew she was late; the others were already assembled and she had once again transgressed on the rules of the harem. She bit her lip, chiding herself, telling herself that she would only call down Pharaoh's wrath and that was not what she had been sent to do. She knew it was no longer possible for her to complete her task. Hattushil's expectation of her ability to charm Pharaoh had been foolish. Still, though, she had no right to abandon her responsibilities. She hurried along, dreading the sight of the man who had treated her with such a lack of regard the night before.

She stepped into the circle of light in the pavilion, aware that her presence seemed to arouse a good deal of attention, that, as it had in the audience chamber, her entry quieted the babble of voices to silence. Pharaoh stared at her with his steely gray eyes, his face immobile, as she neared the cluster of women. The others drew back from her as though she were poison, and she felt exposed and dreadfully alone.

She watched as one of the other women approached him, bowing at his feet, kissing his offered hand, and then his foot, smiling up at him in thanks for the favor of a word. Two others repeated the performance, and all the while

Shanda felt his eyes, cold flames that touched her, gazed at her, thick with expectation.

And then, it seemed, it was her turn.

"Well, Princess, will you not greet me?"

His voice was almost gentle, and it surprised her. She hesitated a moment, allowing her eyes to meet his, to find, unbelievably, that there was no anger in them. She squared her shoulders and told herself that there was no need to fear him. The thought came to her that she had been right the night before, that by refusing to allow him to please her she had made him more intent to prove that he could do precisely that. Perhaps, she thought, the game was not entirely lost after all.

She stepped forward into the circle of bright light the torches cast on the place where he sat. She moved forward quickly, before her nerve left her entirely. She knelt on one knee and bowed her head.

This was not the complete obeisance she'd seen the others make, but she found she could not lower herself so servilely as to kiss his feet. This bow, she told herself, showed more deference than Hattushil had demanded of her. Surely it would satisfy Pharaoh.

And at first it seemed to. He held out his hand to her, and his glance was gentle. He even smiled. For a moment she thought what had happened the night before had been nothing more than a nightmare, that she'd imagined it all, and for him it had never happened. She touched her lips to his hand and began to back away.

"Perhaps you were not watching the others, Princess."

There was a note of warning in his voice, thinly edging his tone. She looked up to find his eyes on her, and she saw in them the triumph, the assurance that here, finally, she would be forced to swallow her pride and show him the deference he demanded of her.

"My ladies kiss my foot when they greet me, Princess," he told her softly. "Come greet me as they do, and I will overlook the reticence I see in your manner."

She told herself she should do as he had bidden her, that he would ask nothing more of her if she did. But somehow she could not force herself forward, could not bow to him as though he were a god.

"Your ladies worship you, lord, as a living deity, and even so base a contact is a blessing to them," she told him evenly as she returned his stare. "To me you are only a man, and I find no ecstasy in your touch."

There was a loud gasp of shock from the others. It rippled through the air like a curtain of impending doom, as though the women expected a thunderbolt to descend from the sky and strike her for her blasphemy. Still, she didn't move, but stared at him, her eyes caught by his, aware of the growing anger in him.

He swallowed once, seemingly trying to force it away.

"Princess, greet me properly and I will forgive this transgression as well."

The gentleness had disappeared from his tone. This was a battle to him, one of pride, and she realized suddenly he would not dismiss her unless she submitted. And even with that knowledge, she knew she could not bring herself to do as he demanded.

She, too, swallowed, but what she tasted in her mouth was fear.

"I cannot, lord. I have sworn to serve you, and I will honor my word. But my blood is as royal as yours, and I cannot demean it by acting like a slave."

He rose, pushing himself from the chair with his hands, the muscles of his arms rippling in the shimmering light. She could see the tension in him, and she knew he would demand payment for her impertinence. Still, she realized she could not have done otherwise if she hoped to ever find any value in herself.

"Here your blood is no better than a slave's," he told her through tight lips. "Greet me as you are told, or I warn you, Princess, you will suffer my wrath."

Shanda felt herself grow cold under his gaze. Do it, a voice inside her screamed. How great can the cost be?

But she only shook her head. "I cannot, lord," she managed to whisper.

Pharaoh knew that he had no choice if he ever hoped to see her come to him as he wanted, meekly, lovingly. He would crush her will and he would have her. And to do that, he had to squash her pride now, before it became even stronger. He turned to the chief eunuch, pointing to the leather whip he wore at his belt.

"That whip is there to be used, not for display," he said to the eunuch. "Use it now."

The eunuch visibly paled with shock. "But, lord," he protested, "no woman has been beaten in my memory. Not in your time or your father's."

Pharaoh's eyes didn't waver. "Use it," he ordered.

The eunuch bowed and motioned to the two others who stood guard by the great doors. They moved forward quickly, to Shanda's side, seizing her arms and nearly dragging her, for she felt too numb to move, to a gilded pillar. Then they tied her hands around it.

"Five lashes," Pharaoh commanded.

She could hear the whip being cracked in the air. And then there was a hand on her shoulder, drawing away the fabric of her gown, pulling it down, baring her to the waist.

She closed her eyes, steeling herself for the first blow. But once again there was the touch of a hand on her shoulder.

"I will forgive you, Princess, even now," Pharaoh told her softly.

She opened her eyes and turned to face him, shocked to discover that there was a look in his eyes akin to pleading. There was a desperation in them that told her he did not want to do this to her but that his pride demanded it.

"I cannot, lord," she whispered.

The look disappeared, replaced once more by anger. "You bring this on yourself," he said sharply as he backed away.

When the first blow landed, she was not entirely prepared for it, and her breath escaped with a gasp, but she managed not to scream. She bit her lips and steeled herself for the rest.

Pharaoh turned away, stalking from the pavilion, reaching out and grabbing the arm of the first woman he passed, ignoring her pleased smile, pushing her along the path into the shadows of the garden.

"She is a fool to defy you, lord," the woman told him with a smirk of satisfaction.

He turned to her angrily, aware of the sound of the second blow falling.

"Perhaps you would like to see if you could bear so much without a cry?" he snarled at her.

She grew instantly silent, bowing her head to him, wondering what the strange woman had done to change him this way, for she'd never seen him with such anger in him before. He took her roughly by the arm and she followed without another word.

Shanda told herself she was beyond pain, but she knew it was a lie. Her back was on fire. She found it was all she could do to keep from crying out with relief when her hands were freed and she found Med beside her, putting his thin arm around her waist to steady her. She could hardly walk, even with his help, and she staggered through the now silent circle of women as he led her back to her room through the darkness. She told herself she would not collapse, but still it surprised her when she found herself back in her room.

She fell on her bed, gasping for air, forcing herself to let nothing but silent tears cry out her pain. And then there was the agony of the boy's hand on her back, but her wounds quickly grew numb as he carefully rubbed a salve on the cuts.

She had won, she told herself as a cloud of pain and dark shadows seemed to fill her brain. For a moment she wondered how many more of these battles with him she would be forced to enjoin, and how many victories she could manage to survive. And then the pain and the shadows seemed to blend, and she fell into darkness.

For three days Shanda kept to her room, venturing out only to bathe in the pool and then returning quickly, unable to ignore the words she heard spoken about her, at first whispered, then voiced more boldly as the days drew on. Pharaoh had not returned to the harem, and the women blamed her. By the evening of the third day, they spoke about her quite openly, even in her hearing.

"The Hittite bitch has soured him," they muttered angrily. "Now we will all suffer for her arrogance."

They longed for the opportunity to hurt her, to cut her advances of friendship, and were only more angered when she refused to give them the opportunity, or even so much as an indication that she was aware of their existence.

She stayed quietly by herself, speaking only to Med, filling her days with the boredom of worry and recrimination, knowing she had failed. She came to accept the possibility that with her failure came the probability that she would never again return to Hattushil's court, never again see Nem.

The raw cuts on her back had begun to heal, the skin

closing and only the deep red weals remaining. That almost distressed her, for she would have preferred to cling to the pain and the marks as reminders, assurances for herself that she had been condemned to serve a barbarian. She dwelt on her pain and her anger, blaming Hattushil and Nem for sending her to be mistreated and demeaned, telling herself that she hated them both for the wrong they had done her by sending her to the barbaric Egyptian king.

Even Med's attempts to amuse her, although tolerantly accepted, met with little response. She had withdrawn into a shell of her own misery and had little desire to have it shattered.

On the morning of the fourth day, half a dozen of Pharaoh's private guard presented themselves to the chief eunuch. He took the message their chief presented to him, considered it thoughtfully before nodding to them and then turning, passing through the heavy, wide doors of the harem to cross the center of the pavilion, then quickly treading the path to Shanda's door. His knock was abrupt, and when Med opened the door to him, his expression was filled with disdain, yet tinged with curiosity.

"You will fetch your mistress and bring her to the great doors," the eunuch instructed, his eyes narrowing as he peered into the shadowed room where Shanda sat, apparently completely oblivious to his presence despite the fact that she could not have missed his entry, especially since he was her first and only visitor since the afternoon she had been brought there.

"Pharaoh has summoned her," he added then, noting with satisfaction that these four words, at least, startled her and attracted her attention.

"Pharaoh?" she repeated numbly.

He ignored her, and turned away, leaving Med to hurry to her and offer her a comb, then a thick woven ribbon to tie back her hair. Her hand shook as she drew the comb through her hair, and she was forced to allow the boy to tie the ribbon. Then she followed him along the path to the pavilion and then to the doors, where he presented her to the guards.

She ventured a quick look back, watching the doors close on Med, noticing his surprised expression before they swung firmly shut. She was surprised to realize that parting from him was painful. She realized she had come to depend upon his kindness and his company. Without him she felt horribly alone.

She ventured a look at the stern faces of the soldiers, but they showed no expression.

"You will come with us, Princess," one told her brusquely. The others closed ranks around her.

She followed numbly, knowing there was nothing else she could do, wondering if Pharaoh had decided she was in need of some new punishment in payment for her sins.

They took her to the wide central courtyard. Shanda vaguely remembered passing through it that first morning when she had been brought to the palace, remembered how she had stood for a moment and admired the tall painted columns that rimmed the open walkway at its edge and supported the roof that provided relief from the unremittingly bright sunshine. That day, the shade had looked pleasant and comforting to her. Now everything appeared threatening. It seemed impossible that her outlook had so completely changed in only a few days' time.

The space was filled with milling soldiers and horses, stamping and anxious, their movements agitating slightly the chariots to which they were hitched. As they entered the courtyard, another guard approached her. Shanda knew his rank was higher than that of the others by the way they saluted him. He was rough looking, his face and body darkly

tanned, his shoulders angular and muscular, his skin marred
in several places by the thickened tissue of old scars. But
when he turned to her, he smiled pleasantly, as though he
saw her uncertainty and wanted to reassure her.

"Will you come with me, please, Princess?" he asked,
bowing to her politely.

She was quite baffled by his deference, the first she'd
been shown by anyone, except Med, since she'd entered
the palace several days before. But more than the deference, she found she appreciated the smile.

She nodded to him, and then he turned and led her out
into the startlingly sharp sunlight of the courtyard, skirting
the stamping horses' hooves and the small knots of soldiers.
He led her to one of the chariots, and Shanda admired the
pair of beautifully matched whites hitched to it.

"We wait here, Princess," he told her with another smile.

"Magnificent horses," she murmured tentatively, not at
all sure what was expected of her, not sure he wished to
converse with her.

But he grinned and nodded agreement, motioning her forward so that she might inspect them.

"The finest in Pharaoh's stables," he replied with obvious
pride. "Perhaps the best in all of Egypt."

Shanda moved forward, patting a smooth, carefully
groomed white rump. Its owner turned his head and
stared at her, then neighed. She wished she had some
fruit to offer them. Given her ease with animals, she might
at least make friends with the handsome horses. She'd had
little success with humans at Pharaoh's court, but with his
animals she knew she could find comforting companionship.
As the second white watched, the first allowed her to raise a
hand to his long, hard nose and draw it slowly downward.
He neighed once more and nudged her shoulder playfully,
snorting and sniffing at her.

"You should feel honored, Princess. He is not usually tolerant of strangers," the soldier told her.

"He is beautiful," she breathed softly. "They are both beautiful."

He had no chance to answer her, for at that moment the soldiers drew themselves briskly to attention. Even the horses seemed to hush.

Shanda looked up at the shadowed portico at the head of the courtyard and saw Pharaoh step out into the sunshine. The golden light turned his bare chest to glowing bronze, and Shanda found she could not help but admire the strength and proportions of his body. Her thoughts startled her, and she pushed them away. Still, she realized that even among the soldiers around him, Pharaoh appeared physically powerful. He moved like a great cat who knew his own strength, with the stealthy assurance of controlled power. She was struck, as she had been on that first afternoon, by the force of his masculinity.

He made his way directly to the chariot where she stood, the soldiers silently making way for him as he passed.

"Good day, Princess," he greeted her when he stood before her.

Shanda bowed as she saw the soldier at her side do, then straightened and looked up at Pharaoh, wondering if the impertinence would be met with the same anger she had managed to rouse in him the last time she had seen him.

But he seemed unconcerned with her lack of obsequiousness, apparently willing to allow her greater informality before his soldiers than he had before the women of his harem. She thought she caught a hint of pleasure in his gray eyes as he stared at her.

"I have decided to show you a bit of Egypt, Princess," he told her before turning to the officer. "Your men are ready, Seti?" he asked.

"We await you, lord," Seti responded quickly. Then he offered Shanda a last fleeting smile and called out the order to mount.

Pharaoh moved to her and put his hand on her shoulder. "Come, Princess," he said and pushed her gently forward, to the chariot.

She flinched. The pressure of his hand brought a sudden hurt to the still sensitive welts on her back, and she had not braced herself for the contact. He saw it and dropped his hand immediately, apparently only then remembering what had happened the last time he had seen her. He said nothing, but offered her his arm, waited for her to grasp it, and then helped her carefully into the chariot. Shanda was bewildered at his chivalrous treatment as he mutely climbed in beside her.

It seemed that he was trying to make peace with her, to pretend there had never been any anger or violence between them. She realized that there could be only one reason for him to want to reestablish a note of accord with her, and that realization made her inwardly smile, feeling an odd triumph. It was, she told herself, a victory for her. She began to feel that she might actually do what Hattushil had sent her to do, that he might be made to fall in love with her after all.

He moved forward, to the front of the chariot and took up the reins. The small procession set off, moving slowly out through the palace gates and along the narrow streets of the city.

Shanda gripped the rim of the chariot's side and stared curiously at the houses and shops and the hordes of gaping people. She had first been brought to the palace directly from the river where the barge had docked, a short journey. She had no idea that the city was so huge, so sprawling. It seemed enormous to her, immense and very crowded compared to the Hittite cities she'd seen.

When they reached the city's edge, Pharaoh turned to her.

"Put your hand on my shoulder, Princess," he told her with a grin, "and hold tight."

She thought he looked a bit like a boy about to begin a much anticipated outing. The expression surprised her.

He turned back to face the horses and snapped the reins. The whites responded immediately, leaping forward at a gallop.

Shanda quickly put her hand on his shoulder to steady herself and held tight. The wind snapped her skirt around her legs and blew her hair into a wild mane behind her. The countryside through which they passed seemed to move with incredible speed. For the first time in what felt like a lifetime to her, she felt almost free.

The pale dun colors of the city gave way to the deep green of well-tended fields and then, with a surprising quickness, to the golden brown of desert sand. Still the chariot raced onward as Shanda held Pharaoh's shoulder. When she looked back, she saw a trail of dust kicked up by their passage and, behind that, tiny now in the distance, the horses and chariots of the royal guard.

Finally Pharaoh drew the horses to a halt, calling out to them and pulling back on the reins. The two whites stilled themselves with obvious reluctance, their sides heaving, and shook their long manes.

Shanda looked down into the valley below the rise where they'd stopped. She could see an army encampment, with shelters at the far end and what appeared to be training grounds close below them. On the open flat directly below were long lines of soldiers, those on foot to the rear, thick lines of manned chariots to the front.

Pharaoh looked back at the slowly growing images of his guards, still far behind, and laughed with pleasure. "No pair can match the speed of these," he told Shanda with pride.

Once again she was struck by the thought that he seemed boyish now, showing his pleasure with his animals and the delight he, too, had felt at the speed of their ride. There was obviously a good deal more to him, she realized, than the small glimpse he had shown her. She even found herself smiling back at him, finding his pleasure somehow contagious.

He turned back to the whites, urging them slowly down the steep side of the slope.

"There will be games today, Princess," he called back to her.

Shanda stared down. Already the soldiers had drawn themselves to attention, waiting for their king to review their ranks. Two men on horseback, seeing his approach, had started up the slope to greet him.

"Generals," Pharaoh called when they were within earshot.

They raised their arms in a stiff salute, then drew their horses back to let his chariot pass. Then they fell in behind him and followed him down to the flat.

When they had reached the open flat, Pharaoh guided the chariot slowly past the ranks of charioteers and foot soldiers, stopping several times to call out a personal word to one man or another. They all answered smartly, and Shanda could hear the pride in their voices. Pharaoh was well liked by his soldiers, it was obvious, as well as deeply respected.

First there was a show of swordplay, with pairs of foot soldiers engaging and filling the air with the sound of iron striking iron. By the time the swordplay ended, the royal guard had made their way to the top of the rise. They fanned out along the ridge and stared down, impassive, at the war games below.

The winners marched past Pharaoh, then fell back to their ranks as the charioteers lined up to display their prowess. The drivers urged their horses to a run along the long, narrow flat while the archers who stood behind the drivers fired at a series of targets. Shanda was amazed at the precision and accuracy of their shooting from the speeding chariots. The targets were feathered with large numbers of protruding arrows when they were done.

"Well done," Pharaoh praised his generals. They smiled and bowed their heads in recognition of the compliment to their men, obviously pleased.

Then Pharaoh turned to Shanda. "Are you impressed with my soldiers, Princess?" he asked her.

His tone was light, but his gray eyes seemed to bore into her, and Shanda knew that he was really telling her something, not asking. His land was not defenseless, he was saying, and any enemy foolish enough to invade it would certainly be defeated.

For a moment she felt afraid, sure that he knew more of what Hattushil and Nem intended, more even than did she. He stood, silently waiting, as though he expected her to confess, to beg for his mercy, to admit she was a small part of some intended transgression against him. She was tempted to do just that, blurt out what little she knew, but managed to curb the words before they were spoken. When she stood silent, he turned back to his generals.

"I will try my hand," he said, then turned to look up at the rise where his guard waited. "Send for my driver."

"There is no need, lord," Shanda said. "I would be honored to drive for you."

He turned to her, clearly surprised at her offer, but no more so than Shanda herself. She hardly realized she had spoken until it was too late, until he was staring at her, and his amusement began to drift into his eyes.

"You, Princess?" he asked.

He thinks me a silly, incompetent fool, she thought, and the realization released a wave of resentment in her. She was determined to show him that she could handle his powerful whites as well as any driver, as well as Pharaoh himself, for that matter.

"Yes, lord," she replied firmly.

His glance was still amused, but he stood aside and let her take up the reins. Then he accepted the quiver and bow that were brought to him.

"I am ready, Princess," he said softly, his voice sounding goading in her ears, goading and superior.

Shanda did not turn back to face him. Instead, she carefully took up the reins and wrapped the ends around her waist, and tied them securely. That done, she grasped them and flicked them neatly against the horses' backs. The beautiful whites took off at once.

There was sharp tension in the leather straps as the horses pulled against the tightened reins, and the delicious feeling of movement, of control. It had been more than two years since she had done this. That was before her mother's death, but still the knowledge was there, in her hands and arms and body, and so was the memory of the sensation. She felt as if she had been born with reins in her hands and filled with the sensation of the powerful movement of the horses pulling her forward.

They sped past the row of targets. Behind her Pharaoh fired rapidly, sending arrow after arrow into them. Shanda heard the sharp thwack of the bowstring, the hiss of the arrows as they flew, and then the dull thud as they found their mark. All that, however, seemed somehow far apart from her, for she was lost in the movement of the horses and the pull of the reins in her hands. When they'd crossed the flat, she slowed the horses with reluctance, pulling back on the reins with her whole body, and then turned them and trotted easily back to where the generals waited. She was still infused with the exhilaration of the run.

When she drew the whites to a halt, Pharaoh leaned toward her.

"Tell me, Princess," he asked her, "do all Hittite ladies learn to drive as well as to sew and cook?"

She turned to him and found he was smiling at her. She returned the smile, too delighted with the thrill of the previous moments to bear him anything but goodwill at that moment.

"No, lord," she told him. "My mother came from the far north, from a land beyond the waters that you call the Great Green. It was the practice of her people to learn to ride, and it was she who taught me." She laughed then. "Indeed, Hattushil's ladies rarely venture beyond their pavilions and practice doing as little as they possibly can."

She had spoken easily, with genuine gaiety in her voice. Thoughts of her mother pleased her almost as much as the ride had. Pharaoh saw the pleasure she felt, in her eyes and in her manner, and wondered who this stranger could be, for she had none of the sharp tenseness he'd seen in her before. What he saw pleased him and reminded him of the thoughts he'd had of her that first afternoon, before their strange war of wills had begun.

"And the women of your mother's people," he asked her, watching her closely, "are they all so well trained?"

She nodded. "Yes, lord. At least that is what my mother told me."

He turned and pointed to a narrow obstacle course behind the open flat where the soldiers had practiced. She followed his hand with her eyes, noting the shadowed heaps of sand, the obstacles made of felled limbs and deep gullies.

"Do you drive well enough to navigate that?" he asked.

"Yes," she replied evenly. "Well enough even for that, lord."

He studied her a moment longer before he spoke. "I would see this, Princess," he told her. Then he climbed out of the chariot and stood staring up at her.

He's challenging me, Shanda thought. He thinks I cannot do it. She raised her chin and swallowed, wondering if perhaps she had not spoken too quickly, too confidently.

"Very well, lord," she answered slowly.

The generals had ridden up to them by now, wondering why Pharaoh had not returned to review the soldiers' exercises. But he motioned one of them to dismount, then swung himself easily into the saddle and sat watching Shanda, waiting for her to start.

Shanda tightened the reins where she'd tied them around her waist, then leaned forward and wrapped her arms around the extended straps.

"Go now, my handsome lords," she whispered to the horses, and flicked the leather against their backs.

They responded to her quickly, leaping forward, almost as though they, too, were as eager to show their skill. Pharaoh rode forward, his generals surrounding him.

"Is this wise, lord?" one of them asked. "She might ruin the horses."

But Pharaoh waved him to silence and continued forward until he reached a good vantage point from which to watch her drive. Behind him the troop of charioteers had pushed forward as well, eager to watch the woman put the Pharaoh's great whites through the hardest of their own training courses.

Shanda leaned toward the whites, whispering encouragement to them. The pull of the reins at her arms and waist was hard, echoing the movement of the animals' hooves as they kicked up a trail of darkly golden sand behind them. The first of the obstacles was a huge heap of tree limbs, and Shanda kept the horses running at full speed until the very last moment, then leaned sharply to the right, pulling the reins to turn the galloping whites to one side. They responded as if they'd always known her hand. From behind her, as the chariot skirted the edge of the heap, she heard a loud cheer. It was then she realized she was being watched not by Pharaoh only but by the company of soldiers as well.

She smiled and leaned toward the horses. "Let us show them all," she called out to the animals, and thought of Althea. "Thank you, Mother," she whispered softly to the wind.

Pharaoh watched her maneuver his great whites through the maze of troughs and rises and piles of branches. By the time she was done, the men behind him were wild, hoarse with cheering. He realized he'd never seen the course traveled so quickly, the turns managed so tightly, without a second wasted, without a single misstep.

When Shanda turned the pair back and returned to where he waited, he could see the horses snorting, their sides heaving from the run. He raised his arm and the noise of the soldiers behind him stilled.

Shanda drew the whites to a halt, nodded to him, and quickly untied the reins from her waist. Breathless with excitement and exultation, she quickly climbed down and ran to the front of the chariot, reaching up to the horses and embracing each of them in turn.

Pharaoh climbed down from his borrowed mount and approached her.

"I am glad your mother's people live beyond the Great Green, Princess. If all their women have as much skill as you, their men must be formidable indeed."

Shanda turned to him and found him smiling at her, but he looked intrigued now. No longer was there even a hint of the superior disbelief she had seen in his eyes before. And there was something more than that, something dark and strong and potent, something that went beyond mere desire. She felt a glow of triumph almost as powerful as the heat and excitement she'd felt with the reins in her hands and the horses' hooves beating against the sand beneath her.

He was beginning to think of her as more than his property, she told herself, more than just a woman to be used and cast away. This, she realized, was what Nem had told her she must do, charm Pharaoh, intrigue him, consume his thoughts. She needed no further proof than the look in Pharaoh's eyes to know that despite that first encounter, she was beginning to do just that. But once it was done, then what? Nem had promised her a future, promised to come for her and take her from the Egyptian's bed. She had no idea what that promise meant, or how long she must wait until it would be fulfilled.

She returned Pharaoh's smile, reminding herself that this man was her enemy, that she must not let down her guard. She felt overwhelmed by the task she'd been sent to perform, aware that she had no talent for duplicity. This all-important feat might well be beyond her.

Her feeling of triumph faded. Please, Nem, she thought, picturing him in her mind, his dark eyes staring at her, his handsome mouth so familiar to hers, please do not leave me long in this place. Until you come for me, I am like a lamb in a den of lions.

# *Five*

SHANDA HELD TIGHT to Pharaoh's shoulder. The chariot seemed to be flying, and when she turned to glance back at the soldiers' camp, she found it had grown tiny with the distance. It looked like a toy settlement now, made for the amusement of some pampered child.

The whites raced with a breathtaking abandon, as if they had been holding back until then, knowing they would be given this chance to show their speed and wanting to prove their prowess. The guard, it seemed, had made no effort to follow, for when Shanda looked back, she could see no second trail of dust racing after their own. For a moment she wondered if Pharaoh had given them the order to remain behind, or if they had merely decided the chase was futile, knowing their lesser animals could not hope to keep up the pace the whites had set, and given it up before it had been begun. Then she abandoned the questions and simply savored the feeling of speed and the passage of the countryside that fell limply behind them.

It seemed to end all too quickly, even though when Pharaoh slowed the whites their sides were heaving and they snorted, breathless with the exertion. Shanda looked back and realized they had traveled farther than she had thought, for she could see nothing of the encampment. Even the line of green that bordered the river had grown thin in the distance.

Pharaoh turned the horses toward the desert and let them walk slowly for a while, until finally he drew them to a halt. He turned to Shanda.

"Come, Princess," he told her as he climbed down to the sand. He held his hand out to her, waiting for her to grasp it. "I will show you something of Egypt."

Shanda did not know why, but she hesitated. As she stared out at the desert, it seemed suddenly endless to her, a great, golden ocean, the air above it shimmering with the midday heat. All she could see was sand, broken in the distance only by a single enormous rock that projected out of the dunes far enough away to seem dwarfed. She had a dully sick feeling that once she set foot on that expanse of shimmering sand, there would be no way to withdraw, no escape, except perhaps in death.

But Pharaoh was standing in front of her, waiting, his look as much of a summons as his words might have been had he chosen to utter them. She realized she had no choice but to take his hand and step down onto the sand.

He walked with her, forward, into the dunes. Shanda could feel the heat around her, rising from the sand.

"This is Egypt's father," Pharaoh said softly but very clearly, as though he were intoning some great, unarguable truth. He pointed to the horizon, to the golden shimmer of the sun on the endless sea of sand. "The desert protects us, keeping back any enemy who might try to steal up on us. A watchful father, he guards us, allowing us to sleep secure in his vigilance."

He turned his gray eyes to her, staring at her, probing

and hard. Shanda knew then that he was not simply showing her the desert, but asking her a question, just as he had done when he stood beside her and showed her his army's camp. And as she had then, she felt a shiver of fear that he knew more of her purpose, of the reason she had been sent to him, than even she did, that he knew and waited only for her confession of guilt, her plea for mercy.

She stood, mute and still, returning his stare, stricken with an inner desire to give him an answer. She felt that if she could unburden herself to him, all of it would end, and he would send her back to Hattushil's court, back to Nem. But the feeling faded quickly, for she told herself she had no answer to his question, and if she had, giving it to him would mean exposing Nem and probably inviting her own death. She saw a flash of anger in the gray eyes before he dropped his gaze from her and turned back to the desert.

Then he knelt and lifted a handful of the golden sand. "This is Egypt, Princess," he told her as he poured the sand into her hands.

Shanda watched the grains pass through her fingers and fall. She was confused now, not understanding his intention in bringing her there, wondering what thoughts were passing through his mind as he stood beside her and stared at her with those knowing, questioning eyes.

When she looked up, she realized he had drawn close to her. He put his hands on her arms, holding them close to her body, and then once more he knelt in the sand, this time drawing her down with him.

He kept one hand on her arm, and with the other he lifted another handful of sand.

"This is Egypt, Princess," he whispered again, and let the sand trickle over her arm and her breasts.

She looked down at the golden grains, then back up at his face as he drew her close. She could read the look in his eyes. If he had been trying to extract a confession from her at the start, it seemed he had decided to settle for something else.

His lips tasted of salt, and his arms pulled her so close she thought she could not breathe. But then his hands began to move against her back, stroking and encouraging, as his tongue pressed against her lips. She parted them, allowing him entry, wondering at the sudden liquid throbbing that his touch had released inside her.

She didn't quite realize what was happening when he pushed her down onto the sand. For a moment she was aware only of the glare of the sun in her eyes. Then she felt the weight of him and tasted his lips against hers. There was the warmth of his hands on her breasts, and she could only wonder at the liquid fire he had loosed within her.

He lifted himself from her and stared down at her, and once again Shanda saw the question filling his eyes. She stared back at him, defiant now, sure of herself as she saw the question slowly replaced by desire.

This time when he lifted a handful of sand, there was no question of his intent.

"This is Egypt, princess," he intoned as he slowly let the grains fall onto her arms and her breasts. "Feel it close to you."

Then he leaned closer to her, his lips seeking hers, then trailing down to her neck. His fingers fumbled for a moment, then freed the clasp that held her gown, and pulled it down, baring her breasts so that his lips might find them, then her belly, and finally casting the garment aside completely. Then he parted her legs and slid inside her.

"This is Egypt," he said again as he began to move inside her. "Feel it inside you." He buried his lips against her neck.

Shanda stared up at a cloudless sky, staring for a moment at the hot golden orb that was the sun, forcing herself to stare at it until she could no longer bear it. It is like that with him, she thought as she closed her eyes against the burning hurt. If she let his passion take hold in her, somehow that would burn her, too.

She would not give in to him, she swore to herself, not yet. She could gain a hold on him only by showing him that she was as strong-willed as he. Strength and control—those, she realized, were her only weapons against him, the only qualities he would truly admire.

But telling herself not to feel was a far cry from accomplishing that end. His hands and lips and tongue set her flesh on fire. The feel of him deep inside her set her throbbing with the surge of strange tides that seemed far more powerful than she, tides that lifted her and tossed her, helpless, in a turgid, throbbing sea. She felt as though she were about to drown, unable even to draw breath, much less awaken the will within her to fight against the flow.

He felt her resistance. This, he knew, was as much a battle of wills as her refusal to kneel to him had been. The knowledge dulled the sharp edge of the desire she roused in him and enabled him to control the flooding throb in his own blood. He would prove to her that he could force her body to admit that he was its master, he told himself, and then she could not but submit her will as well. Determined, he forced himself to find the control, to keep himself from the precipice.

He pressed his lips and tongue to her earlobe, then to the soft pink shell of her ear, feeling her quiver, sure she would have pulled away still, if he let her.

"Feel it, Princess," he murmured as he moved inside her, his movements strong and sure. "You cannot fight me for-ever."

His words aroused only anger in her, and she told herself that she hated him, that his arrogance and his overbearing pride were more than she could bear. He was taunting her, telling her that he could win now that he understood the rules of the battle in which she had engaged him. And she swore to herself that he could not force her to do anything she refused to accept, that he could not make her feel.

But as strongly as she fought against the tide, it was not strong enough. When it enveloped her, it was shattering, and all the more potent for her resistance and her determination to keep it at bay. Her body shuddered, and she felt as though she were falling and yet somehow floating. She felt as though her body were bursting from within and the pieces were being scattered on the wind like the grains of sand on which she lay. The sun had melted her, left her without will or volition or the ability to move, unable to flee from the shattering, encompassing tide. Defeated and wondering, she let it claim her.

He felt her trembling beneath him and knew he had done what he had intended. He gave himself finally to the passion, letting the sweet torture end. Then he held her in his arms, expecting, when the moment had passed, that he would finally have from her the submission he sought.

She lay, hearing the throbbing of her heart like a drum, loud and strong and even, punctuated by the ragged sound of her breath. It seemed forever to her before she could breathe without gasping, before she could think of her body as her own. He had done something to her, she realized, something she could not quite understand, something wondrous and yet frightening. She told herself it was wrong, that he ought not to have this power over her, that no one had the right to make her lose herself as he had.

She opened her eyes and found him staring at her, his gray eyes revealing his satisfaction, the pleasure of his victory. She swore to herself that she would not let him savor it.

He put his hand on her hair, stroking the long golden mane outward around her head, admiring the way the sunlight set it afire. He leaned toward her, wanting to taste her lips once more, to show her that he would be gentle in victory as he had not been in battle.

She stared up at him in defiance. Then she offered him a single word, the greatest condemnation. "Barbarian," she whispered, her voice ragged with scorn.

His eyes found hers and he realized suddenly that he had won nothing. He stared at her a moment, then pushed himself away from her, suddenly enraged, not only with her but with himself, angered that she had refused to give him what he expected of her, but even more that she was able to parry his assault so easily. Straddling her, kneeling in the sand, he studied her, and felt defeated and humiliated in his defeat.

They stared at each other for a moment, her glance filled with disgust, his with steadily growing anger. Even the voice within him that told him she was right, that he'd taken her in the sand like an animal, that she had reason to resent him, could not diffuse the wrath inside him, nor could it sweeten the knowledge that she had again escaped him.

He rolled back onto his heels and stood, as Shanda turned away. The dark red welts that marked her back spoke for her, mute yet powerful accusations she knew he could not deny.

She reached for her gown, lying beside her in the sand, and held it up to cover her nakedness. "Barbarian," she repeated venomously.

It was more than he could tolerate. He turned on his heel and walked away from her, back to the chariot. He climbed inside, taking up the reins in his hand, and stood there wordlessly and waited for her to come to him.

At that moment Shanda felt nothing but despair. Enough! a voice inside her cried. She could not go on with this; she could not fight this battle with him any longer. Hattushil had had no right to demand the pledge of her; Nem had had no right to send her to do this thing. She stared past Pharaoh at the empty sands behind him, as though looking for the reprieve Nem had promised her, as though expecting to see Hittite chariots rushing forward to save her. But she saw only the vast burnished gold of the sky and the sand.

She would not crawl back to Pharaoh; she would sooner die.

Shanda turned away from his expectant stare, dismissing his unspoken summons with a defiant toss of her head.

She heard the snap of the reins against the horses' backs and knew that he was driving the chariot away from her, toward the line of fertile green that edged the river.

For a moment she was too numb to feel fear at his departure. She stood slowly, still grasping her gown in a fruitless attempt to hide her nakedness from the empty desert around her. Then she dully pulled it on, found the silver clasp in the sand, and fastened it with absent, knowing fingers. She watched the slowly retreating figure of Pharaoh for what seemed like an eternity.

She knew he expected her to race after him, to shout to him to wait for her, to beg him not to leave her alone in the desert. It shocked her to realize he was so determined to have his victory that he would use even this crude threat to undermine her pride. And she decided that before she would do as he expected, before she would beg him for anything, she would die.

Shanda hesitated only briefly, then turned toward the endless sea of golden sand and began to walk.

She set out with determination, telling herself that the rock outcrop was as fitting a place as any to wait for death and a far more majestic memorial to her than the endless plane of sand would be. She would go to the rock and wait there for the heat and the sun and the sand to claim her. Surely it would be a kinder fate than to return to Pharaoh, to yet another battle, to a dismal and hopeless existence.

Her concentration made the walk seem so short, or perhaps it was the realization that at its end there would be no place left for her to go, no more paths to take. She had become suddenly very aware of life, of the feel of the dry wind as it pressed the fabric of her skirt against her legs and tugged at her tousled curls, of the dull crunching sound of her sandaled feet against the sand, of the sharp salt taste of the desert wind on her lips and tongue. A voice inside her told her calmly that soon she would feel nothing, hear nothing, taste nothing, that she must savor these last sensations with appropriate solemnity.

For a moment she pressed her eyes tightly closed, wishing she had been able to accept her mother's gods, or even Hattushil's, wishing there was some belief buried somewhere inside her that life, in ending, would begin anew on some fresh path. But where that belief ought to have been there was only a wrenching emptiness. Its absence left a loneliness in her that tore at her.

She tried to think of Nem, to remember how she had felt when she was with him, before all the madness had begun, before she was sent away. But where his image ought to have been, there, too, was only emptiness. He should never have let Hattushil send her to Pharaoh, she thought. She ought to have meant more to him than that. She ought to have meant more to him than anything.

She had almost reached the rock before she noticed the snake that lay curled there in the warmth of the sunshine, its eyes, lazily hooded, stared up at her, dark, shining beads that considered its prey before raising its head and preparing to strike.

The cobra was enormous, its thick, smooth body a seemingly endless coil. Its head rose slowly, moving from side to side, its tongue darting expectantly from its mouth, tasting the air. She froze, her eyes caught by the snake's. The slow, undulating movement of its head was somehow hypnotic, holding her attention, almost distracting her from the terror that faced her. It seemed almost as if the snake relished this preamble, fed on the fear that came before the instant of the bite.

Shanda froze. She was too close to back away from the serpent, too close even to think it would let her escape.

Although she had convinced herself that she was prepared to die as Pharaoh drove the chariot away from her, the presence of a very real, very imminent death so near to her made her suddenly realize just how valuable every moment of life was. She stood, frozen by fear, listening to the sound of her heart throbbing inside her. Now, when it was too late to turn back, she realized that life was far too precious simply to be abandoned.

Her mind filled with the thought of how useless it all had been, how flagrantly she had wasted the gift of her life. It seemed to her that she had made all the wrong choices, that somehow she could have gone on, that if she'd taken a different path there might have been some happiness for her, some future. All that was lost to her now, all possibility, all hope. And somehow she knew, deep inside her, that she had helped to bring about her own destruction.

She stared, motionless, at the cobra, and saw death return her stare.

# *Six*

PHARAOH PULLED BACK on the reins and waited for the
horses to halt before he turned to look for her. He had
assumed she would race after him, that fear of the desert
would force her to him. But he had been wrong about that
as he had been about almost everything else with her.

He saw the flutter of her silk robe as she moved ever so
slowly across the sand, and he saw that she was moving
away from him, not toward him.

The game had gone on long enough, he told himself. If
she would not give herself to him totally, he would settle for what she would give, the small part of herself that
was committed to her pledge to obey her father. Perhaps
he could find in that part of her enough to satisfy him. She
was different from any other woman, he realized. She challenged a part of him that had never been challenged before,
and she fascinated him. Certainly her beauty was part of his
fascination, the amazement he felt at the impossible mass of
golden hair and eyes the color of the sky. But the realization
came to him that he had more than enough beautiful women.
It was more than her eyes and her hair and her skin that

enchanted him. She was an enigma, a constant puzzle, and somehow he found that a far greater attraction than mere beauty alone. The simple fact that she dared defy him set her apart. The knowledge that the strength of her will was a match for his own made her a challenge from which he could not walk away.

He turned the horses, admitting to himself that she had defeated him yet again, that it was he who was going to her and not she who ran after him, begging him to save her. This time he felt a mild amusement. Perhaps, he thought, it was not really so terrible a thing for a man to admit to himself that he was not quite as invulnerable as he would have himself be.

He began by walking the horses, not wanting to reach her too quickly, trying to prepare the stand he would take with her, searching in his mind for words that would appease her without admitting his acceptance of his own defeat. He was, after all, not without pride of his own. But as he kept his eyes on her, she came to a halt and stood motionless not far from the rock outcrop. It suddenly occurred to him that something was wrong. There was no reason for her to stand that way, facing the rock abutment. He could think of only one thing that could be a threat to her.

He slapped the reins violently, urging the horses to race through the deepening sand. When he was still a good distance from her, however, he drew them to a halt, pulling back sharply on the reins. He did not dare get too close, knowing that a sudden, threatening motion would cause the snake to end its dance and strike. He offered up a prayer that she would remain still, that she would not give in to fear and frighten the snake into striking.

As he slipped from the chariot, he snatched the bow and quiver he had used on the practice range. He pulled a single arrow from the quiver as he moved stealthily toward the side of the rock, letting the rest fall, knowing that if he missed with his first shot, there would be no use for another.

Shanda knew he was there. She could sense his presence behind her, although she dared not turn to face him. And someplace inside her that had been overcome with fear seemed to grow suddenly less frightened, less certain that she would die. She felt her heart begin to thud with the sudden rekindling of hope.

The snake seemed to sense the change in her, or perhaps it heard the sharp beat in her chest, the throbbing cadence of life. It stopped its swaying dance, and the dark, round eyes considered her. Then the cobra lunged toward her.

Shanda's heart felt as though it would stop when she saw the movement. One thought raced through her mind, a raging outcry at the cruelty of the fate that gave her hope only to snatch it from her. She steeled herself, waiting for the bite and the bitterness of death.

Time seemed to slow. She saw the arrow fly, saw it strike the snake's head and pass through it, saw it force the head with its venomous fangs backward until the serpent finally fell, twitching in its death throes, on the sand in the shadow cast by the rock.

Shanda stared at it numbly for a second, and then her legs crumbled beneath her and she fell to her knees. She did not realize she was crying, only that the cobra's image was blurred. It was only when she felt Pharaoh's arms around her that she realized she was sobbing, crying as she had cried only once before in her life, at Althea's death. She let herself fall against him, then allowed the wrenching sobs to claim her.

He knelt beside her in the sand and held her close to him, gently comforting her, wondering what had happened between them. He had wanted this of her from the start, this display of weakness that her trembling sobs showed him.

But now that he had it, he realized it in no way diminished her, and only served to lower his own opinion of himself.

"It's over, Princess," he whispered gently, wanting to comfort her, to see the terror leave her eyes and the fear end for her. "You're safe. Nothing will hurt you. I will allow nothing to hurt you."

But she seemed not to hear; her attention was only for the still rope of the cobra's body lying near them in the sand. She lifted her face from where it had lain against his chest, stared at the dead snake, seeing it all again in her mind, the swaying head, the sudden, deadly lunge. She uttered a small moan of pain as the cobra in her terror-filled mind found its mark, sending the imaginary venom into her, and she fainted.

Pharaoh brushed her hair away from her cheek and stared at her still features. He knew how close she had come to death, how close he had come to losing her, and he felt the near loss as a dull pain, a deep, searing thing inside him that burned all the more because he had driven her to act as she had.

He lifted her in his arms and carried her back to the chariot, then, still holding her close to him, turned the horses and started back to the palace.

Pharaoh walked through the room and lowered her onto the bed. For a long moment he stood and simply stared at her. Then he touched her still cheek, letting his fingers move slowly to her lips. He felt her breath against them, a gentle warmth.

He hadn't noticed the boy until he turned and saw him, kneeling on the floor at the far side of the room.

"You, boy, come here."

It seemed odd to Pharaoh to see the boy's wide-eyed terror as he crept forward, darted a quick glance at Shanda, then tore his eyes, suddenly filled with tears, away, apparently believing that she was dead.

"She is not hurt, boy; she only fainted."

There was relief in his eyes, Pharaoh thought. The boy, too, had come to care for her.

He turned to the bed, looked at her one last time, then turned away.

"Tend to your mistress," he ordered as he started for the door. His voice was sharp as he gave the command. He wondered why, for he certainly bore the young eunuch no ill will. Could it be jealousy? he wondered as he darted a quick look back to see Med put a tentative hand on her neck to assure himself that she was, indeed, not dead. Was he jealous of the familiarity she would allow the servant, a familiarity she denied him? He told himself the thought was absurd.

Before he left the room, he turned back one last time and watched the boy fetch a bowl of water and a cloth.

Shanda woke in a room she did not recognize. For a moment she wondered if her mother's gods might really exist, if she had died and then wakened to the promised life that followed death.

"Princess, are you feeling well now?"

She sat up slowly, hardly noticing the damp cloth that fell away from her forehead, and turned to find Med sitting on a stool close to the bed. She realized that she was indeed still alive, that she had not yet passed from the world she knew.

She nodded to Med in answer. "Where are we?" she asked him, gazing around the room.

He stood quickly and offered his arm to her, helping her from the bed. Then he smiled and waved his arm, motioning to the room, seeming to want to show it all to her, to let her see how their position had changed.

"After you left, they told me to gather your belongings and bring them here." He slurred his words in his eagerness to tell her. "Look, Princess, there is a whole apartment and a garden and a pool. All for you."

The importance of this change in their status was apparent in his expression. He had never before heard of one of the pharaoh's women being given such distinction.

He waved his arm again, and Shanda turned to a neatly manicured garden just beyond the room. The waning sunlight had turned the flowers to pale, shimmery shapes. Then she turned her gaze back to the boy and stared at him, not quite comprehending, her thoughts dazed.

If what Med had said was true, she mused, Pharaoh had intended to take her from his harem even before the strange ride to the army encampment, before the terrifying episode with the cobra. The memory returned to her, and she shivered, remembering the fear, the anticipation of death.

"How did I get here?" she asked numbly.

"He brought you, Princess," Med replied brightly.

"Pharaoh?"

He nodded. "He looks on you with favor, Princess. That is why he took you away from the hall and the rest of the women."

Shanda thought of what had passed between them that afternoon. "I think not, Med," she told him evenly, ignoring the questioning look he cast at her. She pursed her lips. "Will you show me our new home?" she asked when she realized he was disappointed that she showed none of the excitement he so obviously felt.

There were two large rooms—the bedroom in which she'd awakened and a sitting room furnished with two large couches, a table, and several chairs. Both opened onto the walled garden, and all the furnishings were finely wrought. Brightly colored birds sang in cages in the garden, and the sound of water falling over rocks on its way to the pool played a gentle background music to their songs. It was, Shanda thought, indeed a pleasant change from the harem with the constant noise of the women's chatter, their bickering, their shrill laughter.

"Where does that door lead?" she asked when he'd shown it all to her. She pointed to the heavy door at the back of the sitting room.

"Out, Princess," Med replied.

"Out?" she asked, raising a brow. "Open it."

"But, Princess—" he began to protest.

She would have none of it. "Open it," she repeated firmly.

He pulled the door open. Just outside, a huge guard turned and faced them, then moved to block the doorway. He bowed respectfully, but did not move away. "Is there something you require, Princess?" he asked.

Shanda shook her head. "No, nothing." She motioned to Med to close the door. Unmoving, she watched the heavy portal swing into place.

"One prison is as good as another," she murmured as she turned away.

"Princess?"

"Nothing, Med," she told him.

It didn't really matter, she told herself firmly. Even if Pharaoh had left her free, she had no place to go.

Her inspection complete, Shanda wandered back to the pool. She stared at the water as she released the silver clasp and let her dress fall to her feet.

She was filled with a sudden weariness. It seemed to her that she had never felt so tired.

"I will bathe now, Med," she said as she stepped out of the circle of silk at her feet. "And then I will sleep."

She watched as he hurried off to fetch her robe and

brushes, realizing that her simple acceptance of her new quarters had in no way diminished his excitement. Then she stepped slowly into the pool, feeling the water against her skin as a welcome caress.

When she put her hand on her hair, she felt the grit of sand that clung to it, and thought of the way Pharaoh had taken her that afternoon, the way he had treated her. No, she mused, Pharaoh did not look on her with favor. There was no question in her mind about that.

She could live with his displeasure, she told herself, survive in his well-appointed prison. Her close brush with death had dulled her outrage and tempered her pride. Far more disturbing was the memory of the way her own body had betrayed her, of the way he had made her feel.

She submerged her head in the water, washing away the grains of sand, wishing she could as easily wash away the stain he had put on her spirit.

Med told her that Pharaoh would bring her gifts as a sign of his pleasure. Shanda scorned his suggestion, telling him that Pharaoh had set her aside not as a sign of his favor but rather so that he would not be plagued by her presence when he looked for his amusement. Med ignored her protests, insisting that she would see.

When three days had passed and Pharaoh still had not come, even Med's certainty began to wane. His stature was tied to his princess's, and he had seen it climb and then fall too many times in the preceding days to accept the loss without regret.

Shanda, however, had her own regrets with which to deal. She had failed in everything she had set out to do— failed with Pharaoh, failed even with her own death. With no diversions to fill the hours, she found herself dwelling on thoughts that brought her no comfort and served only to intensify her misery. She knew she had to find some occupation or she would lose whatever wits were left to her.

She had become bored with the games of senet Med offered her for amusement. She threw the casting sticks haphazardly, letting one fall to the floor.

He scurried after the ivory stick as it rolled across the floor and brought it back to her, a look of mild censure on his face. Shanda ignored it.

"Med, will you teach me to read and write?" she asked him abruptly.

Once spoken, she realized the prospect was the first that had roused any real interest in her. This was something that really might rid her of the boredom that had taken hold of her.

He offered her a look that made her think for a moment that she might already have taken leave of her senses.

"I cannot, Princess," he told her mournfully.

"But why not?" she demanded. "Has Pharaoh forbidden it?"

He shook his head slowly. "No, Princess," he told her. "I cannot because I have not the knowledge."

"Oh." She was disheartened. She had assumed that because his father was a nobleman he had been given an education. His confession reminded her just how young he had been when his life, the life to which he had been born, had been so cruelly taken from him.

She apologized profusely, feeling guilty for having forgotten that his misery was as great as her own.

Med, though, did not dismiss her request. If Shanda was virtually imprisoned in her apartment, he, at least, had the freedom of the palace. The next afternoon he returned from a purported foray to the palace kitchens not only bearing the expected tray of fruit, bread, and cheese but also accompanied by the eunuch scribe to the harem.

Shanda greeted them both with a look of perplexed surprise.

"It is time for your lessons to begin, Princess," Med told her with glee as he set down the tray and turned to his companion. "This is Sesostris, scribe to the harem."

The guards, Shanda mused silently, apparently considered the comings and goings of eunuchs with the same indifference with which they looked upon ants or flies.

Sesostris bowed. A beefy man well into middle age; he was balding and thick, with a fringe of graying hair and wide brown eyes. "It will be a great pleasure to serve you, Princess," he intoned in a full, rich baritone that quite surprised her.

"I have nothing with which to pay you," she warned him, wondering what recompense he might desire.

He smiled at her, then cast a satisfied look at Med. "I require no payment, Princess," he told her as his large eyes turned slowly back to hers.

Shanda shook her head slowly as she considered the look he had offered Med. She would not allow the boy to sell himself so that a whim of hers might be satisfied.

"I cannot accept so generous a gift from you," she told him evenly.

"But, Princess—" Med objected.

Sesostris waved him to silence, then turned to Shanda, considering her for a long moment with eyes that were surprisingly knowing. Then he bowed his head slightly. "As you wish, Princess. Let me first assure you that, much as I admire young Med, I would not barter for his favors so grossly. He asked me if I would be willing to share my knowledge with you, promising me only a few hours in pleasant surroundings and the best meal he could pilfer from the kitchens." He patted his round stomach and offered her a crooked smile. "I ask for no further recompense, nor do I desire it. Should you choose to reconsider, I would consider the meal, your company and Med's, and the tranquility of this lovely garden payment enough for what little of my meager knowledge I might share with you, Princess."

With this doubtful beginning, Shanda commenced her education in the written word of Egypt. They made their way to the garden.

While Med laid out the food and fetched chairs, Sesostris produced a clay tablet and stylus and incised half a dozen shapes on its surface. Then they sat, and as the older eunuch worked his way through a goodly portion of their common meal and explained to her the meaning of what he had written, Shanda worked at copying the shapes.

The lessons continued in the afternoon each day after that, and with familiarity Shanda lost her reservations about the scribe. If he occasionally cast a yearning eye toward Med, he treated the boy with a tolerant reserve. In fact, he showed far greater interest in the roast duck and fine beer Med managed to coerce from the kitchen stewards for Shanda's table. And once a hint of familiarity had sprung up among the three of them, he proved himself an amusing companion, providing a wealth of gossip and delivering it with a sharp-tongued wit.

One bit of gossip he delivered with his usual insouciance was a report of Pharaoh's visits to the harem. Pharaoh, he said, had visited his women but had left quickly without having chosen one or gone with her to her quarters. Med cast a meaningful glance in Shanda's direction. She shook off his suggestion, quickly changing the subject, but Sesostris did not miss the look. When, several days later, he reported the same curious series of events, he seemed to have joined into some conspiracy with Shanda and Med.

He winked merrily at Shanda. "The women are desolate," he told her in a tone that contained nothing if not glee. "They

have nothing with which to amuse themselves except their
own petty bickering. And they have decided this is all your
fault, that you have turned him against all women."

Med joined him in his laughter, but Shanda turned away,
thinking perhaps the women of the harem were right. At
any rate, she had fared no better than the others. Pharaoh's
continued absence told her that only too plainly. And much
as she told herself she preferred it so, she could not quite
make her arguments convincing, at least not when she forced
some measure of honesty upon herself.

She continued to study with a concentration that surprised
her. Never before had she so strongly devoted herself to a
single purpose. She told herself that the reason was simply lack of other means of entertaining herself. She refused
to accept the possibility, although the thought occasionally
occurred to her, that she pursued the study as a means of
trying to understand Pharaoh.

As the days passed, she slowly began to master the intricacies of the written language, and Sesostris even brought
to her a Book of the Dead that he was preparing—at great
profit to himself, he admitted with a satisfied smile—for
Nofret, the pharaoh's vizier. Sesostris and Shanda sat side
by side, and with his help she slowly started to read from
the long scroll of beautifully decorated papyrus.

While the two of them sat, heads together, in the garden, Pharaoh entered the apartment. Med had just entered
the room with a tray bearing their midday meal and had
just started to lay the food out on the table when the door
opened. The boy stared at him a moment, in obvious shock,
and nearly let the tray fall. Somehow he managed to retain
his hold on it as he fell to his knees and lowered his head.

Pharaoh ignored him, moving to the doorway and staring out at Shanda and Sesostris where they sat in the garden.

"Who is that with her?" he demanded sharply, his voice low. Then he clamped his jaw tight with displeasure.

Med realized that Pharaoh had obviously been aware of his presence after all. He left the tray on the floor and scrambled to his feet.

"If it please you, lord," he managed in a shaking voice, "he is the harem scribe. The princess wished to learn to read and write and I could think of no other way to fill her request."

Med's knees were shaking, and he dared not raise his eyes to Pharaoh's face. Instead, he watched in terror as Pharaoh's powerful hand moved to his side and slowly withdrew a jeweled knife that had been sheathed there.

# Seven

MED LIFTED TERRIFIED eyes, finally, to Pharaoh's face, his
courage somehow spurred by his fear. He was bewildered
to find Pharaoh smiling. He hastily dropped his eyes back
down to the knife, expecting to see it pointed at his heart.

Instead, Pharaoh turned it, offering it to him hilt first.
The half-dozen jewels set in fancywork gold shone up at
him brazenly. Med's confusion only worsened.

"Take it, boy," Pharaoh told him evenly. "Consider it
payment for your diligent care of your mistress."

Med only shook his head slowly. "I need no payment to
do what is expected of me," he said slowly.

Once again Pharaoh smiled, this time with real warmth.
"Then it is a gift, offered with my thanks."

Med's hand moved slowly forward, trembling as it
touched the knife. A warmth seemed to come from it,
and he told himself it was the warmth of Pharaoh's touch.
He shook. He could not believe he was being given a gift
by a god.

"And tell the scribe that he, too, will be well rewarded
for the time he spends with her," Pharaoh told him.

Med nodded. "Shall I fetch the princess, lord?" he asked when he'd found his tongue. He wondered dazedly how he dared look up directly into Pharaoh's eyes, wondered why a thunderbolt did not come down from heaven and strike him for such an impudent intrusion on the man-child of the great god Aten.

"No," Pharaoh said. "Let her finish her lessons." He put a hand on Med's arm. "When the lesson is over, this is what I would have you do," he went on, drawing the boy back into the room so that they would not disturb the student and teacher at work in the garden.

Sesostris had decided the lesson was finished. He'd taken the precious papyrus scroll and begun to roll it carefully so that he might return it to his pouch as he launched himself into his daily recital of the harem gossip.

"Tonight Pharaoh leads a procession to the temple of Aten and attends the mysteries of the priests, then makes sacrifice for the abundance of the year's harvest."

Shanda looked up at him, bewildered. "Pharaoh does these things?" she asked.

Sesostris nodded. "Yes, Princess. Each year, just before the time of the rising of the Nile. It is said that without his son's entreaties, the god would abandon Egypt. Of course, there is no record of a year when the sacrifice was not made, so it cannot be said that famine would follow if Pharaoh did not perform the rite." He winked, pretending it was all a game, but something in his tone indicated that he was not quite the heretical scoffer he presented himself to be, that he was unable to separate himself from the beliefs in which he had been raised. His expression grew suddenly serious. "There have been years when the sacrifice did not go well, and it is written that in those years there were locusts or other causes of failed crops. It is said that once the river did not rise, and the fields lay barren for years. I think in any case it is not wise to fly in the face of the gods," he finished, his tone almost reverential.

Shanda was bewildered by his revelation. She found it hard to think of Pharaoh in the same terms Sesostris apparently did, despite his attempt to hide his reverence, as a god, as a powerful intercessor with the sun god of the Egyptians.

Sesostris continued. "After the sacred rites and the sacrifice there is a great banquet. Every noble in all of Egypt attends. The women of the harem are in a great uproar." He smiled at Shanda. "They do not attend, of course, but they gossip about what every woman of the court will wear, what sort of gown, what jewels, and what woman Pharaoh will choose to share his bed on this most auspicious night. And tomorrow there will be even more gossip as the servants the women send out to spy on the guests report to them and describe the banquet to them."

He looked up then at Shanda's sitting room, searching hopefully for Med and the promise of a meal. His hand strayed to his decidedly rotund belly, as though he were checking to see if his hunger had diminished its size.

"Where is that boy?" he muttered petulantly when he saw that the room was empty. He began to move toward the stairs that led from the garden, his eyes quickly finding the half-set table, the partially emptied tray left on the floor.

Shanda, too, found the disarray bewildering. "Med?" she called.

"Probably off playing with the birds again," Sesostris grumbled. "You shouldn't be so lenient with him, Princess. He'll grow spoiled." He considered the contents of the tray with an appraising eye. "And we'll all starve."

Shanda hadn't listened to him. She was beginning to feel concern. "Med?" she called out again, louder this time.

In response, he seemed to suddenly appear behind them.

He was wearing a grin that filled the whole of his face. "You called me, Princess?"

Shanda turned to him and considered his smile. "Has something happened?" she asked.

"Of course something's happened," Sesostris interjected. "The boy's decided he's a great hunter and left our food on the floor as bait, hoping to catch a lion, I suppose." He moved to the tray and knelt clumsily to retrieve it.

Med continued to smile with smug delight and held up the jeweled knife. "He was here, Princess," he crowed with unconstrained glee.

"Pharaoh?"

Shanda was quite bewildered now. She had been there for eighteen days; she knew this, for she had kept track secretly, not letting Med know know her interest. Eighteen days, and Pharaoh had not appeared. Why now? she wondered. And why had he not demanded to see her?

Med nodded, still smug with his superior knowledge.

Sesostris had by now retrieved the tray and brought it to the table. Apparently Med's revelation had superseded even his hunger.

"Don't stand there like a mute, boy," he roared. "Why do you have that knife?" he demanded, his eyes considering the jeweled hilt, weighing the knife's value. "What happened?"

"It is a gift," Med said with a superior toss of his head. Then his eagerness to reveal his secret overcame his desire to keep it. "He said you are to be rewarded for the time you spend teaching the princess," he told Sesostris. Then he turned to Shanda. "And you, Princess, are to drive his chariot tonight in the procession." He grinned, then held out his hand to her. "Come, I will show you."

He led Shanda to the bedroom and pointed to the bed where he'd laid out the things Pharaoh had brought for her. She lifted the skirt of the gown carefully, staring at the shimmering gold fabric in disbelief. She'd never seen anything like it before.

"And there is more, Princess," Med told her. He pointed to a pair of sandals, the leather rubbed with gold until they were coated with it, then snatched up a small coffer and opened it to reveal a hoard of gold jewelry. Slowly he took the treasures out—a necklace of hundreds of carved gold beads strung to form a wide collar, a thick-linked girdle for her waist, and a gold diadem in the form of a snake, its tail grasped in its mouth, its gold head inlaid with blue faience eyes. Shanda stared at it and thought of the cobra, and shivered.

"You see, Princess," Med told her softly, only a hint of an I-told-you-so tone to his voice. "It is as I thought. He looks with favor on you."

Shanda reached out and touched the gold snake, considering it and Med's words in silence. Was it possible that she had not failed after all? she wondered.

Sesostris broke into a peal of loud laughter, dissolving her thoughts. The scribe's amusement was contagious, and soon both Shanda and Med were laughing as well.

"Just wait," Sesostris roared when he'd finally managed to control his laughter. "The women of the harem will have a fine piece of gossip to chew on now, won't they?"

Once again there was a peal of the contagious laughter, but this time Med managed to gain control first. And once he'd sobered, he held his hand up to Sesostris, demanding silence.

"There is no time for this," he said firmly to Shanda, acting the unlikely part of the elder of the group. "You must bathe and dress and your hair must be arranged." He turned to the old eunuch. "Go spread your gossip, scribe," he said with a grin. "We've better tasks to occupy us this day."

Sesostris cast a mournful eye on the food he would not

have the opportunity to enjoy that afternoon. But he seemed willing to endure the hardship, and he turned back to Med and returned his grin, then bowed with mock humility. Then he bowed once more, this time with a more reverential air, to Shanda. "Until our next lesson, Princess," he said as he left.

Spurred by Med's impatience, Shanda went to the pool and bathed quickly, then sat in the warm sunshine so that her hair would dry as Med busied himself with her combs, removing the tangles and arranging the golden curls. When he was done, he disappeared, only to reappear a few moments later bearing a box with paints and brushes.

Shanda peered at his burden suspiciously. "What is that for?" she demanded.

"Pharaoh said you were to dress like an Egyptian woman," he told her, nodding toward the gown he had set out on a bench nearby.

Shanda examined the garment. The golden fabric was sheer, of the sort she remembered the ladies of Pharaoh's court wore. The only concession to her Hittite modesty was the fact that the gossamer fabric would cover both of her breasts.

She let Med paint dark circles of kohl around her eyes, color the lids with dark blue powder, and paint a thick red paste on her lips. But when he brought the polished silver disk for her inspection, she stared at the stranger who looked back at her and then shook her head.

"No, Med," she said evenly. "If it is an Egyptian woman he wants, he can take one from his harem. Bring a cloth so that I can wash it away."

He seemed about to protest, but apparently reconsidered, for he wordlessly fetched her a cloth and a bowl of water. She quickly scrubbed away the paints until she was satisfied that the pink of her lips was brought on by nothing more than friction with the cloth and her eyes stared back at her as she was accustomed to seeing them.

She quickly donned the golden gown and let Med slip the sandals on her feet. Then she stood as he brought out the coffer containing the jewels Pharaoh had brought for her. She carefully secured the girdle around her waist and allowed Med to fasten the gold collar around her neck and place the diadem so that it circled her head and the snake's head hung down over her forehead. She stared at her reflection in the silver disk and suddenly felt the weight of all the gold, an unexpected burden. She doubted that any of Hattushil's women had ever worn quite so great a burden of riches.

Med appeared with a small box and a cotton boll.

"Please, Princess," he said as he opened the box, not waiting for her protest, "Pharaoh had this brought especially for you."

Shanda looked into the box and found it filled with a pale white powder filled with tiny flecks of gold. Med dipped the cotton into the powder and carefully covered her neck, arms and cheeks, all her exposed skin, with it. This time, when she looked into the mirror, she saw her own face staring back at her, but it seemed to glow with the softest sparkle of gold.

She looked up at the young eunuch and found him smiling at her.

"You are very beautiful, Princess," he told her.

It seemed almost as if the words of homage were a cue for the knock at the door that followed it. Med put down the cotton and the box of powder and ran to answer it.

"Pharaoh's guard is here to fetch you, Princess," he told her when he breathlessly returned to her.

Shanda stared one last time at the reflection of her shining face, then put down the silver disk and stood. As she walked to the door, she felt her heart begin to beat in her chest. This would be her last chance with Pharaoh, she somehow knew, and a part of her told her that she would not be able to live were she to fail. She tried to tell herself that it didn't matter, that she was better off with his antipathy than she had been with his attentions. But a voice inside her told her she was a liar.

When she reached the door, she found four guards standing at rigid attention, waiting for her. As soon as she stepped out to the corridor, they formed a circle around her. She wondered from what it was they were there to protect her.

They escorted her to the courtyard. It was far more crowded than it had been the afternoon Pharaoh had taken her to see his troops. Besides the soldiers of his guard, there were dozens of men with shaved heads wearing heavy, dark robes and thick ropes of gold around their necks. They stood apart from the soldiers, as though being subject to the proximity the courtyard forced upon them was an insult they had trouble accepting. One of them—an enormous barrel-shaped man with small, sharp eyes who wore a large golden amulet suspended from a heavy gold rope around his neck—turned to stare at her as she stepped out into the courtyard. Shanda felt his glance, as heavy as a weight, on her. When she returned his glance, he continued his inspection of her a moment longer, then turned away.

As he had that first time, Seti, the general of the guard, approached her and Shanda turned to him, thankful for a friendly face, especially after the strange look she'd received from the priest.

"Is something wrong, Princess?" he asked her when he'd dismissed the guard who had accompanied her.

She shook her head. "No," she murmured, smiling her thanks for his concern. Then she pointed quickly to the priest. "Who is that?" she asked.

He followed her hand with his eyes. "Nekhbet," he told her. "He is the head priest of the Temple of Aten." He grew thoughtful. "Not a pleasant man, but you need have no fear of him, Princess." He turned back to her and smiled once more. "You take my place this evening, Princess. I cannot but think the substitution greatly pleasing to the eye."

Shanda pushed aside thought of the priest and smiled in acknowledgment to the compliment. "What is it I am to do?" she asked.

"Drive his chariot to the temple. Not a great task. The priests will lead the procession, and the guard, as always, follows. You simply hold the reins and keep the whites from trampling upon the priests." His expression suggested that he entertained the thought that perhaps the whites might be serving a useful purpose were they to do just that. Then he smiled. "The horses liked you, Princess. They will be pleased to see you, I think," he added. "Come."

He took her arm and led her across the courtyard. Shanda gasped at the sight of the chariot to which the horses were hitched, a huge, ornate affair, completely layered in gold. Even the whites, carefully groomed and brushed, seemed to gleam faintly of the precious metal.

Seti smiled when he saw her reaction. "The chariot is used only for this procession each year, and for triumphal processions. But there has been no war for quite some time, and now it mostly stands idle in the stables. Come."

He led her forward, and Shanda greeted the great white horses, finding they did indeed remember her. They nudged her with their noses and willingly accepted her offered caress. When she drew her hand away, she found it lightly coated with the gold speckled powder. It seemed Pharaoh's horses had been groomed for the procession with the same careful attention that Med had lavished on her.

Seti spoke with her for a few moments, describing the serpentine path the procession would take through the streets of the city on its way to the temple, but Shanda's attention kept wandering toward the doorway where the priests milled in superior isolation. It was there that Pharaoh would appear, she thought. She found herself wary but unexpectedly anxious for the sight of him.

The sun was just beginning to lower when the door opened and he walked out. The noise in the courtyard immediately quieted, and the priests quickly formed a double line from the doorway to the chariot. They stood in complete silence as he passed them.

Shanda watched him approach with mixed dread and anticipation. He had never before looked quite so formidable to her, not even on the first day when she'd entered his audience room. He was covered with gold—a thick, wide breastplate of beaten gold, a robe heavily embroidered with gold threads, a crown of gold, even gold greaves. She wondered how he managed to stand so tall bearing the weight of so much gold. For a moment she thought she could understand why his people revered him as a god, for, clothed as he was in the shimmering metal, he seemed more than merely mortal.

Seti nudged her from her reverie and silently offered her his arm to climb into the chariot. She did what he seemed to expect of her, climbing into the chariot and taking up the reins. Then she waited as Pharaoh climbed silently up beside her.

If she had expected a greeting from him, he disappointed her. He seemed almost oblivious of her, of all those around him. He stood in his golden chariot, staring unblinkingly forward as the priests re-formed their lines in front of the chariot. They moved in complete silence, even their sandals on the stone hardly making a sound. It struck Shanda that the silence in the courtyard was unnatural. Not a sound arose from the soldiers of the guard, and even the horses did not break the stillness.

The gates of the palace swung open then, and Shanda could see a mob of townspeople standing silent and waiting. The long line of priests began to chant as they walked at a stately pace through the gates. Those who waited without bowed their heads reverently as the line passed them. It seemed eerie to Shanda, that there was no sound from them save an occasional cry of a child, which was quickly hushed into silence. It was only then that she appreciated the awe his people felt for the act Pharaoh was about to perform.

Shanda found she had no need even to guide the whites. Apparently well trained for the occasion, they walked slowly after the priests through the milling horde of silent spectators. A feeling of unreality took hold of her. The silence—absolute save for the chanting, the noise of the great whites' hooves against the dirt of the road, and the muffled footsteps of the priests and soldiers—gave her the impression that she had somehow wandered into someone else's dream.

The feeling only intensified as the procession wove in the last fading rays of daylight through the silent streets, through the unending, mute crowd. When finally it reached the temple, the sky had turned to a pale golden hue, with the sun, a burning semicircle, sitting on the rim of the western horizon. Shanda pulled the horses to a halt behind the priests and turned, expectant, to Pharaoh.

His face as impassive as it had been when he'd joined her, Pharaoh turned silently away, climbing down from the chariot and moving with a near trancelike fluidity through the double line of the priests. He climbed the stone steps that fronted the temple, then disappeared through its open, wide door.

The line of priests followed after him, their monotonous chant fading away as they, too, passed into the temple precincts and the great cedar door swung shut behind them. With the absence of the low murmur of their prayer, the silence seemed to Shanda only more oppressive. She stared at the huge temple door, shut now behind the dark-robed priests, and felt a shiver, almost as if she had witnessed men walking deliberately into their own tomb.

The palace guard, which had made up the end of the procession, now moved forward and circled Shanda and the chariot. When she turned her attention away from the now empty temple portico, she realized the ring of guards was more than merely ceremonial. The wide place in front of the temple, like the streets through which the procession had passed, was filled with people, an unending sea of them. The crowd seemed to feel a communal awe and anxiety, and they pushed forward like a tide, as if seeking some measure of comfort by moving nearer the temple steps and the great golden chariot in which their god-king had ridden. Had the guards not been there to stop them, Shanda thought they would have pushed their way to the chariot and the temple doors.

She stared out at their strained faces and realized that there were no scoffers, like Sesostris and Seti, among the commoners who waited in front of the temple. Their expressions showed tension and fear, and she realized they truly and completely believed that the results of Pharaoh's sacrifice would determine if they would face a year of plenty or one marked by famine and starvation. Their open piety she found strangely moving. In the silence it seemed powerfully contagious, and she began to feel the hum of their mute prayer inside herself, a prayer of humility and abasement, a supplication to those all-powerful deities who controlled their lives to show them mercy.

Shanda found herself wondering just what rites Pharaoh would perform, what means he would use to influence his gods. Her curiosity was like a nagging itch that refused to be satisfied, and she stared at the temple facade with a growing eagerness.

The sun slipped finally below the horizon, leaving a many-fingered hand of color in the darkened sky behind as it disappeared, darting feathers of red and gold and purple that slowly extinguished themselves and fell into the earth. Torches appeared, seemingly from nowhere, and were silently lit to ease the night darkness while the crowd waited, reverent and anxious, to learn its fate.

Shanda found herself staring, as silently breathless as those around her, wondering what omens the mysteries would reveal.

When the temple doors finally swung open, the silence seemed to grow even thicker. Pharaoh walked out, his manner still oddly aloof, his gaze still fixed, as he turned to the crowd assembled before him. Then he raised his arms over his head in a gesture of success.

It was as though a dam had broken. A roar of cheers washed over the crowd like the flow of a great moving tide. And finally Pharaoh smiled.

Shanda gazed up at him, at the glow of gold from his robe and breastplate as they reflected the flickering torchlight, at his lean, handsome face, at his dark eyes shining with his triumph, at the hint of the powerful torso revealed as the robe fell open with his gesture. And just as the silent throb of the crowd had made her almost share their beliefs, so now she pictured him almost as they did, as a man who was somehow more than mortal.

She had no idea how long he stood there, how long the shouts of the crowd continued—minutes, perhaps, or perhaps much longer. It was as though a sort of delirium encompassed the crowd. No amount of shouting seemed to make them hoarse or tire them. She could hear the waves of the cries now, spiraling back through the streets of the city.

Finally Pharaoh slowly descended the stairs. The cries continued unabated as he climbed into the chariot behind Shanda and the circle of his guard elongated to allow the chariot to swing around for the return to the palace.

The chariot began to move, and as it did, Shanda saw that the air around them filled with small pale-colored missiles, dimly indistinct in the darkness. It took her a moment to realize that flowers were being thrown in the chariot's path, lotuses, thousands upon thousands of them, offerings from the people, given with their shouts of joy and gratitude.

The return to the palace seemed to move with greater speed, and Shanda was surprised when she saw the gates and the torches that lit the courtyard beyond. The homage of the people seemed unending, and the entire route of the return was covered with blossoms, an endless cascade of them as the chariot moved through the throbbing, frenzied streets. She caught one flower and held it, wanting to keep the memory of the strange ride.

The palace gates swung open as the chariot approached, and Shanda drove onto the palace grounds, up to the place where she had found the chariot waiting earlier, before the door where Pharaoh had appeared, and pulled the horses to a halt. She stood unmoving, waiting for him to leave her, feeling suddenly as though she had been cheated because he had not even spoken a word to her.

But then she felt his hand on her shoulder.

"Come, Princess."

She turned and saw him smiling at her, offering her his hand. She tied the reins to the side of the chariot and took his hand. Together they climbed down from the chariot and walked to the door, which stood open, waiting for their entry.

The room in which Shanda found herself was not large, and it was almost empty. Only two chairs stood in its center, placed companionably close and facing each other. As Pharaoh entered, a half-dozen servants came forward, hands extended, waiting to help him remove the heavy ceremonial robes and jewels.

It was, Shanda realized, a robing room, having little more function than to offer Pharaoh a few last moments of quiet before he ventured forth on such occasions as this.

"Sit, Princess," he told her firmly, waving her to one of the chairs.

She sat while he allowed the servants to remove the heavy robe, the crown and greaves and breastplate. A lighter robe was brought to him, and he slipped his arms into it as he moved to the remaining chair, then sat facing her and smiling.

"What did you think of the mysteries, Princess?" he asked her when he'd settled himself.

His question startled her, but before she had time to consider it, she voiced the question that had plagued her while she waited in the square. "What happened inside the temple?"

His face clouded abruptly and the smile disappeared. "That is for the priests and Pharaoh to know. No others," he said sharply. "Certainly not a woman, a foreign woman."

She drew back, abashed at the vehemence in his voice, realizing that she had inadvertently transgressed and that the transgression was a serious one.

"I'm sorry," she murmured, looking down, away from his eyes, at her hands. She was almost surprised to realize she still held the lotus she had caught. "I had no idea." She stared at the blossom, trying to think of something to say.

But his moment of anger passed quickly. "It is no matter,

Princess," he said, and his voice was once more pleasant. "You had no way to know."

She looked up at him again and found him once again smiling. "I have never seen anything like the frenzy of the people. The Hittites have no such ceremony, no such offering to the gods."

Once more his eyes turned sharp, but his voice, when he spoke, was without anger.

"Perhaps that is why they suffer drought, Princess, why their king must send away his daughter in place of his tribute."

Shanda felt her heart begin to beat sharply, wondering what it was she saw in his eyes—accusation, perhaps, or something else? She was grateful for the intrusion of servants bearing large bowls of perfumed water and towels. One knelt before Pharaoh and one before her. Pharaoh washed his hands and Shanda dropped the lotus into her lap and followed suit.

He pointed to the bloom in her lap as the bowls were taken away and another servant appeared bearing a tray with goblets of wine. "You admire the lotus, Princess?" he asked as he took one of the goblets.

She took the wine that was offered her and sipped it. It was strong, and it made her a bit light-headed almost at the first sip.

"I've never before seen a storm of flowers," she told him with a smile. "Egypt has many wonders."

"Like everything on this night, it almost seems magical," he agreed as he drank his own wine. "Tomorrow when they've been trammeled and begun to rot, the streets will stink of them. But tonight they are part of the sorcery."

He drained the remaining wine from his goblet, then let his head fall back and closed his eyes. He seemed to be gathering his strength, marshaling his forces for the ordeal that was still to come. Shanda sat mute, wondering what was now expected from her, afraid to make yet another blunder.

"It is time, lord."

Shanda turned and saw that the vizier had entered behind her. He stood, his hands clasped in front of him, looking at her and at Pharaoh.

She realized that she had seen him before, on that first day in the audience room, but she had been far too preoccupied with her consideration of Pharaoh that day to pay him much attention. Now, however, she wondered how she could have ignored so riveting a face. The vizier's eyes were dark and penetrating but somehow guarded, as though he could delve into other people's secrets but never give away his own. The skin was drawn tightly over the bones of his face, making his features sharp and his head seem like a barely covered skull. When he turned his eyes from Pharaoh to Shanda, she was unable to meet his gaze, and she quickly withdrew her glance.

A sudden shiver ran down her back. She was not sure why, but she sensed something malevolent in the vizier's stare, malevolent and ominous.

# Eight

PHARAOH OPENED HIS eyes and straightened. "It seems a god is not to be given the luxury of even a small respite," he said as he stood. He held out his hand to Shanda. "Princess."

She faced him and stood, putting her hand in his, feeling an unexpected wave of compassion for him. For all the bravado she had seen in him, he was not without his own weaknesses. That thought came as a surprise to her. As much as she had scorned the idea that he was a living god, neither had she thought of him in quite mortal terms before.

He led her to the rear of the room, to the door by which the vizier had entered. She glanced at the man as they approached him, wondering what it was about him that seemed so unpleasant to her, unpleasant enough to be frightening. But Nofret bowed as they passed, and she could not explain her reaction to him.

The door was drawn open, and the two of them stepped into the huge banquet room beyond. It was crowded with hundreds of people, all richly dressed, obviously members of Pharaoh's court. Shanda stared at them, realizing that the wine she had drunk made them appear to shimmer slightly, to seem a bit unreal in the flickering light cast by the torches that ringed the room. Their finery flashed in the torchlight as they stood, waiting for Pharaoh's entry, then bowed to him.

He nodded his recognition of his courtiers, then turned to his pet, waiting there for him, the lion that had sat at his feet the day Shanda was brought to him. Its keeper moved forward with the beast, bowed, released the animal to him, bowed once more, and left. Pharaoh bent to his pet, scratching its head and stroking its ears as though it were merely an overgrown house cat. When he walked forward onto the large dais, the lion ambled along at his side. Bewildered, Shanda stood where she was, not sure what was expected of her.

Pharaoh's throne waited for him on the dais, an impressive carved chair with a tall back and arms ending in serpents' heads. Like everything else that evening, the throne was sheathed in gold.

He took one of the cushions from the seat, dropped it on the floor at his feet, and seated himself. Taking their cue from him, the members of the court settled themselves in the chairs that were arranged around the dozens of large tables that filled the room proper.

Only then did Pharaoh realize Shanda was not beside him. He motioned her forward. When she had moved to his side, he pointed to the cushion he'd dropped near his feet. She stared at it a moment, then at the cat that lay on the floor nearby.

The anger hit her like a blow. She had not been chosen to accompany him as a sign of his favor, she realized, but simply as a decoration, chosen for her golden hair, like the chariot and his throne, a mark of his wealth and power. And now he would have her sit at his feet like his animal, a curiosity for his court to admire.

Shanda felt herself grow numb inside as she sank down on the cushion. She would not let herself give in to the anger, she told herself. She would not let herself feel the hurt he had done to her pride. She had no right to pride, she realized. She had lost that when she clung to her life instead of embracing the cobra in the desert.

A servant appeared with a table which he set before Pharaoh. Then the room was flooded with servants bearing huge platters of food and ewers of wine, which they distributed among the many tables. Shanda sat numb and rigid, staring out at the activity in the room.

"Here, Princess, eat."

He pulled a piece of the breast meat from the roast duck that had been set before him and held it out to her. Shanda barely moved her head.

"No, thank you, lord. I am not hungry."

It was a lie, certainly. She had eaten nothing since morning, for there had been no time for the meal Med had brought to her rooms for her and Sesostris. The hour had grown late and she was very hungry. The light-headedness the wine had left with her still bothered her, reminding her that food would be required to calm it, and her stomach churned at the scent of the rich meat.

"Nonsense," he told her evenly, still offering her the piece of duck. "You cannot have eaten since early in the day. And I think your stomach agrees with me," he added as he heard the loud growl her empty stomach made.

"I am not a beast to be fed scraps from your plate," she retorted, the words out of her mouth before she had the chance to think them inadvisable.

He leaned back and considered her thoughtfully, dropping the piece of duck before his lion, who reached out a lazy paw and pulled it into his yawning mouth.

"Why do you serve me, Princess?" he asked her abruptly.

She turned finally to face him, her brows raised in curiosity at his question.

"You obviously have no regard for me," he explained. "Nor do you treat me with reverence, as my other women do. Yet you make an effort to obey me as far as your pride will allow. Why?"

"Hattushil demanded my word," she told him evenly. "I gave it to him. To break it would mean the loss of my honor." She stared up at him. "A woman can have honor, too," she said in a tone that challenged him to deny the possibility.

He didn't. He stared at her in silence for a moment more.

"It must be hard for you, Princess," he said slowly. "How your honor must battle with your pride."

She made no reply, but turned away from him, staring out once more at the chaos of movement in the room. Suddenly she felt the bite of tears behind her eyes and she thought of Nem. She fought back the tears, but she could not push away Nem's image. Pharaoh was right. Her greatest battles were not with him but with herself. And Nem must have known what she was being sent to face. He ought never to have allowed it. If he had loved her as much as he told her he did, he would have found some way to keep her from being sent away. Even if it meant leaving, giving up everything, he should never have let her go.

"I think you left behind more than your promise and your home in Hattushil's court," Pharaoh said gently as he stared at her still profile, at the trace of liquid in her eyes. "I think you left behind your heart as well, Princess."

She turned to face him, this time unable to keep her expression detached, unable to pretend she felt nothing. "There was a young general," she admitted, her voice barely more than a whisper.

"He was a fool to give you up."

She swallowed, remembering the feeling of loss, of desertion. "To defy Hattushil would have meant fleeing, leaving everything behind," she murmured.

She found herself offering Pharaoh the words with a diffidence that was only intensified by her own lack of satisfaction with the excuse. She wondered why she felt the need to defend Nem and his decision when she had come to think of his behavior as unforgivable.

"A man would make a profitable trade were he to surrender the wealth of a kingdom in exchange for your love, Princess."

He'd said the words slowly, his voice very low, and they sank into Shanda with a surprising weight. She turned to stare up at him, shocked and bewildered.

"Would you truly give up everything for such a trade, lord?" she asked him softly.

He stared at her, his eyes holding hers for a moment in silence. Shanda felt her heart begin to pound in her chest, loud enough, she thought, for him to hear.

But he broke his glance from hers and sat back before he replied. "There is no need," he told her, his voice once more as it had been—steady, controlled, a trifle distant. "I have everything, and I have you, Princess, as well."

The thudding in her heart stopped abruptly and was replaced by a wave of cold anger, anger more with herself than with him, for holding an expectation of him that he had refused to meet.

She turned away again, pretending interest in the musicians, acrobats, and jugglers who had streamed into the room in the wake of the servants who still scurried about with ewers of beer and wine and trays of food. She would not face him, she told herself. She wouldn't give him the satisfaction of seeing in her eyes the disappointment she felt at his words.

But as he had already several times that day, he again surprised her. He put his hand on her shoulder. When she turned, he motioned to the chair a servant was setting beside his.

"Would your pride allow you to eat from my plate if you were seated beside me, Princess?" he asked her. "Or would that, too, be taxing it?"

She could hear the amusement in his voice and see it in his eyes, but she was not offended by it. She took his hand, rose, and moved to the chair.

"I think this will satisfy it," she told him with a small smile as she settled herself at his side.

He motioned to the plates of food on the table in front of him and she took a piece of duck, which she ate with relish and great enjoyment. When she'd finished it he held out his goblet to her.

"And will you share this, as well, Princess?" he asked.

She put out her hand to take it and felt his fingers warm against hers. The contact, she realized, was oddly agreeable.

He released the cup and she raised it to her lips, sipping the heady wine. He stared at her as she drank, then leaned back.

"Do you see the looks those women are leveling at you, Princess?" he asked her, nodding toward the room with its crowd of courtiers.

She looked up, surprised by his question, and glanced around. He was right, she realized. A good number of the women stared up at her where she sat beside him, their glances filled with anger and envy.

She sipped at the wine once more and nodded in reply to his question.

He leaned forward, helping himself to a portion of the duck on his plate, talking as he pulled the meat from the bone.

"They are all wives of officials, and they wait each year for the opportunity this night affords them," he told her evenly. "They ruin their husbands providing themselves with gowns and jewels in the hope that I will notice them and ask them to dine beside me." He leaned back and thoughtfully chewed a bite of the duck.

Shanda put the wine down on the table and faced him. "And I have stolen that honor from them?" she asked him.

He nodded.

"But why should it mean enough to them to ruin their husbands?" she demanded.

He swallowed the meat before he turned his eyes to her. "Because, Princess, if the woman pleases me, I will offer to share my bed with her as well as my meal."

"But their husbands—" Shanda gasped.

"Encourage them," he replied, almost as if he had expected her shock. "You see, in the morning, in return for the lady's favors, I reward her husband with a more important position, a chance for greater wealth. Most men's greed is greater than their passion, and I always pay handsomely for what I take."

If his revelation had at first shocked her, the pain she saw in his face as he spoke the last words completely surprised her. It seemed odd to her that she felt a tinge of pity for him after the admission he had made to her, and the revelation he had perhaps inadvertently made. What he had told her made her begin to understand finally the way he had treated her. He expected nothing from a woman; he knew she would always demand a price for the favors she offered, and he was willing to pay it as long as it did not truly touch him. Shanda found something terribly sad in that revelation, in the fact that he expected nothing and gave nothing of himself in return. She wondered if he had ever felt love, or ever received it.

He leaned forward, grasped the goblet, and drained its contents. He motioned to a servant to refill it, broke a piece of bread, and handed it to Shanda with some cheese. When she once more began to eat what he had given her, he spoke again.

"And that woman," he said, nodding to a small dais at the side of the room where a table had been set and a woman and a handsome young man ate in superior solitude.

Shanda looked at the dark-haired, perfect-featured woman. No longer in the first flower of her youth, she was nonetheless still extremely beautiful. She turned back to face Pharaoh. He, too, was staring at the woman, and his features had turned cold and fixed.

"She is beautiful," Shanda ventured.

"She is Queen Tiy, my wife," he told her evenly. It was almost as though he spoke of a stranger, and only the sharp anger Shanda saw in his eyes revealed the depth of feeling within him as he gazed at Tiy. "And beside her sits Prince Amenophis, my son and heir. The two of them have but one thought between them: to see the boy take his place as pharaoh. To that end they occupy their lives, plotting with my vizier, Nofret, to see me dead and the boy sitting on this throne in my place."

"The queen and your vizier?" she repeated in bewildered amazement.

She pictured Nofret's face in her mind—the darkly penetrating eyes, the skull-like countenance that looked so like a death's head. The thought of having such a man as an enemy made her tremble with terror.

Pharaoh nodded. "Nofret is Tiy's lover, and someday she will goad him into an act of violence."

The fact that Pharaoh allowed Queen Tiy to take a lover astonished Shanda. Any one of Hattushil's women even suspected of offering her favors to another would soon have breathed her last. Again she conjured up the vizier's image, and this time felt herself shiver with distaste.

Pharaoh finally turned back to face Shanda, and his expression softened into a wry smile.

"Your father's court, Princess, is a far less complicated place than mine, I think."

She mulled over his words in her mind. Had life really been less complicated in Hattushil's court, or was it simply more brutal? She'd never really given the matter any thought before. Dwelling on things she had no power to change had never seemed fruitful. Althea had taught her that, to accept what she could not remedy and to do what was necessary to survive.

"But your queen . . . " she began to protest, turning her thoughts back to those things Pharaoh had told her.

He shook his head and once again offered her the wry smile. Then he turned toward the acrobats, keeping his eyes on them as he spoke. "I was very young when my father died, Princess. I was not his firstborn son, or even the son of his first queen, but he named me his successor. There were some who would have challenged my right to his throne, and to appease them I married the daughter of my father's firstborn. Tiy's father considered me too young and weak to rule and thought marriage would bring him the power of the throne, if not the title. And he was nearly right. I was too young to rule. But I was not the weakling he thought me. I needed time to learn and find my strengths before I could exercise the power my father had bequeathed me."

"So you wed Tiy only to give yourself that time?" she asked.

He nodded. "It was a union of necessity, to keep Egypt from civil war," he said. "We brought each other no pleasure. She was forced into my bed as much as I was forced into hers." He reached for the goblet and took a long swallow before continuing. "I went to her only enough times to ensure that she was with child. We were both delighted when the infant was a boy, because that meant the exercise would not need to be repeated."

"And Tiy's father?" Shanda asked. "What became of him?"

He drank again, once more emptying the cup, as though he needed to think of the right words for what he wished to say.

"His eyes were keen enough to see my strength growing," Pharaoh said, "but he was foolish enough to try to have me killed and put himself on my throne. Luckily he waited too long before he made the attempt. Instead, he was the one to die."

Shanda watched as his eyes narrowed as he gazed at the jugglers, his attention far too intense for his thoughts to be on the entertainment. He was silent for what seemed a long time, and then, finally, he turned his glance once more to his queen where she sat at the far side of the hall.

"I regretted the act, for her sake, realizing that she had been cheated and through no fault of her own. As a kindness to the two of them, I let Tiy keep the child to raise. I was wrong. I had foolishly given her, not only reason to hate me but also a weapon to use against me. I let them forge their union against me." He turned back to Shanda and shrugged as though throwing off thoughts that were obviously painful to him.

"But why have you allowed her to take a lover?" she demanded, still bewildered at his apparent acceptance of what she would have expected him to find intolerable.

"Nofret?" He seemed surprised by her bewilderment. "Why should it concern me if she can find some comfort in his bony arms?"

Shanda shook her head, not understanding his actions. "But why do you keep him as your vizier if he plots with her against you?" she asked.

This time he grinned widely, obviously amused by her disbelief, her naïveté. "He has far more fear of me than love for her," he told her. "And I think it best to keep my enemy close at hand, where he can be watched." Once more he motioned to the servant to refill his goblet. "Besides," he added as the wine was being poured, "he is a very good vizier, very well organized, meticulous about his work. He saves me from a great many boring tasks."

He broke off another piece of duck and held it out to her. Shanda ate it almost without thought, still confused by his revelations. She wondered what pain he must feel, knowing he was surrounded by enemies, knowing his own son wished for his death.

She also wondered what it had cost him to tell her all these things, to show her his weaknesses, his failures. Surely that was something he did not do easily, and she found herself beginning to see him differently, no longer as distant, cold, insensitive, and arrogant, but as a man who was as human as she, with his own private pains and misgivings, forced to face the consequences of his own mistakes. She was not sure she liked this new understanding; it had been far easier to tell herself she hated him before he made his confession to her. Now she could not deny the fact that she was beginning to feel something for him, no matter how hard she tried to believe otherwise.

"Look at those jugglers, Princess," he said, pointing to two men who were throwing lighted torches and sharp swords to each other as they strolled among the banquet tables.

Shanda stared at the pair, absently accepting the goblet he passed to her and sipping the potent wine, keeping her eyes on the jugglers as they courted what seemed certain disaster with an unbelievable elan.

"I am like those jugglers, Princess," he told her softly.

"As long as the swords and torches fly, as long as they are in the air, I count myself and Egypt safe. But I cannot allow even one to fall, for if I do, everything will end in ruin."

They fell silent again, and Shanda realized how wrong she had been about him. Finally he broke the silence.

"Have you done, Princess?" he asked her. "Have you dined well enough, seen enough of the jugglers, and heard enough of the musicians?"

She looked sheepishly down at the plate. They had devoured most of the food, and she had consumed her full share. She hardly remembered drinking the wine, but there was a pleasantly blurred feeling in her head that could have come from nothing else. Only Pharaoh's words seemed focused to her now; the memory of what he had told her was distinct despite her light-headedness.

She nodded to him. "Yes, lord. Quite enough."

He waved a hand to a servant, and bowls of water were brought to them. Shanda watched his distant stare as he washed his hands and dried them. She reminded herself of his words: "I think it best to keep my enemy close at hand, where he can be watched." Was that how he thought of her? she wondered.

He stood and offered her his hand. She took it and rose, then walked beside him to the door that led to the robing room. The lion followed them, his great mane stirring the air behind them as they moved. The banquet continued, the noise and music and laughter unchanged, as though Pharaoh's early departure was to be expected. But the sounds were muted, as though they came to her from a great distance, and as she stepped into the robing room at Pharaoh's side they seemed to have left the revelers in some place far removed from them.

The small room was empty and quiet, with only the light of a small lamp to ward off the darkness. Wordlessly

Pharaoh led her through it to a door at the far side. He opened it, and they stepped into a long, torchlit corridor.

This was a part of the palace Shanda had never seen before, the corridors here narrower and plainer, far less opulently decorated than those she had traversed before. She followed him through what seemed to be a maze, corridor meeting and crossing corridor, all of it the same dull ocher color in the flickering light cast by the torches.

Pharaoh seemed entirely at home as he silently led her and the lion padded along behind them, his occasional roar more a bored punctuation to their ramble than an indication of excitement at the prospect of an outing. The animal seemed more aware of where they were going than Shanda was.

Soon they came to a flight of stairs set into the stone wall of the corridor. Pharaoh led the way up the narrow steps, turning slightly so that she could hold his hand to steady herself. The lion settled himself on the floor at the foot of the stairs and lowered his head to his paws in preparation for a nap.

Pharaoh saw her consider the beast, and he laughed, finally breaking the silence of their walk. "He will guard our privacy, Princess," he told her. "He will let no one pass."

He helped her up the last of the steps, and Shanda found herself on a wide, flat roof, the dark, starlit sky above them, the cool night breeze pleasant against her skin. It took her eyes a moment to adjust to the dimmer light, and then she stared up, feeling a wave of contentment sweep over her as she was enfolded by the beauty of the night.

The corners of the roof were lit by torches, a servant beside each one keeping careful watch against fire. Near the center was a pale, fluttery form, fairly large, but she could not quite make it out in the dimness.

Pharaoh drew her to one side of the roof, and she put her hand on the waist-high wall and stared out. Below her flick-

ered the lights of the city, the noise from the commoners'
celebration drifting up to her as a distant, pleasant hum.

What most intrigued her, however, was the river. The
view of the Nile from the palace roof was breathtaking.
The water slid by like a huge snake reflecting the moonlight and turning to a great flowing mass of liquid gold. At
its edges an endless parade of tiny lights, fireflies seeking
mates, blinked bravely into the darkness.

Pharaoh stood behind her and placed his hands on the wall
beside hers. She could feel the warmth of his body close to
her, but he held himself apart, near her, yet not touching.

"As the desert is Egypt's father, so the Nile is her mother," Pharaoh said softly. "She succors us, makes our fields
fertile, keeps us from want."

Awed by the beauty of the night sky and the river of
gold, Shanda stared out at the Nile.

"It's beautiful," she whispered.

"More than beautiful."

His voice had turned low and husky, and Shanda turned
to find his eyes were on her now, not on the spectacle of
the river and the star-strewn sky. There was that in his gaze
which told her he had spoken of something other than the
Nile.

She turned away, unable to think of anything to say to
him, and stared down at the water. And then, unbidden,
came a voice inside her, a voice urging her to tell him what
little she knew of the truth: that there was no drought, no
famine, among the Hittites, that Hattushil had sent her to
Egypt to hide from Pharaoh the fact that the Hittite king
was Egypt's enemy.

She gripped the stone wall as she turned once more to
face him.

"Pharaoh," she began.

"Yes, Princess?"

And suddenly the words died on her lips. What foolishness was this? she asked herself. How could she tell him she had been sent to deceive him, that she was a piece in a game she did not even understand? He would think her a fool; he would scorn her.

She stared up at him, then lifted her hand slowly to his cheek.

"Even a god cannot undo what is done, Princess," he said slowly. "We began badly, you and I. If I had it in my power, I would call it all back and begin anew."

"Perhaps we can pretend that you have that power," she suggested.

He put his hand on her waist and drew her to him. She felt herself melting against the hard wall of his chest, surrounded by the muscled bonds of his arms. For the first time, she felt the contact joyously, not as something to be endured for the sake of her oath, but as a gift to be enjoyed, an offering to bring her pleasure. She let herself be pulled close to him, let her body press close to his and feel the communicating warmth.

"Perhaps, Princess, we can do just that," he agreed.

His lips found hers with a gentle hunger, prodding her own, sending a slow tide surging through her veins that set her adrift on a river as powerful as the surging Nile.

He lifted her into his arms. Shanda threw her head back, stared up at the stars for a moment, and felt a bubbling throb of joy fill her. She saw then that the torches had been extinguished and the servants had disappeared. She wondered how they could have gone without her hearing them, for the stillness, save for the distant noises of the city and the soft, liquid sound of the moving river, was complete. All that remained was the great, fluttering, pale form in the center of the open roof—a gauzy tent, she realized, dimly lit now by a lamp within, a translucent room open to the sky.

Pharaoh carried her inside and set her down on a large divan. She lay back against a heap of pillows and stared up at the stars. They seemed to be moving, slowly circling the heavens, but perhaps she was still a bit giddy from the wine.

She watched Pharaoh as he lifted a pitcher from the table beside the divan and filled a golden goblet. Then he sat beside her and offered her the wine.

She took the goblet from him, but did not drink immediately. Instead, she swirled the wine and stared into the dark red liquid, wondering if that was how her blood appeared at that moment, deep and dark and swirling through her veins.

She looked up at him. "Is this where you would have brought the wife of the official, the one you would have chosen to dine with you?" she asked him softly.

His gray eyes returned her stare, but she found no answers in them.

"Does it matter, Princess?" he asked her. "I've brought you here tonight."

She sipped the wine, hardly noticing the few drops that spilled from the cup as she handed it back to him, realizing that he was right, that it didn't matter who else had come here in the past or how many there had been. All that seemed important at that moment was the way she felt, the stirring, liquid throb that began when he leaned toward her and slowly licked away the errant drops of wine from the valley between her breasts. She raised her hands to the nape of his neck and leaned back into the pillows, staring up at the stars, letting herself fill with the feeling of his touch.

"Tonight we begin again, Princess," he said softly as his lips found hers.

When she closed her eyes, she could still see the sky, the tiny, bright pinpricks of stars as they'd appeared through the gauze of the tent above her, the black of the night sky around them, an endless, all-absorbing black that threatened to swallow all the light in the sky, made bearable only by the indomitable tenacity of the jewellike stars and the great golden orb of the moon. She thought of Hecate, the powerful goddess who ruled the moon and to whom her mother had secretly offered sacrifice when the goddess showed her full face, round and golden, in the night sky. For the first time, Shanda felt the goddess's power, the thick racing tide within her, and she regretted the times she had privately scorned Althea's tribute. She offered up a silent prayer, a supplication to be forgiven for her lack of faith.

Slowly Pharaoh stripped off her golden gown, and soon her jewels, too, lay on the floor in a heap like so much refuse cast away in the search for more important treasure. She was aware only of the touch of his hands and his lips on her skin, on her lips and thighs and breasts, and in the warm valley between her legs. That and the sweet, surging tide that seemed ever rising inside her.

She felt him join her more as a need than as a desire, as though he were some lost part of her that she'd unknowingly mourned, finally found, and restored to herself. She felt him inside her, and didn't know where she ended and he began, only that in the joining she felt complete as she had never felt before. And when the tide rose ever higher until it could rise no farther, she welcomed the sudden explosion, opening herself to it and embracing it as she embraced him.

He felt the trembling shudder, heard her moan of pleasure, and knew he had finally received from her what he had wanted all along. This trembling acceptance, this joyful joining—this was what he had longed for the first day when he'd seen her and known he had to have her. He released himself into her, letting their passion meld, realizing the act had never before been quite so sweet to him. That would be something to ponder later, when he could order his thoughts, when his mind cleared and left him time to think. For now he had but one thought, to find her lips again with his, to drink in her sweet, warm breath, to revel in the triumph of having finally won her.

He lay back on the divan, then gathered her in his arms and pulled her close to him. He looked down at the golden hair spread across his chest as she lay, panting slowly, her cheek pressed to his shoulder.

"Have we begun well this time, Princess?" he asked her, although he needed no answer to know that they had.

She turned her eyes up to meet his and she smiled. That pleased him almost more than the passion, to know that she finally smiled at him with real pleasure.

"Indeed, lord," she replied, "very well."

For a moment he wondered idly, now that she'd given him what he'd wanted, if his hunger for her would die. But when she raised her hand to his cheek, leaned toward him, and offered him her lips once more, he knew his appetite was far from sated.

Shanda kissed him, then let her tongue slowly taste his lips. What folly had she fallen into? she wondered. What madness had caused her to feel this way for him? And what pain would she feel when he learned that she was a diversion sent to keep him occupied while Hattushil made his plans and began upon whatever treacherous path he had decided to follow? It would have been better for her if she had ignored the words he had spoken to her that evening, if she had been able to go on thinking him a barbarian. But with his admission of weakness and failure, he had become a man in her eyes, and she had succumbed to him. She wondered if he knew what he had done, if he realized that by confiding in her he had made her vulnerable to him.

She pushed the thought away, telling herself that there

was no future to dread, no tomorrow at all, only this moment, and it was too sweet to be spoiled with such contemplation.

But even as she found his hands once more warm against her skin, his lips once more hungrily seeking hers, she knew the respite was only temporary. Tomorrow would come, and all too soon.

# *Nine*

SHANDA OPENED HER eyes to a dim sky that had just begun to fill with light. She'd never seen a sky quite so pulsing with color—red and orange and yellow to the east where the sun's first fingers rose tentatively upward, fading into a mellow blue-gray where its rays did not yet reach.

"I've been lying here beside you, Princess, wondering if your eyes were really the shade of blue I remembered, or if it was simply my imagination and the effects of the wine last night."

She turned her head slightly and found him, his head propped up on a hand, lying at her side and staring at her.

She smiled, warmed by the sudden memory of what had happened between them the night before. "And have you decided?" she asked him with a smile.

He nodded gravely. "They are as I had remembered them to be. Perhaps even a deeper blue." He leaned toward her, brushing his hand against her cheek, then offering her a kiss, warm against her lips. "And your lips taste as sweet as I remembered them as well." Then he pulled himself away, his expression tinged with obvious regret. "But it is time to leave, Princess," he said. "My father the sun begins his climb into the sky."

She heard a note of irony in his last words and wondered if perhaps he kept his own counsel regarding his belief in a pharaoh's divinity. How painful, she thought, to be considered a god and yet know oneself to be only human.

He stood and offered her his hand. She grasped it, allowing him to draw her to her feet, and then stood for a moment, stretching and yawning in the cool morning air. When she was done, she realized that he watched her. She did not know why, but she felt the blush creep into her cheeks, and she began looking for her gown.

He retrieved it, then held it, still staring at her.

"As comely and pleasant as I find this particular view, Princess, I am unwilling to share it with the palace guards," he told her and he held the golden gown out to her. The fabric hung from his hand, shimmering in the early morning breeze.

She slid it on. When she'd settled it, she turned back to him and found his eyes still on her.

He grinned then—almost shyly, she thought—and turned to retrieve his own robe.

"Come, Princess," he said as he pulled it on. "Neither of us is ready to greet Nofret yet this morning." He looked up at the sky as he took her hand and tucked it into he crook of his arm.

"Nofret?" she asked. The thought of waking to his skeletal grin was indeed less than appetizing.

"He will arrive soon, bearing some bauble as token and the promise of appropriate reward to follow," he answered absently.

She pointed to the heap of gold jewelry she'd worn the night before, which lay scattered near the bed. "What of that?" she asked.

"Nofret will tend to it. If nothing else, he regards my treasures with great reverence," he told her as they moved closer toward the stairs.

She pondered his words as he handed her down the stairs, realizing abruptly that he did not ordinarily stay the night with his chosen woman, that his vizier arrived in the morning to see the lady home and offer assurances that the payment she and her husband expected would be made.

The lion looked up at them as they stepped down the last of the stairs, shook his huge head, then yawned loudly. He roared as he rose to his feet, ready to follow his master, sure breakfast would soon be offered.

Once more Pharaoh led her through the maze of palace corridors, passing guards who came to sharp attention as they neared and cast considering glances when they had passed.

Shanda expected he would bring her back to her apartment, but instead found herself in front of a huge pair of ornate doors barred by two palace guards. They bowed and drew the doors open as Pharaoh approached.

Shanda was amazed by the luxuriousness and size of the room she entered. Blocks of smoothly polished colored stone formed its floor; enormous pillars of painted and decorated stone supported the ceiling, on which a beautifully wrought sky was painted. The furnishings were all of costly ebony, beautifully and finely carved. The lion, apparently entirely at home, ambled toward an opening to the garden beyond, settled himself in a patch of sunlight that warmed the floor beside it, and once again put his head on his huge paws and closed his eyes, clearly having decided to wait there until his food was brought him.

A servant approached and bowed low to Pharaoh. Then he looked up at Shanda, his expression bewildered.

"Bring food, Usha," Pharaoh ordered as he walked past

the man, holding Shanda's hand and drawing her with him.

She glanced back and noticed the servant's unbelieving look before he turned to do as he had been bidden.

"Is something wrong, lord?" she asked him, her tone tentative. "Have I done something wrong?"

He darted a glance back at the servant, then laughed. "No, Princess. It is just that he has never seen a woman in these rooms before."

His words gave her something more to ponder as she followed him into the next room. It contained an enormous bed, swathed with pale, gauzy hangings and heaped with pillows. She had little time to consider the comforts of the room, however, for he continued on without even glancing toward the bed. Shanda decided he had apparently sated his want for her the night before. The thought left her with an unexpected pang of regret.

He led her into the next room, which opened onto the riotously flowered garden. Shanda inhaled the perfume of the blooms on the air before turning to an enormous pool, more than twice the size of the bath in her own apartment. The water was a clear azure blue that magnified the polished stone that lined the sides and bottom of the pool.

Pharaoh removed his robe and let it negligently fall. He then plunged into the water and swam halfway across before surfacing and turning to look at her expectantly.

Shanda slowly pulled off the golden gown and laid it carefully on a marble bench. Then she moved to the edge of the pool and stood for a long moment, her movements deliberate, aware that his eyes were on her. Then she slid into the water.

It felt cool and pleasant against her skin. She treaded water for a second, then filled her lungs with air and plunged beneath the surface.

He watched her gentle downward drift, watched the way

her hair, a mass of pale golden tendrils, fanned out in the water around her and framed her face and bare shoulders. Then he swam down to her and offered her a watery kiss on the lips before catching her by the waist and surfacing once more, with her in his arms.

Shanda was breathless and laughing when they broke out of the water, and she offered him a slightly taunting smile before she wriggled out of his arms and swam to the far side of the pool. He darted after her, laughing now as well, but she slipped just out of his reach as he approached the pool's edge. Again he started after her, and this time his stronger stroke brought him abreast of her as she neared the opposite side.

He put his arms around her, holding her against the side of the pool with his body.

"Give up, Princess," he told her as he moved his face close to hers. "There is no escape for you."

She laughed and pretended to search for a way past his arms. Then she sobered suddenly as he pressed closer to her, and turned her face to his. She put her arms around his shoulders.

"I no longer wish to escape," she told him softly.

He pressed her back against the smooth stone side of the pool, his body close to hers, his lips finding hers once more, licking away the droplets of water that clung to them before darting his tongue into her mouth.

She pressed herself against him, clinging to his shoulders, her hands moving slowly over his hard muscles.

"Why is it, Princess, that there is no end for my want of you?" he asked her.

It was true, he realized, slightly bewildered as he contemplated the fact. Possessing her had in no way diminished the fascination she held for him. If anything, it had made his desire grow.

She smiled up at him, feeling suddenly very knowing, very sure of herself. She pressed her lips to his, tasting first the lower, then the upper, her movements very deliberate and tauntingly slow. Then she lowered her head to his neck, letting the warmth of her breath precede her lips and tongue as her hands slid slowly down his chest to his hips. She felt the dull, heavy thud of his pulse beneath her lips and realized that their game had grown suddenly serious.

She slid under the water, letting her hands and lips trail down his torso, moving slowly, releasing the air in her lungs in tiny bits, wanting to make it last as long as she could. She found his tumescence, thick and hard, and the bed of dark, wiry curls.

She pressed her lips to him, touching him tentatively, and then was forced to surface, for her lungs were empty and had begun to ache. He was waiting for her, his arms ready to catch and hold her, and she willingly wrapped her arms around his neck and her legs around his hips.

He had not expected her actions, not expected the sudden and strong reaction of his body to her touch. The need she'd roused in him would not simply disappear. Nor did he want it to.

He loved her there in the pool, the movement of their bodies sending out eddying circles of waves into the water. Shanda clung to him, feeling him deep within her, sure that the moment would never end, that this sudden unsought passion he'd wakened in her would burn from her all vestiges of the past which she now yearned to forget. She pressed herself close to him, her nails biting into his back, letting the shuddering release fill her.

After a moment he lifted her out of the pool, carried her to a low couch, and laid her on it. He leaned over her, kissing her belly and then the golden thatch between her thighs. Then he smiled down at her.

"Do you remember, Princess, that evening when you would not kiss my foot?" he asked her with a crooked smile.

She nodded slowly. "Yes, lord."

He smiled again and circled her foot with his hand, slowly rubbing the arch with his thumb. "I am not so proud as you, Princess." He lifted her foot to his mouth and slowly pressed his lips to the place he had massaged.

The contact sent a small shiver of fire up her leg.

"Perhaps my pride has diminished, lord," she said with a smile as she pushed herself up and leaned on her elbows. Her eyes sparkled with amusement as he once more pressed the arch of her foot to his lips before releasing it. She sat up and swung her legs off the couch. "I no longer find the prospect demeaning," she said as she knelt on the floor in front of him.

He put his hands on her shoulders and held her until she looked up at him.

"I think, Princess, that your kisses are far too precious to be wasted so profligately." He slid his hands into the silk of her hair and drew her to him.

Shanda wrapped Pharaoh's robe around herself, laughing as she saw the way it dragged along the floor, pushing up the sleeves so that her hands were freed of the excess fabric.

"Come with me, Shanda," he said. "I have something to show you."

She padded after him, tugging at the too large robe, as he led her to a door that was blocked by a long table. This he pushed aside with an impatient shove, his expression speaking more of his desire to be rid of it than of the effort of moving it that its weight certainly required. He put his hand on the latch, hesitating only a moment before he drew the door open and motioned to her to pass through.

She gasped softly. This, too, was a bedroom, not nearly so large as his, but incredibly beautiful. The walls were painted with river scenes, monkeys romping by the shore, playing in beds of lotus flowers, hanging from trees and vines, and reaching for small flocks of fancifully feathered birds which flew just out of their reach. Beneath her feet was an incredible mosaic of colored stones arranged in the shapes of fishes and shells so as to resemble a riverbed. It was so real that she could almost feel the splash of the water against her legs.

"My father had these rooms decorated for his third queen," Pharaoh said. "Her family was not so noble as the families of his other wives, and she was a good deal younger than he. But she was comely, and she was the only woman he ever really loved. When she died, he had the rooms closed off. No one has lived in them since. Only servants come in here, to clean and tend them."

He then took her hand and showed her through the remaining rooms: a dressing room with an enormous slab of polished silver against one wall to reflect the lady's image, an ebony dressing table fitted with inlays of lapis lazuli, carnelian, and gold; a sitting room, the table set with a game of senet as though waiting for the dead queen to come and play, a box of paints and brushes set out on a table by the window overlooking the garden, should she wish to write or draw; everything beautifully decorated. But the room that most surprised Shanda was beyond this, a small chamber that contained a child's bed, a chest, and toys. The walls, here, too, were beautifully decorated, with quizzical-faced monkeys swinging through the branches of trees.

She watched as he absently lifted a carved figure of a hippopotamus from one of the shelves of toys and fingered it. His hand moved without the need of his sight, for he kept his eyes riveted to her expression. She realized that he knew the toy well, that his hands had held it many times. He was the child who had played in this small nursery, and it was his mother for whom his father had prepared these rooms and, after her death, turned them into a temple to her memory.

"But you," she asked softly, "you have never brought someone to live here with you?"

He shook his head. "I remember how my father grieved when she died. I told myself that this place I would hold until I found a woman who would mean as much to me as she had to him. There never was anyone." He put his hand on her shoulder and pulled her close to him. "Until now."

He put his free hand on her throat, his fingers caressing, his breath warm against her cheek.

"Would you be content here, Princess?" he asked her softly.

This, then, was what Hattushil had sent her to do, to make Pharaoh love her, to cloud his vision. But Shanda felt no sense of victory, no sense of having conquered him. She swore to herself that she would never again think of Hattushil or of Nem, that the part of her life to which they had belonged was past and she had no desire to return to it. She had conquered Pharaoh's heart, but he had made a conquest of hers as well, and the knowledge that he loved her filled her with happiness.

"Yes, lord," she replied. "I would be more than content here."

He enfolded her in his arms and kissed her.

He sat facing her and ate hungrily, occasionally making an offering to his lion, who lay at his feet. Shanda smilingly considered the enormity of his appetite and then, just as objectively, her own. The pleasant exertions of the night before and the morning had roused a prodigious hunger in her, which had not been sated by the sumptuous meal

Pharaoh's servant had set for them.

"If I continue to eat like this, I shall grow as large as a cow," she said.

She seemed unconcerned, however, as she turned her attention to pulling the juicy seeds from a pomegranate, popping them into her mouth and then licking the sweet, sticky juice from her fingers.

He reached across the table for her hand. "Your resemblance to that beast would make you dear to the goddess Hathor, deity of love and joy. The cow is her sacred beast." He raised her hand to his mouth and licked away the last drops of pomegranate juice.

"I think, lord, it is not to any goddess I would be dear, but to a god. One very particular god."

He turned his eyes to hers, but kept hold of her hand. She felt the weight of those searching gray eyes, felt as though they could make their way inside her, probing her, searching for answers to questions he chose not to ask. It surprised her to find that she welcomed their entry, that there was nothing any longer inside herself that she wanted hidden from him.

"Excuse me, lord."

Usha, his servant, had entered and now bowed low. His expression, when he dared to raise his face, mirrored his distaste of the reason for this intrusion. He let his eyes dart briefly to Shanda, but he withdrew them quickly, as though the sight of her might somehow prove dangerous to him.

"What is it?" Pharaoh demanded.

"Lord Nofret begs audience, Pharaoh," Usha replied.

Pharaoh groaned softly and released Shanda's hand. "Show him in," he ordered.

The servant bowed and left the room.

Shanda stood.

"What is it, Princess?" Pharaoh asked her.

"I will leave you to your audience, lord," she replied.

But as she turned to go, he reached out and caught her hand.

"There is no need for you to leave, Shanda," he told her. "Nothing will be said that you may not hear." He grinned at her. "And I would much rather look at you than at Nofret. Sit."

She nodded and reseated herself, pulling the robe close over her breasts, then turned her chair so that she faced away from the door by which the vizier would enter.

Pharaoh smiled as he watched her cover herself and avert her face, assuming her action to be a part of her foreignness, a display of Hittite modesty.

"My lord."

Pharaoh looked up. His expression lost any trace of amusement. "Nofret," he said tersely, "why do you bother me here?"

The vizier bowed his head. "I regret the necessity, lord, but I thought perhaps you had forgotten there were to be audiences this morning. The emissaries from the provinces have already assembled and await you."

Pharaoh considered his vizier in silence for a moment, watching the way the man's eyes darted to Shanda's golden hair, then slipped away to meet his own before they were averted in an apparent display of subservience. He leaned back in his chair before he spoke. "These emissaries from the provinces, no doubt they are grateful for the opportunity to see so great a city as Thebes and to sample of its pleasures?"

"No doubt, lord," Nofret agreed.

Pharaoh's glance fell upon Shanda's face. He found her eyes on him, and he smiled at her a shade lecherously.

"Then you may tell them that their pharaoh has graciously decided to prolong their holiday by postponing their audiences and thereby their return to their homes. Tell them they may enjoy themselves for one day more, and at Pharaoh's expense." He smiled once more at Shanda, then turned back to Nofret. "No, tell them two days more," he amended. "Is there anything further?"

Nofret clasped his hands and bowed. "No, lord, nothing further," he replied.

"Then I will not detain you." Pharaoh dismissed him with a wave of his hand.

When the vizier had gone, Pharaoh looked at Shanda. Her absent, concerned expression startled him.

"Why did you turn away from him, Princess?" he asked. "It was almost as if you hoped he would not recognize you. Surely you realized he would know you the moment he caught a glimpse of your hair."

"I was remembering the things you told me, lord," she replied, "about Nofret and the queen, and the fact that you have never before brought a woman here." She turned away from his gaze. "Nofret will tell the queen he saw me here."

Pharaoh shrugged. "But why should you be concerned with such a triviality, Princess? I've told you that Tiy leads her own life and I lead mine. She has no reason to concern herself with whom I bring here, what I do."

Shanda turned back to let her eyes find his and shook her head slowly. "I think, lord, you are knowledgeable about a great many things, but of women you know very little," she told him evenly.

Tiy would hear about her, hear that Pharaoh had brought her to his rooms, and Shanda knew that the information would not please the Egyptian queen any more than Hattushil's women had been pleased at the entry of a foreign woman to his court and his bed.

Pharaoh noticed her worried expression. "You have no reason to fear Tiy, Shanda," he told her evenly.

But Shanda knew better. She knew just how dangerous a queen's jealousy could be. And despite Pharaoh's assertion, she knew Tiy would bear her ill will even though she herself had no love for her husband. The Egyptian queen, in this matter at least, would be no different from Hattushil's women. Shanda had a new enemy with whom she would some-day have to deal, and the prospect did not please her.

Pharaoh reached across the table, put his hand under her chin, and pushed her head up until her eyes met his.

He smiled. "Come, Princess," he said. "Tell me how you would spend our holiday. What of Egypt would you like to see?"

She returned his smile, pushing away the thought of Tiy, aware that she could do nothing at that moment to change matters.

"The sky, lord," she murmured, thinking of the way the stars had shone through the gauzy tent the night before and of the beautifully painted ceiling in his apartment, and feel-ing a blush begin to warm her cheeks. "I would like to see a bit more of the Egyptian sky."


"She *is* beautiful," Tiy said slowly. "I wonder how she gets her hair that impossible color."

"The ladies of the harem say it is natural," Nofret informed her dryly. "It seems those portions modesty prohibits baring are also golden."

His news did not please Tiy. She frowned at him, then pursed her lips. "I had no idea you were privy to harem gossip," she told him with a tartness that surprised her. She wondered why she cared.

He was unruffled by her show of ill humor.

"A good vizier hears everything that might be worth hear-ing," he told her, venturing a white-toothed grin.

He wondered why his news had so disturbed her. The

Hittite was, after all, nothing more than Pharaoh's new plaything. Surely he would tire of her quickly. And even if he did not, Tiy certainly had no reason to be distressed at losing something she had never desired to keep. But when the queen glowered at him, his smile disappeared.

Tiy stood and wandered aimlessly about the room. When she found herself beside a table set with a bowl of fruit, she seemed to waken. She stared at the contents of the bowl, then lifted a large bunch of grapes from it.

"Perhaps this Hittite princess should fall ill," she said thoughtfully as she plucked one of the grapes from its stem and put it in her mouth.

Nofret shrugged. "It could be done," he agreed. "But I see little value to the effort."

Tiy turned on her heel to face him once again. "Little value?" She seemed amazed that he did not see it immediately, as did she. "You are not the only one who listens to gossip. Pharaoh, it seems, has not once gone to his other women since he took the Hittite from the harem. And you yourself told me he has taken her to live with him. He has never done that before. This woman may prove dangerous."

"Dangerous?"

"You fool," Tiy said. "This Hittite is young and presumably not barren. If he were to give her a child . . . "

Nofret showed no concern. "He has given others of his women children," he replied. There was a slight note of disgust in his tone, as though he thought the indiscriminate spilling of so much seed a great act of folly.

"And shown no interest in either the children or their mothers, beyond providing what they require," Tiy finished his thought for him. "But this one is the first he's brought to live with him. It is said his father had but one woman to live with him, and she was Pharaoh's mother," she added thoughtfully.

Nofret's complacency was unshaken. "I think, my queen, it is time for me to offer you a bit of gossip to which you have not yet been privy."

She crossed the room to stand beside the chair where he sat. "And that is . . . ?"

"Pharaoh does not believe the lies she has told him. He has sent spies to verify or disprove her claim of drought and famine among the Hittites. And he has heavily reinforced the garrison at Shunem."

"Which means . . . ?" she asked.

"Which means that he does not trust her, that he suspects there is no drought, that he thinks Hattushil holds back the grain he owes in tribute to use for another purpose—to feed his army. In short, my queen, Pharaoh thinks Hattushil plans to invade Egypt. Should that happen, do you really think he will keep a Hittite as his favorite?" He grinned. "He loves Egypt more than he can ever love any woman. Far from stealing your crown, she will end without so much as her life."

Tiy smiled and bent toward him, offering him a grape and her lips.

He took neither, instead putting up his hand to push away hers.

"There is one last word I might offer you to ease your mind," he said, and this time his smile made his face look only sinister.

"Yes?"

"The spies have returned, my queen," he said as he put his hand on the back of her head. "There is no drought, no famine." He drew her face close to his. "You have nothing to fear from this Hittite princess."

Tiy smiled, pleased by his words, and dropped the grapes, unmindful, to the floor as she pressed herself against him.

# Ten

SHANDA WAS MOST pleased when Pharaoh took her with him on outings. Soon after she went to live with him he took her to the river to ride on his barge. He sat at her side in the shade of an awning, amused at the way she stared, spellbound, at the strange animals inhabiting the shore and the water. Intrigued, she pointed at the great monsters of the river: the hippopotami, which floated, all but submerged, then suddenly raised their enormous heads and sent up sprays of muddy water; the large lizardlike crocodiles with their spiny, armored backs and huge jaws, sunning themselves in the mud on the banks and occasionally opening their mouths to reveal rows of pointed, sharp teeth, then suddenly lurching into motion, snapping at an unwary bird or turtle that ventured too close. But most of all she enjoyed the less ferocious creatures that ventured to the riverbank to drink—the ibex and oxen and baboons, and especially the birds. He pointed out an ibis to her, the bird his people held sacred, and she watched curiously as the long-legged creature waded in the reeds at the side of the river, searching for insects to eat among the leaves in the shallow water.

Later, he hunted, killing an enormous crocodile with his spear while she watched, terrified that he would be hurt, and guiltily aware that he probably had chosen to hunt the beast for no more pressing reason than to show her he had the skill, strength, and courage to perform such a feat. Flushed with his victory, he took half a dozen waterfowl, shooting them with bow and arrow with an ease that belied the skill required.

Servants took the game to the shore, cleaned and cooked it, and then Shanda and Pharaoh ate their evening meal on the river, watching the night settle over the Nile. It seemed to her that she had never felt quite so much at peace with herself or quite so pleased with the world around her.

The lion hunt, the next day at dawn, however, was an entirely different matter. Pharaoh required her to stay well back, in a chariot surrounded by several guards to ensure her safety, and she watched the hunt from a dun-colored hillside overlooking a plain.

Soldiers served as beaters, surrounding and finally forcing the lion into the circle in the plain below where Pharaoh waited to confront it with sword and spear.

Despite her fear that Pharaoh might be hurt, it still seemed to Shanda a mean, bloody encounter, and she shuddered as the great beast, mortally wounded, dragged its bloodied body off to a rocky ledge to die. It was an old lion, and probably sick, doubtless the reason it had taken to prowling among the peasants' settlements by the river during the night to seek food. Although she knew the hunt was a necessity, that the animal had already killed two children, still she saw the lion's death as ignoble. Better for it to have found its end off in the wilderness, she thought, among its own kind, than to be surrounded and frightened by the soldiers so that Pharaoh could end its life.

That evening, as she washed the bloody scratches on Pharaoh's arms and shoulders, she realized that he felt the same disgust as she did at what he had done that day.

"A king's responsibility, Shanda, is to his people, even if the actions required of him differ from those he would otherwise have chosen," he told her. "Everything has a price, especially kingship and divinity."

His expression as he told her these things was set and determined. She realized then that he would sacrifice anything, even his life, to protect his people and his domain. She had no doubt that he would also sacrifice his love for her, however powerful it might be, if he felt it was necessary for the safety of his kingdom. She prayed that the need to do so would never arise.


"I have a surprise for you today, Shanda."

Pharaoh seemed pleased with this pronouncement, and Shanda found herself pleasantly perplexed at the prospect.

"What sort of a surprise, Lord?" she demanded.

But he only smiled and shook his head, as he helped her climb into his chariot. "You must wait until the moment is ripe."

"I fear you are cruel, lord," she accused, but willingly accepted the kiss he offered her, then put her hand on his shoulder, holding tight as he took up the reins and urged the horses into motion.

The chariot sped off, the powerful whites easily outdistancing the royal guards. As they left the city behind, Shanda realized that the scenery was familiar to her. He was heading toward the army training encampment where he had driven her the afternoon he took her from his harem, the afternoon she had faced the cobra in the desert.

This day, however, she had no feeling of trepidation as she rode behind him in his chariot, holding his strong shoulder, watching the manes of the great whites fly in the wind. This day she knew she had nothing to fear.

At first the review of his army seemed much as it had that first day, with the generals riding out to meet him and escort him forward. That first afternoon the men had all been strangers to her, but now Shanda recognized several of the generals. Most of them nodded to her pleasantly by way of greeting, but one in particular offered her an openly evaluating stare. Shanda recognized the young man. She had seen him sitting at the side of Queen Tiy the night of the banquet. He was Pharaoh's son, Prince Amenophis.

She saw the interest in the prince's eyes as he watched her, and she knew she had been right. Nofret had told the queen of Pharaoh's affection for her, and Queen Tiy had told her son. She sensed in the prince an antipathy that shocked her, even though she had assumed his mother would bear her no goodwill. She wished she could assure Amenophis that she represented no threat to his position or the queen's, that she had no desire to share Pharaoh's crown, and that she had no desire to have a prince and a queen as her enemies.

She watched curiously as Pharaoh greeted his son, noting that he treated this youngest of his generals with aloof tolerance and that the boy returned his greeting with diffident formality. She wondered if either of them mourned the loss of the love that might have flourished between them had the circumstances been different.

Pharaoh reviewed the ranks of the charioteers as he had on the previous occasion when he'd brought her to watch them, then he returned to her where she waited with Seti, the general of his guard.

"Now, Princess, your surprise," he told her as the charioteers formed into ranks.

Shanda stared, more than a little perplexed, and watched as the chariot drivers wound their reins around their waists.

"Why would they do that, lord?" she demanded.

He turned and smiled down at her. "They follow your example, Shanda," he told her with a wry grin.

"But I do it because I have not the strength in my arms to control the horses when they race, because I need the weight of my body as well. Those are strong men; surely they have no such need."

He put his hand on her waist. "Watch, Princess," he directed.

And she did. The chariot drivers started their horses on the race toward the row of targets, then dropped the reins from their hands altogether and leaned from side to side, using their bodies to guide the horses while they reached for their bows. When the chariots passed the row of targets in single file, both the drivers and the bowmen fired arrow after arrow at the marks.

"It was your example that gave me the idea, Princess," Pharaoh told her.

"You see, when they use their bodies to guide the horses, they leave their hands free to handle bow and arrow," Seti explained to her. "It doubles the power of each chariot, as now two men can fight from it rather than one." Seti smiled at her. "It gives our charioteers a great advantage."

Shanda turned back to watch the charioteers practice. Hattushil and his generals had seen her and Althea drive many times, but had never thought to use the women's example to their own advantage. Pharaoh's ingenuity impressed her enormously.

When they had viewed the exercises, Pharaoh spoke to the soldiers, congratulating the charioteers on their mastery. They accepted their king's praise with silent pride, then broke into loud cheers when he rejoined Shanda in his chariot and she drove him past their ranks for a final review before he left them.

"Their cheers are for you, Princess," Pharaoh told her. "You have given them a valuable advantage in war. They look on you now as a good luck charm."

Shanda felt him press close to her. She turned back to find he was smiling at her.

"I think they have good reason," he added as he reached past her, his arms surrounding her, and took the reins from her hands. "When I am beside you, I cannot but help feel the gods are smiling."

They left the army encampment behind, and Pharaoh drove to the river. There a boat waited for them, its crew dressed in the uniform of the royal guard.

"Where is it you take me now, lord?" Shanda asked him as he handed her into the felucca.

"For a view of eternity," he answered, then turned to direct the ship's captain, leaving her to ponder his words in silence.

The ride on the water was a short one, slightly upriver and to the far embankment, but it took a fair time, for the oarsmen had to fight against the Nile's flow as well as the breeze. When their craft finally reached its destination, Shanda saw they were expected. There were chariots and a group of Pharaoh's guard waiting for them.

Shanda looked around curiously as Pharaoh handed her into the chariot. There were no fields here edging the river; the countryside turned quickly to desert and ragged cliffs. It seemed to her a forbidding and inhospitable place. She was surprised to see a small village huddled at the desert's edge, and she wondered why anyone would choose to live in so bleak a village when there was far more fertile soil so near.

They rode off slowly, leaving the Nile behind them, moving into a series of rocky valleys sided by tall dun-colored cliffs. When Pharaoh pulled the horses to a halt, she looked up, surprised to see half a dozen men treading what appeared from below to be a treacherously narrow path up the side of a steep rise.

"What place is this, lord?" she asked him, surprised to hear her own voice so muted, so apparently awed. There was something about the place, she realized, that stifled any thought of levity.

Pharaoh stepped down onto the rocky ground, turning to offer her his hand.

"This is the place, Shanda, where Egypt's gods follow the path to eternity," he said as he lifted her from the chariot and set her down on the rock-strewn ground.

She heard in his voice the same reverence she felt as she stared at the tall cliff faces around them. He pointed up at an opening in the wall of rock at the end of the path the men had climbed.

"What is up there?" she asked, feeling her tongue grow thick in her mouth and her throat go suddenly dry. Even before he answered her, she already knew.

"That is my tomb, Princess," he told her.

She had expected this revelation the moment they'd entered the valley. Somehow she'd known what he intended to show her. There was a feeling around her, an aura of death and eternity, and it had hushed her voice and dampened her spirit.

"Come, Princess," he said as he took her arm and led her toward the path up the cliffside. "I will show you the work that is being done to prepare my tomb."

She made herself walk to the place where the path began its steep climb. But then she came to a sudden halt. She could not bear the thought of seeing his tomb, could not contemplate the possibility of his death.

"What is it, Shanda?" he asked when she made no move toward the path.

She shook her head. "I cannot, lord," she told him. "I beg you, do not ask me to step inside your tomb."

He stepped down to her side and stood for a moment mutely considering the terror in her expression.

"There is nothing to fear, Princess," he told her gently. "It is only the place where I will someday begin the long walk to the afterlife." He pointed to where the men had disappeared into the dark hole in the rock. "Even now the artisans decorate the walls with pictures and prayers to the gods."

She told herself she was behaving like a fool, but she could not make her feet move forward, could not shake off the sense of doom she felt at the prospect of climbing to that particular cave. She closed her eyes and in her mind saw Pharaoh's body, dead and cold, lying surrounded by all those dun-colored cliffs. She was filled with fear and heavy with her own guilt.

She shivered and shook her head. "I cannot go there, lord," she said numbly.

Shanda felt cold, even though the sun beat hot against the masses of rock around them.

He was silent for a moment, then reached out to her.

"I will not force you," he said as he wrapped his arms around her shoulders and held her close.

She felt the warmth of him and found it comforting to know he was there beside her, to feel the life that still pulsed, strong and vital, in his body.

They stood as they were for a long moment, until the specter of his death passed from her. When she finally looked up at his face, she found him considering the cliff face a bit farther along the valley.

"I will show you something else, Princess," he said evenly. Then he turned his eyes to her, and there was a smiling challenge in them. "That is, if you can manage a small climb?"

She accepted the challenge with pleasure, glad that he no longer wanted her to go to his tomb.

"You forget, lord, I am not one of your idle Egyptian ladies. I can drive your chariot, and I can follow any path you care to set for me."

He laughed. "We shall see, Shanda," he told her. Then he turned and began to walk along the cliff side. "Come."

She ran after him, realizing that he was moving quickly to test her resolve. She was determined to keep up with him at any cost.

The climb was easy at first. The path he followed was not too steep, but it was narrow and she had to stay close to the rock face lest she fall. But as they moved upward, the incline grew sharper, and she willingly accepted the hand he offered her to steady her. When she looked down, she saw that one misstep would prove fatal, but she was not really afraid of falling. As long as Pharaoh was beside her he would keep her steady and safe.

He stopped on a small ledge to let her rest, and Shanda turned her glance upward and realized they were almost to the top. But the path hewn into the rock face ended at the ledge on which they stood. Save for a smooth, narrow fissure in the stone, the remainder of rise, the last eight or so feet, seemed totally featureless, almost as though it had been polished. She could see no hand- or footholds in the smooth stone.

Pharaoh, too, turned his eyes to the last of the climb, but there was no bewilderment in his expression. He moved to the far side of the ledge, and eased his body sideways into the fissure. Shanda could not understand how he intended to climb here, for, like the rock that overlooked the valley below, the sides of the fissure were smooth and unmarred.

He smiled at her. "Now the interesting part," he said. He began slowly to inch his way upward, his back against one side of the rock fissure, his feet pushing against the other. The fissure grew wider as he rose until, as he neared the top of the rock face, his legs were extended almost straight out. When he had covered the last few feet, he grasped the lip of the rock with his hands and pulled himself upward.

The prospect of following his lead was not at all appealing to her. Even if she managed to inch her way up as he had, she doubted her legs were long enough to keep her steady when she neared the wider part at the top. She wished she had held her tongue instead of boasting that she could follow any path he set for her. Perhaps she really was no better than the idle women she had scorned.

He seemed charitably uninterested in chiding her for her boast. He lay on the rock above and stared down at her.

"You need only climb into the crease, Shanda," he called down to her. "I will pull you up."

She did as he directed, climbing into the fissure in the rock and reaching her hands up to him. He lay above her, and caught her hands. For a moment she dangled suspended, staring down at the valley below, gripped by the sudden terror of falling. Then he pulled her up beside him.

She sat, panting as the fear subsided, and stared out at the valley and the river. The view was breathtaking, the valley and the sand beyond a deeply burnished gold in the waning afternoon sunshine, the Nile in the far distance a slender winding snake of intense green-blue with a bright green fringe along its sides. And above it all hung a sky of pure, unblemished blue.

He was standing beside her, as taken with the scenery as she was. But his thoughts were not on the wonders around them.

"Why do you fear to enter my tomb, Shanda?" he asked her, turning to look down at her.

She shrugged and turned her eyes back to the fields on the far side of the Nile. "I do not know, lord," she whispered.

"Does death frighten you so much?"

He'd knelt down close beside her, put his hand on her chin, and turned her face to him. She saw pity in his eyes, and compassion. She knew that she could not evade his question, no matter how much she hated the thought of speaking of a subject that, since the day she'd faced the cobra, had come to hold more terror for her than any other.

"How could it not, lord?" she replied, her voice low and filled with uncertainty. "To step off into blackness, to close one's eyes knowing that they will never open again. How could that not make one fear?"

"Our priests tell us that death is only the doorway into another life, Shanda. If our lives in this world are worthy and if, when Osiris weighs our hearts he finds them not heavy with sin, we are granted another life, a life the gods make for us. Do the Hittites have no gods? Is there no other world to which you will go?"

She turned away from the pity she saw in his eyes.

"Yes, the Hittites have their gods, and my mother had gods as well," she said bitterly. "But her gods could not protect her from the poison one of Hattushil's wives gave her. And the prayers I offered, to her gods and to the Hittite gods, neither brought her back to life nor carried away the one who killed her. I have no more prayers for gods, nor can I believe in them."

She felt a hard ball of bitterness inside herself. She wished it were otherwise, for a part of her wanted to believe as he did.

"Perhaps if you could accept my gods, Princess, you might lose your fear."

She smiled at him sadly, knowing it could not be so easy.

"I need but one Egyptian god, lord," she said even as she wrapped her arms around his shoulders.

It was true, she realized. Despite her dismissal of the notion that he was divine, she was not afraid when she was near him, when she could reach out and touch him. For as long as she kept his love, she was safe. And if she ever lost it, her life would mean nothing to her, and she would be better off without the burden of it.

He returned her smile and pressed his lips to hers.

"It has been a long climb, lord," she said, her expression mischievous, as she lay back and pulled him down with her.

They made love there on the mountaintop overlooking the valley that held the tombs of his ancestors, the kings and gods of his people. Shanda at first regarded it as an act of defiance, an affirmation of life over death, even a death that purported to be nothing more than a doorway into a new life. But when she gazed up and saw his head and shoulders framed by the golden orb of the setting sun, she thought only that he seemed to her at that very moment very much a living god, a god who ruled her heart.

It would be a cruel fate if he proved to be an inconstant god, if he turned his back on her.


The valley was growing dark by the time they neared the end of their descent. With her back pressed to the rock face and her hand firmly grasped in Pharaoh's, Shanda made her way down toward the valley floor.

Then the valley seemed suddenly to plunge into blackness as the sun set below the rim of the mountain behind them. There was but one source of light, a tiny flicker in the absolute darkness, and Shanda kept her eyes on it, gauging her descent by the way it seemed to grow ever so slightly with each step she took.

When they finally reached the valley floor she could see that the tiny light was actually a substantial fire. Several of the royal guard stood near it, warming themselves against the chill of the night air.

Before they reached the soldiers, however, there was a noise among the rocks a few feet from the path, and a tiny glint of light. Pharaoh pushed Shanda aside, and crouched, knife in hand; Shanda saw the glint of the blade.

"Who is there?" he whispered, his voice low, hard, and sharp in the night silence.

The noise grew to a loud scrambling among the rocks.

"Mercy, lord. It is I, Hesirat, leader of the artisans who labor in your tomb."

The workman scrambled closer and lifted a small lamp so that it illuminated his face. In the darkness, the flickering light made his features look grotesque.

Pharaoh straightened and his stance relaxed. "Yes, Hesirat. You may approach."

When the artisan neared them, Shanda realized she had seen him before. He was the commoner who had been brought before Pharaoh the day of her first audience, the one who had stood witness against a lord in defense of his fellow workmen. She assumed the lord had been found guilty of having stolen from the workmen placed beneath him, after all, for Hesirat had remained. She was glad she had taken the artisans' side.

Hesirat bowed very low. "We were told that you would come to see the progress of the work, lord," he said. "The painters and the carvers still await you in the tomb."

Shanda felt a twinge of conscience, realizing that by keeping Pharaoh from his tomb, she had been the cause of disappointment to so many men.

Pharaoh, too, obviously regretted his missed tour, for he nodded gravely to the man.

"I will come as soon as I have taken the princess to stay with the guards." He pointed to the fire at the far side of the valley, then motioned for Shanda to come forward and stand beside him.

Hesirat's face lifted at the promise of the visit, then fell when he realized it would take a good while for Pharaoh to travel to the fire and back. He smiled at Shanda tentatively as he remembered that it had been her advice Pharaoh had asked during the trial.

She considered his hopeful stare for a moment, then realized her fears were no longer quite so strong and her curiosity had grown. She turned to Pharaoh.

"Perhaps you would permit me to accompany you, lord," she said.

He gave her a questioning look. "You no longer fear the tomb, Shanda?" he asked softly.

She shook her head. "I have a god to protect me," she replied.

He seemed pleased with her response, for he smiled down at her, then turned to Hesirat. "We will go now," he said.

Hesirat nodded, smiling happily, then scrambled up the rock-strewn path to the place where he had been waiting and found the torch he'd left there on the ground. This he lit from the small clay lamp he held, watching as the tar-soaked reeds sprang into a sharp flame. He held the torch aloft to light their way.

This climb was easier than their first. The path along the rock face was wider, and much cleaner, smoothed by the feet of the laborers who traveled over it each day. As she walked, Shanda tried desperately not to think of the fact that she was being led to a tomb.

Once they'd reached the opening, Shanda was surprised to find the interior of the tomb filled with light. Torches and clay lamps had been lit to illuminate the work and allow Pharaoh to examine it.

Shanda was stunned by the brilliance of what she saw. The first room in the tomb, a large square chamber, had been carved from the living rock. Its walls were alive with pictures of Pharaoh, hunting lions and crocodiles, fowling, waging battle, receiving tribute from his subjects. All the art was beautifully wrought, finely detailed and vibrantly colored. Beneath the pictures were detailed accounts of his life, the writing far more beautifully drawn, certainly, than the scribblings Shanda made in her lessons with Sesostris.

Pharaoh made a careful inspection, then turned to Hesirat. "This room is nearly completed?"

Hesirat nodded. "Yes, lord. The drawings in that corner"—he pointed to a blocked out but as yet unpainted depiction of Pharaoh spearing fish from his barge—"are going a bit slowly. My son, Hesire, has been given that piece, and although his work is adequate, he is a bit slower than the more experienced draftsmen."

Pharaoh crossed the room to the scene in question, nodding brusquely to the boy who knelt beside it. The boy seemed to have trouble keeping his head bowed as Pharaoh considered his work. Shanda could almost feel his fear, and she pitied him.

When Pharaoh finished his inspection, he turned to Hesirat. "Your son's work is well wrought," he said. "And if the gods will it, he has still many years to complete it."

Hesirat glowed with the praise of his son, and the boy finally looked up, relief bringing a wide, boyish grin to his face. Shanda watched Pharaoh's reaction to the boy and his father, the mutual pride and joy the praise had elicited. There was, she thought, almost a hint of envy in Pharaoh's glance, a longing for the sort of closeness this laborer and his son enjoyed. It struck her that Pharaoh, like any other man, yearned for a son to love.

He nodded to her to follow as he walked through the remaining rooms of the tomb. There were several small storerooms that would one day hold his personal belongings as well as food, grain, wine, and oil—all he would need on his journey to the afterlife.

There were also temples where pictures of the gods covered the walls. Hathor with her cow's head; Anubis, the jackal god waiting to guide Pharaoh's *kah* to judgment; Maat, weighing truth with her feather; Isis together with her husband and brother Osiris, fertility crowned by the sun beside the great lord of the underworld—all held places of honor. The drawings and prayers on the walls of these rooms were just roughly sketched; the painting had not yet begun. Pharaoh and Hesirat discussed the progress of the decoration and the continuing work of carving more rooms from the rock.

Finally Shanda followed them into a small room that was already fully decorated with pictures of all the gods and prayers to them. Pharaoh pointed to a stone platform in the center of the chamber.

As Shanda stood in that chamber a cold cloud settled over her, a feeling of being enfolded by death. Unlike the fear she'd felt earlier that day when she contemplated Pharaoh's death, this was a bitter certainty, the sure knowledge that death was inescapable. For the first time in her life Shanda considered the futility of her own existence.

"This is where I will lie," he told her softly. Then he took her hand and led her out of the room.

She stood near him as he talked to the artisans, but she no longer heard the words that were spoken. Her mind was filled with the image of the room where his body would one day lie, and in her imagination she saw his coffin lying in the darkness surrounded by the images of his gods, waiting for his resurrection and the start of his afterlife, a life in which he would know only happiness.

She forced herself to remember the look she'd seen on his face at the sight of Hesirat's pride in and love for his son. That happiness, she told herself, was one he deserved in this lifetime, one for which he should not be forced to wait any longer. That, she told herself, was a gift she could give him. A gift of life.

She shivered as he led her back out into the night air. A gift of life, she thought, might remove the cloud of death that still clung to her.

Tiy stalked around the room, looking very much as she felt, like a caged animal. When she reached the far side of the room, she turned back to face Nofret, who lay naked on her bed.

"You said he would be done with her once he knew," she said angrily. "But still he keeps her with him. And now you tell me he took her to see his tomb."

Nofret arched a brow. He had been wise, he decided, to keep his news to himself until the visit to her bed was satisfactorily concluded.

"He has even given word to the women of his harem that they are to prepare themselves to leave," he told her, aware that this information would not please her but not sure at that moment that he cared. He swung his legs over the side of the bed and looked on the floor for the clothing he had cast off an hour earlier.

"Leave?" she demanded. "To go where?"

He lifted his robe. "They are to be returned to their families," he told her as he pushed a long, thin arm through a sleeve. "They will be rewarded for their services, of course, but it seems he has lost his interest in them and has no further need to keep them near."

"The Hittite bitch!" Tiy shrieked.

Nofret turned to stare at her curiously. He had never seen the queen quite so angry before, never seen her lose her control so completely.

Tiy noticed his stare and carefully gathered her shattered wits. Uncontrolled anger, she knew, would not help her.

"It is time she fell ill, Nofret," she said sharply. "A long and lingering illness, I think. One that inevitably leads to death. There are poisons . . . "

He shook his head as he put on his ornately tooled leather sandals.

"There will be no need of that," he told her with the same disinterest with which he might have discussed the weather. "I have received word from my spies that will push him to do what you want of his own will."

"Your spies brought word of Hattushil's lies," she returned sharply, "and still the bitch sleeps peacefully in his bed."

Nofret smiled.

"I assure you, my queen, the Hittite will not sleep peacefully for long." He offered her his death's-head grin.

She turned away, displeased by his ugliness. There was much about Nofret she admired, she told herself, but once he was no longer useful she would rid herself of him, and choose as her companions men who were more pleasing to the eye. But when she turned back to face him, she found him considering her with a knowing stare. She wondered, not for the first time, if he had the ability to read her thoughts. The possibility was unsettling.

"And why not?" she asked.

"Because Hattushil's army has begun to move south. It can only be a matter of time now."

Her displeasure—indeed all thought of his lack of physical appeal—disappeared. She smiled at him with genuine pleasure.

"Indeed," she agreed thoughtfully, "it is only a matter of time until he kills the bitch with his own hand."

The prospect pleased her.

# *Eleven*

"YOU ARE SURE, Princess?"

"Yes. I have counted very carefully. I am sure."

Med considered her words thoughtfully before he replied.

"When will you tell him?" he asked.

Shanda finished twining the string of faience and gold beads around a thick rope of her blond hair. She had seen beads of this sort woven into the narrow braids of the Egyptian women's dark hair. She liked taking bits of their fashions and adapting them to her own distinctive style. Shanda considered her reflection in the shiny slab of silver; then, reasonably pleased, she turned to face Med.

"I intended to tell him this morning. He said we would go to the river," she replied, her words tinged with a hint of regret. "But then Nofret came and spoke to him and he went off." She was disappointed that the outing had been canceled.

She stared up at Med, well aware that the boy knew all about Nofret's visit and Pharaoh's sudden departure. She did not quite understand her nervousness, the need to talk. Nor did she understand the unsettled feeling she'd had since

Nofret's visit. It was like the tension that filled the air just before a storm. But she had left storms behind her in Hattushil's court. In Egypt, there were no storms, no clouds lying heavy and ominous overhead. In Egypt there was no rain, only fair weather and clear skies.

Med wrinkled his nose in distaste at the mention of Nofret's name. He, too, seemed to have an instinctive dislike for the vizier with his sunken-eyed stare, his look of death.

She put her hand on her belly, wondering how long it would be before she felt the first movements inside her. She'd seen enough of women carrying babies to know what to expect, but she had no idea how it would feel, and consideration of the possibilities had taken up a good portion of her time over the previous days. But today even consideration of this fascinating matter did not chase away the unpleasant cloud that had settled around her.

Med spoke, trying to cheer her up. "Whatever ill news the vizier brought him, Princess, I am sure your news will please him well enough to make him forget."

She stood and walked to the doorway, then stared out at the garden. It was fragrant and cool and pleasing to the eye. She wondered why it did not ease the trepidation she felt, why today she took no joy in its beauty.

"So you think he will be pleased, Med?" she asked the boy, wanting very much to hear his assurances, to be told that her fears and trepidation were nothing more than symptoms of her condition.

But she could not deny that Pharaoh's sudden departure had seemed an ill omen to her. Any matter broached on a day begun so badly would proceed grievously, she thought. What if the news that she would bear him a child did not please Pharaoh? Ever since the day she visited his tomb, she'd been sure he yearned for a son. And yet she had never spoken of it with him, and he'd never broached the subject. Perhaps, she had been wrong.

"Of course he will be pleased, Princess," Med told her firmly, aware of the worried expression on her face and determined to rid her of it. "*Her* son brings him no joy; you've said so yourself."

Shanda *had* spoken against the queen to Med, something she ought never to have done, and Med's antipathy was only a mirror of her own. But there had been mornings when she had not felt well, times when she desperately needed to talk to someone, and there had been no one else to whom she could speak the words.

She turned to face the boy. "You must never refer to Queen Tiy in that way again, Med," she told him sharply. "Nor of Prince Amenophis."

He looked away, stung by her sudden and unexpected criticism.

"No, Princess."

"It is for your own safety," she explained as she saw his dejection. "And should I ever again refer to either of them in a less than reverent manner, even between the two of us, you must remind me of my folly."

Her voice trailed off and she turned to stare once more at the garden.

Med went to her. "Princess," he ventured, putting his hand on her arm.

She turned to him and smiled wanly. "Our safety, as well as the life of this one," she said, putting her hand on her belly, "can rest on a word, Med. Believe me, I know."

"But surely Pharaoh . . . " he began.

She raised a hand to stop his words. "As powerful as he is, Med, there are some things that even he cannot prevent. The queen has power of her own." She put a hand on his shoulder, surprised at how tall he'd grown in the past few months. "Enough of this. We have more important matters to discuss. I will tell him this evening. Ask Usha to serve Pharaoh's favorite wine with dinner. And we must choose the appropriate gown for me to wear."

"Where is she?"

Usha looked up, surprised at Pharaoh's expression, at the sound of thunder in his voice. He had known his master to be angry in the past, but he had never seen such a storm in his eyes. So much wrath poured from him now that it seemed to taint the very air around him.

"She is in the garden, lord." Usha bowed low and backed away, wishing only to remove himself from the path of that bristling wall of anger. As Pharaoh swept past him, he felt relieved that he was not the target of his master's rage.

Shanda was startled by the sharp tap of Pharaoh's sandals against the stone walk. She had never before heard him move with such sharply directed steps when he approached her.

She looked up from the basket of flowers she was arranging and ventured a smile. "My lord," she murmured. Then, when she saw his expression, "Is something wrong?"

Shanda was bewildered. She immediately recognized the anger in him when she saw the way his jaw hardened as he stared at her, the way he fought with himself to maintain his control.

"Perhaps *you* could tell *me* what is wrong, Princess," he hissed at her through clenched teeth.

She took one step toward him, then stopped, not daring to go farther. "I don't understand, lord," she said. Her voice was shaking. She heard her own fear in it and knew he must hear it, too.

"Then let me explain, Princess," he said, his voice dripping bitterness now. "Let me tell you how your father sent you to me, pleading famine in his land, knowing there was no famine, knowing he intended to save for his soldiers the grain he owed me as tribute. Soldiers, after all, need to be fed well if they are to fight a war."

She was bewildered by her own lack of surprise at what he had told her. So this was what Hattushil and Nem had intended all along! His words faded and she heard the beating of her own heart in her ears. She felt weak, felt her legs tremble. She feared she might collapse.

"There is to be a war?"

His face grew dark as he moved toward her. "Tell me you knew nothing of his intention to invade my land, Princess," he hissed at her. "Tell me you knew nothing of the army he has sent across my border."

"I—I knew nothing . . . " she began, but her words faded into silence.

She found she couldn't say more, couldn't plead innocent. For she had known. Hattushil had not told her, but deep inside she had known. She had always known.

He stood, glaring at her. Where she looked for love, she found nothing but hatred in his eyes. She felt herself trembling, suddenly afraid.

She put her hand on her belly, thinking of the child inside her, wondering what would happen to this baby she had conceived with such joy.

"I love you," she whispered.

"Love?" he roared back at her. "I want none of your love, Princess. You mix it too easily with lies and deceit. Your love is a cancer inside me. I would sooner embrace my own death than your love."

She saw pain in his eyes then, and she knew the hurt he felt was as great as her own. She was a traitor to him. He had given her a part of himself that he had always before kept safe, only to find it ill used and destroyed. Better for both of them if she had never come to love him.

"What will you do?" she asked him, her words as dull and lifeless as she herself suddenly felt.

"What do you think I will do, Princess?" he demanded. "Do you think I will lie here languishing in your arms while your father brings his armies to my palace gates? Do you think I am so blinded by love that I cannot see how you've betrayed me?"

He turned away, unable to face her any longer, telling himself he never wanted to look at her again. Then he saw her eunuch standing at the far end of the garden path, trembling.

"You, boy," he shouted, glad to have someone else on whom to focus his attention.

Med crept closer and bowed deeply.

"Pack your lady's belongings," Pharaoh commanded. "She will come with me and my army. I want her to see battle, to smell blood, to know that she was the cause of death and misery."

He stalked away without turning back to glance at Shanda, pushing past Med as though he were an insect on the path beneath his feet.

She stared dully after him, hoping this was a horrible dream from which she would soon awaken. But when she looked down, there were the flowers, still in her hand; she could feel them, just as she could feel the warmth of the sun on her back. It was real, she told herself, with a dull finality. She should have known at the start that it would someday come to this. She ought to have steeled herself for the pain.

She looked up finally to find Med standing in front of her.

"What shall we do, Princess?" he asked, his voice, like his face, filled with fear and uncertainty.

She carefully set down the flowers, realizing that there would be no quiet dinner for her and Pharaoh, no pleasant evening surrounded by the scent of the blooms, no perfect moment to tell him about the child inside her. She ought to ache, she thought, to be consumed by pain. Instead, she felt numb, as though she had been washed clean of the ability to feel anything ever again.

She stepped past Med into the beautifully painted room with the images of the river on the walls and floor, staring at the pictures as if seeing them for the first time. She stood for a moment and admired the mischievous faces of the monkeys. Then she turned back to face Med.

"We will do as he bids us, Med," she said finally, her voice dull and flat, almost as if she had said these words a hundred times before, as if she had rehearsed them in her mind. "We must ready ourselves to follow Pharaoh to war."

It was still dark when she felt Med's hand on her shoulder.

"I'm not asleep, Med," she told him as she sat up. There had been no sleep, no freedom for her from the thoughts that filled her mind and tortured her. "Is it time?"

Med nodded. "Yes, Princess. The guards have come."

"Tell them I will be only a few moments," she told him.

He nodded, and she watched him as he moved, obviously reluctant, to the door. She could see the fear in Med's eyes; she knew that she, too, should be terrified, and yet she felt no terror, only the numbness that still filled her.

She rose quickly, washed with the bowl of water he had set beside her bed, then hastily donned the clothing that lay ready for her. For a few moments the illness in her stomach seemed determined to gain control of her, but she fought it, refusing to let it detain her. She would not be thought a coward, hiding away, without the courage to face her fate.

She looked around one last time, then followed Med to the door, passing Usha, nodding to him. Before he turned away from her, she saw the look of accusation in his eyes, and knew that he thought as ill of her as his master did, but she did not condemn either of them.

Med was waiting for her by the door. Half a dozen of Pharaoh's guards stood behind him in the corridor, their manner uncertain. They were no longer sure how much deference they owed her.

She pointed to the small casket Med held in his arms.

"What is that?" she asked.

The chest containing her clothing had been taken the night before. Nothing of hers remained in Pharaoh's rooms to remind him when he returned that she had once lived here with him and shared his bed. The place had been swept clean of all evidence of her presence. Nothing remained of her to defile his sanctuary.

"Your jewels, Princess," Med told her.

She shook her head. "Open it," she told him. When he opened the casket, she quickly rifled through it, found the gold cuff that had belonged to Althea, and put it on her wrist. "I will take only what I brought with me," she said evenly. "This is mine. The rest belongs to Pharaoh. Leave it here."

He seemed reluctant to part with the chest, as though the jewels were a mark of Pharaoh's favor and by leaving them behind he could no longer deny the withdrawal of that favor. But he did as she directed him, setting the casket on a table, then moving to her side as she turned to face the guards.

"I am ready," she said, then stood still while they encircled her.

When they began to move, she kept step with them, but she was hardly aware of their presence. She knew only that she would never return.

She had not expected the walk to be so long, had not thought she would be marched all the way to the river. But as the morning wore on and the sun climbed into the sky, she realized that a traitor did not warrant the luxury of a chariot to bear her to her destination, and she told herself that she deserved no better.

She was hot and covered with dust by the time they reached the river. She looked about curiously, surprised at the number of barges tied there, and the endless ranks of soldiers who filed onto them. Egypt and Pharaoh, she suddenly realized, were well prepared for war. She was surprised at the satisfaction she felt when she realized that Hattushil would not find the easy victory he had expected.

The guards conducted her directly to one of the barges. They had obviously been given strict orders. They stood aside as Med helped her aboard, then directed her to a canvas tent in the center of the open barge.

The midmorning sun was hot. When Med drew back the tent flap and Shanda stepped into the small shelter, she was enveloped by a wave of heavy, still air. She had to force herself to move into it, knowing that by late day the tent would be an oven.

She looked out through the open tent flap and saw Pharaoh, standing on the riverbank, his eyes on her. Even from this distance, she saw his jaw grow hard as he stared at her, and she could almost feel the anger pouring out at her. It would have been far easier for her, she thought, if she had been spared the sight of him, the confirmation of his hatred.

She lowered her head and stepped farther into the tent. It was devoid of the luxuries she had enjoyed on Pharaoh's barge. There were no comfortable divans, no heaps of soft pillows on which to recline. Only a hard chair, a pitcher of water, and a bowl had been left for her. She had once traveled on the Nile as Pharaoh's pampered favorite; now she was his prisoner.

She settled herself in the chair and felt the heat and heaviness of the air beat down on her, weighting her, making her light cotton robe stick to her damp skin like a burden she was condemned to bear.

"You cannot stay here, Princess," Med told her. "This air will make you ill."

She shook her head, even though waves of nausea had already begun to wash over her. "I am fine, Med," she told him firmly, "and far more comfortable than the soldiers." She waved her arm toward the deck outside where the soldiers were seated on the planks, one close upon the next with barely room to move their legs. "You will stay outside." She motioned for him to leave, since there was no reason for him to endure the heat and confinement with her.

He began to protest, but she stopped his words with a movement of her hand. "I will call you if I need you," she told him sharply. "Now go outside."

She managed to control the sick feeling in her stomach until he left her. Then she emptied her stomach into the bowl. She held herself still until the movement inside her quieted a bit. But the air inside the enclosure, already hot and heavy, became quickly fouled by the odor of her vomit. Her stomach began to heave again, but as there was nothing in it, she could find no release from the discomfort.

By the time she felt the barge begin to move and heard the muffled movement outside, she was too ill to care that she was leaving Thebes.

The barge was tied up at the river's edge for the night. Med had come to the tent, wrinkled his nose with distaste at the foul air, then wordlessly borne away the bowl and ewer and returned with fresh water and bread and cheese. But she was still too ill to eat, and she just lay weakly on a blanket he spread out on the deck for her bed.

"The first of the soldiers have reached the mouth of the river and started the march to the border," he told her.

"Have you spent your day spying on the soldiers?" she asked.

He shook his head. "Not spying. Just listening," he replied. "They all talk. There is little else for them to do but gamble among themselves and talk."

"And Hattushil's army?" she asked. "Do they talk of that, too?"

"They were stopped at the border by the troops there," he told her. "Pharaoh had them sent there soon after the harvest."

Shanda closed her eyes. She had come to Thebes just after the harvest time. If Pharaoh had sent troops to the border then, it was because he had doubted her loyalty from the very start. So her fate had been sealed from the day Hattushil had demanded that she give him her word, from the moment he had decided to send her to Pharaoh in place of the tribute.

"The Hittites have made camp at the border, and are undoubtedly planning their attack," Med continued. "They can go no farther unless they defeat the garrison at Shunem or are willing to attempt the long march around the mountains and through the desert."

"But surely they realize that Pharaoh will not wait calmly for them to enter Thebes. They must know he is bringing his armies to face them?" she insisted.

Med shrugged. "Perhaps they do not know his armies are so great, Princess, or they may think he is unprepared for war. They might hope to seize the garrison at Shunem and then move into the heart of Egypt before more troops can be readied to face them. The soldiers laugh and say they hope the Hittites will not flee before they have had a chance to draw blood." He added quietly, "I am sorry, Princess."

"You have no need to be, Med," she told him. "Hattushil made his own fate. Pharaoh only brings it to him." She stared up at him, wondering if Med, too, had come to think of her as the enemy. "I will sleep now," she said. "Thank you for bringing food and water."

"But you've eaten nothing, Princess," he protested.

"I have no hunger, Med."

The thought of food, despite the grumbling in her stomach, was unbearable. And the prospect of the morning, with the barge's return to the river and the resultant motion, only intensified her resolve not to eat.

"But your baby . . . "

"Better for it that it had never been conceived," she told him bitterly.

He considered her words in silence for a long moment. "Then you will not tell Pharaoh?" he asked finally, realizing that she would not, and that her decision ended the last hope for her reprieve.

"No. I will not use his baby to force him to grant me mercy. Whatever my punishment, this baby will share it with me."

She spoke with a bitter certainty, knowing what kind of life the child would have, surrounded, as she had been, by hatred and envy. She, at least, had had Althea to comfort her. There would be no mother's loving arms for this child, if Pharaoh let her live long enough to bear it.


The next day brought them to the beginning of the great fertile plain at the mouth of the Nile. Med knew that beyond the delta was the Great Green, the sea that seemed never to end, and beyond the sea lay the land about which Shanda had told him stories, the stories Althea had once told her. But he was not to see the Great Green, and he would catch only a brief glimpse of the fecund river delta.

Instead, he stood on the deck of the barge as Pharaoh's great army streamed ashore, legions of ferocious black Nubians and seemingly endless ranks of tough, lean-muscled Egyptians. The soldiers loaded their weapons and supplies

onto carts and, once their companies were assembled, began
to move off to the east, row upon row of them, a long, moving
river of men.

Finally Seti, the general of Pharaoh's guard, came aboard
the barge with orders that Shanda be conveyed to one of the
covered carts. Relieved that she was at last to be released
from the stifling tent, Med hurried to her.

Seti stood by the rail and waited for her to emerge. He wondered why Pharaoh had sent him to perform this unimportant
task when there was much significant work for him to do
before his troops began the march north with Pharaoh and the
generals. Perhaps Pharaoh expected him to bring word of the
princess's condition when he returned to the royal entourage.

His own feelings regarding Shanda were sharply divided.
He admired her both for her beauty and for the horsemanship
she had displayed at the army encampment. He allowed himself the luxury of a smile as he admitted that his admiration
owed more to her golden hair and finely chiseled features
than to her skill, however great, with Pharaoh's great white
horses. But he, too, had heard that she was part of the
Hittite invasion, and this made him feel suspicious and hos-
tile toward her. No wonder, he mused, that Pharaoh seemed a
bit mad when he spoke of her. This was a madness sent by the
gods to torment men, he told himself. Seti, too, had felt it.

When Shanda appeared, though, Seti was unprepared for
what he saw. Gone was the healthy glow that had always
emanated from her. She leaned on her servant's arm as
though she lacked the strength to hold herself erect. It seemed
to him that she had grown decidedly thinner, and her skin was
far paler than he remembered.

He was thankful that she made no effort to greet him,
beyond a smile and a nod, for he did not want to be tempted to
express his sympathy for her. When she thanked him for his
arm as he handed her ashore, however, his resolve began to

crumble. He became aware of an unexpected weakness in the grasp of her hand on his arm when he caught her as she nearly stumbled, and despite his instructions, he could not suppress the compassion that welled up in him.

As they walked to the waiting cart, he found himself darting quick glances at her face, certain now that she was not well.

"I am under orders not to speak to your lady," he said to Med. "But I have had no orders with regard to you, boy." He turned his eyes then to Shanda. "Your lady," he went on softly, "does not fare well?"

Med's expression grew suddenly animated. "She has been ill," he said, ready to begin a catalog of the agony she had endured, to blurt out that she was with child and that the heat and motion were unbearably oppressive to her.

Shanda pressed her fingers into Med's arm sharply. She had no need of anyone's pity, nor did she deserve it. And she had done enough harm. Seti had shown her only kindness. There was no need for him to bring Pharaoh's anger on himself out of concern for her.

Med's words were choked off abruptly, and he offered her a startled look, then dropped his eyes. "The trip on the water did not agree with her," Med finished sheepishly.

Seti nodded and turned his eyes back to the boy. "If she needs anything," he said, "bring your request to me. To me, personally. Do you understand, boy?"

Med nodded. "Yes, lord," he murmured. Then he helped Shanda into the cart and climbed up after her.

Seti stood watching as the cart lurched into motion. It seemed odd to him that Shanda would have become so ill from the ride on the barge. He'd seen her travel on the river with Pharaoh several times, and never had she shown any indication of distress from the motion. But then he shrugged and turned to find his horse among the confusion on the riverbank. He had a war to think about, and women were strange and changeable creatures at best. If there was anything seriously wrong with her, the boy would bring word. For the time being, he had important matters to which he need attend.

# Twelve

TO SHANDA, THE march to the border garrison at Shunem seemed endless. The cart in which she rode lurched and bumped its way along rutted, uneven paths, leaving her each night more tired and pained than she would have been if she had been allowed to walk. But Pharaoh, it seemed, had decided that the sight of her would somehow taint his troops, and he apparently wished to be spared the necessity of seeing her himself. She was confined inside the covered bed of the cart just as she had been shut in the tent on the barge.

She made no complaint about her treatment, however, and allowed Med to make none on her behalf. Although she longed for a few hours' exercise, she felt she had no right to request it. Each time she grew discontented with her situation, she reminded herself that although she'd had no sure knowledge of Hattushil's plan to invade Egypt, she had been a party to his deceit nonetheless. She was as guilty in her own eyes as in Pharaoh's.

And the wagon trip, although tedious, was far easier on her than the barge ride had been. Once the long stretch of desert had been traversed, the army proceeded into the mountainous regions along the coast of the Great Green. Here the winds blew heavy with the scent of water. As Pharaoh's army moved into the cooler air of the mountains, Shanda was finally able to cope with the nausea. And the boredom combined with constant jostling left her so exhausted by evening that she found respite each night in deep slumber.

As the army approached Shunem, the soldiers became more and more excited, for they were hungry for a taste of battle. Each evening when he brought her food, Med told Shanda the latest gossip and gave her an enthusiastic if florid description of the scenery.

Through Med she learned that the garrison at Shunem was housed in a fort on a narrow plain between two mountainous ridges—a strategically perfect position from which to hold an invader at bay. She was relieved to hear that Hattushil was unsuccessful in his attempts to take the fort. Aware that Pharaoh and his army approached, Hattushil had waited with his army at the mouth of the plain, certain that his soldiers, well rested and fed, would defeat the Egyptians, who would be forced to fight after a long and arduous march.

Hattushil quickly changed his mind, however, once the first of Pharaoh's army reached Shunem and engaged the waiting Hittite troops. The violent skirmish that ensued proved a complete rout. The seemingly endless flood of Egyptian forces pushed Hattushil's army back into the mountains to the north. Pharaoh's troops had triumphed over the Hittite army even before the whole of the Egyptian forces had reached the plain at Shunem.

But Pharaoh was not content with this easy victory. He was determined to pursue Hattushil to his own country, to his capital at Kadesh, if necessary. It would be unthinkable to leave Hattushil unpunished for his attempt to invade

Egypt, however unsuccessful. As soon as all of the Egyptian forces had arrived and reassembled at the fort, Pharaoh and his army set off again, leaving a strong contingent to guard its rear at Shunem.

Through all those long days of traveling, Shanda waited, expecting word to be brought to her that Pharaoh had tired of the effort of maintaining her. Each time her cart stopped, she half expected a soldier to enter, sword in hand, to carry out her execution. She had slowly begun to lose her fear of death, to see it as a release from this torturous life. She sometimes felt she would embrace it gladly, if only to end the torment of waiting.

When at last a soldier arrived and ordered her to leave the cart, however, it was not to her death that he hurried her, but to a small tent. She tried in vain to catch a glimpse of the surroundings as she was hurried through the graying twilight gloom into her new prison. She noticed that guards were stationed around her tent, a grim reminder that any attempt to escape would prove fruitless.

She spent her few moments in the open enjoying the feel of rain on her cheeks. It had been so long since she had felt the cool, wet drops on her skin and smelled the scent of pine in the air. It brought her a painful memory of her childhood and of Althea. It would have been kinder of Pharaoh, she thought, to have taken her life before they reached this place, before she could think of that time when she still had hopes and expectations, when still she dreamed.

Later, when Med came to her with food, he said they were now in Hattushil's land. Pharaoh's army had chased the Hittites all the way to Kadesh; they were now camped on a rise overlooking the great walled city. His manner, she realized, had unconsciously come to resemble that of the soldiers, the swagger, the unalterable certainty that he and his fellows were not only superior to their foe, but deserved that superiority by right of birth. Still a boy, and one doomed never to know real manhood, she realized he longed desperately to share their anticipation of victory and glory. She hoped, for Med's sake, that the victory would be quick and complete, that the end would come before he saw the reality of war.

She nibbled absently on a piece of bread while she considered what he had told her. Some part of her had known where they were even before he told her. She had known the second she stepped out of the cart and smelled the forest and tasted the rain on her lips. She could close her eyes and describe the whole of the surrounding countryside— the wide open plain outside the city of Kadesh, the narrow stream that wound its way through the sward, the dull gray stone of the city's walls. She would have the memory of Kadesh with her as long as she lived. It was in the palace there that Althea had died.

For some reason, she could not accustom herself to her newest prison. This tent was larger and more comfortable than her lodgings on the cart and the barge, but she felt cramped and suffocated nonetheless. She was unable to eat so much as this chunk of bread. She dropped it on the table, stood, and began to pace the small area in the dim light cast by the single clay lamp. She sensed that something was about to happen. The taste of it was on her tongue as vividly as the flavor of the rough-grain bread.

"Come, Princess. You must try to eat."

Med was treating her the way a nurse would treat a small child or someone who was very ill. She had noticed his attempts to cajole and bully her into eating and resting, and like a child or an invalid, she had acquiesced to his gentle commands. It seemed to her that her mind had slept during the long days they had traveled.

Now, however, she was able to consider her current

situation. She could see things crisply and clearly, with an awareness that she had managed to avoid until then. Faced with the prospect of an eternal sleep, she had wasted the last precious moments of her life, letting her mind be lulled by her own misery. It was a loss she now regretted.

Med's suggestion that she eat she met with a sharp stare. She found she could no longer be absently acquiescent. She shook her head and turned away from the platter of food he'd set out for her on the rough plank table.

"It will all end here, Med," she told him, her manner agitated, distracted. "Whatever is meant to happen will happen here. And soon. I can feel it in the air."

Med shook his head. "The city is well fortified. Pharaoh might lay siege here for months before there is a battle."

Shanda shook her head again. "No," she told him firmly. "The battle will come soon. Hattushil's nobles will not accept the presence of an invader at the gates of Kadesh. They will force the king to do battle, for it was his ambition that drew the Egyptian army to the gates of the city."

Med seemed unconvinced, but made no further argument, apparently unwilling to dispute with her a point on which she seemed so certain. She seated herself on the edge of the small cot that he had made for her bed and stared thoughtfully at him.

"Shall I tell you what it was like to live here, Med?" she asked him softly.

He turned to her, surprised at the suggestion and beginning to recognize the change in her.

"Yes, please, Princess," he said avidly and lowered himself to the ground at her feet.

"Hattushil has a palace here," she began. "It is said to have a thousand rooms."

She got no further. A movement by the tent flap attracted her attention, and she looked up in time to see Pharaoh enter.

All thoughts of storytelling left her mind. She rose, trembling, to her feet. Now, she thought, now is the time. He has come to carry out the execution himself. This was the event she had felt would soon come to pass; it had been a premonition of her own death.

She stood slowly, then bowed her head to him, unaware that Med had scrambled to his knees and tremblingly waited there.

Pharaoh stood in silence, staring at her, not quite believing what he saw. He was stunned by the changes in her, by her drawn, pale face, and by the thinness of her body. For a moment his anger melted and all he could see was the woman who had touched him as no other ever had, who had meant more to him than anyone else. He was filled with pain at the thought of losing her. He felt pity for her and remorse for the hardships she had obviously endured at his behest.

"You have been ill, Princess?" he asked her.

Shanda wondered if the words had been choked from him, they sounded so strained. At that moment, she felt more pity for him than for herself. His gray eyes, shining in the dim lamplight, were gentle and caring. What he was about to do might cost him more than it cost her, she thought. After all, when the act was done, her misery would be at an end. His would go on and on.

She shook her head slightly. "I am well, lord," she replied, surprised at how controlled her voice sounded in her ears, how uncaring.

Perhaps it was the control he heard in her words that swept the concern from his eyes. They grew suddenly cold; the warmth he had felt for her was abruptly extinguished. He was staring at his enemy and he would waste no pity there.

"That is well," he told her evenly. "There will be a battle

tomorrow, your father's armies against mine. You will be compelled to see it all. You will smell the blood in the air, taste it on your tongue. It is only fair that you know what your duplicity has wrought."

He moved his hand, directing a servant who waited behind him to step forward and deposit a pile of thick leather objects on the ground at her feet.

"Your armor, Princess," he said, his manner brusque now, even distant. "You will drive my chariot into battle. We will see if your skills remain when you are the target of your father's soldiers' arrows and swords."

He turned and started to leave. But when he reached the tent flap, he turned for a moment, offering her one last glance.

"Be ready at dawn, Princess," he said.

And then he was gone.

Med seemed to have turned to stone. Still on his knees, he stared wide-eyed at the place where Pharaoh had stood. He seemed rooted to the spot, as if his knees had planted themselves in the cool, damp ground.

Shanda moved forward to the heap of heavy leather armor Pharaoh had brought to her. She lifted first the cuirass, then one of the greaves, considering the dark, heavily padded leather, weighing each piece in her hands.

Med managed, finally, to stand. He moved slowly to her side and stared down at the dark leather. "He can't have meant it, Princess," he said dully. "He can't mean to take you into battle."

He knelt and lifted a greave, obviously completely confused by the thick, padded leather pieces with their trailing leather ties. Shanda was almost amused by his bewilderment, realizing that she had greater knowledge of these things than did he.

She smiled humorlessly at him and handed him the cuirass, then set the rest of the armor aside. "He meant it, Med," she told him flatly.

Med dropped the cuirass as if the leather burned his hands. "But what will you do?"

Shanda considered his panic, realizing that all the swagger he had learned from the older, wiser soldiers had fled him. He was, after all, nothing more than a boy who had been thrust into a situation he was too young to understand and too powerless to change.

"I will eat a bit more bread," she told him. She felt calmer than she had since the day Pharaoh came to her in anger and accused her of treachery. "And some cheese, I think, and then I will sleep. It will not do for me to be light-headed in the morning."

"But you can't go into battle, Princess," he protested. His voice broke into a muffled sob. "You might be killed."

She shrugged, then moved to the table and picked up the piece of bread. She considered it for a second in silence, looking at the thick, dark crust, at the pebbly grains of coarse ground wheat.

"I will die soon, in any event," she told him. She took a bite of the bread, surprised at how calm she felt, at how the prospect of death held no real terror. She ate the bread slowly, contemplatively. "At least a death in battle is thought to be an honorable death. Perhaps that will in some way redeem what I have lost in life of late." She lifted a piece of cheese, scraped away a bit of mold that clung to its edge, then consumed the cheese with more determination than pleasure.

"But you can't!" This time Med's cry was a wail of pain, a child's protest at the prospect of loss.

Shanda turned to him and spoke sharply. "You can serve me best by thinking well of me, Med, and by helping me accept my fate with dignity. I cannot do it alone."

His face fell, and his eyes filled with remorse. "But if you told him about the baby, Princess . . . " he ventured. "Surely he would not endanger his own child."

She shook her head slowly. "You've seen the way he looks at me, the hatred in his eyes. He would hold this child in utter contempt, Med." She went to him and took his hand. "Some things are worse than death, Med. I understand that now. I will take this baby with me wherever I go tomorrow. And I need you to help me. If you do not, I fear I will lose what little strength I still have."

"What will you have me do, Princess?" he asked in a choked whisper, apparently resigned now, as was she.

"I will sleep now. You must wake me well before dawn. I will not have him think me a coward, Med," she told him.

She stared at him evenly, holding his eyes with her own until he finally nodded.

"As you wish, Princess," he replied.

"Good," she told him, then dropped his hand and turned away, moving to the cot at the side of the tent. She pushed the sandals from her feet and lay back, suddenly very tired.

When Med entered the following morning and set a lamp on the table beside her, she was already awake, lying quietly, wondering if Hattushil's gods, or Althea's, would give her courage if she offered a prayer in payment. In the end, her indecision kept her from the prayer. She thought it was just as well, knowing that the gods, if they did exist, would consider her bribe a paltry one.

She rose immediately when Med came to her, puzzled by the absence of the nausea she'd come to expect in the mornings. She stripped and washed in the bowl of cold water he brought her.

"Bring the golden gown, Med," she told him. "I will have his soldiers see me and know I am not afraid."

"Yes, Princess."

She was surprised and relieved at Med's quiet acquiescence. She knew she could not face his panic when she was still unsure if her own would suddenly emerge and displace the calm.

She sat naked on the bed and pulled her brush through her hair, watching Med open the trunk that contained her clothing and search through her garments until he found a glimmer of gold. He pulled out the golden gown she'd worn when she drove Pharaoh's chariot in the procession to the temple. She gazed at the shimmering fabric and remembered that that was the night she had fallen in love.

She stood and let Med lift the gown over her head. It slipped down, settling easily against her skin. She had grown considerably thinner, and the gown was looser around her breasts and waist than it had been when she first wore it, but the roundness of her belly took the place her fuller hips had filled before.

She sat at the table where Med had placed her breakfast of bread and beer. She had no appetite, but she broke off a piece of bread from the loaf and bit into it. It was tasteless, just hard, dry stuff, and for a moment she thought the morning nausea might return to plague her after all. But then her stomach settled, and she forced herself to consume all of the bread, then swallow the bitter beer.

When she was done, she turned to Med. "Is there much time?" she asked him.

Med went to the tent flap and looked out at the first meager lessening of the gloom in the sky.

"Yes, Princess," he told her. "There is still time."

His expression was as determined as her own. He seemed to have decided to make her task as easy for her as he could. She was filled with gratitude for him, knowing that he did not tread his path easily.

"Will you sit with me for a moment?" she asked.

He settled on his knees at her feet.

"Pharaoh is not an unfair man, Med," she began softly. "He will not blame you for my actions, so you need not fear."

He looked down, not wanting to meet her eyes. She leaned toward him, putting her hand on his head.

"If it were in my power, I would free you. But that choice is not mine to make," she went on gently.

He nodded. "I have no wish to leave you, Princess," he murmured.

She pulled the golden cuff from her wrist and held it out to him.

"This was my mother's," she told him. "She took it from my dead father's wrist."

"But Hattushil still lives, Princess," Med protested, bewildered.

She shook her head. "There is no time to explain it all now. Perhaps there will be an opportunity later. Perhaps not. But it will please me if you take this cuff. I have nothing else of value to give you, Med, as a thank-you token for your kindness and your friendship. Please wear this, and sometimes think of me."

He shook his head vehemently. "I cannot take it, Princess," he protested. "It should one day belong to your child."

She stared at him silently for a moment, realizing that he had dealt with his fear by refusing to believe that she and her baby would die, by telling himself that they would all soon return to Thebes and resume their lives. She thought it would be cruel to try to convince him that Pharaoh would not take her back with him, that she would die in this battle or at its conclusion.

She put her hand on her belly, seeking the faint stirring

she'd begun to feel in the last few days. That was the hardest part, to feel the child move inside her and know it would never live.

"Then keep the cuff safe for my child," she told Med gently as she slipped the golden cuff on his wrist. She stood then, not giving him time to protest her gift. "It must be time now," she said briskly.

"No, not yet, Princess." Med jumped up and moved to the pile of armor, lifted the cuirass and held it out to her. "I will help you with this," he said doubtfully, looking at the breast and back plates and wondering how the armor was to be worn.

Shanda took it from him and shook her head. "It is impossible," she told him evenly. "Even if I had the strength to support the weight of all this leather, I certainly couldn't control the horses."

Med's jaw fell. "But you can't go out there without it!"

She dropped the cuirass on the heap and turned away. "I'm afraid I must," she said. "Pharaoh expects a driver, not a statue. Weighted with all that, I would be useless."

She turned back to face him and smiled encouragingly. "Go to the guards, Med," she ordered him. "Tell them I am ready."

# *Thirteen*

SHANDA HARDLY NOTICED the way the guards stared at her as they escorted her to the chariot that waited, ready for battle, before Pharaoh's tent. But they did stare at her and at the golden gown. They had not expected her to make so magnificent an appearance.

When she'd decided to wear the gown, she had not considered the palace guard, who would of course know everything, who would have heard every word of palace gossip. If she thought of them at all, it was only with the distant realization that they most likely knew her fate more plainly than did she, knew the moment when Pharaoh expected her to meet her just punishment.

Instead, she had thought of the charioteers and foot soldiers whom she'd watched at practice, the ones Pharaoh said had come to think of her as a good luck charm. The dress was her gift to them, and she hoped they would see her in it and once more consider her a symbol of good fortune. Perhaps in their expectation of good fortune they might actually find it.

She sniffed at the dampness in the morning air, and looked

up at the sky, searching for the sun. There was a dim light-
ening above, but none of the golden sunlight for which she
searched. Only a few pale red and orange fingers of light
darted into the sky from below the horizon to the east.

After all those long days of being closed up, she was
disappointed that there was no sunshine to greet her when
she finally returned to the world. It seemed unfair. She wondered if she would live long enough to see the sunlight at
all. Surely, she thought, no matter how great her sins, she
deserved at least to feel the sunlight on her face once more.

The guards stood aside, letting her move forward, away
from them, and she walked up to the great white horses.
They greeted her with the warmth of old friends, stamping
and shaking their heads as she neared, then nuzzling her in
welcome. She found an unexpected pleasure in their affection after having felt friendless and deserted for so long. It
was good to find that some creatures were still willing to
openly show her their affection. She offered them a caress,
stroking their long, smooth necks.

She then climbed into the chariot, which was unlike any
she had driven in the past. There was a high wooden shelf
in the front, clearly designed to offer a measure of protection for the driver. Two movable circular shields, one on
either side, had been designed to slide along ridges in the
chariot's body. The shields would provide the swordsman
with some protection, if he had the time and presence of
mind to push the heavy leather-covered disks to the place
where they would be most effective when they were most
needed. The two shields could be locked on to the front of
the chariot, as they were at that moment, by a small wooden
latch; when that latch was lifted, the shields would be free
to roll along the ridge. If left as they were on the front of the
chariot, they would provide the driver with some protection,
but the swordsman behind the driver would be exposed.

It was a highly sophisticated conveyance, extremely well designed for battle. Shanda knew that Hattushil's charioteers were not nearly as well protected.

She untied the reins and carefully wrapped them around her waist. When she'd finished tying them, she checked to ensure that her knot was fast, for if it came loose in the midst of the battle she would be unable to control the horses and disaster would ensue.

She had just finished securing the reins when the guards stirred and came to attention. She saw the flap of Pharaoh's tent being drawn open. Her heart seemed to stop as she watched him step out into the damp morning gloom. Seti emerged behind him, followed by a half-dozen other generals.

Pharaoh looked neither to the right nor to the left, but strode directly to the chariot. Shanda was transfixed by the sight of him, by the way his hand rode lazily on the hilt of the sword that hung by his side, by the sight of the thick muscles in his arm as he carried his helmet. She could almost feel those muscles beneath her fingers. The memory of his body close to hers was so sharp it hurt.

He paused for a second, staring at her, then climbed into the chariot behind her. She knew he was surprised at the way she'd chosen to present herself, and she wondered what his reaction would be.

"I brought you armor," he reminded her evenly.

She met his eyes, wondering at the indifference in his tone. It seemed to her that even his hatred was easier for her to bear than the distant way he stared at her.

"It is too heavy for me to wear, lord," she replied. Unable to meet his glance any longer, she turned to face the front of the chariot and took up the reins nervously.

She had felt a glimmer of hope that he might say something further, that he might insist she don the armor or suggest she was not up to performing as his driver, but he seemed to expect her services without regard to the danger in which he was placing her.

Seti glanced at her and, when Pharaoh was ready, motioned to her to follow him. She slowly turned the chariot in his direction, maneuvering it through the ranks of Pharaoh's guards. Then she drove slowly through the encampment where charioteers and foot soldiers stood armed and ready for the battle. They followed the chariot, their long ranks quickly swelling until their number was beyond counting.

They left the encampment behind and began the climb up the long rise Shanda knew shielded the Egyptians' camp from the wide plain outside the great walls of Kadesh. She had driven along the valley and over this long hillside many times before, but the memory was unclear, as though it had come to her secondhand and was not quite her own. She felt as though the years she had spent at Kadesh had been erased from her mind, as though that life had been lived by someone else. All her life, she had felt alien, apart, but at that moment she was more alone than she had ever been before.

As she drove, she almost felt the eyes of the soldiers who had fallen in behind the chariot. It was not, however, until the chariot reached the summit of the rise that she heard the growing swell of the cheer behind her.

Pharaoh leaned toward her. "My men still think of you as their talisman, Princess," he told her.

She looked back, only then realizing the cheer was for her.

Pharaoh's voice turned bitter and hard: "Let us hope you bring them more luck than you have brought to me."

Shanda did not mistake the bitterness in his words. For a moment she could feel the sting of tears in her eyes. She had to force herself to look at Kadesh, the place that once had been her home.

The walls of the city were lined with soldiers, as if they had grown hundreds of tiny heads and hands that held bows already fitted with arrows. Hattushil and his people were prepared for this battle.

Pharaoh's foot soldiers and chariots moved up to the top of the hillside on either side of the place where she and Pharaoh waited. Even as the Egyptians formed a long line across the ridge, the huge gates of Kadesh swung outward. Armed men, a great, thick stream of them, charioteers and foot soldiers alike, poured out onto the wide plain below her. From the distance, they looked like minuscule men holding toy weapons.

Once more Pharaoh leaned forward to speak to her. "My spies were right when they said your father's lords would force him to immediate battle. They obviously have as little love for him as I."

Shanda knew he was right. Hattushil's power lay in his ability to keep his lords at one another's throats, letting them dwell on petty differences among themselves to keep them from banding together to challenge him. But no differences could keep them from uniting in the face of an invader at the very gates of Kadesh. She had known, as she had told Med the night before, that they would not tolerate a siege of their city brought about by Hattushil's foolish attempt to invade Egypt. They would countenance their king's ambition only so long as it served them and the cost was not too great.

Soon two long rows of chariots faced each other on the plain as the horizon slowly filled with the dully glowing light of day. The horses began to stamp their hooves and snort their impatience, forcing their drivers to struggle to keep them in ordered lines. Behind them, foot soldiers raised their shields and readied their bows. Already the scent of fear and sweat, a precursor of battle, filled the air.

Shanda leaned forward to release the wooden latch,

freeing the two shields so that they could be drawn back
on either side. But Pharaoh seized her wrist and stayed
her hand.

"Leave the shields where they are," he ordered.

For a moment she thought it might be concern for her
safety that had prompted him, a last attempt to mete out a bit
of mercy despite his knowledge that she had betrayed him.
And for that instant, a brief throb of hope rose in her.

It was quickly extinguished. He put on his helmet and fastened it, raised his sword over his head, then leaned toward
her, his lips close to her ear.

"You will drive as I direct you," he whispered. "If you
deviate from my instructions it will not be a Hittite sword
you feel in your side, Princess, but mine." He raised his
sword, a signal for his soldiers to ready themselves. "Now,"
he shouted to her sharply. "Forward."

Shanda did not allow herself to think of her disappointment, to feel that last hint of hope ebb slowly from her. She
forced herself to think only of the horses, leaning toward
them and slapping the reins against their backs, urging them
into a run. She hardly heard the wild cries of the soldiers
on either side as they, too, started in an uneven wave down
the long hill.

On the plain below, the Hittite soldiers moved forward,
weapons drawn, to greet them.

At first, Shanda was aware of only the sensation of speed,
the scent of grass and pine needles in the air, and the dull
roaring noise around her, the sound of the soldiers' shouts
mixed with the dull stamping of hooves in the soft soil, and
the horses' labored breath. But soon there was another sound
added to those noises, one Shanda had heard many times
before, but never from precisely that position, the sound
of arrows in the air, approaching and striking all around
her, first the whine and then the dull thud when they met

armor or shield, or the sharp, pained cry when one found its mark.

She drove the chariot forward, into the meaningless melee, and quickly the scent of grass and pine were over-powered by stronger odors, the smell of horses and sweat and one other that grew constantly stronger—the sickly sweet scent of human blood. The noise, too, had changed in timbre. The challenging war cries were slowly muted and finally overpowered by groans and grunts as the fighting came hand to hand, the clash of sword against sword sharp on the air, the cries of pain growing ever louder and more frequent.

Unable to bear the horror of what she saw and heard around her, Shanda slowly grew numb, and the images began to blur. She was still in command of her senses, but their messages had grown dim and weak, as though they came from a great distance.

She kept her attention on the horses, moving them forward, finding space in the mass of humanity around her to turn when Pharaoh shouted for her to do so, driving toward one of the Hittite warriors if that was his command. He was a tireless fighter, she realized dully, and a strong one. None of the Hittites he challenged long withstood the relentless assault of his sword.

The Egyptians, following their pharaoh, pushed the Hittite soldiers back toward the city walls. By midmorning, they were within a few hundred paces of the great cypress gates of Kadesh. As the Hittite soldiers lost heart, they began to waver under the pressure of the aggressive assault. Shanda felt certain that the easy victory Pharaoh's army had won at Shunem was about to be repeated.

But then the marksmen on the city's walls loosed a heavy volley of spears and arrows, forcing the Egyptians back. When they had fallen back, the huge wooden gates swung open a second time, and fresh forces swept out of the city. At their head was a tall, dark charioteer wearing a brightly plumed helmet. His cry of bristling challenge sent the men behind him into a frenzy as they charged out to meet the embattled Egyptian forces.

The Hittites had given ground easily at Shunem, but here at the gates of their own capital they seemed determined to die rather than surrender. The volley had forced the Egyptians back, and the appearance of fresh soldiers joining them had renewed the other Hittites' spirit and energy. The fresh troops plunged into the battle with vicious determination and with energy unsapped by hours of fighting. Slowly the Egyptians were being pushed back.

Pharaoh, however, refused to give ground. Shanda, who had kept her attention centered on the horses, hardly noticed the Egyptian retreat until she looked around and saw that Pharaoh's chariot was nearly surrounded by Hittite foot soldiers.

It occurred to her at that moment that the Egyptians might actually lose the battle, that Hattushil had gambled and won. And the thought was not hers alone. There was a feeling in the air, a sense that the battle would soon be over. That feeling had started with the first retreating steps the Egyptians had taken. The Hittite war cries even then had been tinged with a note of victory.

"There. Drive toward him!"

Shanda did not even need the gesture Pharaoh made, pointing his bloody sword toward the chariot in which the officer with the plumed helmet rode. She could see the Hittite's weapon, bright in the morning sunshine, flashing as he brandished it, encouraging his soldiers forward to pursue their advantage. She could hear his soldiers shouting vicious challenges to their enemy, surer now as they forced the Egyptians back.

She put her mind to guiding the horses through the pulsing throb of humanity. All around her were the results of battle—men fighting with bloodied limbs, bodies fallen in improbable positions on the trammeled blood- and mud-spattered ground. Her own arms were speckled with dark droplets of blood thrown off by Pharaoh's sword. Their color, varying from bright red to dull rust, attested to their relative freshness and to the duration of the battle.

Slowly she maneuvered the chariot toward the beplumed leader of the Hittite forces. Apparently the Hittite general had seen Pharaoh's advance. He seemed more than willing to meet the leader of his enemy, for he shouted to his soldiers to pull back and leave space for Pharaoh's approaching chariot.

"Take us close to him," Pharaoh shouted.

His words seemed impossibly distant above the din of the battle, as though he were at the far side of the plain rather than directly behind her.

But before she could reach the general, another Hittite chariot drew close to her left side, and the warrior behind the driver leaned forward, brandishing his sword.

Pharaoh turned to meet the warrior's first heavy blow, parrying the deadly thrust with his own sword. Shanda heard the clash of metal against metal close to her ear. She dared not turn, fearing the movement would bring her into contact with one of the deadly blades.

The officer with the plumed helmet—too impatient to wait for the combat to end, or fearing his prize might be taken by another—ordered his own chariot drawn up close to the right side of Pharaoh's.

Shanda saw the second chariot move near and realized they were trapped between the two. Pharaoh, still occupied with the fighter on his left, was unaware of the second men-

ace drawing close to his other side and then falling slightly
behind him.

Shanda turned to face the driver of the second chariot.
He returned her stare, obviously surprised at the sight of
a woman. Then he gave her a wide, lecherous smile that
spoke of his intensions at the conclusion of the battle.

She turned her eyes to the Hittite general behind him.

Suddenly time seemed to stand still for her. The events of
the past few hours had overwhelmed her, had tumbled one
upon the next until they had blurred and lost their distinc-
tions. The battle, until that moment, had been a long, wea-
rying succession of sights and smells and sounds, frightening
perhaps, but too confused in her mind to mean much to her.
Her mind had captured certain images for her to take out at
some time in the future and examine at her leisure, but until
then they were buried in a dull and clouded blur.

But at that moment her senses became starkly clear. The
images of the soldiers around her were suddenly so sharp
she could see the thick hair on their muscular arms, the
beads of sweat dripping down their cheeks. It came as a
tingling shock to her that she was actually there, that she
was in the midst of a battle, and that all around her men
were dying.

And as she watched the young general raise his sword,
ready to bring it down on Pharaoh's back, she knew without
a doubt that he was about to die.

She stared into the Hittite general's eyes, searching for
that part of a man that would allow him to strike another,
even an enemy, from the rear, to mete out death without
the courage to face his victim's eyes.

And she gasped. The dark eyes, the long, narrow nose,
even the grimly determined set of the thick lips—they were
all familiar to her, more than familiar. There had been
nights, and many of them, when she'd gone to sleep with

the image of that face in her mind, the taste and the feel of those lips still warm on hers. This was the man in whom she had placed her hopes, the man who had once said he loved her.

"Nem."

She mouthed his name, but no sound came from her lips. And he, intent on Pharaoh's back, had apparently taken no notice of her.

She put her hand to the latch that held the shield and pulled it away. But then her hand trembled, and she found herself unable to push the heavy shield along the ridge. If Nem killed Pharaoh, the Egyptians would surely be defeated. Without their king, the already wavering soldiers would lose what little spirit they still held. They would scatter and retreat.

And if that happened, Nem's promise to her would be fulfilled. He would be responsible for Pharaoh's defeat, and Hattushil could no longer object to his marrying a royal princess. She would have what she had wanted so desperately before she was sent away to Thebes—marriage to Nem, release from Hattushil's court, a real home of which she would be mistress. She would also have a man who had sworn his love to her.

While Pharaoh, if he survived the battle, would reward her with death as punishment for her part in the Hittite duplicity. She glanced briefly at Nem, then at Pharaoh as he struggled still with the Hittite swordsman on his left. She glanced once more at the movable shield. She could decide which of these men would live and which would die.

She had thought once that she loved Nem. Now she knew she loved Pharaoh. But was her love for him strong enough to persist even in the face of the knowledge that he now hated her, and that saving his life would mean the end of her own? And had she really lost the feeling she had once had for Nem, as she'd told herself she had since the day he'd let her leave for Egypt?

Nem began to lower his arm. She had no time to think, no time to make decisions that would have far-reaching effects. She had only her feelings to rule her, only her heart to make her choice. It seemed far too heavy a matter to be determined by so uncertain an instrument.

It terrified her to realize that her choice would determine not only the future of her own existence and that of these two men but also the outcome of the battle that raged around her.

# *Fourteen*

SHANDA WATCHED THE blade in Nem's hand begin to fall, and she pushed against the shield with all her weight, sending it around to the right side of the chariot. Once set in motion, it moved with surprising ease, slipping into a position where it protected Pharaoh's back as he faced the left side of the vehicle.

She felt a sharp sense of relief. She had made her choice and she was glad of it. She had no regrets.

Nem's blade fell with a heavy thud against the edge of the shield. Carried along by its own weight and the force with which Nem had thrust it, it slipped down the side of the shield. Shanda felt a wave of fiery pain as it plunged into her side.

Her cry of pain was muffled by the death cry of the swordsman on the left. Pharaoh pulled away his weapon and turned just as Nem withdrew his sword.

Only then, as he pulled back the bloodstained blade, did the young Hittite general turn his eyes to Pharaoh's driver. He saw her face, contorted with pain, and realized only then what he had done. His hand shook as he stared at her.

"Shanda!" Nem's voice was filled with shock and with the sure knowledge that it was her blood that slowly slid along the shining surface of his blade. His hands trembled. His eyes found hers, and only then, when he saw that her eyes were filled with pity, did he realize he had lost his one opportunity to kill Pharaoh.

While he was staring at Shanda, Pharaoh turned and swung. Nem looked down, unbelieving, at the blade buried in his chest. He looked up again, searching for her, his expression now filled with surprise.

"Shanda."

This time there was reprimand in his voice as well as remorse. And then he slumped forward against the side of the chariot, his body suddenly ugly in its awkwardness. Shanda stared dully at his sword as it fell to the ground.

"Forward, Princess," Pharaoh shouted in her ear.

His words roused her, and Shanda tore her eyes away from Nem's body. She gasped with sudden pain as she turned back to face the front of the chariot and put her hands once more on the reins. She knew that if they had not been securely tied around her waist, she would have fallen. She slapped them against the horses' backs, urging the great whites forward.

Nem's death marked the beginning of the final phase of the battle. The force of his confidence had roused the Hittite soldiers after the humiliating defeat at Shunem. His death at the hands of the enemy king now became a symbol of the futility of their cause. The soldiers saw their general's retreating chariot, his body slumped unmoving and flaccid over the side, as a fateful omen.

Meanwhile Pharaoh's chariot moved relentlessly toward the gates of Kadesh, and his advance spurred the Egyptians' hopes. His soldiers saw the bewilderment Nem's death had caused among the Hittites and used it to start their second forward thrust. And their advance was merciless.

The battle continued until well into the afternoon, but the Hittite defense had begun to shatter long before that. The Egyptians had taken the whole of the plain and had begun to pursue the scattered, fleeing Hittite soldiers back as far as the wooded rise to the north.

Pharaoh, intent on the battle, called his directions to Shanda without a single glance her way.

Shanda's only thought was to keep control of the horses. She had been forced to wind the reins around her forearms to keep herself from dropping them, and she leaned heavily against the protected front of the chariot. She managed to follow Pharaoh's directions through the remainder of the battle. When finally he was satisfied that the plain was in his own soldiers' hands and he knew the battle won, he ordered her to turn the chariot and return to the encampment.

When she pulled back on the reins and turned the horses, her torso was racked with agonizing pain. Somehow she maintained control of the horses even though the hillside had begun to undulate and sway before her like a blood-spattered green seascape. She could feel something warm and sticky slipping slowly down her side and leg, and knew, if a bit remotely, that it must be her own blood.

As the chariot climbed the rise at the end of the plain, Seti called out from across the field. "A great victory, Pharaoh," the general of the guard said in a voice that gave evidence to his elation at the outcome of the battle.

"Now to take the city," Pharaoh called back to him, his own voice grimly determined.

Seti seemed undeterred. "They have not enough forces left to provide any real defense, lord," he replied. "I will wager they'll sue for peace rather than prolong their own misery."

Shanda heard their words through a thick mist. It hurt her now even to breathe, and she felt terribly cold despite the heavy heat of the late afternoon sun. The odor of blood and sweat, overpowering in their intensity, filled her nostrils. The hillside, no longer sharply green now but stained brown and red and spotted with the grotesque shapes of the dead and wounded, spun around her crazily.

The only thing that seemed real to her was the sharp bite of the reins where she had wound them around her wrists. She knew that if she lost the feel of them she would lose everything. She had to hold on to the reins even if nothing else she saw or felt was solidly as it ought to be.

Bands of Egyptian soldiers began to return to the encampment, following behind Pharaoh's chariot. They herded along with them small, miserable groups of Hittite prisoners. As their king passed them, they roused themselves to frenzied shouts. The awareness of victory was sharp and intoxicating to them.

Shanda maneuvered the chariot through the encampment and drew it to a halt in front of Pharaoh's tent. Behind her she was dimly aware of the raucous shouts of the soldiers who had fallen in behind the king. Pharaoh raised his blood-smeared sword in a gesture of triumph, which they echoed with enthusiasm. Shanda was vaguely aware that the camp was filled with hordes of soldiers drunk on victory and that hundreds of bloody swords were being waved in the air. Already the prostitute camp followers had emerged from their tents and began to circulate among the victorious soldiers, eager to earn their share of the gleanings of the battle.

But as Shanda grew weaker she saw only the pale, dim blur of the horses' rumps and felt only the reins wound around her arms and grasped tightly in her hands.

The whites, their work finally done, stood shaking their long manes. Their necks and legs were lathered, their beautiful coats marred with dark drops of blood, and their sides heaved as they waited for the water that was quickly brought to them.

Shanda let her hands drop the reins and stood, forcing herself to concentrate as she slowly removed them from her arms. But when she tried to unwind them from her waist, she found the effort too great. Exhausted, she dropped her hands to her sides and listened to the roaring buzz that filled her ears.

She realized she was gasping for breath even though each mouthful sent a burning line of fire through her side. Then suddenly the sunlight disappeared, and everything around her began to spin as she fell.

At first, Pharaoh only knew that the cheering of the soldiers around him had stopped. And then he turned and saw her slumped over the side of the chariot. She was covered with blood.

"Shanda!"

He used his sword to hew away the blood-smeared reins still tied around her waist, then let the weapon fall as he took her in his arms.

He felt the warmth of her blood, hot and sticky against his hands. And when he lifted her, she was too still, too light in his arms.

He wondered when and how she had been hurt. He recalled only the battle, the seemingly endless succession of Hittite soldiers, the ceaseless challenge of their advance.

And then there was the stark memory of turning to see the Hittite general pull back his bloodstained sword, the realization that the shield had been moved back to where it would protect Pharaoh, leaving Shanda exposed. He realized she had saved his life and in doing so had taken the blow meant for him.

And he had not so much as noticed, leaving her to continue to drive for him despite the wound, letting her bleed until the floor of the chariot where she stood was slippery with her blood.

He felt a keen, searing stab of remorse. When he'd learned

that she was part of her father's plan to invade his country, he'd told himself he could tear her from his heart, that he could cut away his love and feel nothing for her ever again. But that had been a lie. He'd known it then, even as he had tried to shut himself off from the pain of losing her. But that pain had been nothing beside the knowledge of what he had done to her, nothing compared to the emptiness that filled him at the thought that had let her protect him while she bled to death.

He held her close to him, aware of the faint throb of the pulse in her neck, sure it was far too weak, too slow.

"Bring the physician!" he shouted at the confused guard who stood by the opening to his tent.

Shanda awoke to the sensation of pain. It seemed to start in her side and spread all through her body. She had never known anything like this before, this burning hurt that filled her and seemed only to grow stronger and more potent.

A man was leaning over her, tearing away the filthy strands of bloodstained fabric that had once been the beautiful golden gown. She knew his face; he was Imhotep, Pharaoh's physician, the one who had come to him the day of the lion hunt to inspect her work of washing and bandaging the bloody scratches on Pharaoh's shoulders and arms. He'd been kind to her that day, she remembered, praising her, telling Pharaoh she could be trained as a physician.

She painfully reached out to him. "Let me die," she begged him softly. "Have enough mercy on me to let me die now."

He shook his head, and continued to cut away the bloodstained fabric.

And then Pharaoh's face appeared beside the physician's. Behind him she saw other faces, Seti's, and that of Amenophis, Pharaoh's son. They were all dark and begrimed, and Seti's, she thought, wore an expression of grim pity. She wondered numbly why she felt so calm, why her vision seemed clearer than it had been since the start of the battle.

She turned her eyes to Pharaoh. "Let me die—" Her words caught in her throat as a spasm of pain seized her. After it passed, she met his eyes. "Surely you cannot hate me so much as to force me to live any longer?"

The physician put his hand on her now bare belly, the one rounded part of her otherwise spare torso. She looked up at him and realized quickly that he knew.

"Is it not better to live, Princess?" he asked her gently. "If not for yourself, then for this one?"

She turned her eyes back to Pharaoh and read the surprise in his expression. Then Imhotep was lifting her head, putting a cup to her lips.

"Drink, Princess," he whispered encouragingly.

Too weak to resist, she swallowed the bitter liquid he offered her. Before she'd finished it, the pain seemed to lessen and his face began to swim in front of her.

A moment later it disappeared completely.


"What did you mean?" Pharaoh asked sharply.

The physician turned to him. "She's with child, lord," he said evenly. Once again he put his hand on the small rounded hillock of Shanda's belly. "This is your baby."

Pharaoh put his hand where Imhotep's had been. Her skin felt cold and damp beneath his hand. It was a surprise to him. Always before when he touched her, she had felt so warm.

He pulled his hand away and stepped back, stunned. Then he grasped the physician's arm, his fingers biting into it sharply. "You will not let her die."

"She has lost a great deal of blood, lord," Imhotep told him evenly. "I can do only what is in my power to do."

Amenophis stepped forward, his face sullen and angry.

He had fought that day and fought well. His own arm hung limp by his side, and a bloody bandage encased it. Yet Pharaoh had not so much as noticed his presence, had made no effort to offer the praise he deserved at the conclusion of this, his first battle. Instead Pharaoh wasted his concern on this alien woman, this witch who had enthralled him. She was dangerous, he thought. To let her live was dangerous. And if she indeed carried Pharaoh's child, she became a greater menace still.

"You heard her. She wants to die. Let her," he said, his voice sharp and filled with anger. "She's one of them, a Hittite. If she lives, you will only invite a serpent into your bed."

Pharaoh turned to face him. "Get out of my sight," he hissed angrily. "But for her I would be dead. Or would that have pleased you better?" he demanded, his voice cold with disgust. "How many prayers did you offer that I might not live to see the sun set today?"

Pharaoh watched Amenophis struggle to choke down a cry of rage. For a moment he felt regret, thinking he should have praised the boy for the part he had had in the battle, wondering if this might be a chance to somehow bridge the rift between the two of them. But then he saw the look of open hatred Amenophis leveled at him, and he knew what he had said was true, that his own son had prayed for his death in the battle.

Amenophis turned on his heel and left. Pharaoh watched him go.

Seti moved to his side. "He will one day become very powerful, lord," he whispered to Pharaoh. "It would be well for you to keep a watchful eye on him."

Pharaoh shrugged. "I am very powerful now," he said diffidently. "It would be well for him to keep a watchful eye on me."

He turned his attention back to the physician who was examining the gory cut in Shanda's side. He shuddered as he realized the blood that slid from it had slowed to a trickle. Perhaps she had already bled beyond the point where she could survive, and the blame was his, all his.

He settled himself grimly in a chair, determined to watch as Imhotep opened some vials of foul-smelling unguents and began treating the long gash in Shanda's side, layering it with the ointments and what appeared to be spiderwebs. When he was done, he called to Med.

"You, boy, help me with the bandages."

Med crept out of the shadows in the corner where he had stood watching the procedure with mute horror. He remembered when Shanda had talked of death, but he had never really believed she would die; he'd never believed Pharaoh would let her die. But now she lay there, still and paler than he'd ever seen her. And the bed linens beneath her were stained red with her blood. It made him shudder, the sight of so much blood.

Med held her shoulders as the physician wrapped bandages around her, his eyes on the physician's hands but his mind filled with the thought that her body seemed to have suddenly become fragile to the touch. The thought frightened him.

Imhotep tied off the bandage and turned away to wash his instruments and place them in their leather pouches. But Med stayed beside Shanda, touching her cheek from time to time to assure himself that she still lived. She was the one person who had shown him kindness, and he loved her for it.

"I've done what I can," Imhotep said to Pharaoh, his manner brusque, as though he had no time for sentiment, even a Pharaoh's sentiment. "I'll go out to the wounded now. There are others who need me."

"No!"

The two men turned to Med, quickly recognizing the fear in his expression, then looking down at Shanda. Her body had arched and become rigid.

Med looked up at them. "What is happening to her?" he cried in terror.

The physician crossed quickly to the bedside. He touched her belly and his expression grew grim.

"Fetch clean water, boy. And more bandages."

Med hesitated, not wanting to leave her.

"Go now, boy!" Imhotep shouted at him.

But still Med could not move. "What is it?" he cried once more.

The physician seemed to take pity on him. "She's lost too much blood," he replied evenly. "Her body is giving up the baby. But perhaps we can save her life if you will do as you are told."

Med set off at a run.

Pharaoh moved to the bedside. Sickened by what he saw but unable to turn away, he watched as Imhotep took the small bloody thing from her and placed it reverently in a bowl.

The physician looked up at him. "It would be better, lord, if you were to wait outside. I will send for you if there is any change."

"Can you tell . . . ?" Pharaoh asked in a hoarse whisper.

Imhotep nodded. "It was a son," he said gently, then quickly turned back to his work.

Pharaoh stepped back, but did not leave. He'd killed his own unborn son, and possibly the only woman he'd ever loved. Perhaps it would have been better for him if Amenophis's prayers had been answered. If he'd died in the battle, he would not be doomed to endure this pervasive pain, this feeling of remorse that threatened to overwhelm him.

When Imhotep was finally finished, he turned to wash his hands in the bowl of water Med had filled for him.

Med moved to the far side of Shanda's bed, knelt on the floor beside her, and grasped her hand. It was cold and slack, and he almost let go of it, sickened by the thought that he touched the hand of a dead woman. Forcing himself to banish the thought, he took the gold cuff from his wrist and placed it on hers. He felt better then, as if the bit of gold was a talisman that could protect her. It even seemed to him that her hand grew a bit warmer.

"What is that?"

Med looked up. He'd forgotten Pharaoh was there, forgotten everything save for her. He bowed his head respectfully, but stayed beside her, his hand on her wrist. Even his fear of Pharaoh had fled him, leaving him with but one fear—that she might die.

"It is hers, lord," he replied. "She gave it to me, to keep it safe for her child."

He shuddered then, suddenly aware of what he had said, realizing too late that there no longer was a child. He darted a glance up at Pharaoh's tortured face, contorted now with misery that had grown with Med's words. Then the boy turned away, putting his head down on the bloodied sheet at Shanda's side, filled with a sharp misery of his own.

He felt Pharaoh's hand on his shoulder and lifted tear-filled eyes. "You're a god!" he cried out. "You can make her live."

Pharaoh drew his hand away, then turned and stared miserably at the thing that would have been his son. It was frightening to look down at the tiny creature and feel no kinship to it, even knowing it was his own. But when he looked back at Shanda the pain inside him grew sharp.

"Not so powerful a god as you think me," he replied to Med, wishing that he had, indeed, the ability with which the boy thought him endowed.

He had never felt so powerless, and it was not a feeling he accepted easily. He turned to Imhotep. "Tell me, physician, will she live?" he said, but there was no force in the question. It seemed almost a supplication. He was Pharaoh, and yet he was begging for word that she would live.

Imhotep looked up at him sharply, then shook his head. "I have done what can be done," he said slowly and, for the first time, showed a bit of regret. "If she lives, it will be of her own doing, not mine."

"Pharaoh?"

He looked up and saw Seti had returned. Pharaoh had not seen or heard him enter and wondered how long he had been there.

"What is it?" he asked wearily.

"The Hittite lords have sent a party to speak to you," Seti replied.

Pharaoh flashed him an angry look. "Send them away or deal with them yourself, but do not disturb me now," he said through clenched teeth.

Seti bowed his head but made no move to leave. "I regret, lord, but it is necessary. They have brought you King Hattushil's head."

# *Fifteen*

SHANDA WOKE TO dim lamplight softening the edges of the darkness. She was aware of the dully throbbing pain that filled her, but it seemed far away; all her perceptions seemed distant and unclear. She felt as if she were suspended in a cloud, thin and hazy, that obscured everything in a vaporous mist yet still let her see and hear and feel. She wondered if she was still dreaming, if all the pain and horror had been a nightmare. Perhaps she would soon awaken and find herself gazing out to the soft morning light in the garden, and turn to see Pharaoh wakening at her side.

If it was a dream, she thought, it was very different from the one that had preceded it. That dream had been filled with horrors—blood, sticky and thick, flowing everywhere, and the vision of bodies, mutilated corpses that rose up from the sickly red-tinged ground to turn sightless eyes on her and offer her chilling, terrifying cries. Now that she'd escaped from it, she was sure that that vision could only have been a nightmare. But this dim stillness and the oddly distant, floating feeling . . . she was not quite sure about this.

A face swam slowly into her vision. It was familiar, but

she had to struggle with her memory to put a name to it.

"Med," she finally whispered hoarsely.

He put something cool on her forehead, and the sensation was pleasant against her warm skin.

"Princess." He ventured a smile, but she could see, even through her confusion, that he looked afraid.

Now another face appeared beside Med's. This face cost her no effort to identify. It had swum in and out of that first dream, chasing her across the corpse-strewn field, accusing her, telling her she was the cause of all the horror around her.

But the face was not staring at her with eyes that accused this time. She had never seen it so drawn and tired and filled with regret. She realized abruptly that this was not a dream. The expression on Pharaoh's face was one she could never have imagined.

Her eyes found his. "Has the battle been lost, then, lord?" she asked in a weak whisper, unable to think of any other explanation for his anguish-filled stare.

She felt him grasp her hand, raise it slowly, and enclose it between his palms. The pleasing sensation sent a sliver of heat through her arm. She marveled that she was still able to feel this way merely from the touch of his hand. Surely, she thought, the dull pain should chase away this warmth; surely it ought not to be able to reach her through the pale cloud that surrounded her.

He shook his head slowly. "No, Shanda," he assured her softly. "The battle has not been lost. The lords of Kadesh have surrendered."

She managed a weak smile. "Then all is well," she said. Her eyes narrowed and she peered at him intently. Surely his expression spoke of tragedy, not victory. "Were you wounded, lord?" she asked. "I do not remember you being wounded."

"No, Shanda," he replied. "I am unhurt."

She sighed with what might have been contentment had it not sent a thick stab of pain along her side. "Then I have paid my debt to you," she whispered as she closed her eyes. "I can step into the eternal darkness in peace."

"No, Shanda, you cannot," he told her sharply. Her eyes opened at the strident sound of his words. "You cannot leave me alone," he said when she met his eyes. "You cannot leave me here, dead inside. If you go, you take with you the only part of me that was ever really alive."

She stared up at him, suddenly filled with pity for him. "My poor love," she whispered.

Med put a cup to her lips. "You must drink this, Princess," he told her. "The physician says it will help to heal you."

"No." She tried to push the cup away.

Pharaoh put her hand gently down, took the cup from Med, and lifted her in his arm.

"Drink, Shanda," he told her gently. "Live. Do not condemn me to go on without you."

Warmth filled her at his words. And she realized that the anger and hatred she'd come to expect to see in his eyes was completely gone. She moved her hand to her belly as she sipped the bitter liquid. There was this child, she told herself, for whom to live as well.

The cloud began to grow thicker around her, and the pain somehow lessened. She realized the haziness she had recognized when she'd wakened had been caused by this medicine. But despite the blurring in her mind, she felt something, some lack, and knew something inside her was terribly wrong. She struggled to identify it before the cloud obscured thought altogether.

The truth struck her like a blow. She knew with absolute certainty that the baby was gone. When she'd thought there would never be anything for her but Pharaoh's hatred, she'd told herself that it would be kinder never to let this child come into a world where he would not be loved, that at least he would have her beside him as he stepped into the eternal darkness, that he would not go alone. The knowledge that her baby had gone on without her was shattering.

She grasped Pharaoh's arm and pulled herself forward.

"My baby!" she cried. "What has happened to my baby?"

The cloud grew thicker and began to pull her away. She could not keep her eyes open any longer. Pharaoh's tortured words came to her from a great distance, and she had to fight to hold on to them.

"Forgive me, Shanda. Don't leave me alone."

His plea followed her into the darkness.


There seemed only to be the nightmares, the horrible dreams filled with the anguished cries of a child she sought constantly but never found. Gone were the terrible images of mutilated soldiers. Gone were the horrible cries and Pharaoh's accusing pursuit. In this nightmare she ran sightlessly on in the darkness, hearing the child's wails but never finding him. And somehow this dream was far more frightening than the other.

In those two days while the dream haunted her, Pharaoh stayed by her side, doing what little he could, washing away the sweat of her fever, gently holding her still as she thrashed. He placed an ankh, a life symbol, reverently around her neck, and offered up prayers, the most sincere of his life, that she might live.

The physician had given him little hope. Her fever steadily worsened, and the sleep potion had offered her little peace. In her drug-induced slumber she fought with spirits, and the encounters left her ever weaker. The rest that Imhotep had intended to leave her body free to heal had been of no value. He thought there little possibility she would survive.

Shanda awakened when the cries ceased and she heard only silence. She felt weak and. dizzy, and her body was intolerably hot, as though there were fires inside her, fires that ate away at her and threatened to consume her altogether.

Pharaoh was still there, looking even more haggard and grief stricken. When she opened her eyes, he put his hand gently on her cheek.

She could only look up at him and whisper, "My baby."

It was her child's cries that had filled her dreams, she knew, the wailing of the unborn baby for whom she'd searched in that endless darkness.

He pushed away the strands of damp hair from her cheek.

"His *kah* haunts me, too, Shanda," Pharaoh told her solemnly. "Set him free so that he may rest in peace. Set him free and return to me."

Her eyelids seemed too heavy for her to keep open, and they drifted slowly closed again. But her mind clung to his words. Perhaps what he said was true. Perhaps the cries in her dreams were those of her unborn baby's *kah*, his spirit. Perhaps her own *kah* pursued it, refusing to release it, to give it up. Shanda knew that her spirit still longed to join with her child's, to go with him into the endless darkness.

But then she thought of Pharaoh's tortured stare and knew what her death would cost him. She loved him far too much to cause him such misery, she thought. She had decided once to die so that he might live. Surely she could live for him instead.

For his sake she would fight, she decided, not for her own death, but for life. She could only pray her baby's spirit would forgive her.

* * *

"Am I dead, then?" she asked when she looked up and saw Med's hollow-eyed face, his expression of deep mourning. She didn't expect an answer. She assumed she had not even spoken aloud. But he smiled at her, and his worried eyes brightened.

"No, Princess. It pleases me to say you are alive."

Med motioned to someone behind him, but she lacked the energy to raise herself to look. Then he rinsed a cloth in a large bowl of water and wiped her cheeks and forehead. The cool cloth felt good against her skin.

"Alive," he repeated with a smile, "and much better."

She *was* better, she realized, and the recognition surprised her. She felt stronger now, stronger, and the pain had lessened greatly.

No dreams had marred her rest since Pharaoh begged of her to let her baby go. Perhaps he had been right. Perhaps by ceasing to search for her child's *kah*, she had freed him to find his own peace. She only knew that by releasing him, she had found rest of her own.

Meanwhile, her eyes roamed. She was in a large room with thickly carved furniture and heavy woven hangings on the walls. She was no longer lying in a camp bed, but rather in a huge bed surrounded by dark silken curtains. With an unpleasant shudder, she recognized the room. This was Hattushil's bedchamber. It was Hattushil's bed in which she lay.

She raised her hands to Med's, surprised at the effort it cost her.

"Why are we here?" she demanded.

He held her hands reassuringly. "The Hittite lords have surrendered, Princess," he told her. "Pharaoh was given the palace as a gesture of their goodwill." He moved the cloth from her cheeks to her neck. "Prince Amenophis wanted you to be sent to be tended by the Hittite women, but Pharaoh would not have it. He said no one was to touch you but the physician and me."

"How did he know?" she murmured. Left to the care of Hattushil's women, she had no doubt but that she would have met the same end as had her mother—poison slipped into her medicine, then a slow, lingering death. None of them had any desire to have the foreigner's whelp among them again, and the opportunity would have been too fortuitous for them to ignore.

"How did he know what, Princess?" Med asked, more than willing to talk to her, aware that for days he had longed to hear her voice.

She shook her head. "No matter," she told him.

He began to comb her hair, spreading the golden strands out over the heap of pillows on which her head lay. "Pharaoh left orders he was to be sent for if you woke. He will be here soon," he told her, his voice low and conspiratorial. "It will please him, I think, to see you look beautiful."

She stifled a smile. "You are as bad as a plotting procurer, Med," she accused him.

But she made no protest as he finished with her hair and then smoothed the silken bed clothes, artfully covering the thick bandages and yet leaving her shoulders and cleavage bare.

She stared down at the small golden charm that hung from a golden chain around her neck. "What is this, Med?" she asked.

"Pharaoh put it there, Princess," he told her. "It is called an ankh. It is a life symbol."

She held out her wrist, the one on which he'd placed her gold cuff. "And this?" she asked. "I gave it to you."

He shook his head. "You meant to *bequeath* it to me, Princess," he replied softly. "I am happy there was no need."

The door was drawn open then. Med darted a quick, conspiratorial smile at Shanda, then bowed to Pharaoh and silently slipped away.

Pharaoh crossed the room to her and sat beside the bed. He put his hand on her cheek tentatively, as if he was afraid to touch her, afraid the pressure of his fingers might cause her pain.

She smiled. "My lord," she said. Her voice sounded husky to her own ears, her tongue felt thick and clumsy, and she had no idea what to say.

"The physician says you are much better," he told her with a smile.

She lifted the ankh. "Perhaps it is due to this," she suggested.

He stroked the pale golden hair that lay spread across the pillows, lifting the locks and letting them fall through his fingers as he felt their silken softness. But then his smile faded suddenly. "I was afraid you would die," he murmured. "Nothing ever frightened me so much as the thought that you might die."

"There have been lies between us, lord," she whispered. "I would wish it were otherwise."

He shook his head. "It doesn't matter now, Shanda," he told her.

"It does," she insisted. "I was never told that Hattushil intended to invade Egypt. I swear that to you. But I knew there was no drought, no threat of famine, and I knew somewhere in the back of my mind that he must have intended to keep the grain for his army."

"Why didn't you tell me?" he asked her softly.

"At first because I hated you," she replied, the words sounding as though they were torn from her lips. "And then because I loved you."

"It's in the past now, Shanda," he assured her.

"Then you've forgiven me?" she asked. "You no longer hate me?"

"I never hated you," he told her. "I wanted to, but I knew I would never be able to hate you."

She smiled and tried to sit up, but a sharp pain in her side stopped the movement.

He gently pushed her back against the pillows.

"You must rest now and get well," he told her. "The charioteers have made offerings and prayers for your recovery. When you are well enough, you must go out to greet them."

"It would please me," she told him.

"They think of you now, more than ever, as their golden good luck charm. As do I." He leaned forward, to touch her lips with his.

A few days later Imhotep proclaimed her well enough to venture outside the palace gates to greet the soldiers and thank them for their prayers and offerings. The prospect pleased her enormously, as did the knowledge that she had returned to Kadesh as one who belonged, no longer an outsider. Hattushil's women would hear of it, she knew, and regret the wrongs they had done to her.

Pharaoh carried her in his arms to the palace gates, refusing to let his guards take her in a sedan chair.

When they reached the gate, however, she asked him to put her down. "A good luck charm cannot be broken," she told him with a smile.

"Indeed, Pharaoh," Seti agreed as he stepped forward. He and the rest of the generals had assembled inside the gate. They would review the soldiers after Pharaoh and Shanda left the field. They had insisted that the soldiers continue their training, in part to keep them from becoming lax, but mostly as a warning to the citizens and lords of Kadesh.

Pharaoh set her on her feet, putting his arm around her to allow her to lean against him. Several of his officers came forward to greet him, and all but one, young Amenophis, offered her a pleasant word and a smile. Pharaoh had told them how she had saved his life. They knew the effect that had had upon the battle, and realized they owed their victory partly to her. She had won them; they would never again look upon her as a foreigner, certainly not as an enemy.

All of them except Amenophis.

Shanda was not surprised at the antipathy that flowed toward her from Pharaoh's son. She knew he considered her his enemy, and she would one day be forced to confront him. But for that moment, she tried not to think of him.

The palace gates were drawn open, and Shanda walked out to the filled square at Pharaoh's side.

The afternoon was warm and bright, with sharp sunshine and a pleasant stirring of wind. On afternoons like this one, Shanda remembered, Althea had taken her to ride out on the great plain beyond the city. She had sat at her mother's side in the tall grass and listened as Althea told her stories about a land far to the north where she had once lived, a land where sometimes the rain fell from the sky white and cold to the touch, where there were rugged mountains that were the homes of strange and powerful gods. Shanda had thought those stories were simply tales thought up to amuse a child, but she was no longer so sure. She had seen enough to know that many things existed beyond the realm of her own experience.

As she stepped forward beside Pharaoh, she raised a hand to the throng of soldiers assembled in the square. Their shouts filled the air, and Shanda felt for the first time in her life that she truly belonged somewhere. She had been handed a great challenge and had met it with success.

And then her eyes settled on two tall spikes at the far

side of the square. She squinted into the sunlight to see the objects impaled on their points.

She cried out in sudden pain.

The air no longer seemed bright and fair, but was tinged with the smell of death that still lingered in the plain beyond the city. She had lain in Hattushil's bed but had not once wondered what had become of him.

And now she was staring at his head impaled on one of the spikes. His eyes were gaping sockets picked clean by birds; his face was a dead, dull gray. And beside his severed head, staring down at her in sightless reproach from the point of the second spike, was Nem's.

Pharaoh knew immediately what it was she had seen. The Hittite lords had brought the heads to him in a basket, a gesture of their surrender, assuring him that the insult done him and his country had been Hattushil's and the young general's alone, that the lords had had no part of it and had seen to it that Hattushil paid for his folly. He'd had them set the gory trophies on the poles as a warning, and they had willingly complied. Then Pharaoh had forgotten about their existence.

But now he realized what a shock it must have been to Shanda to see her father's head suspended over the square, a grisly, eyeless monstrosity, its dark curling beard and hair bristling, framing the empty sockets and the gaping mouth.

He caught her as she fell and shouted to Seti to have the heads removed as he carried her back into the palace. He was standing over her when she opened her eyes again.

She stared at him a second, then closed her eyes tightly as though trying to force away the image of what she had seen.

"I'd forgotten about them, Shanda. I would not have let you see your own father that way if I had remembered."

She shook her head sharply and opened her eyes. "It was not my father," she told him firmly.

She pushed herself up until she was sitting against the mound of pillows, knowing that Hattushil had sat as she now did, that the heat of his body had warmed these pillows. She felt tainted by the touch of them against her skin.

Pharaoh was confused by her comment until, for the hundredth time since the battle, he recalled the moment when he'd turned to see the young general draw back his sword. He'd been haunted for days by the image of that sword, by the sight of Shanda's blood sliding slowly along its shining length. But always before the memory had stopped there. Now it did not. He saw the young general stare at the blood and then at her, saw his shock and watched him mouth her name. And Pharaoh knew why she had fainted at the sight of those two gruesome offerings the lords of Kadesh had brought to him.

"He was the young general you loved before your father sent you to me, wasn't he?" he asked her softly.

She stared up at him in silence before she found the words to answer. "I never really loved him," she managed finally. "Not as I love you. I knew that when I saw him raise his arm, when I knew he would have killed you."

Pharaoh sat beside her and gathered her up into his arms. "I didn't understand how much it cost you," he told her, "how much you lost when you kept him from burying his sword in my back."

"I could not let you die," she whispered. She closed her eyes and saw Nem's head staring down at her once more. "It was seeing him like that . . ."

She pushed herself away from him, and as she did, she felt a sharp pain in her side. The fall, or perhaps the movement, had opened the wound in her side. But she had something to tell him, something she could hold inside her no longer. She pressed her hand against the hurt and looked out at Hattushil's private garden. She remembered playing among those carefully tended flowers while Hattushil was entertained by Althea.

She turned back to face Pharaoh. "I told you there were lies between us," she began.

He reached out to her. "You explained, Shanda," he said.

She shook her head and drew away from him. "No. I once told you my blood was as royal as yours, but that was a lie, too. I was nothing but coin to Hattushil, a means of payment that would cost him nothing to lose. You believed the Hittite king sent you his favorite daughter. But that, like the rest, was nothing more than a lie." She turned away and her expression grew hard and grim. "It did not pain me to see his head on that spike. I was glad. He was not my father. And I have never felt anything but hatred for him.

"I told you my mother came from beyond the Great Green," she went on, her voice calm now, determined. "She was the daughter of a king who planned to marry her to a neighboring prince as a means of cementing a treaty. But she was in love with a young man, and the two of them ran off, hoping to find sanctuary with her mother's people to the south. On the way they were set upon by bandits, and he was killed. My mother was taken by the bandits and sold to Hattushil."

"And the young man who was killed was your father?" Pharaoh said.

She nodded. "Hattushil had never seen a woman like my mother, with golden hair and pale blue eyes. She pleased him well enough to force him to make a bargain with her: She would come to him willingly only if he would accept as his own the child she was carrying. He accepted her conditions."

She looked down at Hattushil's gardens, searching for beauty there, but finding only memories. "I suppose if I had been a male child I would have met with some accident or illness to save him from giving another man's son his name, making another man's son his heir. But I was only a girl, and he saw no reason not to let me live. And by the time I was born, he was infatuated with my mother and determined to keep her. He accepted me as his own. But everyone in his court knew the truth.

"And Hattushil hated me. I felt it even when I was very small. He never hurt me for fear my mother would hold it against him, but as I grew to look more and more like her, his hatred increased. I was a reminder to him that he had wanted a child from her and she had managed to keep herself from giving to him what she had given to my father.

"When Hattushil decided to invade Egypt, he was glad to send me to you, glad to be rid of me in a manner that he thought would bring him some profit."

She took her hand away from her side and looked down at her palm, at the thin line of blood that had seeped through the bandages and her gown to stain it. "Please take me away from here," she whispered. "I don't belong here. I never did."

She wondered idly how many times her mother had lain with Hattushil in that bed selling her body so that her child might live. The room was like a tomb to Shanda. She could detect the scent of death in the air.

Pharaoh noticed the deep red stain on her gown and reached for her. This time she did not pull away.

"There is only death here," she whispered.

There was a dull certainty in her words that shocked him. But he accepted them without argument.

"As soon as it can be arranged," he told her, "we shall return to Egypt."

He held her in his arms and she fell against him. Dizziness and weakness overpowered her, and she was glad of the solidity of his arms around her.

"I will not heal here," she told him. "There are spirits here who would gladly see my end." Perhaps they were Hattushil's and Nem's ghosts, she thought. Perhaps this was to be her payment for what she had done. She thought of the heads staring down at her from the bloody pikes.

"If I stay here, lord," she murmured, "I will die."

# Sixteen

"IF WE LEAVE now," Amenophis said, "we might just as well tell the Hittites they have leave to move south again whenever it pleases them. I say it is foolish to return to Thebes. We should strike to the north and show the Hittites what it means to rouse the ire of Egypt."

Amenophis glared at Pharaoh. The boy enjoyed his position of command, and it pleased him to have a say among the council of generals. Returning to Thebes would mean the end of that authority. He had no intention of giving it up without a fight.

"When we leave, we take the royal treasury with us," Pharaoh replied without rancor. "The Hittites will not soon forget the cost of my anger."

Pharaoh considered Amenophis's outburst the ramblings of a spoiled boy, something to be ignored. It had been a mistake to give him an active command, however unimportant. He had made another error in his relationship with his son. Having command of his own phalanx had reinforced his belief in his own superiority without rousing in him a spirit of responsibility. It had been painful for Pharaoh to know he would bequeath his crown to an heir for whom he had no love, but it was agony for him to contemplate leaving Egypt in the hands of one who was entirely incompetent to rule. He thought dully of the son Shanda might have borne him and wondered if the child's death was not only a personal loss but a tragedy for Egypt as well.

"The Kadesh lords have given me their king's head and sworn fealty to me," he went on, addressing Amenophis and his other generals. "That and the surrender of nearly a thousand talents of gold, I think, speaks for their recognition of the seriousness of their crime. I have done what I intended to do." His tone was authoritative, and he was obviously in no mood to entertain further discussion of the matter. "The army will begin preparations to withdraw."

"Militarily, it would not be inappropriate to pursue our advantage, lord," Seti suggested mildly.

Pharaoh turned a withering glance on him. "I said we return to Egypt," he thundered.

His response was enough to impress his seriousness upon all but Amenophis. The young prince seemed determined to show Pharaoh his folly, to throw it up to him in the company of the generals.

"It's for *her* sake you spare her people," he cried. "For your Hittite whore."

Pharaoh turned on him, anger coloring his cheeks. "You go too far, boy. Unless you have grown tired of drawing breath, you would be wise to keep your own counsel."

The room became completely silent around them, as if the men had drawn a breath and waited to see how far their king's ire had been raised before they dared to release it.

Amenophis's complexion grew dark. He felt the eyes of the generals on him and thought that to back down would lose him what little respect he had earned. Ignoring Pharaoh's warning, he stepped forward.

"You have taken this woman to your bed and treated her like a queen, ignoring the one who truly deserves your respect. I do not forget the insult you do to my mother and to me."

Pharaoh grew suddenly outwardly calm, controlling his anger, pretending it had fled. Seti took a step back, knowing this appearance of calm hid a rapidly growing rage that might erupt unexpectedly and not wishing to find himself in its path.

"What you choose to forget or remember is of little interest to me," Pharaoh said evenly, his tone dismissive, as though he spoke to one so far below his station he could not be bothered to waste his energy on anger. But then his eyes grew suddenly sharp as he studied Amenophis. "You think yourself already pharaoh, boy, but you are not yet so great that I cannot crush you like the gnat you truly are."

Amenophis shuddered with rage, but somehow managed to swallow it, realizing perhaps that he had already dared far too much, that his open rebellion had earned him, not the respect of the generals but their dismissal and, more dangerously, Pharaoh's open antipathy. Even his anger could not blind him to the fact that he was not yet in a position to challenge his father openly.

He bowed stiffly, then turned on his heel and stalked out of the room, leaving the other generals in embarrassed silence.

Pharaoh scanned the faces of his men. One or two of them, he thought, showed signs of sympathy with Amenophis, so his son's opinions were not entirely his alone. A few of the others would have continued the battle against the Hittites, given the option. He would have to watch those men, he decided. Their defiance was not yet open, but the fact that they harbored thoughts of it meant they might one day be a danger to him.

The rest of his generals were entirely willing to accept his decision. As long as the war had been one of retribution, it had been popular among the soldiers and they had fought bravely and well. But they had no desire to fight their way deeper into an unfriendly country. Already the taste of spring was on the wind, and the soldiers talked about returning home to their families. For all his delusions of command, Amenophis had no understanding of the intricacies of dealing with these men.

And Pharaoh had other matters to concern him. He would deal with Amenophis and his few sympathizers after they had returned to Thebes. It cost him nothing to postpone a confrontation. They were certainly in no position to pose a serious danger to him. At least not yet.

"You will begin the preparations for withdrawal," he told his generals, then dismissed them with a motion of his hand. He stood with Seti and watched them bow and file from the room.

When they were alone, Pharaoh turned to the general of his guard.

"You think, like the prince, that we should move north, wreaking vengeance on the Hittites?" His voice was mild now, amiable, even a bit amused.

"I think we should not lose sight of the possibility that they might have been a more potent enemy had you not thought to reinforce the fort at Shunem," Seti replied evenly.

"But omnipotent and all seeing man-god that I am, I foresaw Hattushil's duplicity and so sent soldiers to Shunem and kept the border safe." Pharaoh grinned. "Perhaps you, like the Hittites, have forgotten that a Pharaoh is a powerful foe."

He grinned again when he saw Seti's frown at his irreverent reference to his own godhead. But he sobered abruptly.

"Do not assume, as does my foolish son, that I have not considered the possibility of pursuing this war," he said evenly. "But continuing north would mean constantly leaving large contingents of troops to guard our rear. Were we to move even so far as Carchemish, we would need to station more than half of our forces behind us to secure our retreat. Add to that the number who would be needed here, to hold Kadesh. The oath of fealty the lords here swore to me would be worthless if I chose to continue this war, and subduing this city would require a strong garrison. Would you have me invade a country with only the handful of soldiers left to me? What kind of battle do you suppose those few would be fit to make?"

Seti finally smiled. "Perhaps it is not without reason that you are Pharaoh and I am a lowly servant, lord," he suggested. "Or does the crown of the two Egypts endow one with perception as well as godliness?"

Pharaoh laughed, surprised at the unexpected irreverence. It was the first laughter Seti had heard from him in weeks. It pleased him that he had given his lord cause. But when the laughter ended, both men grew sober.

"Imhotep says Shanda is not well enough to travel," Pharaoh said. He seemed not to be speaking to Seti but merely saying aloud the words that were foremost in his mind. "He tells me the trip back would surely kill her." He looked down the length of the now empty reception hall. "And yet she tells me the only thing that will make her well is to leave this place. From all I have seen, I cannot say I disbelieve her."

"The physician is a wise man, lord," Seti ventured, not at all sure his advice was being sought.

"But there are matters of which even wise men are ignorant," Pharaoh countered.

It occurred to Seti that Amenophis had been right to say

that Pharaoh's decision had little to do with battle tactics and a great deal to do with his passion for the Hittite princess.

"Then we return to Egypt?" he asked.

Pharaoh nodded. "As quickly as possible. I will not leave her to lie in a Hittite grave as I have left our son."

There was bitterness and pain in his words, neither of which Seti could mistake. Perhaps, he thought, this war of Hattushil's had cost Pharaoh more than he was able to lose.

"We leave in two days, Seti," Pharaoh said abruptly.

The eyes he turned back to Seti were once again sharp. It was apparent that whatever his motives, Pharaoh was once again completely in command of himself.

"See that all preparations are made. And keep an eye on Amenophis. He grows bolder as he becomes a man. I think him still unready, but there will come a day when he will move against me, and I wish to be prepared."

Seti bowed his head. "Yes, lord," he replied. "I will see to everything."

Shanda was almost as pale now, Pharaoh thought, as she had been when he lifted her bloodstained body from his chariot. Imhotep had told him that despite all his efforts to stanch the wound, she continued to bleed. And there was no questioning the infection that fought to claim her. Pharaoh could feel the heat of it when he touched her.

Perhaps she had been right when she told him there were evil spirits in Kadesh that would watch her die with pleasure. When he lifted her in his arms she seemed so light he wondered how her frail body could hold even so little life as that to which she now clung.

He carried her to the waiting wagon and watched as her eunuch made her comfortable on the cushioned bed he'd made for her.

"Shall I ride with you?" Pharaoh asked as he gently touched her cheek and found that her skin was hot and damp. The fever that seemed beyond the physician's medicines once again raged within her.

She took his hand and brushed it with her lips, smiling at him.

"A pharaoh rides at the head of his army, lord," she told him with a smile. "Not at the bedside of a foolish woman."

"A brave, beautiful woman," he countered.

"But foolish still."

She watched him in silence for a moment. He could see that she had to struggle to keep her attention from wandering as the fever threatened to consume her thoughts.

"I know you are leaving Kadesh because of me, lord. I also know that this hasty departure has cost you a great deal," she said softly.

He shook his head. "Not so much. The lords of Kadesh have emptied their king's treasury to bribe me to leave the city intact and venture no farther into their kingdom," he told her with a grin. "I return to Thebes far richer than I was when I left." He kissed her lips softly. "In many ways," he said.

She leaned back into the heap of pillows, suddenly spent. "This place speaks to me only of death," she whispered. "I can even taste death in the air here. It frightens me." She looked out at the city square and through the open city gates to the field, still muddied and stained, where the two armies had met in battle.

"We leave it all behind us now, today," he assured her.

He touched his lips to her cheek once more, then motioned to Med to sit beside her.

Shanda saw him climb into his chariot and lead the long procession of his army out of Kadesh. As her own wagon lurched through the city gates, she saw the great mound that was the communal grave of many of the soldiers who had died in the battle.

She felt a dull lurch of pain as she realized the lords of the city, in their rage and spite, must have buried Nem and Hattushil there. In failure and death they would not have been considered worthy of loftier tombs. The sight of that uneven heap brought her more hurt than she had expected. No matter what they had done, she thought, surely they had deserved more respect from their own people. A burial with dignity was the least any man deserved.

The stream that ran beside the mound was no longer clear and colorless as it had been the morning before the battle. Now the water ran rust-colored, as though forever stained by the blood that had been shed on the plain surrounding it. She could almost taste the water and smell the sweet scent of human blood that had mixed with it.

She turned her head away, not wanting to see any more.

"Close it," she told Med.

He silently drew the side of the wagon closed, shutting away her last sight of Kadesh.

The return journey seemed endless to Med. But to Shanda, lost in a fevered haze, it was only another cloud that filled her mind. The days and nights blurred, one slipping unnoticed into the next. She began to believe that she had never been without the sharp pain and the fever that ate at her. She tried unsuccessfully to remember how she had felt before she returned to Kadesh.

Through the long days Med sat beside her, trying vainly to cool the fever that had so strong a hold on her, wondering if Pharaoh had made the wrong choice in taking her from Kadesh while she was still so weak.

Pharaoh, too, had begun to question the wisdom of the

sudden departure from Kadesh. Often he left the lead of the army to one of his generals and came to sit beside her, to stare into her glazed eyes and remind her that they had left Kadesh behind, that now she must do as she had promised him and grow stronger.

When finally they reached the fertile delta at the mouth of the Nile, Pharaoh had camp set up for himself and his guard as the barges were readied to carry the soldiers back upriver to Thebes. The plain was turned into a vast army camp, with hundreds of small fires holding off the onset of darkness as the soldiers settled in for their first real rest since they'd left Kadesh.

Pharaoh had his tent set up on a small rise overlooking the Great Green, where the breezes could bring the taste of the sea. He carried Shanda to it from her wagon, wishing she would wake and speak to him. He was filled with the fear that it was too late, that he had waited too long to take her from Kadesh, that she no longer had the strength to fight for her own survival.

That night he sat beside her, terrified that she would not live until morning.

But when dawn finally came, she stirred and opened her eyes. For the first time since he had taken her from Kadesh she smiled at him with clear, bright eyes.

"We are home?" she asked tentatively.

*Home*, she thought. How good the word sounded. Until she came to Pharaoh, she'd never really had a real home.

He nodded and then smiled. "Yes, Princess." He pointed toward the entrance to the tent. "Out there is Egypt. We sit at the mouth of the Nile, waiting for the barges to be readied to return us to Thebes."

She struggled to sit up, and he sat beside her and gathered her in his arms. He kissed her forehead, telling himself it was not as hot as it had been the night before.

She pressed herself close to him, comforted by his body near hers.

" 'The Nile is Egypt's mother,' " she told him, echoing the words he had spoken to her that night on the palace roof. " 'She succors us, makes our fields fertile, keeps us from want.' " She looked up at him then, finding his eyes with her own. "May I see it?" she begged softly.

"Do you not accept the word of Pharaoh, woman?" he asked, but smiled at her as he spoke.

"Yes," she replied solemnly. "But it would please me to see the Nile."

"If it will please you, my love," he agreed.

He called to Med to bring a cloak. Pharaoh wrapped it around her shoulders, lifted her in his arms, and took her outside into the early morning light.

The soldiers camped on the plain behind them were starting their day, and she heard shouts and movement, smelled the breakfasts being prepared over the fires. There was the bite of smoke on the air and the aroma of bread being baked and fish being grilled.

Shanda tightly clasped Pharaoh's neck as she looked out over the lush green plain that seemed to stretch on forever, alive with movement of soldiers. And beyond the camp were fields of grain and vineyards bearing the first buds that would grow to be fruit. Soon the soldiers would board the barges that lay far off at the river's edge like tiny toys. The smells, the noise, the movement—it all seemed so normal to her, as though she had wakened to these same sights and sounds and odors her whole life.

In the far distance the sea gleamed brilliant with the first bright fingers of morning sun. The sparkling water struck a note within her, filling her with a contentment she'd never felt before. She tasted the crisp air and felt the wind tugging at her hair and whipping Pharaoh's cloak about him.

"You have seen Egypt," he told her. "Now you must fulfill your promise to me, Shanda. You must grow strong and well."

She nestled her head against his shoulder. "In such a place as this," she whispered to him, "it would be impossible not to grow well, lord."

"Then we shall stay here," he told her, "until you have kept your word."

This place offered sunlight and warm sand in which to lie and, at least for a while, a respite from the intrigues of Amenophis and Queen Tiy. Soon enough, he would have to deal with matters that might prove even more unpleasant than the expedition to Kadesh. But he would have this time alone with her before he returned her to Thebes as healthy as she had been when he took her away.

"Is it wise, lord, to allow Prince Amenophis to return to Thebes while you remain here?"

Seti was obviously disturbed at the prospect. The first barges were being loaded, and Amenophis and his soldiers were to be among the first to return to Thebes.

Pharaoh watched the long line of soldiers slowly boarding the waiting barge. The sun, low on the horizon behind him, was hot and languorous on his back. It was an altogether pleasant feeling, one he had missed since he'd left Egypt and ventured into the cold, damp mountains to the north.

"Prudence is not always the best path to follow, Seti," he finally replied.

"Pharaoh?"

"Have you seen her these last few days, Seti?" Pharaoh asked. "Just being here has done her far more good than all the potions Imhotep can offer. Each day she grows stronger."

There was no need for Seti to ask to whom Pharaoh referred. He had seen the princess several times in the preceding days, and on each occasion he was surprised at the changes in her. "Yes, lord, but each day you leave Amenophis to his own devices in Thebes allows him to grow stronger as well."

Seti spoke with regret, but he was determined to perform his duty as he saw it, and that meant reminding Pharaoh of the folly of leaving Amenophis and Tiy free to conspire against him.

"Do you honestly think a few months will give Amenophis and Tiy enough power to challenge me?" he asked.

Seti shook his head. "No, lord. Especially since the defeat of Hattushil, you are certainly beyond their reach. And Nofret is too much the conscientious vizier to allow them to make a move before the moment is ripe."

"Then leave the pup to his play," Pharaoh responded, more than anxious to dismiss the matter even though he knew he could not afford to ignore it for long.

"Pups grow quickly, lord," Seti insisted. "Some grow strong enough to challenge their masters. And this particular pup has gained two powerful friends," he added, reminding Pharaoh of the generals who were less than pleased with the decision to withdraw from Kadesh.

Pharaoh sighed as he watched the slowly moving line of soldiers. "Then you think Amenophis will use this opportunity to make allies he will one day be able to use against me?"

Seti nodded. "Yes, lord."

"Perhaps I will send spies to keep an eye on them, Seti, but unless the need to return becomes urgent I will stay here with Shanda. I've given all my life to Egypt. Surely I am owed a few moments of rest."

Seti bowed. "It will be as you say, Pharaoh," he said.

Pharaoh kept his eyes on the line of soldiers as they slowly boarded the barge and arranged themselves on the deck.

Seti, of course, was right, as he usually was. Pharaoh had no doubt that Amenophis and Tiy would someday strike at him in the hope of placing his crown on his son's head. But he knew he was more than secure for now, especially since his victory at Kadesh. When the time came, he would be ready for whatever blow they might care to strike against him. In the meantime, he would not endanger Shanda's recovery by taking her back to Thebes, regardless of the consequences of his decision.

# Seventeen

SHANDA SAT IN the center of a large sheet spread out on the sand. Above her, the thin tent Med had constructed to protect her from the sun fluttered in the late afternoon breeze. She stretched lazily and lay back against a disorderly heap of pillows.

She waited for the pleasant lassitude that used to come over her as she sat in the late afternoon sunshine and watched Pharaoh take this last swim of the day, the indolent laziness that had once claimed her as she lay warmed by the heat of the sun and the sand and soothed by the scent and taste of sea air on her lips. Today, however, the feeling eluded her, as it had for the past few afternoons. She tried unsuccessfully to expunge the thoughts that had become steadily more bothersome as the days passed.

She felt extremely, almost impossibly, well. The fever was gone, leaving her memories of the preceding weeks confused, but with little other ill effect. And aside from the thick, red scar on her side that reached from just below her breast to her lower hip, the wound from Nem's sword had completely healed. She had fulfilled her promise to Pharaoh, she thought.

She let her fingers trail through the warm sand as she searched among the waves for the sight of a dark head. Pharaoh had so far refused to allow her to swim with him, telling her that the currents were strong and the waves pounding. He said she was not yet strong enough to engage in strenuous activity, and he treated her with the deferential tolerance one allowed invalids.

The only problem was that she no longer felt like an invalid. She had so far humored him, splashing about in the knee-high water while he swam or lying on the beach and letting the sun fill her with pleasant, languorous lassitude. But the desire for strenuous activity, especially activity of a particular kind, was growing ever stronger inside her. It was as though there was a void within her that needed to be filled. And the sight of his naked body as he entered the water to swim only accentuated that need, making it all the stronger.

The night before, as she lay unhappily alone, she had wondered if his remoteness stemmed not from consideration for her health but from a simple lack of interest. She thought of how they walked along the beach when he finished his swim and how he refrained from touching her except to keep her steady as she walked through the sand. Always he pulled back from her, as though he found the prospect of touching her unpleasant. And his reticence had grown more pronounced as she had become stronger.

She had stood naked in the lamplight, studying the ugly scar that marred her pale skin. She had gingerly touched the swollen, uneven thickening of the flesh. This was hardly a pleasure to be anticipated with relish. Perhaps, she'd mused miserably, it was simple physical revulsion that kept Pharaoh at a distance.

Shanda had returned to her bed and spent a good portion of

the night miserably considering that possibility. She told herself that he cared for her and that he would never abandon her. But the prospect of spending her life as a tolerated pet was not one she envied. Better to have died and been buried in Kadesh than to know he maintained her only out of gratitude and an absent fondness.

This is foolish, she thought, and she pushed herself up out of the sand. She stood for a moment, watching Pharaoh as he began the long swim back to shore. His head was a small dark dot in the distance that seemed to bob with the rise and fall of the waves.

When he'd returned from his morning ride with Seti, she had been waiting for him. Twice during the course of the morning she had tried to ask him the question that was in her mind but found herself unable to utter the words. And each time he'd noticed her troubled, questioning stare, but he had not pushed her when she lost her courage.

His apparent willingness to leave the words unspoken between them had disturbed her even more. Because he did not want to hurt her, he would avoid her questions if he could. She began to search for the right words, rehearsing them in her mind so the next time she would not lose them in her confusion.

She did not see any of Seti's men on the beach today. For the first few weeks there had always been two or three guards with them, but as the summer drew on and the possibility of danger faded, Seti had allowed his men to grow lax. Shanda was delighted to find the long beach completely deserted.

There was but one way to do this, she told herself firmly as she unclasped the brooch that held the fabric of her gown together at her shoulder. The fine linen fabric fell to her feet, and she stepped out of the circle of it, leaving it where it had fallen in the sand.

She walked carefully into the water, feeling the sand,

warm and smooth, underfoot, carefully avoiding a spiny sea urchin that the tide had brought in and abandoned on the sand. The water was cool and pleasant, and she moved purposefully forward, enjoying the sensation as it rose from her ankles to her knees and then to her hips, letting the waves splash against her belly and breasts and neck, unheeding of the impact as the water raced into shore, or the pull as it fled back to the place from which it had come.

She was standing in waist deep water when Pharaoh saw her.

"Shanda!"

There was a note of warning in his voice and she wondered if she had angered him or if he was simply afraid she might be swept out to sea by a particularly strong wave. For a moment she felt her determination wane. Would it not be better to go on not knowing than to learn that Pharaoh no longer wanted her?

She had to force herself to stay where she was rather than return to the beach. But she desperately wanted to know the truth. She watched as his strong arms rose out of the water in even cadence, bringing him steadily closer. Her body swayed slightly as the waves pushed against her.

When he was a few feet from her, he stood and slicked the water from his face and hair. Then he moved slowly toward her. "Shanda, what is it? Is something wrong?"

She stared at him steadily, refusing to drop her eyes, knowing she would see the truth in them, knowing they could not lie.

"Lord," she began, and then found, just as she had before, that the words refused to be said. She simply stared at him dumbly.

He moved a step closer to her.

"Is something wrong, Princess?" he asked her gently.

She took a deep breath, gathering up her courage.

"My lord"—she pointed to the jagged, angry line of red on her side—"does this make me repulsive to you?"

He stared at her for a long moment, his eyes searching. "Is this the question you've tried to ask me all day?"

She could only nod. There was a thickness in her throat that terrified her. She thought of all the times when words had been so easy for her. When she'd first come to him, she'd been full of angry words, defiant words. Why, she wondered, was it so much harder to love than it was to hate?

"No part of you could ever be anything but beautiful to me," he said as he moved toward her and put his hands on her shoulders. And then, as though to prove what he told her, he bent down and pressed his lips to the angry red weal where it began beneath her breast. Then he slowly slid his tongue along the thick, irregular line.

Shanda thought she had forgotten what his touch was like, that her body had forgotten what power lay in the contact of his lips, but the first touch of his lips on her skin immediately awoke the fires within her that had been banked for so long. Her heart began to race, and a sharp, deep, regular beat filled her.

He straightened and drew away from her instead of pulling her close, as she had wanted. He was once again establishing a distance between them.

"Have I answered your question, Shanda?" he asked.

"Yes," she replied miserably, wishing she'd never asked and turning away from him.

He took her arm and made her face him.

"Shanda, what is it?" he asked her, bewildered by her look of dejection.

The words, it seemed, had been waiting to be released. She heard them tumbling from her lips even as she wondered who had spoken.

"I have waited for you to come to me," she told him, suddenly fierce in the face of his rejection, "only to have you avoid touching me. Have you so quickly tired of me? Is that why you hold yourself apart from me? Because you cannot bear to touch me?"

He looked at her in silence for a moment before he spoke, and she thought his reluctance stemmed from a fear of hurting her, a desire to bring her no further pain. She would, she thought, have preferred cruelty to this strained regard.

"You think I have held myself apart from you because I no longer want you?" he asked finally.

He was smiling at her with the tolerant hidden amusement one ordinarily reserved for conversation with precocious but slightly spoiled children. Had she been less upset, she would have bristled at the expression. Instead, she could only think his amusement confirmed what she had feared. She felt certain that she was no longer the object of his passion, that he had enough unscarred women to amuse him.

She began to walk through the water, back toward the beach, unwilling to play the fool any longer.

He moved after her quickly, took hold of her shoulders, and turned her to face him.

"Do you think I no longer desire you, Shanda?" he asked as he pulled her close to him. "Do you really think what I feel for you could simply die?"

But words were no longer necessary. She could feel strong and ample evidence of his desire.

She put her hands on his cheeks and brought his lips to meet hers. At first his lips were warm and hungry against hers, the way she remembered them. But when she parted hers to invite him in, yearning for the sweet taste of him, he pulled back abruptly.

"Why?" she cried, the single word sharp with anguish.

He looked down at her. "Shanda, I have never in my life

been so afraid as I was when I thought you might die," he told her, his voice thick with emotion.

She shook her head, bewildered. "I am not going to die," she promised.

"I know myself," he told her evenly. "One kiss, one taste of you, would not be enough. Once I begin, I will not stop."

She took his hand, raised it to her lips, and pressed an eager kiss on his palm.

"I do not want you to stop," she told him, then looked up to find his eyes, dark and hard with longing, gazing down at her.

"But if I hurt you, Shanda . . . "

She shook her head. "The only way you could hurt me is by not loving me," she told him as she kissed his palm once more, then guided his hand to her breast.

Pharaoh was not certain that he could trust her words. But his own yearning spurred him, as did the warmth of her flesh beneath his fingers.

She smiled up at him, then raised her hands to his neck. "Love me," she whispered as she pulled him down to her kiss.

She felt his hands slide over her wet skin as his arms enfolded her, felt the heat of his body as he pressed himself against her. And then he was kissing her, his lips tasting of salt as his tongue gently probed hers, calling up the sweet yearning within her.

She clung to him, her hands on his shoulders, lost in sensation as he lowered his lips to her neck and breasts and once again, slowly, teasingly, to the thick line of scar. And then his hands fell to her hips and he lifted her, pulling her against him.

She wrapped her legs around him, letting his hands and the buoyancy of the water hold her, feeling the waves within her rise in a tide of longing as he entered her.

All the world, it seemed, had turned to sparkling gold, the sun glinting off the water liquid gold and the sand at its edge a great long path of burnished gold. Everything around her was filled with a sharp brilliance she'd never seen before. It seeped into her, made her feel as though she were part of it, her body sharp and lustrous with the fire that burned inside her. She pushed herself against him, then held still, gasping softly with sweet pleasure as he filled her.

"Have I hurt you, Shanda?" he whispered.

She saw the concern in his eyes, heard it in his words. She smiled, aware that pain, even the memory of it, was entirely gone from her body.

"You give me only pleasure," she told him softly.

He smiled and began to move slowly within her, watching her face, searching for signs that he might be causing her some hurt and finding, happily, that she showed only the same passionate ecstasy he felt within himself. Then he buried his lips against her neck, letting the tide within him sweep through him.

Shanda clung to him, pressing herself against him, feeling like a part of him, knowing that all of her suffering had been part of her fate, a test of her love for him, a trial to determine her worthiness to receive the gift he offered her. And she had survived only because she loved him.

The tide within her, like the waves lapping against her, rose higher and higher, carrying her upward until it finally crashed down upon her, leaving her shattered and feeling as liquid and insubstantial as the golden sunlight that floated on the water around her.

He held her close and she leaned against him, spent and filled, as her heartbeat began to slow. A wave splashed against her, wetting her cheeks and lips. She sighed with a tired contentment, unmindful of it, then leaned closer to him, kissing his chest, tasting the sharp bite of the seawater that she licked from his nipples.

He smiled, wondering if she could feel the beat of his heart against her lips. Then she raised her head and kissed him, hard and sure, full on the lips, and he knew she had.

He released her slowly. Then, just before she found her footing in the rock-strewn sand beneath the water, he changed his mind and lifted her once more in his arms. Carrying her, he began to walk toward the shore.

"I am no longer an invalid, lord," she told him with a laugh as she wrapped her arms around his neck. "You need not carry me."

"It is not as an invalid I find myself thinking of you at this moment, Princess," he told her with a smile.

She threw her head back and laughed again, filled with sheer, unfettered delight, certain that nothing could mar it.

He carried her over the sand and set her down on the large linen sheet, settling himself beside her as she, oblivious of the water that clung to her, leaned back against the heap of pillows.

"I wonder, lord, if I might ask something of you."

He leaned forward and slowly licked away the drops of salt water that clung to her breast before he answered. "What would you have of me, princess? Jewels? A palace of your own?" He raised his head, and his expression grew serious. "Would you have me place a queen's crown on those beautiful golden curls?"

She shook her head. "No, none of those things," she replied, wondering how she could broach this subject, which would probably cause him hurt. "I would have you give me a baby, lord," she said slowly, searching his eyes, wondering what thoughts they hid. "A son."

Pharaoh was silent, and she knew he was thinking of the baby they had left behind them, in Kadesh. As much as that loss hurt her, she knew it hurt him more, for he bore the weight of knowing he had been the cause of that baby's death. But just as the need for his love had driven her, so too did this need, this odd emptiness within her that she knew could be filled only by a child.

She reached up to push away a damp lock that had fallen across his forehead.

"That is a gift not for yourself but for me," he said slowly.

"For us both," she whispered in reply.

He gazed into her eyes, then kissed her softly on the lips. "I will do all in my power," he said, finally smiling, "to grant your wish, Princess."

He leaned forward, offering her his lips, eager to fulfill his promise.

Pharaoh lay beside her, watching her sleep. He put his hand on her arm, touching it softly, admiring the gentle golden hue her skin had turned in the long days of sunshine. He remembered how pale she'd been when he took her from Kadesh, and compared the memory to the warm body lying beside him, her face now pink-cheeked and glowing, her flesh warm and silken soft beneath his fingers.

He thought idly of what it would be like to live alone with her here where the Nile flowed into the Great Green, where all of their days could be like the one they had just spent, making love, lying together in the sand, holding each other close as they watched the sun slowly sink and turn the sky to flame. How much easier life would be, he thought, if he were an ordinary man, if there was no duty for him, no court at Thebes waiting for his return.

Such thoughts were just foolish, idle meanderings, he knew. And it pained him to realize that there would be little more time for him to spend there with her before he had to return. It was an eventuality he contemplated with regret. He would have liked to stay there with her, watching the orange and apple trees grow heavy with fruit.

But there was little chance he would be able to remain even until harvest time. Already Seti's spies had sent back word that Amenophis had entered the city at the head of the army, proclaiming his part in the victory over the Hittites. It would not be long before Tiy would have him seeking support from those who had supported her father in his long-ago failed attempt to seize the crown. Old enemies, he thought with a shade of bitterness, should have the good manners to stay buried. Unfortunately they seldom did.

The support Tiy and Amenophis could gather, he knew, would be decidedly limited, certainly not enough to challenge him. But the longer he was gone, the greater would be their intrigues, and by remaining absent he would appear to have grown weak, unable to control even his own wife and son. And the appearance of weakness could be as dangerous to him as the most powerful of adversaries.

Shanda stirred at his side, distracting him from his thoughts. He leaned toward her and kissed her.

"It is time you were fed, Shanda," he told her firmly when she opened her eyes. "It grows late and the sun has nearly set."

He looked up at the sky, dim now, with long, thick fingers of red and orange reaching out from the horizon and coloring the growing darkness. Clouds, dim and gray in the waning light, floated peacefully above the water. It was strange how pleasant he found the sight of clouds in the sky, he thought. Perhaps because they were rarely seen in Thebes.

"I will miss the clouds when we return to Thebes," she murmured softly, echoing his own thoughts.

He stood and extended a hand to her. "There is no need

yet to think of returning," he told her as he helped her to her feet. "Now it is time to think of food."

"I think you would have me grow fat, lord," she teased as he pulled her to him.

"Indeed, Princess," he agreed amiably. He put his hand on her belly, wondering if they had already begun the child for which she had asked. "I would have you grow great and round."

Shanda put her hand on his and held it close to her belly, feeling the warmth of it seeping inside her. She had absolutely no doubt that she had conceived that day.

"I shall," she told him confidently, with a seriousness that seemed to surprise him but which was quite justified in her own mind.

He drew her to him and buried his lips in her hair as he gazed off at the darkness that was quickly filling the sky. His father had bequeathed to him a crown and all the privileges and responsibilities that entailed. He had held on to his inheritance by whatever means he could—by taking a bride he did not love and, when the need arose, by force. It was not a past of which he was entirely proud, but it had been justified. What he had done had been necessary not only to secure his own life but to keep his empire whole.

He wondered what would be left to bequeath to her child. What inheritance of deceit and violence would he pass on to their son? More than that, he wondered if, with Amenophis as his enemy, this child would live long enough to do what was necessary to keep what would one day be his.

# Eighteen

SHANDA'S RETURN TO Thebes was far different from her departure. She spent the voyage upriver at Pharaoh's side, not in semidarkness, hidden from view like the criminal and traitor she had been considered during the passage to Kadesh. On this voyage she was pampered and indulged, with Pharaoh apparently determined to make amends for everything she had been forced to endure.

Their passage was celebrated with great enthusiasm by the peasants who farmed the long fertile strip by the river. News of Pharaoh's approach spread before him. All along the river, groups gathered to catch a glimpse of their king. Many threw flowers into the water as his barge passed, offerings that left the barge's wake iridescent with floating blooms of lotus, hibiscus, heliotrope, and jasmine. A reign marked by stability and plenty had made Pharaoh popular among his people, and his victory over the Hittites had served to strengthen their awed veneration. They were more than eager to pay homage to him as he passed.

"It is a shame, Pharaoh," Seti remarked as they neared a particularly enthusiastic group who shouted and waved from shore, "that peasants cannot be lords and lords peasants."

Pharaoh grinned. "It would be a pleasure to make a few of those who spend their days fawning at court actually labor for their bread," he agreed. "Or take them into battle and let them face violent death from an immediate and personal viewpoint."

He turned and looked at Shanda, who was dozing in the late afternoon heat. The first month of her pregnancy had not been easy for her. She had been plagued by nausea in the morning and sometimes late at night. Instead of growing round, as he had thought she would, she had become even thinner, which caused him considerable concern despite the physician's assurance that such occurrences were entirely normal and the passage of time would soon correct the condition.

"But this is not the moment to talk of death," he said as he turned back to Seti. "Now I wish to speak only of life, new life."

Seti grinned. He had never seen Pharaoh quite so delighted as he was at the prospect of this child's birth.

"I think the worst is past, lord," he said. "She looks much better this morning."

"She tries not to let me see," Pharaoh replied, "but the travel on the river unsettles her. Once we are back in Thebes, I think she will be more comfortable." He suddenly became thoughtful. "But Thebes will have its own dangers," he added softly.

Seti understood him immediately. "If this child is a boy, Queen Tiy will consider him a threat to Amenophis."

"And a queen who feels threatened is more apt to act than one who is not?" Pharaoh prodded.

Seti nodded. "It is not wise, lord, to dismiss an enemy before you are sure just what his capabilities might be."

Pharaoh offered him a crooked, humorless smile. "Just when, Seti," he asked, "have you ever known me to ignore a threat? Or to face an enemy unprepared?"

Seti shook his head. "Never, lord," he replied. Then he added, very softly, "But you have never been in love before, either, lord."

Pharaoh noted his worried expression, then smiled as he clasped Seti's shoulder.

"Do not worry, old friend. I have confidence that you will keep me, as you always have, forewarned of dangers, and help me steer clear of them. If we are careful, the tide will not carry us so swiftly that we cannot control the destiny of our craft."

"Only the gods control destiny, lord," Seti warned him solemnly.

Pharaoh laughed. "Need I remind you that I am a god?" he asked with a grin. "I fear you have lost your reverence, Seti."

Seti, however, was not amused by his levity. "You are a man-god, lord," he amended evenly. "A god with a man's failings and a man's weaknesses. A god who can be hurried on the road to his death like any other mortal."

Pharaoh sobered at his words. "Then I will depend on you to keep me treading that path at only a moderate pace." He looked once again at Shanda. "I find myself with a great deal for which I would choose to live," he added softly.

To Shanda's eye, the riverfront was chaos. Every inhabitant of Thebes had come to witness Pharaoh's return to the city. The water's edge was thronged with people, and as far as she could see from where she stood, the streets behind were equally crowded. She was reminded of the procession from the temple when Pharaoh had sacrificed for the harvest. There was the same joyousness in the air, the same controlled yet potent adulation.

Seti's soldiers had already disembarked and formed a cordon, holding the crowd at a respectful distance. As Pharaoh helped Shanda climb down from the barge onto the dock, the air was suddenly filled with a shower of pale missiles, lotus flowers thrown on the ground before Pharaoh by the people who stood behind the ranks of soldiers.

Shanda smiled when she saw the flurry of blooms. She almost wished she could repeat that night of the procession, drive his chariot as she had then, sleep with him once again on the palace roof, with the clear, dark sky above them filled with countless shimmering stars. She tingled as she remembered the potency of their passion.

"Come, Shanda," Pharaoh said, raising his voice so that she could hear him over the noise of the crowd. "Seti tells me the soldiers have been assembled and waiting since early morning."

She nodded and took his hand, then walked with him to his chariot and climbed up to stand behind him when he took up the reins. It was the golden chariot she had driven in the procession to the temple. She remembered that Seti had told her it was reserved for the annual religious ceremony and for triumphal processions. This, certainly, was the latter.

Seti's guards moved into formation around them, and the procession started to move forward through the crowded streets.

This was the army's victory procession, Pharaoh had told her, as much as his, and the soldiers would be part of it. Thus the soldiers had stood, in full uniform and carrying their shields and swords, since early morning, waiting for the arrival of Pharaoh's barge. Far from showing their impatience, they had broken into loud and enthusiastic cheers when she and Pharaoh stepped from the barge. Shanda noted, with pleasure and surprise, that the charioteers called out her

name as well as that of the king. They had not forgotten
the part she played in the victory at Kadesh, and they were
anxious to display their gratitude.

The procession began, the soldiers forming orderly ranks
behind Pharaoh's chariot and then marching slowly through
the city to receive the homage due them.

Once again the townspeople threw flowers in Pharaoh's
path, a seemingly endless shower of them. Pharaoh caught
a lotus blossom and gave it to Shanda. Then he put his arm
around her, pulled her forward to the front of the chariot
and he drove with his arms on either side of her. She
leaned back slightly, feeling the warmth and strength of his
body close to her. Never, she thought, would she forget
this day, this moment. Never would there be another like
it.

The sun had begun to wane by the time the procession
approached the palace. Shanda looked at the gates, remembering that the last time she had seen them she had been
certain she would never see Thebes again. Certainly she had
not expected to be part of a triumphal procession any more
than she had expected ever again to stand with Pharaoh's
arms around her and to hear the joyous welcome of the people of Thebes. This second chance, she told herself, was
a gift for which she would be properly grateful, one she
would treasure.

The great gates swung open to admit the guard and the
royal party. Behind them, the soldiers and townspeople
alike cheered wildly as Pharaoh's chariot passed through
into the palace courtyard. The wide open area, like the
city streets outside the wall, was crowded to capacity.
Here, though, there were no peasants, but only lords of
the kingdom, summoned to swear fealty upon their king's
triumphant return. And overlooking the scene, like a great
bejeweled spider, stood Queen Tiy, waiting on the steps

at the far end of the courtyard that led to Pharaoh's audience hall.

As Pharaoh drew the chariot to a halt, Shanda saw that the queen was flanked by Prince Amenophis and Nofret, the vizier. But it was Queen Tiy who held her eye, magnificent in a gown of black and gold, with jewels sparkling on her hands and ears and around her neck, wearing the crown of Upper and Lower Egypt on her mass of ebony hair. If there was a deity of darkness in Egypt, it was not Anubis or Osiris. Surely, she thought with a shiver as the queen stared directly at her, the throne of darkness in Egypt was occupied by none but Tiy.

This woman was cold and determined and would make a formidable enemy. There would never be an outburst of anger from her, never a threat of harm, only the act of retribution performed with emotionless and pitiless violence. If circumstances made this woman her enemy, Shanda doubted that even Pharaoh's power was great enough to protect her.

She thought of Althea. By enthralling a king, her mother, too, had made a queen her enemy, and that enemy had eventually engineered Althea's death. Was she condemned to repeat her mother's life, to face the same agonized end? Shanda saw that she would have to convince this woman that she presented no threat to her position or the prince's. Otherwise neither her life nor that of her unborn child would ever be safe.

She felt Pharaoh's hand on her arm, startling her out of her reverie. He climbed out of the chariot and waited for her to step down beside him. Shanda felt a moment of confusion. She glanced up at Queen Tiy, feeling the woman's eyes as she had felt Nem's sword in her flesh, sharp and impersonal and deadly. Then Pharaoh's hands were on her waist, lifting her down beside him.

He put her hand on his arm, and they began to walk toward the long flight of stairs. Pharaoh nodded occasionally to the courtiers who lined their path, but seemed completely unaware of the queen and his son who stood waiting for his approach.

When they reached the stairs, he stopped and turned to Seti.

"Will you escort the princess, Seti?" he asked as he placed Shanda's hand on his general's arm.

Seti smiled. "With great pleasure, lord."

Pharaoh offered Shanda a wry smile, then turned and began to climb the stone steps.

Shanda stared up at Queen Tiy. "She stares at me as a dog does at a bone," she murmured. In comparison to the queen's dark beauty she felt pale, thin, and wan. "A beautiful, dangerous dog."

Seti placed his hand atop hers. "A dog without teeth, Princess," he told her evenly. "You need have no fear of her."

His words, she knew, were intended to calm her, but they were not true and she was not comforted by them.

Pharaoh had stopped on the step where the queen and his son stood waiting. Tiy stepped forward to meet him. Aware that she was performing for all the court, she bowed with theatrical care, moving so that the dark, rich fabric of her gown draped becomingly against her breasts and thighs.

"We greet you, lord, and hail your victory." She offered him a pale bejeweled hand.

Pharaoh took her hand with no outward show of the distaste that washed over him at the sight of her.

"Your welcome honors me, lady," he said evenly.

She stood. "As your triumph over the Hittites honors us all," she responded smoothly, as though she'd spoken the words many times before in preparation for the moment.

Then she turned and glared down at Shanda. "We honor you," Tiy continued, her tone suddenly sly and sharp, "and applaud your mercy in sparing the Hittites even though a continuance of the battle would have brought Egypt more glory."

Pharaoh's eyes narrowed. "You would do well to confine yourself to women's affairs, lady. Your knowledge of both mercy and warfare are limited."

Tiy's face darkened with the rebuke, but she pretended to ignore it, attempting a smile.

"As a gesture of welcome, I offer you the hospitality of my table this evening, lord," she said, smiling alluringly. When he made no immediate response, she continued. "Perhaps an evening together with our son, united as a family, would serve to heal old wounds that have too long separated us."

Pharaoh was wary of this new stratagem. Never before had she made even the smallest gesture toward reconciliation. Still a beautiful woman, she had been magnificent in her youth. He wondered what their life might have been like if she had made an effort to charm him twenty years before. Perhaps, he thought, she felt weak in the face of his victory over the Hittites. Perhaps she felt this was the only way to preserve her position and her son's. Of only one thing was he certain: The chasm between them had long ago grown too wide to cross, and any weakness he might once have felt for her charms had long since passed.

"Old wounds, left untended, fester until they are past the possibility of being healed, lady," he told her. "I regret I must decline."

Tiy cast a hate-filled glance at Shanda. "It is said that Hittite whores are the most accomplished," she hissed. "Does yours so enchant you that you cannot endure an evening's separation from her?"

For the first time since the conversation had begun, Pharaoh's expression showed his rage. He took a step forward, the movement threatening, and saw the sudden fear in her eyes. He found it perversely pleasing. "I tell you this," he said, his voice low and tinged with contempt. "It would serve you well to offer prayers and offerings for the princess's health. For if some accident befalls her or if she grows mysteriously ill, if any harm whatsoever comes to her or to the child she carries, I promise you, lady, you will not live to see the sun rise even one time more than does she."

With that he turned away from Tiy and continued to climb the stairs. Nofret, who had stood too far away to hear their exchange, and ever the conscientious vizier, raced forward to stand beside the open door to the audience hall.

Pharaoh, however, climbed only a few steps before he stopped once again. He spun around and stared at Tiy for a moment, then descended the steps to where Shanda stood with Seti.

"I fear I must deny you the pleasure of this," he told Seti as he took Shanda's hand and placed it on his own arm. He raised his head and met the fury in Tiy's eyes.

"Come, Princess," he told Shanda as he once again started up the steep flight.

Shanda hesitated. She did not have to look up to feel the hatred with which Tiy and her son glared down at her. But Pharaoh's grasp was firm, and she was forced to choose between moving forward or pulling away from him. Reluctantly she climbed the steps at his side.

She kept her eyes straight ahead as she passed Tiy and Amenophis, who stood like marble statues on the steps, nor did she glance at Nofret, who waited at the entrance. She could hear movement behind her and knew the courtiers were moving toward the audience hall as well. She wondered if Tiy and Amenophis would lead the procession.

Pharaoh strode directly to the gold and lapis throne on the dais at the far end of the room. Beside it stood a second throne, smaller than his but also elaborately decorated with gold and precious stones.

Shanda turned to Seti, assuming he would escort her to Pharaoh's apartment before the audience began.

Pharaoh, however, made no move to release his hold on her hand. He climbed onto the dais, and Shanda mounted the last few steps at his side. Then Pharaoh stood for a second, staring at the queen's throne that had been set beside his.

He turned to Nofret. "Who had this placed here?" he demanded.

"Queen Tiy thought it appropriate, lord, that she sit beside you on this occasion," he said, his long death's-head face completely expressionless.

Pharaoh stared down the length of the hall as Tiy and Amenophis entered. Then he put his hand on Shanda's arm and guided her toward the throne.

"You will sit beside me, Princess," he told her, his words clear and loud so that Nofret could not miss them.

Shanda shook her head. "This place is for your queen," she replied, her tone entreating. "It is not right that I should occupy it."

"I decide what is right, Princess," he said sharply.

She knew his anger was not directed at her, but still it sent a shiver through her. She sank reluctantly into the chair and watched him settle himself beside her.

She heard the murmur of voices from those who had entered the hall and seen her, the foreigner, seated beside Pharaoh in the place that rightly belonged to their queen. To his court, Shanda realized, she would always be a foreigner, a Hittite. And at that moment, to be a Hittite was to be an enemy—a defeated enemy but an enemy still. Pharaoh's lords, she knew, would not like seeing her seated beside him, nor would they approve of the insult to their Egyptian-born queen.

She stared down the length of the hall to where Queen Tiy walked slowly toward them. In this moment of open rejection by her king, Tiy moved among the courtiers with the grace and dignity of one betrayed but unbeaten. Shanda thought she saw Tiy smile, almost as if the queen was secretly pleased with the impression the court must have of her as a wronged woman who nobly accepted her fate.

Shanda leaned toward Pharaoh.

"I beg you, lord. Let me leave now. Give this place to your queen, to whom it belongs, or leave it empty. But my presence here is an insult to her, one she will not forget."

He turned his gray eyes on her. "I am Pharaoh, Princess," he told her evenly. "It is I, not the queen, who dictates here."

The eyes into which she stared were as hard and as cold as they had been the day he came to her and told her of Hattushil's invasion.

He reached out and grasped her hand. "Shanda," he whispered.

His eyes, no longer hard and cold, were telling her she must understand, must accept what he asked of her.

"I think it time Egypt had a new queen," he told her softly.

"Egypt already has a queen, lord," she murmured.

"Then I shall take a second wife," he said evenly.

She stared at him a moment, her eyes pleading. "Do not ask this of me, lord. You would make me and my child her enemy. I have no desire to wear a crown. I have but one wish, and that is to be with you."

"You have no reason to be afraid, Shanda," he told her softly. "No one can hurt you."

"Then dismiss my fears as a woman's folly, lord," she persisted. "But to make me your queen and my child your heir will only bring us danger."

"I have told you," he replied sharply, refusing to accept the possibility that Tiy could reach beyond his protection, that there were forces from which he might be unable to shield her, "that you are safe. You need have no fear." His tone softened, and he smiled at her. "We shall speak more of this later."

He turned away from her, his expression growing hard and determined as he faced Tiy and Amenophis, who now approached and bowed stiffly before him. The hall grew silent as the court waited to hear what would be spoken between them. But no words were uttered. Tiy and Amenophis, having completed their obeisance, turned wordlessly and left the hall.

When they were gone, the silence ended. The hall grew busy with whispers and glances at the throne where Tiy ought rightfully to have sat. Shanda felt their eyes on her and knew they thought her an interloper who had stolen Tiy's place. They might once have admired her as their king's uncommon possession, but they would not accept her as his queen.

Shanda sat, frozen and numb, at Pharaoh's side. She neither saw nor heard anything of the long procession of lords who approached Pharaoh, hailing his victory over Hattushil and swearing their allegiance to him. Instead, she saw only his face. His profile, strong and fixed, seemed to her almost carved, as though he were a statue and not a man. Even when he spoke, his glance did not waver or his expression soften. He was, she realized, far more complicated a man than the one she knew, the one she had come to love.

He would show no weakness before his court, nor would he allow their wishes to sway him. He was pharaoh, and his commands were absolute and unarguable. She wondered only that he had brought himself to be simply a man with her, had shown himself as something less than the royal deity his countrymen thought him.

Perhaps he was right, she told herself. Perhaps Tiy's power was too weak to reach her or the child she carried. It was a thought she clung to, desperately telling herself it was true.

But even so, she was unable to sit comfortably beside him. The precious gold and stones of the throne seemed to glow with a heat that burned her.

Amenophis walked over to a long table laden with food and ewers of wine and decorated with huge bowls of flowers.

"You did not think he actually would come, did you?" he asked Tiy, reaching for a large hand of grapes. "I told you she had bewitched him, that he thinks of nothing but his precious Hittite bitch." He fell lazily into a cushioned chair and stared up at his mother as he indolently raised the grapes, one by one, to his mouth.

Tiy glanced at the sumptuous meal she had had her servants prepare and set out. She shrugged and walked past the table to the entry to the garden beyond, without wasting so much as a glance on her son.

"Of course I didn't think he would come. He's never once taken a meal with me, never once trusted me not to serve him poison with his sweetmeats." She smiled at her own words. "If nothing else, he is not a fool."

Amenophis straightened and stared at her quizzically. "Have you ever tried?" he asked in a whisper.

She turned and faced him for the first time since he'd entered her apartment. "You are, despite all attempts to remedy the situation, still a foolish child," she told him evenly.

Then she added, as if the words hardly needed to be said, "Of course I have tried."

He wondered why her response surprised him, why he had not been prepared for the dull, matter-of-fact way she'd said the words. Still, he realized, her reply was far from unexpected. For the first time in his life, he found himself wondering just what his mother was capable of doing and how far her determination would drive her.

"Then why all this?" he asked, waving his hand to the table.

"For effect. The court will learn how I have tried to please him, the efforts I have made for him. Combined with that bit of theater this afternoon, this will garner us sympathy."

"Then you knew he would put the whore beside him?" he asked, incredulous. "You had Nofret place your throne on the dais, knowing he would have her occupy it, and not you?"

She smiled. "Certainly. He could do nothing else."

Amenophis regarded her with an objectivity he'd never allowed himself before. It occurred to him that he'd returned from Kadesh changed. Absence had endowed him with new, unclouded eyes with which to see the queen. He had never questioned her before, and he had no real knowledge or understanding of her.

"Why do you hate him?" he asked her abruptly.

She glared at him, her eyes cold. "Have we not enough reason?" she demanded.

He shook his head. "I know why *I* hate him. After all, you saw to it I drank in hatred of him with your milk. But you, why do you hate him?"

"Because he stole my father's throne," she snapped back at him, speaking a shade too quickly, as though she had no wish to examine her motives too closely or to allow him to do so. "Because he killed my father."

Amenophis put a half-dozen grapes into his mouth and chewed them thoughtfully. He spat out the seeds, unmindful, on the floor.

"It was rightfully his throne," he said finally. "Your father tried to have him assassinated." He watched her calmly as she grew flushed with anger.

"Why don't you go to him, grovel at his feet, and beg his indulgence?" she snapped. "Perhaps this new mercy he has grown will extend not only to his whore's people but to his son as well."

Amenophis only shook his head. "I have no desire to grovel, nor do I want his mercy," he told her. "There is but one thing I want from him—his crown."

"And you shall have it," she assured him. She fell to her knees before him and took his face in her hands. "My beautiful boy, you will be Egypt's most magnificent Pharaoh." She drew his face forward, close to hers, and stared into his eyes.

He felt himself begin to grow weak at her touch. Always it had been this way for him, the melting inside, the knowledge that he would give her anything, agree to anything, if only to deflect her anger. But this time he drew away before she could touch his lips with hers. He was a man now, he reminded himself. Other lips were sweeter to him than hers.

He stood abruptly and stared down at her. "Then we shall kill him," he said. "We shall kill them both. Now."

She shook her head. "Not yet." She raised herself to her feet. "It is not yet time."

"It is time. I am the only rightful heir to the throne. But if she gives him a son—"

She pressed her fingers to his lips. "She is his whore," she told him evenly. "I am his queen." She smiled. "And you are his only rightful heir."

His eyes narrowed. "You fear him," he accused. "His words today frightened you." His voice grew thick with scorn. "You will sit aside while he marries this Hittite bitch and gives her son what is rightfully mine."

Once again her expression grew fierce. "We need support. Do you think he will simply stand quietly while you push a knife into his back? Or that the lords will simply let you take his crown unchallenged? Until we can assure ourselves enough of them are behind us, we wait."

"We wait," he cried, "while the whore breeds?"

She nodded, unconcerned with the note of hysteria in his voice. "Yes," she told him. "We wait while his whore breeds."

"How long?" he asked, his voice controlled now, but demanding.

"Until Nofret tells us the time has come," she replied.

"Nofret," he repeated scornfully. "Does your monster come to you tonight?" The idea revolted him, that she would lie with the vizier, that she would let him touch her with his bony, cold hands. Waves of jealousy engulfed him.

She smiled and shook her head. "No," she whispered, her lips close to his ear. "Tonight, my love, I am entirely yours."

She darted her tongue into his ear, then waited, sure of herself, as he turned to face her, wavering before he decided to offer her his kiss. She knew, as she always did, that he would give in to her, knew even before he did that he could not deny her anything. She knew, as she always did, that she had won.

# *Nineteen*

"PHARAOH WOULD NOT approve." Seti's expression said quite clearly that he did not approve, either.

Shanda nodded, agreeing. "I know," she replied. "And so you must not tell him."

"You would have me lie to him as well?" he asked her, almost amused. He had no intention of granting her request.

"I do not ask you to lie to him, Seti," she replied. "Only to keep word of it from him."

"That would still be a lie, Princess," he insisted.

She put her hands on the arms of her chair, pushing against them to help herself rise. When he extended his strong arm to help her, she took it gratefully and got to her feet.

She grew more awkward and clumsy from day to day. It was an odd sensation, this inability to feel comfortable with the strange bulk that was her own body, this feeling almost like an alien within herself. She paused, reminding herself that she was not alone, that she shared her body with her child. She smiled inwardly, as though she were guardian of some wonderful secret. It was a thought that, no matter how commonplace, never ceased to give her wonder, as did the sharp movements of tiny limbs she felt within her belly.

She pressed her hand to that magnificently swollen part.

"Try to understand, Seti," she said softly, "that I must speak to her soon, before this baby is born." She looked past him at the pool and then at the large cage filled with songbirds, languid and almost silent in the late afternoon heat. "I want this child to live, Seti. Nothing is more important than that."

"Do you think Tiy so strong, Princess?" he asked her gently.

She nodded, still staring off into the garden but aware that Seti had moved to her side. "She is determined," she replied. "That gives her power."

Seti's look was almost sympathetic. He made no attempt to reassure her, for as much as it displeased him to admit it, he knew she was right.

"Do you really think you can bargain with her, Princess?"

"Am I so transparent, Seti, that you can look into my mind?"

He smiled. "Perhaps my eyes are a bit keener than most, Princess," he suggested. He seemed, for a moment, undecided, as though unsure it was his place to speak. But finally he said, "Have you really the right, Princess, to barter away your child's birthright?"

She was startled that he knew her intent and would state it so bluntly. But then she realized he knew that she had little else to trade in return for Tiy's promise to spare her child's life.

"I have the right and the obligation to do anything that will ensure this baby's safety," she cried. "Anything."

"It is for Pharaoh to decide," he insisted. "It is his right to bequeath his power as he sees fit."

"Some things are more important than power, Seti. A

man cannot always understand these things. But a woman does."

He stared at her in silence for a moment. She had grown decidedly more beautiful over the past few months, he thought. Even the clumsiness she could not quite overcome in no way diminished that beauty. He felt a surge of jealousy for Pharaoh, which he quickly squelched. He knew he would eventually give in and do as she asked. Looking at her made him ache inside, made him realize that there was nothing in his power he would not give to her.

It was foolish to go on arguing with her, he knew. He wondered if she knew it as well, if she understood just how much power she could wield if she so chose.

"There will be conditions, Princess," he said reluctantly, as though he had trouble forcing the words past his lips.

"Then you will do it?"

"You must promise to stay within my view. You may speak so that I do not hear—I do not wish to hear—but you will not venture out of my sight."

She nodded. "I agree."

"And you will not touch her or take anything from her hand," he went on, his tone sharper than he intended.

"But surely—"

He interrupted her, stifling her objection. "You yourself have said she is determined, Princess. Agree to this or I shall withdraw my complicity." He stared at her, almost hoping she would not agree and thus give him an excuse not to be part of what she asked.

She nodded. "Very well," she replied.

He grimaced. He had made his reluctance more than apparent. There was now nothing more he could do to dissuade her. "I will send you word when I have made the arrangements," he told her.

Then, before he had time to think about what he was doing, he bowed to her and left.

"She actually came to you here alone?" Amenophis was intrigued by this unexpected occurrence. "Is she a fool, then?"

Tiy shook her head. "She is no fool," she replied. "And she did not come alone. Seti was with her, and she did not move beyond his view. She also made a point of keeping a distance between herself and me, and she refused the wine I offered her." The queen shook her head slowly. "No," she added thoughtfully, "either she knew what to do or she was counseled by someone who knew. Either way, she is no fool."

Tiy smiled, then took the ewer of wine that was still on the table and emptied it onto the ground.

"Why did you do that?" he asked, staring down at the red puddle as it slowly seeped into the dark soil.

"To ensure that you would not drink it, my love," she told him brightly. "If you were to die, all of this would have been for naught." She carefully removed a ring from her right thumb, taking pains not to touch the elaborate design on its face.

Amenophis watched her in silence and, when she'd removed it, held out his hand to her.

"What is that?" he asked, reaching for the strange piece of jewelry. "I have never seen you wear that ring before."

She pulled it away, out of his reach. "Do not touch it!"

He dropped his hand. "Why not?"

She smiled her almost innocent smile. "The workmanship is crude," she said. "You wouldn't want to prick your finger."

With that she dropped the ring on the ground near the place where she'd spilled the wine and, with her sandaled foot, pushed it into the moist earth. He watched her, wondering just how deadly a prick from that ring would have been.

"You should have killed her," he said under his breath. His own words startled him, as did the vehemence with which he'd spoken them. Had he said them aloud so that the thought could not lurk like an unwholesome ghost in his mind?

She cocked a brow. "I told you Seti was watching us the whole time, and she kept her distance."

He was suddenly angry. "You fear him," he accused. "You fear he would act as he threatened."

"Why do you always refer to Pharaoh as 'him'?" she asked. "Do you think that by uttering the word 'Pharaoh' or calling him 'the king,' or"—she smiled at him, but there was no humor in her expression—" 'father,' you will call down his anger upon you?"

His face contorted, but he pretended to ignore her question. "You *do* fear him," he repeated, and this time the words were tinged with bitterness.

Her expression grew dark. "Of course I fear him. And if you were less of a boy, you'd learn to fear him as well." She turned her back to him. "I know him," she murmured. "I have lain with him. He does not make idle threats."

Unlike you, he thought, hearing the words although he did not say them. He wondered why he could not be what she would have had him be, and he suspected that, although she might hate Pharaoh, a part of her longed for him as she had never, would never, long for another man. Perhaps that was why she hated him so.

"What did she want?" he demanded.

"To strike a bargain with me," she told him, but stopped there, enjoying the fact that she knew and he did not.

"What bargain?" he asked when she did not continue, his tone tense now, like his mood, from waiting.

"We both gave our word, my love," she told him blithely. "She gave her word that she would not wed Pharaoh, and in return I gave her my word to let her child live." Tiy smiled at him easily.

"He speaks openly of taking a second queen," he reminded her.

"She has given me her word it will not be so," Tiy responded.

"And just how can she keep him from recognizing the child?"

Tiy shrugged. "Unless she is made his queen, her child will be just another of his bastards and you will remain his only rightful heir." She turned back to face him. "She's not nearly so pretty now," she told him after a moment. She sounded quite pleased with the fact. "She's grown awkward with the child, and I think she is a bit afraid, not only of me but of the birth as well." She looked off thoughtfully. "Someone must have told her that things sometimes go wrong when a woman gives birth," she added with an unpleasant smile.

"Who told her?" he demanded.

She shrugged. "I didn't ask. Perhaps she just felt it. However it came about, she knew." She sat down on a bench and offered him her falsely innocent smile.

"And you agreed to give her what she asked?" His tone told her clearly that he did not like the prospect.

"Yes, I agreed."

"Why?" Amenophis demanded. "We might have been done with her. It was all arranged."

"Because it was not without risk," she said. "Because Pharaoh would think of us when it was done. Because Imhotep might see what was happening and stop it, or confront the midwife with the act once done. Because she might talk, might incriminate us before we could silence her.

For many reasons. But mostly because the Hittite made it unnecessary for us to run the risk of Pharaoh's taking his revenge on us after it is done."

"We should have used the physician," he mumbled angrily.

"Imhotep is incorruptible," she reminded him. "It had to be the midwife. In any case, it is of no consequence any longer."

"Then you intend to keep your word?" He was incredulous.

"Certainly. At least for the time being, we shall let her have her child and think herself safe."

"We agreed," he said angrily, turning on her one last time.

She shrugged, obviously unconcerned.

"How do you know you can trust her?" he demanded, refusing to allow her to end the conversation. "What is to keep her, once the child is born, from changing her mind and agreeing to the marriage? If he makes her his queen, there is nothing to keep him from naming her son as his heir."

"She gave her word," Tiy told him, "and she is the sort who would die rather than break it." Her voice turned thoughtful. "You must realize, my love, that she and her child can be dealt with easily enough. Our problem is finding a way to eliminate Pharaoh. Once he is dead, the woman and the child can be dispatched with ease."

Amenophis tried to hide his anger. "How much longer do we wait?" he demanded. "I shall grow old waiting for him to die."

She moved silently to where he stood, put her hand on his arm, then moved it slowly up to his shoulder and his neck. "Soon, my love," she whispered. "The time will be right soon."

*   *   *

The first cry, angry and startlingly loud, filled the room.
The sound of it surprised Shanda. She had not expected it
to be so strong.

The pain in her hips and back slowly eased. Never had
she known such hurt, such a feeling of being torn apart.
She was limp and drained by it, but now, as it passed, her
memory of it began to fade.

The midwife leaned over her and placed the child in her
arms. The woman stared at her strangely, she thought, but
then she turned her eyes to her baby and forgot everything
but the small miracle she held in her arms.

"A son, Princess," Med told her with a pride that implied
he had had something to do with that fact. "A fine, noisy
son."

The midwife scowled at him, then turned away when she
found herself ignored, and directed the servants to clean up
the mess of bloody linens and the afterbirth that still fouled
the floor.

Shanda smiled at the loudness of her son's cry. He was,
she thought, his father's child, only too willing to express
his dissatisfaction.

"Help me, Med," she said as she tried to push herself up.

He quickly brought pillows and placed them at her back,
then helped her put the angry, red little mouth to her nipple.
The room was immediately plunged into silence as the baby
took her breast and began to suckle with as much vehemence
as he had put into his crying.

"You must send word to Pharaoh," Shanda said to Med.
Then she drew away the linen cloth, intent upon examining
her son's small body herself. It seemed unlikely to her that
this creature, with its loud, squalling voice and tiny, busily
waving arms, had somehow come from inside her. That
reality filled her with wonder.

"He waits in the next room, Princess," Med told her. "I will go immediately." He seemed reluctant to move, however, and kept a proprietary eye on the baby as he turned.

"No need, boy."

Shanda looked up to see Pharaoh standing at the foot of her bed. He was hollow eyed and unusually intent.

She smiled. "Have you been here long?" she asked. She had not seen him enter.

He nodded. "Since I heard the cry," he told her as he moved around the bed to sit beside her. He pushed a tangle of thick, damp hair away from her face. "It would have been easier, I think, to be in here with you, rather than waiting out there, wondering."

"My poor love," Shanda whispered.

She felt her eyelids falling and had to fight to keep her eyes open. She had never felt so tired before. Still, she forced herself to watch as Pharaoh lifted his son's hand and then his foot, carefully counting the tiny fingers and toes. The baby suckled noisily, unmindful of his touch. The feel of his mouth on her breast, the drawing of the milk, was an oddly pleasant sensation.

She looked up at Pharaoh. "Does he please you, lord?" she asked, although there was no need for him to answer as she could see how very much their baby pleased him by the delight in his eyes.

He smiled with sudden pleasure as he turned his glance from the baby to her.

"You please me, Princess. And our son pleases me." He pressed a finger to his son's cheek, dark against the pale golden hue of baby's skin, touching it tentatively, as though afraid of hurting this much-longed-for stranger. "We will name him, Hera-rah—the face of the sun." He smiled again and moved his finger slowly, touching a tiny, perfectly formed ear.

Shanda looked down at her nursing infant and at Pharaoh's finger near his son's pale cheek. She knew then that the baby, for all his loud male cries, was more hers than his, with a pale complexion only slightly more golden than hers. Even the wisps of hair on his head were the color of afternoon sunlight. His face was like the sun.

His head fell back suddenly. Spent and finally sated, he was asleep, his mouth agape, still making tiny suckling sounds.

Shanda laughed softly, and Med took the sleeping infant from her arms. She lay back against the heap of pillows, no longer fighting the urge to let her eyelids close, knowing the attempt would be useless.

She felt Pharaoh's lips, warm against her forehead. And then she fell into a deep, sound sleep.


Amenophis stormed into the room and looked around for an object on which to vent his anger. Finding nothing else, he swept his arm along a table, sending a bowl of flowers crashing to the floor.

Tiy turned away from her mirror and waved her hand at the servant who had been arranging her hair. The girl put the comb down on the dressing table, bowed, and hastily retreated.

The queen surveyed the mess of potshards, water, and flowers on the floor near her feet. Then she stood and carefully stepped through the rubble, taking care not to let her gown drag through the damp.

"We are not pleased?" she asked with a small laugh as she passed Amenophis and stepped out into the sun.

"She's been delivered of her whelp. A boy."

He realized when he heard the echo of his own words that he had shouted. Why, he wondered, did thought of the Hittite woman so unbalance him, make him lose control?

"Do you think me so deaf that I would not have heard of it?" she asked as she waited for him to come to her.

"Already he boasts of his golden-haired son," he raged.

"You sound like a jealous lover," she accused.

"And you act as though none of it matters," he shouted back at her just as accusingly. He strode toward her.

Once he was beside her, she moved to a bed of heliotrope and plucked a handful of blooms absently. She put them to her nose and inhaled their fragrance.

He considered her apparent lack of interest, wondering what she thought. "There is more," he told her. "He talks again of making her his queen."

She turned once more to face him. "She will refuse," she told him flatly. "I told you she gave me her word. Besides, Nofret says Pharaoh's councillors will not accept the foreigner's whelp. They will have only a real Egyptian for their Pharaoh." She smiled. "They will have only you."

He waved his hand in a dismissive motion. "He is above them. He is Pharaoh and will not let them sway him."

She smiled. "All the better," she said. "That will make our task easier when the time comes." Again she sniffed the handful of blooms, crushing the petals absently between her fingers to release their fragrance. After a moment she dropped the mass of ruined blossoms on the ground at her feet.

"Talk!" he shouted at her, refusing to be appeased. He was filled with impotent rage and suddenly wished he could vent it on her. "All you offer is talk. You tell me we will watch him die, and yet still he lives, and his Hittite bitch breeds. And he talks of giving my crown to her bastard."

"Talk," she said with a shrug, aping his words. "All Pharaoh has is talk."

"You yourself told me he does not make idle threats."

"He knows that without the support of his lords his words

are of no value. There is, after all, an end even to a pharaoh's power."

Amenophis was unconvinced. "The army would be enough," he told her.

She considered what he said in silence before turning back to him. "Then you, my handsome and strong general, must see that the army will have no one but you." She absently picked another flower, not even bothering to sniff it but simply tearing it from its stalk and dropping it on the ground. "And meanwhile it is time for me to find the means."

He put his hand on her shoulder. "What will you do?" he asked.

"There is only one way," she murmured, "to get close enough to him."

"How?"

"The palace guard," she replied.

"Seti's men?" He grimaced. "No. That is impossible."

"To one who is determined," she told him, "nothing is impossible."

His fingers tightened on her shoulder. "What have you done?"

She offered him her almost-innocent smile. "Nothing, my love," she told him. "But the time grows ripe." She slowly rubbed her hands together, ridding them of the ravaged petals that clung to them. "The question we must ask now," she said softly, "is what will I do?"

She stared up at him. And then she laughed.

# Twenty

"HE IS ALREADY a warrior, Princess."

Med seemed delighted at this revelation, even though Shanda was not so sure it deserved to be lauded. She could not hide her laughter, however, when young Hera waved his wooden sword in the air and crowed with delight at the way Med, pretending to be an unruly mount, bucked and reared. He held on to Med's dark hair and shouted with joy.

"You are soon to be made human once again, Med," she said, when the boy paused, exhausted from his race around the garden with the child on his shoulders. "Pharaoh intends to present Hera with his own pony soon. I think that will save you from further duty as the royal horse."

"Good," Med said as he reached up to his shoulders and lifted the boy down. "He grows too heavy to carry about like a sack of onions." He put his hand on Hera's belly as he set him on his feet and then tickled him. "Don't you, my fine young prince?"

Hera whooped with laughter, broke free, and ran to the side of the pool. There he dropped down onto decidedly dirty knees. His sturdy little legs seemed oblivious to the impact of flesh against stone. Immediately intent, he began to play with a collection of tiny carved wooden soldiers, chariots, and horses, arranging them in two crooked lines and pushing them toward each other in mock battle.

In an attempt to regain his ruffled dignity, Med adjusted his tunic, straightening his sash and resettling the elaborate leather knife sheath he wore tucked inside it. Since their return to Thebes from Kadesh five years before, he had taken to constantly wearing the jewel-hilted knife Pharaoh had presented to him that afternoon long ago when he'd discovered Shanda in the midst of a lesson under the tutelage of the harem scribe.

Med followed Hera and sat on a low stone bench near where the boy played, apparently intent upon observing the toy battle. It was not long, however, before he was sprawled on the ground at Hera's side, offering an occasional word of advice and a helpful hand as the battle progressed. Shanda realized he was hardly more than a boy himself, and she often found herself wondering if his interest in the young prince's toys and games might not be more than tolerant caretaking. He seemed to take far too intent an interest in the games for her to feel he did not, at least occasionally, consider himself really part of them. There was, however, no question in her mind of his love for her son. She was sure he would gladly give up his life to keep Hera from hurt.

Shanda pushed herself up and out of her chair. Already, she realized, she had grown ungainly, and this second child would not be born for some time still.

She wondered if she would feel for this second child what she felt for Hera. It seemed impossible to her that she could ever love another baby as she loved her firstborn son. But she had begun to realize that love grew upon itself. She had never thought she could love Pharaoh more than she did on the day they returned to Thebes, and yet, with Hera's birth, she had found the bond between them grown ever stronger. Perhaps it would be the same with this new child as well.

"It is time for you to bathe, my young lord," she said as she crossed the garden to where Med sat with Hera.

Hera's large blue eyes looked into hers, then back to his toys, and his round young face grew mournful.

"I do not like to bathe," he said very carefully, watching her face for any sign of weakness, hoping, perhaps, she might be dissuaded.

Shanda kept her expression stern. "Nonetheless, Sesostris will be here soon," she told him firmly. "A young lord does not receive his tutor with dirty knees and elbows." She stared pointedly at those particularly offending appendages.

He looked down at his grimy knees and rubbed them vigorously with equally dirty hands, then darted a look up at her, his eyes asking if the effort would suffice. She shook her head.

"I will be a general," he said brightly. "A general does not need to know how to read and write."

He seized one of the toy horses and offered up a snorting sound as he made the small carving shake from side to side in questionable imitation of a real horse.

"Even a general cannot be harmed by a bit of schooling," Shanda insisted, removing the tiny beast from his hand. "You might ask Seti, if my word on the matter is not sufficient."

He scowled, but got to his feet without further protest. Second only to his father, Seti was his idol, and the mere mention of his name in discussions of this sort, Shanda had found, was certain to bring about prompt and unquestioning compliance.

Med offered her the smile of an accomplice, jumped easily to his feet, and held out his hand to Hera.

"Come, I will help you find Sukhrete," he said as Hera took his hand. "She has hidden your boats and will have to be asked to retrieve them."

"She is too neat," Hera said and turned for a moment to glance down at the scattering of toys on the ground, wondering to what fate of ordered neatness they would be subjected should the nursemaid happen upon them.

"All nursemaids are neat," Med told him. "That is why we have them."

Hera nodded sagely at the wisdom of these words and allowed himself to be led off to the nursery.


"Seti, I wish you would make an effort not to appear quite so worried. I find it makes me uncomfortable," Pharaoh complained.

"I look worried because I am, lord," Seti told him evenly.

"Then at least have the courtesy to hide that fact."

"Sethos has been with Tiy four times of which I am aware," Seti told him.

"A fact that must make Nofret burn with jealousy," Pharaoh replied dryly. "You say he is young?"

Seti ceased his movement, much to Pharaoh's relief, and nodded. "Young enough," he said, "but not handsome enough or intelligent enough to merit such devotion from her. This is unprecedented. I think I should have him removed."

Pharaoh shook his head. "I do not think that would be wise. We must first learn if he is alone with her or if there are others. If we take him and are unable to elicit from him what we need to know, we only warn them and make them more careful."

"But if he should make the attempt—" Seti protested.

"We will be waiting for him," Pharaoh interrupted. "How many times have you told me it is better to have an enemy you know than one who is hidden?"

Seti started to move again, pacing silently for a moment. Then he turned, his expression filled with anger, to face Pharaoh once again. "She corrupted one of *my men*!" he fumed, as though the insult was the greatest wrong of which he could conceive.

"The fact that it is one of your men is significant," Pharaoh told him.

"Lord?"

"It tells us that I am their target. Why else should she seduce one of my own guards?"

"Of course you are their target," Seti replied. "Who else?"

Pharaoh's eyes grew sharp. "Shanda," he said. "My son."

Seti felt a surge of rage at the prospect. How, he wondered, had this woman and child who were not even his own come to mean so much to him? "Perhaps we should increase their guard?" he asked.

Pharaoh nodded. "But only with men of whom you have absolutely no doubt," he instructed.

Seti frowned. He had once felt sure of all his men, confident enough to place his own life and even the life of his king in their hands. Now his confidence was shaken. It would take a few days to choose the men and check on their recent activities, to assure himself he was not assigning potential assassins to guard their intended victims. He did not like the prospect in the least. "Of course, lord," he replied.

Pharaoh tilted his head back and stared up at the ceiling. "As for this Sethos, Tiy's new young friend, we will let him think we are ignorant of his actions." He smiled. "How important he must think himself. How powerful he must think his rod. After all, he cuckolds Pharaoh." He sat up and looked at Seti once more. When he continued, there was disgust in his tone. "Perhaps before it is over, we should inform him that the prize he has stolen was cast out long ago and has lain on the dung heap these last twenty years with a legion to appease its appetites."

"How long do we let it go on?" Seti asked.

Pharaoh shook his head. "Not long," he replied. "It would not do to let the viper grow great with venom. When we know who his accomplices are, we will arrange an opportunity for them."

"That path could prove to have pitfalls, lord," Seti warned.

"Few paths worth traveling are smooth, my old friend," Pharaoh replied with a wry smile.

"When I was alone I found it almost amusing to watch Tiy's maneuverings," Pharaoh said thoughtfully. It had been interesting, if not precisely amusing. But then he had held on to his life only with dogged determination and could consider the interplay a game, even accept the possibility that it was a game he might one day lose. Tiy had, if nothing else, made his life interesting. Now, however, he had new and compelling reasons to live, and the game had lost its excitement. Now he saw Tiy's actions as an open challenge, a threat. "Lately, though, it seems to me," he went on, "I have more than paid the price of her father's blood."

Seti understood immediately what Pharaoh meant to do. "To put her aside, lord, will not be easy. Tiy still has the support of those lords who would have given the throne to her father," he said quietly.

"Then perhaps they, too, must be shown the error of their alliances," Pharaoh said.

Seti shook his head slowly. "Even those who support you,

lord, will not easily accept a queen who is not Egyptian-born," he said softly. "And now the priests have become troublesome."

Pharaoh sobered. "They are more powerful than I would have them be."

Seti nodded. "They are concerned, lord. They feel you are not devout enough, that you do not observe the rites."

"I am no less devout than I have ever been," Pharaoh retorted. "It is only since Kadesh they have begun with this nonsense." He pushed himself from his chair. "They fear the victory makes me too strong with the people, that they lose their hold."

Seti shook his head. "They fear you will turn to new gods, lord, and take away their place."

Pharaoh's brow furrowed. "What new gods?" he asked.

Seti's expression grew tolerant as he offered Pharaoh the look one gave when presenting a lesson to a slow student. "You have a foreign woman in your bed, lord. They fear she brings her gods with her."

"Fools. Shanda has no gods," Pharaoh said. "It is she who is in danger of having my gods supplant her beliefs."

"But the priests have no way of knowing these things, lord," Seti told him calmly. "Perhaps, if you were to make a greater appearance of devoutness, perhaps introduce Prince Hera-rah to the mysteries . . ."

Pharaoh's face fell into a grimace of distaste, but he quickly swallowed it. "Perhaps you are right, Seti," he agreed. "Perhaps it would be useful to go to the temple and offer sacrifice."

Seti suddenly grinned. "You have grown quite reasonable of late, lord," he said.

Pharaoh smiled in return. "I have," he agreed, "have I not?" Then he sobered. "See to the guard for the princess."

Seti nodded. "Yes, lord."

*       *       *

Shanda stood with Prince Hera at her side, his warm little hand, slightly damp with the perspiration of excitement, in hers.

Hera loved watching the soldiers, seeing the horses racing, their manes flying, but most of all he was fascinated by the charioteers as they raced along the long practice court, the reins made fast around their waists to steer the galloping horses, and shot arrow after arrow into the targets. It was a feat, he was sure, that was beyond the capacity of mere mortal men. He ached with the desire to do as they did.

Shanda leaned down to speak close to his ear. "Your father told me he might ask you to ride with him today, Hera," she told him. "Would that please you?"

He looked up at her, wide-eyed with excitement. "In his chariot?" he demanded, just to be sure he had not mistaken what he'd heard.

Shanda nodded. "He said he might even let you drive," she said.

Seti knelt down to him and pointed to where Pharaoh led the group of charioteers.

"Did you know your mother drove Pharaoh's chariot?" he asked Hera, his tone very solemn. "It is a grave responsibility."

Hera looked up at Shanda and then returned his gaze to his father's chariot, his expression tinged with disbelief.

Seti nodded gravely. "It is true," he said. "It was Princess Shanda who taught the charioteers to drive that way, so that they could shoot and control the horses at the same time."

Once more Hera looked up at Shanda, who nodded silently and then turned to watch Pharaoh. The boy was not sure he could believe what he had been told, although he knew Seti would never lie. To his eye Shanda's swollen body seemed incapable of exercising the control and strength such a feat required.

Her attention was centered on Pharaoh. He was, she thought, still the most accomplished of his soldiers, still the strongest. Age would one day take that distinction from him, but he would not give it up without a hard-fought battle.

She felt a sudden stab of yearning, remembering the day she had first driven his chariot, the feeling of freedom and mastery. She had thought herself so certain that day, so sure of what she must do, what she must and must not feel. She was no longer sure of anything except her love for Pharaoh and her son. Perhaps, she thought, that should be enough.

The military exercise was soon finished, and the soldiers lined up into long, even files to be reviewed. Pharaoh drove to where Shanda stood with Hera and Seti. He pulled the great whites to a halt in front of them and offered Shanda a quick smile before he turned his gaze to his son.

"What have we here, Seti?" he asked. "A soldier who has not yet demonstrated his skill to his king?"

Seti nodded soberly as he took Hera's hand and led him toward Pharaoh's chariot.

"It is time you earned your keep, young prince," Pharaoh said solemnly as he gazed down at Hera.

Seti lifted Hera and handed him to Pharaoh, who settled him on a step that had been installed in the very front of his chariot. Hera seemed about to burst with delight as his father showed him how to hold the reins. Then Pharaoh turned the chariot and with his son beside him, began a slow, methodical review of his soldiers. Behind his chariot, his generals followed on horseback.

"I think young Hera is pleased," Seti commented as he watched the chariot moving slowly past the soldiers.

"He is more than pleased," Shanda replied. "It was kind of you to suggest it to Pharaoh."

He waved away her thanks with a movement of his hand. "It delights me to see Pharaoh so happy, Princess," he told her. He stared at her a moment in silence. "Him and you," he added softly.

Shanda considered his tanned, rugged face, his dark, thoughtful eyes. His face was not comely, but still he was certainly a handsome man. More than that, she knew him to be a kind and generous one. The affection he showed Hera was but a hint of the love he would lavish on his own children.

"Why have you never married, Seti?" she asked him. "Why have you not had sons of your own?"

He turned away quickly and then shrugged. "I had a wife," he replied slowly. "A long time ago. She died in childbirth. I never thought to take another."

He might have wished to say more—that there was only one woman who meant anything to him now, and she out of his reach. Still, he had no regrets. He could not possess her, but he knew himself to be important, even necessary, to her. He could content himself with that.

"I'm sorry," Shanda murmured, wishing she hadn't asked. Seti was the last person to whom she wished to cause pain.

She had no time to offer further apologies for Seti pointed toward the long rows of soldiers. "Look, Princess."

Shanda followed his pointing hand. Having completed the review, Pharaoh had turned his chariot and begun to return. Instead of maintaining their military calm, the soldiers, as the chariot passed, were smiling and shouting. Their voices were loud and raucous, and she had to strain to make out their words.

After a moment she realized they were cheering for Hera, calling him the Golden Prince. Just as they had thought her lucky at Kadesh, so now they considered Hera a symbol of good fortune. Hera, with his pale hair and fair complexion, was Pharaoh's son, but he was also a combination of the two who had brought Egypt victory at Kadesh.

She could see him standing in front of Pharaoh, his small round face glowing with pleasure. She could not help but feel his happiness, almost as if it were contagious, nor could she stop smiling with her pride in him.

Her smile vanished, however, as the chariot, followed by the small procession of generals, drew closer. Amenophis, riding in the midst of the other generals, was staring at Hera with a look that sent a shiver of fear down Shanda's spine. There was anger in the prince's eyes, anger and jealousy and a hot, burning hatred.

She knew that Pharaoh had never presented his first son to his troops as he now presented Hera. He had never taken such pride in Amenophis, and never once had the soldiers shown Pharaoh's heir the affection they now lavished on her son. She felt a wave of panic and wished she had not brought the boy to this place to be cheered as the Golden Prince. She had been stupid to allow herself to grow complacent, to think her son safe, to assume Amenophis would honor the bargain she had made with Queen Tiy.

She turned to Seti. "You must make arrangements for me to see the queen," she told him. Then she turned back to watch Amenophis with a transfixed horror.

Seti frowned at her, bewildered by the change in her mood, by the sudden fear he read in her expression.

"But why, Princess?" he demanded. "There is no need—"

"There *is* need," she interrupted. She stared with a fixed intensity at Amenophis. "There has never been greater need," she said.

Seti waited for her to offer him an explanation. When she did not, he felt pained by the distance she had established between them. "I will see what can be done, Princess," he told her, then looked away from the fear in her eyes.

Pharaoh faced the long line of troops and lifted Hera to his shoulders. Once more a tide of shouts broke out from the soldiers as Hera raised his arms over his head and shouted with childish glee.

And Shanda watched Amenophis who sat on his mount, gripping the knife at his side, as he, in turn, watched her son.

Tiy had never seen her son so angry, never before felt that he was beyond her power to control.

She stood aside, thinking only to keep out of the path of Amenophis's anger until it had spent itself, and watched him prowl the room, pausing from time to time to break something, to throw or crush or slash. There was an animal ferocity in him that she had never seen before. It repulsed her, even frightened her, but it also fascinated and attracted her. She knew then that there was much that he had managed to hide from her, much that she would still have to learn if he was not to someday grow too strong for her to control.

When finally he paused to consider the ruin he had made of the room, she dared to approach him.

"Hera is only a child," she said quietly.

He looked up from the mess of her cosmetics he'd thrown to the floor, the paints and their ruined boxes mixing in a confusion of azure, pink, and black.

"He held his bastard on his shoulders so the soldiers could hail him as the Golden Prince," he retorted. "Golden Prince!" he shouted. "Nothing more than his Hittite whore's bastard!"

She touched his arm. "Soon, my love, very soon we will be ready."

He shook off her hand and stared at her for a moment, noticing the dark circles beneath her eyes, and the way the skin on her neck seemed too large for the matter it contained. She has grown old, he thought, surprised that he had not seen the signs until that moment.

His thoughts scattered however, when she pressed her lips to his. With the contact, his anger began to dissolve and was quickly replaced by a longing greater than any he had ever felt before.

Tiy was the only one who ever really cared about him, he told himself, the only one who ever really loved him. He put his arms around her and crushed her to him, then suddenly pushed her away.

He studied her for a moment, wondering why he could no longer see those signs of age that only a moment before had repulsed him. She was suddenly beautiful to him, as beautiful as any young girl he had ever taken, more beautiful. He put his hand on her arm and pulled her toward her bedroom.

"Wait, my love," she begged him softly, trying to pull back, but powerless against his grip and the force with which he led her.

He ignored her, moving quickly, until they stood in the entrance to the room. Then he stopped, frozen where he stood, his hand still grasping her arm.

He stared at the naked man in her bed, a young man, not much older than he was, large and well muscled with a coarse, dull face and a bewildered, sluggish expression. Amenophis thought the expression must be permanent, that this goat-man Tiy had taken to her bed never quite understood what was happening around him and never ceased to be bewildered.

Sethos pulled the linen sheet up to cover his nakedness, then stood slowly, his eyes never leaving Amenophis's face as if he feared the prince might lunge at him and rip out his heart. Amenophis could hear his breath, the ragged panting of fear.

"What is this?" Amenophis turned on Tiy. "How can you befoul yourself with such as this?"

She was, he noticed suddenly, nearly naked, wearing only a thin robe. He wondered why he had not seen that before. Had his anger numbed him to the fact that he had taken her from her bed, that there was the sharp, raw odor of sex about her?

She didn't answer him, but instead smiled at Sethos. "Wait here," she directed, and Sethos obediently moved back to the bed while she put her hand on Amenophis's arm.

This time it was she who led him. "Come," she ordered.

Both his anger and his passion had dulled with bitter shock, and he let her lead him back to the other room with its litter of ruin on the floor.

He dropped into a chair as though felled by sudden weariness. "Why is that—that animal in your bed?" he finally managed.

She fell to her knees beside him and grasped his hands with hers. "He is one of Pharaoh's guards," she whispered to him. "Don't you see, my love? That animal, as you call him, will kill *him* for us."

He straightened and stared into her eyes, looking for the lie. "When?" he demanded.

"Tomorrow," she whispered, conspirator revealing conspiracy, delighting in the thought. "Pharaoh is to go to the temple tomorrow morning to offer sacrifice." She offered a strange, almost innocent smile. "Only it will not be a ram's blood he offers, but his own."

"How?" he asked in a whisper, finally caught up by the urgency he heard in her words.

"The priest Nekhbet will help us," she said.

He nodded. The chief priest, Nekhbet, had been carefully prepared. Both Tiy and Nofret made sure that he received word that Pharaoh had grown lax in his faith, that the Hittite had infected him with the belief in her foreign gods.

"When Pharaoh goes to the temple for the sacrifice, Nekhbet will see that only Sethos is with him. The guard will strike as they walk through the temple, before they reach the altar."

Amenophis nodded toward the bedroom. "He is prepared?" he asked.

She nodded. "He will let Pharaoh pass and then strike when they are alone." She lowered her voice. "He has been told he will be led to safety by the priests and that he will receive a fortune in gold and safe passage to the south."

Amenophis leaned close to her. "But he won't?" he whispered.

She shook her head. "It would not do to let a pharaoh's assassin outlive him," she replied softly.

He smiled at her, then leaned back in the chair and stared sightlessly up at the ceiling.

"Tomorrow you will be pharaoh, my love," she told him.

He straightened, then stood, taking her hands and pulling her to her feet with him.

"Go to him," he said evenly. "Make his last night worth the price he will pay for it."

# Twenty-one

SHANDA LAY WITH her eyes closed, refusing to face the prospect of day. Only this one day to be gotten through, she told herself. One day and then she would see Tiy and there would once more be an understanding as there had been before, this time with the assurance that Amenophis, too, would honor his mother's vow. Seti had promised to go to the queen that afternoon and arrange the meeting. Only this one day to be gotten through, she told herself, and then Hera would be safe.

She felt Pharaoh stir beside her. She turned to him and forced her eyes to open. She was surprised to see that the room was still dark, a silvery shaft of moonlight offering the only illumination.

Pharaoh caressed her cheek. "Go back to sleep, Princess," he told her. "It is not yet dawn."

He pressed his lips softly to her forehead before he rose.

She lay watching him in the darkness as he found his robe and pulled it on. She never tired of watching the way his body moved, the sleek muscles of his back and arms and chest were a constant source of wonder to her, his body so different from her own, so pleasing to her eye. But as he tied on the robe her thoughts returned to where they had been before she'd opened her eyes.

"Must you go?" she asked him.

The bewilderment in his expression at her question made her realize that she was truly afraid. He sat down on the bed at her side and took her hand.

"What is it, Shanda?" he asked her softly.

She shook her head, trying to deny the feeling to him if she could not deny it to herself.

"Nothing," she told him. "There is only this"—she paused —"this strange foreboding I feel." She suddenly felt foolish as she watched the tolerant smile come to his lips.

"Foreboding?" he asked. The tolerance in his expression turned to amusement.

"A feeling that something will happen," she continued thoughtfully, knowing that he was thinking that women who were soon to give birth were prone to such feelings, that the feelings were transient, like the condition. "Something unpleasant," she said slowly. "Something worse than unpleasant."

He said nothing for a moment, just sat staring at her worried expression. His look of tolerant amusement, however, had vanished.

"I have sent word to the priests that I will come to make sacrifice this morning," he told her finally. "I must go. But when it is done, I will return." He smiled again, this time fondly and a shade lecherously. "It has been too long since I have spent an afternoon alone with the woman I love."

She managed to smile back at him and patted the growing mound of her belly. "This, I think, lord, will require some consideration."

He shook his head. "Fear not, Princess. I am an imaginative man."

She laughed softly. "So I remember," she assured him. "Unless that was a stranger who crept into my bed last night."

He stood and considered her sternly. "A pharaoh does not creep, Princess."

She nodded, more than willing to agree. "No, he prowls and then leaps, like a lion."

"A lion who is hungry for prey," he amended.

Her smile faded. "I could not live without you and Hera," she whispered.

"There will be no need," he replied. "We are not about to leave you." He kissed her once more before he quietly made his way from the room.

Shanda watched him leave, then lay motionless for a moment. It almost surprised her to find herself standing, pulling on her robe, and following him to his own bedroom, which served as a dressing room now that he spent all his nights with her. She stood in the doorway, looking in at the pool of lamplight that brightened the center of the room where he stood.

His servant, Usha, was holding out his clothing to him as he dressed. When Usha looked up and saw Shanda, he momentarily took on, as he always did, the same unbelieving expression he had worn the first time Pharaoh had brought her to this apartment. It was, Shanda thought, as though he still did not quite believe a woman now lived there as well.

But Usha recovered quickly, bowing to her. Shanda waved him back to his task as Pharaoh turned to find her there.

"Shanda?"

She held up a hand. "I come to assure myself you are robed befitting the seriousness of your task," she told him.

He grinned, then sat to allow Usha to strap on his sandals. "And do you approve?" he asked.

She considered him thoughtfully, her expression very solemn, taking in the gold-trimmed blue tunic, the belt with its lapis adornment and the dark blue robe. Finally, the inspection completed, she nodded.

When Usha had done, Pharaoh stood, crossed to her, and put his hands on her shoulders. He could still see a tinge of fear in her expression, although she was obviously trying to hide it from him. For a moment he considered not going to the temple, staying there with her instead. He'd never before seen her so strongly affected by a feeling. He wondered if it might be a real warning. Perhaps the goddess Maat had whispered in her ear as she slept.

But then he realized he had little choice. If Shanda's fear was an omen, then he was, at least, forewarned and ready for the attack. The priests were growing more restless day by day. He had to show them he was not, as they feared, falling away from his faith in the ancient gods. To do otherwise would be the same as pushing them into Tiy's waiting arms. Even now the head priest, Nekhbet, was speaking in ways that would have been considered traitorous in any other man. Tiy had chosen her allies well. In all of Egypt, only the priests were beyond the reach of Pharaoh.

He put his arms around Shanda and drew her close. "I will return soon," he told her softly. "Go back to sleep and I will waken you." He grinned at her. "Pleasantly, I assure you."

She nodded, but did not return his smile. Nor did she move when he released her, but stood where she was, watching him as he made his way to the door and left the room.

Shanda heard a low hum and realized with absent surprise it was the sound of her own voice softly murmuring a prayer she had often heard Med offer, a prayer to the great father god Ptah, to protect Pharaoh, the most sacred of his children. When she saw Usha turn and stare at her curiously, she stopped, shook herself as though forcing herself to waken, then started toward her own room. When she was out of Usha's hearing she finished the prayer, not quite sure why she offered it to a god in whom she had no belief. But for the first time in her life she was unable to tell herself the effort was valueless.

She had not reached the door before she stopped, turned, and instead made her way to the nursery, needing to assure herself that Hera was safe. She opened the door silently, then stepped inside, taking care not to wake the nurse who slept on the floor at Hera's feet. She moved silently to the side of his bed and stood watching him sleep.

She was struck by his beauty, as she always was when she saw him asleep. His blond hair lay disheveled around his face; an unruly lock had fallen across his brow and reached nearly to his eye. She would have to see that Med trimmed it soon, she told herself, suddenly practical, maternal. Then she reached down and neatly arranged the sheet he had kicked away as he slept.

She turned and made her way to the garden, knowing she would be able to sleep no more. She sat beside the pool, ignoring the chill of the stone chair beneath her. Then she looked up at the sky, waiting for the sun to rise and tell her it was day.

Pharaoh stepped out into the courtyard to find Seti, as always prompt, waiting for him. Behind him were a half-dozen soldiers. Pharaoh looked them over quickly in the dim light cast by the handful of torches set around the courtyard. Sethos, he noticed, was not among the soldiers Seti had brought as his guard.

He strode directly to his chariot, motioning to Seti to ride with him. Seti climbed up beside Pharaoh, then signaled for his men to follow.

Pharaoh took up the reins and started the horses immediately, without so much as offering Seti a word of greeting. The great gates swung open to allow the small procession to leave the palace grounds and move out into the still dark streets of Thebes. The sound of the horses' hooves echoed eerily in the silence of the morning.

Seti respected Pharaoh's silence as they rode through the city, but eventually his curiosity overcame his reserve. As they were approaching the hulking shadow that he knew to be the temple, he ventured finally to speak.

"You are bothered, lord," he said evenly. "This accommodation to the priests—"

"It is not the priests," Pharaoh broke in. "It is Shanda. She was filled with a prescient dread this morning. She didn't want me to leave. She would not admit it, but I know she was afraid."

Seti considered his words in silence as they neared the temple and Pharaoh drew the horses to a stop. They were obviously expected, for a door opened as soon as the chariot came to a halt and a brilliant shaft of lamplight darted out, cutting through the early morning darkness.

Seti put his hand on Pharaoh's shoulder, then removed a knife from the sheaf in his belt and held it out.

Pharaoh looked down at the pale shine of the blade. "It is forbidden to carry a weapon into the temple," he said evenly.

Seti nodded. "I know. But I think the gods will understand that these are not normal times," he replied.

Pharaoh considered the blade an instant longer before he took it and placed it carefully in his own belt, then obscured it beneath the folds of his robe. "You think, then, this feeling of the princess's is more than the hysteria of a woman whose time grows near?" he asked.

Seti nodded. "Some prescience is a whisper from the

gods, lord," Seti replied. "And I think the princess's time is not so close as to invite such madness."

"So I believe, too," Pharaoh said. "Sethos?"

Seti's expression grew hard. "He went to her again last night," he replied. "My spies did not see him leave."

"So he lies still in her arms, or else he was smuggled out and waits nearby to do her bidding."

Pharaoh scanned the shadows around the temple, vainly searching the darkness for some sign of the assassin. Abandoning the task as hopeless, he climbed down from the chariot.

Seti grasped Pharaoh's shoulder. He was gripped by a fear he did not quite understand, but it held him powerfully and he felt himself bending to it.

"Let me come with you, lord," he begged.

Pharaoh shook his head. "It is forbidden," he said. "Only Pharaoh and the priests may attend."

"Then leave. Come back some other day."

Pharaoh put his hand on top of Seti's, grasping it firmly. "A man cannot spend his life running from fears, Seti. If they are not faced, they will grow until they rule him."

With that he turned and climbed the long flight of stone steps that led to the temple doors.

Nekhbet was there, beside the door, waiting for him. His shaved head shone dully in the lamplight that escaped from within, a pale orb floating above the long black robes that covered his corpulent body. His fingers caressed the golden amulet, the mark of his office, which he wore suspended from a gold chain around his neck. Pharaoh had often seen the priest fondle the shining disk, his long, thick fingers moving sensually over the carved surface, touching, warming, cherishing.

Pharaoh watched his fingers, fascinated, and wondered if Nekhbet had even once in his life offered so much tenderness to a woman. He felt a sudden surge of pity for the temple prostitutes who offered their services to the priests in return for the prayers that would smooth their path to the afterlife. Only grievous sins would require such an act of repentance.

"Your presence honors us, lord," Nekhbet greeted him, bowing his head in reverence. The round face bobbed, then resettled itself, and the dark eyes found Pharaoh's with a challenging stare.

"It is I who come to honor the gods," Pharaoh replied, then strode past him, careful to avoid touching so much as a fold of the priest's robe, and made his way into the great hall of the temple.

It took his eyes a moment to adjust to the sudden blaze of light that glowed from the many torches lining the central gallery of the huge room. It seemed odd to him that, with so much light, still there were corners in which shadows held on to the darkness like lovers clutching in ecstatic embrace. Two long rows of pillars were guardians of the night; beyond them was an unrelieved blackness the torchlight could not touch. He thought it odd that he had never before noticed how much darkness remained in the temple despite the attempts to banish it.

Behind him, Pharaoh heard the doors to the outside swing shut with a thud and the heavy bolt sliding home with a high metallic scrape. In the silence of the great room, the sounds reminded him of a door being closed on a tomb.

His eyes no longer stung by the light, Pharaoh looked around, at each of the dozen dark-robed priests. He could see little of them beyond their shaved heads, the thick sweep of black fabric in which they were enfolded, and their dark eyes staring at him. They seemed not men to him, he realized, but creatures that clung like parasites to the temple walls, taking sustenance from the offerings of piously shed

blood. Surely, he thought, the gods could have little use for
creatures such as these.

These underlings bowed to him more reverently than had
Nekhbet, falling to their knees and touching their heads
to the floor by his feet. Then, rising as though they were
one, they silently formed a double line and faced the gold-
sheathed doors that led to the gods' sanctuary. There was
a moment when all was silent. Then their voices rose in a
chant as they moved toward the holy place.

Pharaoh stood where he was, hardly aware that Nekhbet
remained at his side like a shopkeeper keeping a sharp eye
on his wares lest they be stolen. Pharaoh silently watched
the lines of dark robed priests. Then he let his eyes roam the
length of the long room, trying to penetrate the shadows that
cloaked the corners and niches behind the massive columns.
He was not sure why, but he somehow knew someone was
hiding there in the darkness. The back of his neck prickled,
and his senses had become sharply aware. He told himself
he could scent the man, then wondered if it might be his
own fear that assaulted his nostrils.

The golden doors were pulled open and the first of the
priests entered the sanctuary. Pharaoh began to move forward as well. He forced himself to keep his step firmly
determined, aware that if he gave in to fear, he would never
again be free of it.

He hardly noticed when Nekhbet paused, then moved
away from him. Instead, he concentrated on the sound that
came from the supposedly empty darkness behind the columns. It was a noise like footsteps, not boldly honest footsteps, but the near silent pad a man's sandals made when he
moved with stealth. Had Pharaoh not been alert and searching for danger, had his ears not been seeking the noise, the
sound would have been lost in the depth of the huge hall
and the dull chanting of the priests in the sanctuary.

Pharaoh paused and let the sound grow a bit stronger, aware that the one who stalked him could no longer be hidden by the darkness but had been forced into the light by his approach. Then he turned on his heel, surprising the man approaching him from behind.

Sethos stopped for a moment, startled by the realization that he had been seen, obviously having expected to draw close to Pharaoh undetected, unheard, and to strike without being forced to face his victim. The sword in his hand grew unsteady.

Pharaoh stared at him, at the black priest's robe that hung, oddly ill fitting, over the uniform of the royal guards. From the corner of his eye he saw Nekhbet draw back, either reluctant to dirty his hands with a pharaoh's blood or wishing to remove himself from the act that was about to take place. He dismissed his thoughts of the fat priest, telling himself Nekhbet was too fond of his own pampered existence to take a hand in regicide. Nekhbet was not a threat to him, he decided, although the priest would certainly not raise a hand to help him. He kept his attention on the sword in Sethos's hand, on the way the lamplight darted off the blade as it shook with the assassin's sudden fear.

"Are you not afraid you will enrage the gods," Pharaoh asked, his tone surprisingly mild, "by bearing arms within their sanctuary? Does the thought of facing Osiris with not only my blood on your hands but sacrilege as well raise no fear in you?"

He grinned pleasantly, as though accustomed to having this sort of conversation with his guards. He watched Sethos's face and saw fear in his eyes. With the recognition of Sethos's fear he realized his own was suddenly gone.

"I had not thought, Sethos, you were so brave a man as to risk the wrath of Osiris. Perhaps the rewards you expect to receive in this life are great enough to compensate you for the lack of another?"

Sethos opened his mouth to speak, but no words came from it. His wits, always dull, had fled entirely when Pharaoh turned to face him. He had not been prepared for this. Tiy had promised him he would not be forced to look into his victim's eyes. And now here was Pharaoh, facing him, taunting him, as though it were he who held the sword in his hand. The thought came to him that this was not a mere man he faced, but a god whom he'd been sent to kill. He was filled with a sudden panic, recognizing the folly of what he'd agreed to do. How could he have been trapped this way? he wondered. How could he have been so great a fool as to trade his life for admittance to a woman's bed?

"Do you do this for riches, Sethos," Pharaoh went on, "or as payment for admission to the whore's bed?" He paused, as though in thought, and then smiled suddenly. "Do you really think they will let you live once you have given them my blood?"

Sethos dropped his eyes, unable to bear Pharaoh's stare. But his grip on the sword steadied suddenly as he found his faltering courage, and he began to move forward step by step, moving purposely as though he thought Pharaoh would flee from his blade like a hare who realizes he is caught in a trap.

Instead Pharaoh swept his robe aside, seized the blade Seti had given him, and withdrew it from his belt. Then he steadied himself, leaning forward on the balls of his feet, waiting for the lunge of the assassin's sword.

Sethos's eyes fell to the dagger in Pharaoh's hand, and for a moment he hesitated. He had but one thought, the wish that he had never allowed himself to be seduced by Tiy. He was not so dull as to think he could escape now.

Even if he surrendered his sword, he knew he faced death. The attempt, once begun, could not be wished away. He had but one chance, and that was to do what he had been sent to do. He lowered his head, bull-like, and charged.

Sethos's intent was to use the length of his sword, to slash and draw back before Pharaoh's dagger could come close enough to cause him damage. He knew himself limited in many ways, but a sword in his hand made him the equal of any man, perhaps even a Pharaoh.

But he was so intent on his lunge that he did not see Pharaoh's arm draw back and then suddenly dart forward.

He never saw the dagger fly. He saw nothing, only Pharaoh's eyes, sharp and cold, until he looked down and saw the blade embedded in his chest.

His arm jerked, suddenly useless, and the sword flew from his hand off into the darkness. There was now only surprise in his eyes, and terror. He was filled with the certainty that he was going to die.

He staggered backward, seeking the darkness where he had earlier lain in wait, as if it could offer him refuge from the inevitability of his fate. Pharaoh strode slowly toward him, the look of determination in his eyes sharply piercing, seeming to inflict almost as much pain on Sethos as the blade in his chest.

"Are there others?" Pharaoh demanded, his words turned hard now, like daggers themselves. "Has Tiy sent others as well?"

Sethos tore his eyes away and with his hands grasped the knife, trying vainly to withdraw it. He gasped with the pain, then raised his hands and stared at the blood that covered them. Then he fell back against one of the huge pillars. From his throat there erupted a low, animal sound, and then he slowly slid to the floor.

Pharaoh watched him fall, saw his bloody hands lying

limp, his arms outspread, his eyes, dark and dull, staring upward. He realized Sethos was dead.

He started toward the body.

"Unless you have twice sinned and brought a second blade into the gods' house, Pharaoh, it is time for you to meet Osiris as well."

Pharaoh stopped in midstride as Nekhbet stepped out of the darkness behind the pillar against which Sethos's body lay. He moved between the pillar and Pharaoh. His dark eyes shone, sharp and determined, from his thick, round face. His lips curled into a humorless smile.

In his hand he held the sword Sethos had dropped. The reflection of his golden amulet shone from it, dazzling in the torchlight.

Slowly he raised it to strike.

Pharaoh cursed himself for having dismissed Nekhbet as too cowardly to take a hand in his death. The fat priest had come to possess some courage after all. It was hardly a realization from which he drew any comfort.

He kept his eyes on the sword. "Surely you cannot think that what you do here in the gods' own sanctuary will be overlooked in your judgment," he said as he slowly backed away from Nekhbet. "A priest would be the first to know this act will deny him entry to the afterlife."

"The gods will reward me for shedding the blood of a king who spurns them," Nekhbet responded. He moved forward, too, trying to close the distance between them.

Pharaoh eyed Sethos's body where it lay on the floor behind Nekhbet. If only he could reach it and retrieve the knife, he would have a weapon with which to defend himself. But the priest's bulk stood firmly between him and his hope of rearming himself.

Pharaoh pulled off his robe and wrapped it around his arm.

"You tread a dangerous course, priest," he hissed. He held up the arm he'd wrapped with the robe as though to ward off the expected blow.

"Not so dangerous as you," Nekhbet replied, as he threw himself forward, the sword preceding his huge body like a standard of death.

Pharaoh crouched and then darted to one side, aware only when he felt the sharp pain that the sword had bitten neatly through the robe and into the sinew of his arm. With the sudden spurt of blood, he felt the sting of the blade in his flesh, sharp and hot.

But the force of the lunge had sent Nekhbet beyond the place where Pharaoh stood. The priest was no swordsman; his advantage had lain in the fact that he alone had a weapon and in the surprise his willingness to use it created. Surprise was gone now, and he was about to lose his advantage of facing an unarmed foe. For as he stumbled past, Pharaoh ran back to where Sethos lay.

Pharaoh fell on the body even as Nekhbet turned and started forward, ready to renew the attack. The sword struck against the stone of the pillar just by his ear as the priest struck out wildly. The noise seemed to fill Pharaoh's head, echoing the threat of death it promised.

The priest paused, gathering his wits and his confidence, forcing himself this time to aim his thrust true to the mark. He put the weight of his huge body behind the thrust and brought the sword down once again.

Pharaoh rolled away, ignoring the pain in his wounded arm as it was crushed against the cold stone floor. He grasped the knife that protruded from Sethos's chest and carried it to him. Nekhbet's sword, rather than finding the victim it had been intended to find, embedded itself in the dead man's side.

Nekhbet put his foot on Sethos's body and withdrew the

sword angrily, then moved forward again, aware that this would be his last chance.

Pharaoh lay on the floor, looking up at the sword, and readied the bloody knife in his hand. As Nekhbet raised the blade, he threw the knife.

He knew it was wrong as soon as the knife was out of his hand, knew that his one chance was gone. His wounded arm was not perfect in its control, and his ungainly position had made the throw all the more difficult. The blade caught Nekhbet in the shoulder.

The priest hardly seemed to notice the invasion of his flesh. He stared down at Pharaoh with the same indifferent eye with which he observed the rams brought to the altar for sacrifice. He put both hands on the sword hilt, grasping it firmly, and prepared to offer Pharaoh's blood to the gods.

# Twenty-two

SHANDA SAW THE first tentative rays of sunlight begin to lighten the sky. It turned the foliage in the garden from dull, dark gray to a muted green. The dreaded day had begun, and there was little she could do but face it as she would any other.

She pushed herself out of the chair, regretting the lethargy that filled her and compounded the clumsiness of her thickened body. She felt as if she were being crushed beneath a burden far too great to bear. It was, she told herself with calm logic, nothing more than the weight of the child growing within her. Until that morning the baby had hardly seemed a burden to her at all, but now she found herself straining with the effort of drawing breath.

She would spend the morning with Hera, she decided, perhaps let him play with the box of paints Pharaoh had given her. It was his favorite pastime, if one that produced a decided amount of disorder. Then she would bathe, arrange her hair, and dress for Pharaoh's return. She felt she had to treat this day like any other or go mad with worry.

When she returned to her room, Med was already there,

busily straightening the bed.

"You look tired, Princess," he told her. "Perhaps you would like still to sleep a bit?"

She waved his suggestion aside.

"Med, when Hera wakens, I would have you bring him to me. I do not want him to be left alone today. Not for a moment."

Med offered her a bewildered look. "Princess?"

She shook her head. "Just do as I ask," she replied sharply, aware that the exasperation she felt at his questioning her had more to do with her own fears than with his lack of understanding.

"Yes, Princess," he replied, his tone slightly hurt.

Shanda looked away from him. How could she explain to him how she felt when she was unable to explain it to herself? She would make her peace with Med later; she would beg him to ignore her moodiness and make some excuse. He would accept her apology, she was sure.

She only knew she could not leave Hera unguarded. Only with him and Pharaoh beside her would she feel any measure of safety on this day.

And she also knew that only when this day was past, would her fears be banished and she left in peace.

Hera woke and sat up in his bed. He had been dreaming, he realized, and his mind was still filled with the images of his dreams. He had been a general in his reverie, leading his armies in a great battle, driving his chariot as his father's charioteers drove theirs. He was the greatest general who had ever lived, the very bravest of all.

The dream was so appealing to him and so vividly implanted in his mind that he wished he could return to sleep and find it once again. But he was completely awake, although there was just the mildest hint of light in the sky.

His body was filled with the energy of his dream battle. He could not lie still and quiet in his bed.

He climbed out of the bed very quietly, taking great care not to waken Sukhrete, the nursemaid, sure she would insist he bathe and dress and then sit quietly with his morning milk and bread. Although the prospect of milk and bread was not without appeal, he told himself a general had no need of a nursemaid's presence. And bread and milk could always be found later, once the battle was won.

He would tell his father he had grown too old for a nursemaid, he decided as he stole to the door that led to the garden. He was sure Pharaoh would agree. After all, hadn't he driven Pharaoh's chariot? Surely that meant he was too old to be bullied by a gray-haired woman whose only thoughts were that her prince's knees must be kept clean and that he must drain the contents of his cup of milk in the morning.

He stepped out into the garden, intoxicated by the freedom of the early morning quiet and solitude and by the scent of the garden, damp and brown and green, that came to him when he tasted the air. A cry of absolute happiness came to his lips, but he managed to stifle it before it could shatter the quiet. He knew that if he wakened Sukhrete, his freedom would be lost.

The memory of his dream returned to him, and he thought of the toy armies, the carved soldiers and chariots and horses, that he'd hidden beneath a bush by the pool so that the nursemaid would not come upon them and put them away where he could not find them. The bush had tiny thorns that had scratched him when he stowed the toys beneath it. But the threat of the thorns had made the bush all the more worthy a guardian of his armies, ensuring that Sukhrete would not venture near. He was quite proud of his own deviousness.

He ran, choking back his laughter, along the path that led to the pool. When he reached it, he climbed up on the stone chair beside it, panting more from the effort of holding back his laughter and maintaining the quiet than from the run. The stone felt unusually warm beneath him, for the sun was still low on the horizon and ought not to have warmed it yet. Unaware that Shanda had only moments before vacated it, that it was the heat of her body he felt, he pondered the mystery, but finally abandoned it in favor of retrieving his hidden armies.

He stood, ran along the edge of the pool to the bush, and dropped to his knees in the damp soil, reaching under the bottom branches and feeling about in the dirt for the toys. For his effort he received a scratch on his forearm. He looked at it with a rapt concentration, then smiled. He now had shed blood in battle. Surely that was the mark of a true soldier.

He found the tiny army easily enough, however, and drew the pieces out one by one, taking care after the first warning scratch not to brush against the thorns. After all, he told himself practically, a wise soldier did not shed his own blood needlessly.

The toys retrieved, he carried them to the side of the pool, dropped them to the ground, and immediately became totally engrossed in his game, oblivious of the movement in the bushes behind him.

Amenophis stared at the sky. He had been standing in the same spot since long before dawn. But he had wanted to be there and ready before the time came, so he could savor the moment when the sun rose, knowing that with the dawn would come Pharaoh's death.

He waited beside the fence that backed the royal apartment's garden, Pharaoh's private domain. It was by the gate in this fence that the workmen entered to tend the small garden paradise, to trim away dead leaves and branches and keep the flower beds fresh and filled with blooms. On this particular morning, however, no gardeners would arrive to tend the royal grounds. Amenophis had seen to that himself. In their place, he would enter the garden and use his own knife to perform a task of pruning that had long needed to be done.

The sky began to brighten, and with the growing light, he felt a thrill of strength within himself, felt his own power slowly growing inside him. He stared up at the small rim of sunlight that hovered at the horizon, refusing to close his eyes against the glare, reveling in the first moments of this particular day. He told himself it was a sign, that what he felt growing in him was his father's power bleeding from his body and finding its way into him, the new Pharaoh. It had been done, he told himself. He regretted only that he had not been there to watch Sethos perform the deed. It would have brought him pleasure to see Pharaoh's death, to watch his eyes, to know that Pharaoh knew who had sent him to offer his *kah* to Osiris for judgment.

The time had come, he told himself, and he moved along the tall fence toward the gate to the garden. He saw, as he approached, the guard whom Sethos had brought to Nofret, the one who had been so easily bribed. It was obvious the man had had no difficulty persuading the true guard to offer up the task. It could not have been difficult. Such duty would be, for the most part, extremely boring.

Amenophis smiled. The guard's duty would not be boring this morning, he thought.

The man lowered his spear as he saw Amenophis approach.

"All is quiet?" Amenophis asked softly.

The guard nodded, then turned to look to the sheds where

the gardeners kept their tools to assure himself that they, indeed, had not come that morning. "All is quiet, lord," he whispered hoarsely in reply. He spoke as though the words were a secret password, a means of initiation into the plot about to unfold and thereby qualifying him to a share of the rewards to be reaped at its conclusion.

Amenophis swallowed his distaste at the guard's manner. He moved close to him and put his hand on the man's shoulder. "Remember," he whispered, "you saw nothing, heard nothing."

The guard nodded, and Amenophis smiled at him even as he drew his knife and thrust it into the guard's back.

For a moment Amenophis stood holding the guard's shoulder, steadying him as the sudden sharp pain ran through him and the look of shocked bewilderment filled his face. Then he pulled the knife up sharply and finally withdrew it as he released his hold on the man's shoulder.

The guard reached out to him and mouthed a single word: "Why?"

Amenophis stepped back and away from him as he crumpled, his hands reaching out to Amenophis and grasping convulsively at the air one last time as he died.

Amenophis looked down at him, his expression devoid of emotion. He shrugged and then knelt, pushing the dead guard's body aside so that he could open the gate.

"Because you betrayed your master for gold," he explained, as though the man could still hear him. "Because a traitor will never be anything except a traitor." He carefully wiped his blade on the guard's tunic, then opened the gate and slipped into the garden, pulling it closed behind him. He could see the outline of the roof of Pharaoh's quarters at the far end of the garden, and walked directly toward it without wasting another thought on the man he'd just murdered. He had, after all, far more important prey waiting, prey for which he'd cultivated a taste that was now demanding to be satisfied. And now that Pharaoh was dead, it was prey he could take with impunity.

Hera was intent as he pushed the soldiers forward into the mock battle. He made soft noises, tiny snorts and clanking sounds, as if he could not quite decide whether to provide his army with the sound of the horses or the clash of sword against sword. He took no notice of the movement in the bushes or of the intruder's approach until a large foot was suddenly thrust into his field of battle.

He looked up, at first angry, then surprised.

"Do you know who I am, boy?"

Hera nodded and stared up at him, wide-eyed. "Yes, lord," he replied, suddenly careful and for some improbable reason remembering to be polite as he had been taught. "You are my brother, Prince Amenophis."

Amenophis smiled, pleased and yet not quite sure why he should be. After all, the boy had seen him many times, and it should be no surprise to him that Hera had been told who he was. Still, it gave him a perverse pleasure to know that the boy knew him, that he would see who did to him what was about to be done.

"Shall I call you brother, then?" Amenophis asked.

"Hera," the boy replied as he scrambled to his feet. "Everyone calls me Hera." He looked thoughtful, then smiled. "Would you like to join my battle?" he asked hospitably, pointing down to the now scattered toys at his feet. It was all he had to offer.

"Hera," Amenophis repeated, looking down at the toys, then back at Hera. "I think we have other battles to fight," he said slowly, and then he smiled an entirely unpleasant smile.

Hera grew suddenly uncomfortable, aware that Amenophis was playing with him, laughing at him, and not sure why. He realized he was dressed for sleep in a short, thin tunic, wrinkled now and stained with dirt, from which his arms and legs hung naked and gangling. It must be his clothes, he thought. Amenophis was attired in a robe trimmed with gold braid and a thick jeweled belt. Hera wondered why this man had come to his garden so early in the morning dressed as he was. It seemed as though something was about to happen, but no one had told him of it, and he was unprepared to respond properly. The whole matter seemed entirely unfair to him.

"Why are you here?" he asked softly, surprised at his own boldness with the man his mother had told him would one day be pharaoh.

One side of Amenophis's mouth turned up in a weak grin. "To see you, Hera," he replied. "To bring you this." And then he held out the knife he had used to kill the guard.

Hera stared at it, dumb. There was a thin smear of blood on the blade, and he almost reached out to touch it, but then he drew his hand back, suddenly afraid. He turned his eyes back to Amenophis's face, and somehow he knew why Amenophis had come.

He backed away slowly, stepping on his toys with his bare feet but unaware of the hurt. Then Amenophis's hand shot out and grasped his arm, pulling him back.

He cried out, a high, thin, childlike cry that was quickly cut short by Amenophis's knife.

Shanda felt a sharp pain in her stomach. It made no sense to her at all, but it filled her with fear. She put her hand on her belly and felt the baby kicking. The movement was comforting.

And then came the cry. It wasn't loud, and it stopped almost as quickly as it had begun, but it sent a shiver of fear through her.

"Hera!"

She stood and ran from her room to the nursery, hating the way her size made her ungainly and slow. When she reached the nursery and saw Sukhrete still sleeping on the floor at the foot of Hera's empty bed, the fear grew to a raging panic.

She ran blindly forward to the garden. She was sure the cry had been Hera's and that it had come from somewhere in the garden.

"Hera!"

Her cry had the sound of terror in it. She could hear it herself, even in her distraction, and knew she had lost control of herself, that until she found her son she would not regain it.

She ran along the path, stumbling and twice nearly falling, but managing to stay on her feet. She kept calling out his name, listening for an answer that never came. The fear grew sharper within her, sharp enough to cut, and she felt the pain again, only this time she knew it was not her own pain but Hera's.

And then she was standing beside the pool, staring at his small body lying face down beside the water. He was still, she realized, too still.

She fell to her knees beside him and pulled him into her arms. It was then she saw the blood, his blood, and his open, unseeing eyes. There was no breath in him, no movement, nothing but the last of his blood draining out onto the stone around her.

"Hera!"

It was a wail of agony Shanda heard echoing back to her. She hardly recognized it as her own. She pulled Hera's body close to her, as though the contact could force life back into him, infuse into her child her own life just as she had once given it to him when he lay inside her. But there was no movement, no stirring, and she felt the tears streaming down her cheeks as she leaned over him and put her lips to his, still not accepting her child's death.

"He should have let you die at Kadesh."

She lifted a strained, grief-contorted face to Amenophis, barely seeing him through the tears in her eyes, but able to discern the bloody knife in his hand.

"Monster!" she cried. "To murder a child!"

Her words seemed to amuse him, or perhaps it was the misery he saw in her face that he relished. He smiled with obvious pleasure.

"I should have killed you when he was still in your belly, whore. I have waited too long for this, far too long."

He raised the knife once again.

Shanda made no move to draw back, no attempt to flee from his blade. She grasped Hera's body close to her and lowered her head, burying her face in her son's bloodstained tunic. Death at that moment seemed an acceptable end for her grief.

# Twenty-three

"STOP, PRIEST."

Nekhbet was startled by the cry. The voice rang with the authority of a man who was used to being obeyed. Nekhbet was shocked that someone had ventured into the temple to give an order to the high priest of Rah. No man dared speak to him that way, certainly not in his own domain. Here he ruled, and once past the doors of the temple, not even Pharaoh held greater sway.

His hands shook slightly, and he glanced up to see Seti slip through the temple doors and run toward him. One of the priests stood by the door, having drawn back the bolt and pulled the heavy door open for the soldier. Nekhbet wondered dimly how he had gotten there from the sanctuary. He did not even remember seeing the robed priest in the hall and yet he had to have run past him from the sanctuary to the door.

Nekhbet darted a glance toward the sanctuary and saw the remaining priests standing by the entry staring at him. Their eyes, wide and round, showed only disbelief.

Nekhbet turned back to face Seti.

"Out!" he screamed. "Sacrilege!"

But Seti continued forward, and now his sword was in his hand. "You are a dead man, priest," he cried.

Nekhbet looked down again, at Pharaoh, and realized his chance was lost. His victim had used the diversion to slide just beyond the range of the sword. The general of the guards was right, he realized with an oddly objective clarity. He was a dead man.

He looked down at the sword, at the thin trickle of Pharaoh's blood, then up at the vengeance in Seti's eyes. He had no chance against an armed, trained soldier. And he had no doubt as to what his fate would be were he to surrender. A fast death would be far preferable.

He pointed the sword at his belly and fell upon it.

But Nekhbet did not give up his last breath with silent dignity. The hall was filled with the sound of his scream. When it ended, the silence seemed deafening.

Seti ran to Pharaoh's side and looked at the thick stream of blood that seeped from his arm. "You are not badly hurt, lord?" he asked.

Pharaoh shook his head. "You and your blade saved my life today, Seti," he said as he grasped Seti's arm to pull himself to his feet. "I will not forget."

He stood and turned to the young priest who had dared to admit the soldier to the temple.

"You," he called. "Come here."

The young priest, visibly trembling, started forward. Tall and skeletally thin, he was the antithesis of Nekhbet. His shaved head and long, narrow, hawk-nosed face made him resemble yet another corpse as he fell to his knees and touched his head to the floor by Pharaoh's feet.

"What is your name, priest?" Pharaoh demanded.

"Siptah, lord."

He made no move to raise his head, and his voice quavered, as though daring to say even so much might be an affront.

"Have you been here long?" Pharaoh prodded.

"No, lord. I am the youngest of the priests," he said, daring to raise his head just enough to look up at his king.

Pharaoh realized he was hardly more than boy, certainly a good deal younger than Amenophis.

"And the only one brave enough to come to my aid," Pharaoh told him, with a disdainful glance at the black-robed priests who stood gaping with horror by the door to the sanctuary.

He nodded to Seti. "Get the amulet," he said, pointing to the ungainly heap that was Nekhbet's body.

Seti moved to where Nekhbet lay, pushed the body over negligently with his foot, retrieved the gold chain with its heavy golden amulet, and handed it to Pharaoh.

Pharaoh motioned to Siptah, and the young priest straightened his back but remained kneeling while Pharaoh placed the chain around his neck.

Siptah stared down at the amulet with disbelief, touching it to assure himself it was real. Then he looked up once again at Pharaoh.

"I—I am not worthy, lord," he murmured.

"Few are," Pharaoh replied dryly. "Do more good with it than did your predecessor," he warned.

"I will do my best, lord."

He bowed low once again, touching his head to the floor at Pharaoh's feet. A drop of blood from the slash in Pharaoh's arm fell onto the back of his neck, but he made no move to wipe it away. It stayed there, quickly drying to a dull rust color, dark against his skin.

Pharaoh motioned to Seti.

"Tiy may have begun this skirmish, but it is I who will see its end," he said. "First we go to Shanda, so that I can assure

myself she is safe. Then I will show the queen that she has
made a serious mistake in thinking me easy to kill."

When Med heard Shanda's cry, he thought at first of an
animal caught in a trap and aware it was about to die, but
he quickly cast off the image. There were no animals and
no traps in these gardens. Then he realized the cry had come
from a human, not an animal. And he knew it was Shanda.

The breakfast tray he had been carrying fell to the floor
with a loud crash. He ignored the noise and the wreckage
and ran to the garden.

He stood for a second, not sure where the sound had come
from. Then his feet started to move almost of their own to
the path that led to the pool. He ran along blindly, knowing that Shanda was in danger, that something was terribly
wrong.

He came upon them from behind, Amenophis holding
the knife over Shanda, and Hera lying still, too still,
in his mother's arms. Med knew immediately that the
young prince was dead. There was so much blood and
the boy was so quiet, it could not possibly have been
otherwise. And he also knew that Amenophis had killed
him.

He shouted, a dark, agonized scream of pure hatred, and
darted forward, his hand seizing the jewel-hilted knife he
wore at his side. Amenophis had not even enough time to
turn before Med was upon him, grunting with the effort as
he thrust the knife into Amenophis's back.

Amenophis straightened up and gasped, then spun around
to face Med. The bloody blade dropped from his hand. Then
he fell forward, first to his knees, and then to the ground.

It was not until the act was done that Med realized what
had happened, realized that he had killed Pharaoh's heir.
The deed, he knew, would buy him his own death. He told

himself he didn't care. He stared down at Amenophis's bloody back and knew that if ever a man deserved to die it was this one. If he, too, must die for the deed, at least he would die with honor.

He turned to Shanda. She knelt still on the ground with Hera in her arms, and stared up sightlessly at him. He thought at first she was dazed, for she seemed not to realize that he was there. Her eyes were wide, but were looking elsewhere. Perhaps, he thought, she was searching for the *kah* of her son.

He dropped to his knees beside her.

"Princess," he whispered as he put his hand on her shoulder.

He could hear her breathe, could see she was gasping for air as if she were suffocating. She put her head down and held Hera's body close to her.

Med began to put his arm around her, but then he saw movement from the corner of his eye, saw Amenophis reaching for his fallen knife. It shocked him for a moment, to realize the prince was not dead. And then he understood that Amenophis intended to make one last try.

Med lunged for the knife just as Amenophis did. The prince's hand encircled Med's wrist, the grasp strong, refusing to be shaken free. But Med reached out with his free hand and took the knife, then threw himself forward and plunged it into Amenophis's back beside his own blade. The hand fell away from his wrist, but Med did not stop. He stabbed again and again until he was spent and panting for breath.

He stood then and stared at the knife in his hands and at the blood that seemed to be everywhere. He dropped the blade and gazed with disbelief at what he had done.

A scream brought him back to reality. He looked up to see Sukhrete standing on the path not far from the pool, obvi-

ously afraid to come closer. She was barefoot and still wearing her nightdress. Her hair, mostly gray, coiled wild and
uncombed around her face and neck. Her hand was raised
to her mouth and she seemed about to scream again.

"Go find the guards," Med told her, cutting off the noise
before it was repeated. "Tell them to send for Pharaoh. Tell
them I have killed the prince."

The horror of this revelation stifled her scream. Her head
bobbed, and she turned and started to run, her thick and
aged body moving with a speed of which he would have
thought her incapable.

Med assured himself she had gone, then knelt at Shanda's
side and put his arms around her shoulders. "Princess," he
whispered gently.

Shanda looked up at him and seemed about to speak. But
words were lost to her, leaving only tears. She fell forward
and began to sob.


Pharaoh needed only a glance to know what had happened. Med pulled away from Shanda and stood, letting
Pharaoh take his place.

Pharaoh laid a shaking hand on Hera's still body, searching for warmth and life and finding none. Then he put his
arms around Shanda's shoulders and pulled her to him.

"You were right, Shanda," he whispered. "I should never
have left you this morning." His words, his face, were filled
with grief.

"My baby," she murmured, her face against his chest,
the words muffled by his body and ragged with her tears.

Then she looked up at him, her eyes puzzled and bewildered, silently asking him why anyone would do this thing,
how anyone could plunge a knife into the body of a child.

He knelt beside her for several minutes, holding her close
to him, but aware that there was no comfort for her, not even

in his arms. Finally he drew back and tried to take Hera's body from her.

She shook her head, reluctant to yield up her child. "No!" she cried. Then she met his eyes. "If you take him," she whispered, "he will be dead."

He understood her anguish, feeling the same unreasoning refusal to accept the fact of Hera's death, yet aware that he must.

"It must be done, my love," he whispered. "Already his *kah* has left him."

Once again he reached out to take the still body from her arms, and this time she reluctantly released it. He lifted Hera and handed him to Seti, feeling as if a part of himself had died and now lay cold and limp, a part of himself he had never hoped to find, and had now been taken from him. He could not look at that still, small body. The hurt it made in him was sharper and more painful than Nekhbet's sword and far more difficult for him to bear.

He lifted Shanda into his arms, then glanced quickly at Amenophis's body. This, too, was his son, but the only pain the sight of it gave him was the realization that he had sired a creature capable of doing what Amenophis had done. To kill in war or in defense of one's life or the lives of those one loved—that was one matter. But to kill a child for no reason but pure malice, that was entirely another.

Three men had died that day, three men and a young boy. Only the child would be mourned.

He carried Shanda to her bed and held her in his arms until the doctor was brought to her and gave her a potion to make her sleep. Then he left her reluctantly, aware that there was one matter still to be settled. Tiy had begun this battle with him, and it was not yet done.

As he left, he found Med standing, white faced and trembling, by the door to Shanda's room.

"Tend to her, boy," Pharaoh whispered, putting a hand on the eunuch's shoulder.

Med shook his head. "I have killed Prince Amenophis, lord. I cannot stay here."

"Where else would you stay?" Pharaoh demanded.

"The guards should take me," Med muttered. He was not sure precisely what punishment was meted out to murderers of royalty, only that death would eventually follow.

Pharaoh released his hold on Med's shoulder and turned away. Med's tears made the pain of his own grief sharper. "Tend to your mistress, Med," he said softly as he left the room. "Watch over her until I return."

Then he called out to Seti to follow with his men. There was still a last matter to be tended to before he could allow himself to mourn as well.

The servant who waited at the entrance to Tiy's bedroom was serene.

"The queen awaits you, lord," she murmured as she bowed and then stepped aside.

Pharaoh's impressions were strangely sharp. He had not stepped inside Tiy's house for more than a dozen years, and yet he walked through the rooms as though he had been there only hours before, sure of his way, stopping only to wave aside the confused servants who stood in his path. Even before the door to her bedroom swung open, he remembered the thick scent of the oils she wore, the memory returning with a clarity he found decidedly unpleasant.

The bedroom showed no sign of disorder. Tiy lay propped up with pillows in the center of her large bed. As he entered the room she lifted a gold cup and drained it of its contents.

He moved toward her, burning with his anger but still able to see she had arranged herself carefully for his inspection, her long dark hair loosened and brushed against the pillows around her, her pale gown baring her abundant breasts, her face painted with as much care as if she had prepared herself to attend a feast. Her lips formed themselves into a smile as he drew near.

At first he thought she had planned a seduction, hoping to escape his wrath by offering him her body. The thought sickened him. It was with relief he saw the malice in her eyes and knew that it was not her body she was prepared to offer him, but something else.

"We knew you would come," she said, pointing toward a figure seated in a chair at the far side of the room.

When he looked, he saw that Nofret was there with her. It came as no surprise to him that the vizier had come to her. It had most likely been Nofret who brought her word that her plan had failed. What did surprise him was the way the vizier sat, so still and quiet, his eyes wide but dull. It took him a moment to realize Tiy's visitor was dead.

Tiy smiled when she saw his expression. "Yes, he, too, sleeps his last sleep. He came to me with word of what had happened. He told me you would know we were behind Sethos's attack. Nofret was a coward, after all." That thought seemed to displease her, for she frowned. "He asked me for poison and I gave it to him," she said flatly.

Pharaoh was suddenly choked with anger. The thought that she could lie there so calmly, as though she were guiltless, and condemn Nofret for the acts to which she had pushed him filled him with disgust. He drew his knife and pointed the blade at her.

She seemed amused by the threat.

"Amenophis is dead," he told her coldly. He wanted to hurt her, to make her feel the same pain that ate at him.

She nodded complacently and turned her attention back

to Nofret's still body, as though the answers to her questions could be found in his dark, sightless eyes.

"I know," she told him. "I have lost my son." There was, finally, pain in her words, the first real emotion other than hatred he had ever sensed in her. But she recovered quickly and turned her eyes back to him. "I have lost one son," she told him spitefully, "but you have lost two." And then she smiled once again, with undisguised malevolence, delighted to see the pain her words had brought him.

The knife made his hand ache. He yearned to plunge it into her belly, to let her feel the pain Hera had felt, to let her know precisely how the boy had suffered.

Her head fell to one side, and she pulled it up sharply, almost as if the effort cost her a good deal. And then she smiled her nearly innocent smile.

"You would gladly sink that blade into my heart," she told him evenly. "To feel my life leaking out of me and know you were the cause of it." She breathed heavily for a moment, then settled herself. "But I have cheated you one last time." Her eyelids started to drift closed, and she forced them open sharply to stare at him. Then she lifted the gold cup as though in salute and smiled one last time. "You cannot take from me what I no longer possess," she said, her voice fading to a low whisper.

Then her arm dropped and the cup fell from it, letting a few last drops of brownish liquid spill onto the bedclothes near her, discoloring the white linen. Pharaoh walked toward her, his movements slow, as if he was reluctant to go near her. He put his hand on her neck and felt for the pulse which was no longer there.

He pulled his hand away abruptly, as though he had touched something unclean.

"I curse you, bitch," he hissed at her, staring down at her sightless eyes. "Let my curse be with your *kah* for eternity."

# Twenty-four

"SHANDA. SHANDA, LOOK at me."

Pharaoh knelt beside the chair where she sat and forced her to face him. She was pale and drawn, and there was an emptiness in her eyes that he had never seen there before.

Since that first day, she had not wept. Instead, she had withdrawn, burying herself someplace where he had been unable to reach her, unable to touch her. At first he had been willing to let her deal with her loss this way if she found it necessary, despite the hurt it caused him, despite the fact that it left him alone to deal with Hera's death. But it had been nearly ten days now, and she'd hardly eaten or slept. This withdrawal, he knew, was not healthy for her. And he needed her. More than he had ever needed anyone, he needed her to comfort him as much as he needed to comfort her.

"Shanda, please come back to me," he whispered.

For a moment she looked at him and he thought he had reached her. Then she lowered her eyes again, turning them back to her lap where one of Hera's toy horses lay tightly clasped in her hand.

Shanda felt his pain as sharply as she felt her own, and she wanted to help him. More than anything, she wanted to help him. Had it been done the way her mother's death had been handled, the body put quickly into a coffin and taken to the royal tomb soon after death, she might have managed to endure it. But this she could not face, she told herself. The thought of what the embalmers were doing to Hera's body made her tremble with revulsion. The natron baths, the assaults they made upon him. As if what Amenophis had done to him had not been horror enough.

She shook her head. "I cannot," she whispered raggedly, her words barely discernible. "Do not ask this of me."

"I cannot bury him alone, Shanda," he said softly.

She finally looked up into his eyes, letting him, for the first time since Hera's death, come close to her, letting him see inside her. She was filled with pain, a deep, consuming hurt that seemed to leave room for nothing else.

But as she showed him her pain, she saw his, and realized she had hurt him by leaving him to deal with it alone. She had been so filled with her own agony that she had neglected to realize that he suffered as well.

"My poor love," she whispered softly, and put her hand out tentatively to touch his cheek.

He ventured a smile, thinking she was returning to him, thinking her gesture a reaching out to him as he would have her do. But then she looked back at the small carved bit of wood that she grasped so tightly her knuckles were white with the pressure.

"It must be done, Shanda. You must bury him and go on. If not for your own sake, then for that of the baby you now carry within you."

"No!" she cried, her voice loud and anguished. Her eyes, when they again met his, were wild. Then she closed them and drew breath, fighting for control. "No," she whispered.

This new child, she thought, was an interloper. How could Pharaoh expect her to think of it when Hera had been snatched from her in this horrible manner? How could he expect her ever to love another baby when she felt dead inside herself?

But he refused to leave her alone with her misery. He again forced her to face him, holding her until finally she opened her eyes.

"Help me, Shanda," he begged her softly.

"I cannot," she cried. And suddenly all the words that had haunted her, accusing her, during those last days were on her lips and she spoke them, pushed them out as though they bore the poison that infected her. "It was my fault," she cried. "If I had gone to Tiy, if I had not waited for Seti to arrange for it to be done safely, if I had gone to her and made the bargain . . . "

At her words, he tightened his hold on her. "What bargain, Shanda?" he demanded.

"That I would not marry you," she whispered. "That I would not let you make Hera or this new child your heir. That we would recognize Amenophis. Anything. Whatever she asked. Just as I did the last time."

He stared at her, silent, for a long moment.

"You had no right," he told her finally.

She saw the hint of anger in his eyes and knew it was warranted. "I know," she whispered. "But it was all I could do. I had nothing else to offer her."

His anger dissolved. It was this guilt that ate at her, he realized, the feeling that she was responsible for Hera's death. And it was, after all, wrong, completely unnecessary.

"Listen to me, Shanda," he said evenly. "Even if Sethos had killed me, as Amenophis thought he had, he would have killed you and Hera, not out of fear that you might take something from him, but simply out of malice. And he would have done it despite any bargain you could have made with Tiy." He grew thoughtful, remembering, painfully, the woman who had once been his wife, remembering the malice with which she'd spoken of Hera's death. "And despite her word, she would have given him her blessing for the act. Tiy's hatred was like a sickness, and it ruled her. She could do nothing but encourage it in her son. Amenophis hated you, and he hated Hera. Tiy's hatred was of her own making, but if Amenophis had a reason for his, it can only be laid at my feet."

She stared at him, uncomprehending. "Why?"

"Because I love you. And I loved Hera. And, because of Tiy, I stopped even trying to love her son long before he was old enough to understand why I kept my distance from him and his mother."

He walked to the door and stared out at the garden as though it were an alien landscape, a place that was forever spoiled for him by the violence that had been committed there.

"If there is guilt to be borne for Hera's death, Shanda," he went on, "it is my guilt. It is my fault for never having loved Amenophis as my son, for showing him only the hatred I felt for his mother. It is my fault for not recognizing the depth of the hatred he returned to me as payment in kind."

Shanda stared at him for a long moment, at his bowed head and his stooped shoulders. She had never seen him look old before, had never thought there was a weight too heavy for him to carry.

She dropped the wooden toy on the floor beside her chair and went to him. When she put her hand on his shoulder, he turned to her, and she could see pain in his eyes, and tears that he would never allow himself to shed, tears for

Hera and perhaps even for the innocent child Amenophis had once been.

"I love you," she told him softly. There seemed, after all, nothing else to be said.

He put his arms around her and she let herself fall against his chest. And finally all the tears she had been unable to shed poured from her, a great, endless flood of them. She wept silently and knew that the tears eased not only her own pain, but his as well.

And when the tears were finally gone, she looked up at him. "Will you love me?" she asked him softly.

She had no idea where the words had come from, but once they had been spoken, she realized how right this was, how much they needed to be with each other.

He wiped away her tears. Then he lifted her in his arms and carried her to her bed.

They made love with a gentle tenderness that was new to them both. It was as though their passion were a conduit, a path for the pain to take so it could be shared and thus diminished, not much, but enough to allow them both to understand that it might be borne. And for a few moments it brought forgetfulness as they left thought and memory behind and floated on a sea of simple shared rapture.

Shanda had never felt so much a part of him or felt him so close, so deep within her. She knew then that their love-making was more than a simple release from anguish. It was in fact a way they could help to heal each other, a means of ensuring their own survival, the ultimate affirmation of life over death. And as she clung to him, she found a strength she had thought she lacked, and knew she would be able to do what he had asked of her, if only because she loved him.

Later, as she slept in his arms, Pharaoh put his hand on her rounded belly and felt their child kick inside her, strong and angry and fierce, the unexpected power of life waiting its turn to draw breath. This child she carried within her already grappled and fought, proclaiming himself, asserting his indomitable will. It had been that same force within her that had first drawn him to her, he realized. More than her beauty, it had been the surge of life he saw within her, a throb as powerful and as determined as his own.

He felt a spring of relief swell up inside him as he felt that movement inside her. It was as though a room that had been kept closed and locked for too long had been opened suddenly and allowed to fill with warm sunlight. He knew at that moment that the wound of Hera's death would heal. He would bear the scar of this wound forever, as would she, but they would grow whole again, and well. And they would both be stronger for having endured.

Shanda's hand trembled as Pharaoh pressed the carnelian scarab into her palm. She looked at the words that had been inscribed on its belly, but her vision was blurred by unshed tears and she could not decipher their meaning.

"What does it say?" she asked.

He had only to look at her to realize why she stared so intently at the message and yet needed to ask him what it said. He put his hands around hers, pressing them gently.

"It says, 'Pray, my heart, you that are closest to me, do not betray me,' " he replied.

She nodded. She had asked about the funereal rituals, and the young priest, Siptah, had come to instruct her. He had explained that Osiris would place Hera's heart on one side of a scale. On the other side he would lay a feather, Maat's feather, the measure of truth. Thus judgment could be made as to Hera's worthiness to enter the afterlife. She did not yet know if she could accept Pharaoh's beliefs, but she was determined to understand what was being done to

Hera, and why. Much of it seemed cruel to her, for certainly Hera had been an innocent, and his heart pure. But still the rituals would be adhered to, for he had been the son of a king.

"It is time, Shanda," Pharaoh whispered.

She turned to the small form swathed in white that had once been Hera. She forced herself not to think of what had been done to his body, what horrors, surely, it had been subjected to so that it might lie there, so quiet and stiff and alien to her. She had not wanted to look at it before, refusing to think of it as Hera for fear she might not be able to maintain control of herself as she had sworn she would do. But now, as she looked at her son's body, she realized it was no longer Hera lying in the mummy case, but merely a shell he had shed and of which he had freed himself.

Together she and Pharaoh placed the scarab on the chest of the small white-shrouded body. Then the priest nodded, and wrapped the last layer of linen over it, carefully covering the stone and then tying the white fabric securely. Then the jewels were laid over Hera's mummified body, a collar and breastplate of beaten gold, and bracelets and rings, the mass of it dwarfing his small form.

Through it all the priest chanted. Shanda found the dull, droning sound annoying, like the endless hum of bees. She concentrated on it, however, and by keeping her mind on the priest's drone she managed to stand and watch quietly, without turning away.

Finally the top was placed on the coffin. Shanda gasped when she saw it, for on it had been painted Hera's eyes and features. A beard had been added, as though he were a child and a man at the same time. Pharaoh put his hand on her arm, but she forced down the cry that had come to her lips when she saw Hera's face on the coffin. She had sworn to herself that she would endure this, that she would do what Pharaoh expected of her.

The top was hammered into place and the case sealed, and the priests stepped forward, four of them lifting the coffin, the rest forming a line. Pharaoh took her arm, and together they followed the priests out into the hard, bright sunlight as the funeral procession began the long trip to Pharaoh's tomb.

Surrounded by stone and away from the glare of the sun, the tomb was surprisingly cool. After the long climb, Shanda was grateful for the respite. She had begun to feel a bit dizzy and had been forced to steady herself by holding tightly to the arm Pharaoh offered her.

She had been surprised as she stepped into the small side room that had been hastily prepared for Hera's tomb. While one of the walls bore a procession of solemn-faced gods, like the walls of Pharaoh's own tomb room, the remaining three had been decorated like the walls of Hera's nursery, with monkeys and birds and flowers. She found the paintings comforting. If Hera awakened to the afterlife here, as the priest assured her he would, he would be comforted by a familiar sight. The thought comforted her as well.

The small room was crowded. In addition to the heavy stone tomb into which the coffin had been set, there were grave goods—Hera's bed and chair, the box of paints he had so enjoyed using, a nearly life-size wooden pony Seti had had carved and set there for him in lieu of the live one he would one day have had.

Shanda moved forward slowly and set down by his sepulcher the small wooden army, the soldiers and chariots and horses, which Med had carefully wrapped in linen. Then she stepped back, took Pharaoh's arm, and clung to it while the priests droned on endlessly with their chants.

Finally the chanting ended and the tomb fell into a heavy silence. Then Pharaoh put his arm around her waist and guided her out of the room.

Shanda stood trembling as thick slabs of stone were laid in the entry, one atop another, the workers quickly closing up the doorway. And then it was done: Hera's tomb was sealed for all eternity. She closed her eyes and pictured him in her mind, her beautiful golden-haired child. She bade him a final good-bye and let his image fade slowly away.

Shanda hesitated. Med tugged slightly at the hem of her gown so that it would hang correctly. Then he looked up at her and smilingly offered her his encouragement.

The young priest, Siptah, nodded. "The time has come, Princess," he told her.

She nodded. She realized she was more frightened than she had been the first time she had walked the length of this same audience room. In her mind she had long ago decided this day would never come, and now that it had she could not quite believe it was really happening.

She felt large and ungainly despite the finery and jewels she wore. She would be delivered of this child soon, she knew, and it amazed her that she could think of the event with such impassivity. She had anticipated Hera's birth with great enthusiasm. But she could not push from her mind the thought that this new child was an interloper who came to take the place of Hera. She only hoped she could be an adequate mother to him. She did not believe she would love him as she had the child she had lost.

She wished Pharaoh had been willing to wait until after the child had been born. But he had been adamant. They would marry before the birth, he had insisted, and this baby, if it proved to be a son, would be recognized as his heir. And so she stood, trembling slightly, not so much with fear as

with uncertainty, and nodded to Siptah, the priest, that she
was ready.

After Hera's funeral, when Pharaoh had asked it of her,
she had agreed to study with the priest. And when, for the
sake of his throne, he had asked her to accept his gods, she
had agreed to that request as well, if for no other reason
than it pleased her to think that Hera might be enjoying
another life somewhere, as Pharaoh's religion taught. Her
acceptance had put an end to any objections, appeasing the
priests and those lords who might have disapproved of a
foreign queen.

She thought about those lords as she walked the length of
the long audience hall, and as she passed them she wondered
which of them had supported Tiy, which had approved of
the murder of her son. But when she approached Pharaoh,
she forgot all that and saw only the pleasure in his eyes as
she neared the dais where he stood waiting for her.

The priest stood aside. Shanda knelt in front of Pharaoh
and bowed her head as she had done that first day. And as
he had done that first time, Pharaoh put his hand beneath
her chin and lifted her face.

She watched his eyes as he set the crown upon her head.
Once it was done he seemed at peace with himself, more so
than she had ever seen him. It was as though their marriage
wiped away the years of unhappiness he'd known with Tiy
and perhaps even some of the remorse he felt over his failure with Amenophis. It was a beginning for him, something
shining and new and untainted that he started with her. She
promised she would do all in her power to live up to his
expectations of her.

He put his hand out to her and she grasped it, letting him
help her to her feet. The priest offered a prayer to bless their
union, and then Pharaoh led her to the queen's throne that
had been set beside his.

Shanda sat and then watched Pharaoh seat himself beside her. He gazed out at the crowd of courtiers, but he placed his hand over hers and she knew he was thinking not of them but of her. His expression was calm and certain. He had eliminated any threat to his power in the weeks after the attempt on his life at the temple. For the first time in his reign, he ruled absolutely. He would bring Egypt peace and abundance, she knew. She only hoped he would find his own happiness now as well.

Shanda grasped Med's hands and screamed out the pain. It was over far more quickly than it had been with Hera, but still when it was done she wanted only to sleep.

Imhotep told her the child was a boy and brought him to her, but she turned away, feigning exhaustion. She knew Pharaoh would be pleased to learn he again had a son, but she had secretly wished it would be a daughter, wished this baby would in no way challenge her memories of Hera. She was not yet ready to look at this child, not ready to see Hera in another face, to hear his cry from another child's mouth.

But this baby's cry was determined and strong and angry, demanding attention. It was a summons she was not quite prepared to ignore, and despite herself, she turned to him.

Imhotep put him in her arms and she tentatively drew away the cloth in which he'd been wrapped, not quite certain she could love this baby, and almost afraid to find she did not. But the moment she saw him, she knew this child would never try to steal the place she had kept for Hera in her heart. There was no question in her mind but that this baby would make his own place.

He was dark, like Pharaoh, and much larger than Hera had been, with strong arms and legs that he thrust angrily into the air at the affront that had been done him by forcing him from the comfort and warmth of the womb. Shanda touched his face and then his belly and his arms, and then, finally, she smiled at him and put him to her breast.

When Pharaoh entered, he found her lying with the baby in her arms, watching as he hungrily suckled at her breast.

He leaned over her and kissed her forehead, then smoothed away the tangle of her perspiration-dampened curls.

She looked up at him.

"It is a boy," she told him.

He smiled and nodded. "So the physician has told me," he said.

He pushed aside the cloth and studied his son's body, personally verifying what he had been told. Shanda watched his expression and saw that he, too, had expected this child to be fair and blond like Hera. He seemed surprised to see the baby's tawny complexion and fine, dark hair.

She smiled up at him. "He is indeed your son, lord," she told him.

He nodded, then took his glance from his son and turned it to her face. "He is *our* son," he told her firmly.

She looked spent, he noticed, barely able to hold her head upright. He sat down on the bed beside her, and put his arm around her shoulders, letting her rest her head against him.

"We will name him Sekhem," he said, watching his son reach for Shanda's breast. "It means 'the powerful.' And he will one day be a great pharaoh."

Shanda nodded her head drowsily, and her eyes slowly closed. Pharaoh looked down at her as she and the child peacefully drifted into sleep. He felt a wave of well-being spread over him, a shower of pure contentment. He had sought only to survive, to keep his fate in his own hands as far as the gods would allow him, to walk the path of his life with strength and pride. But somehow he had gained more than he had sought from life, a great deal more, and the riches he possessed seemed far greater than he could ever have hoped to attain.

Pharaoh sat on the bed beside Shanda, holding his queen and his son in his arms and knowing for the first time in his life what it meant to be truly immortal.